THE SEPA PROJECT

J MOODY

REVIEWS FOR THE SEPA PROJECT

"The SEPA Project is an unequivocal dystopian tale. Keeping readers entranced, Jillian creates a comprehensive scene of vast terrains, exquisite palaces, desolate wastelands, and everything in between. Include a storyline of unimaginable pain, deception, courage, and strength; this is a novel that keeps you coming back."
— *Literary Lioness Reviewer*

"This is already one of my indie reads of the year. An epic, sweeping SFF debut that incorporates intricate world building with subtle, complex characterization. Cannot wait to read Book 2."
— *Stephen Black, Author of The Kirkwood Chronicles*

"The story brings up paralleled truths in our own existence in such a seamless, natural way that I have to applaud Ms. Moody. She certainly has a way with foreshadowing and ending chapters that all but guarantee the reader's continuing on immediately because there really is no choice in the matter. A master storyteller at work!"
— *Vivian Dunn, Author of For The Love of Many*

"This is easily the most gorgeous sci-fi story I've ever read. Moody displays an artist's eye for color and detail, presenting a carefully-crafted world that captivated me before I realized what was happening. SEPA is a deeply satisfying experience."
— *Cassandra Yorke, Author of <u>Mary, Everything</u>*

ALSO BY J MOODY

THE SEPA PROJECT

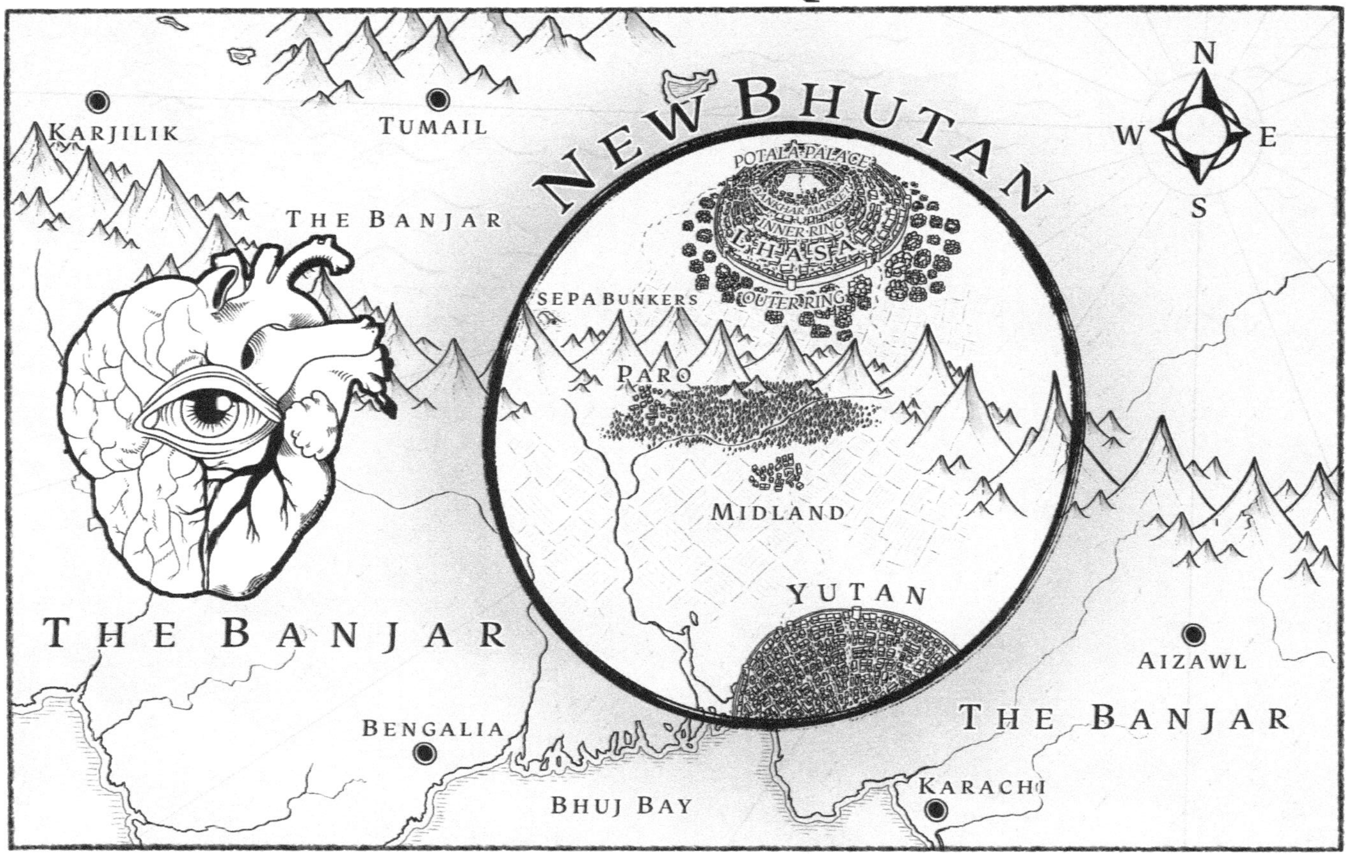

THE SEPA

288 tried to catch her breath as the helio lifted into the air. Recognizing signs of panic had been part of her studies, of course, but she'd never experienced hyperventilation herself. It was *highly* disconcerting. She looked at the blood on her hands. Just beginning to dry, it was crusting under her fingernails and cracking around the lines in her palms.

The Sepa mantras played on repeat in the helio's cabin as they flew toward New Bhutan.

We are the water bearers.

The lifeblood of the Banjar.

She tucked her hands under her legs to staunch the trembling and looked out the window. The Broken Ocean was disappearing from view. She craned her neck to keep it in sight for as long as she could before the broiling hills of the Banjarian desert swallowed it whole. Bhuj Bay wasn't far from the dome's southwestern edge, so it wasn't long before the view changed to the bouquet of decadence that was New Bhutan.

Her hands came out and flexed into fists, punching the seat beside her as if there was a person she could blame, a physical form she could punish. The glory of the dome before her was shadowed by

Jule's hollowed eyes. Jule's voice, thick with blood, telling her to stop this. "When you get to New Bhutan, you can stop this."

We work for the betterment of the planet.

We offer our lives for the lives of so many.

There was blood on her Sepa robe. The once blue toga, meant to signal that she was a water bearer, had long since been bleached to a dirty yellow, stained with mud, and was now covered in coughing bursts of clotted red. She tried to listen to the mantras, blocking out Jule's voice from her mind. She repeated them in a low murmur, letting the words regulate her breathing.

We bear true faith and allegiance to the Family.

We are one in our mission.

They entered the barrier through a hatch built high in the sky, and she realized that the Banjar, and everyone in it, was now only a memory.

They flew straight to one of Potala Palace's many courtyards and 288 watched the world below her with an ache growing in her chest. The Sepa mantras cut off abruptly when the helio touched ground. *We are the life—*

She took a deep breath, finishing the line in her head.

—blood of the Banjar.

Stepping out of the helio into the city of Lhasa felt like stepping onto a new planet. The rush of a different kind of air, cool and fresh, ignited her lungs with life. Shades of green winked in every corner; greens she could touch and smell. It was all too much to accept in one moment, and her steps slowed involuntarily.

The palace pilots didn't bother to get out of the helio and verify her delivery. After she'd cleared the blades, they shot off again without a word. They knew by now that they could trust a Sepa to do exactly as she was told. A Sepa doesn't question an order.

The courtyard was a mecca of tall, wide leafed plants casting their shade across a pathway of cool tiles and white sand. Small, raised pools of water mocked and tempted her, the rainbow of green hues glittering across her vision. The urge to reach out and touch it rooted her feet in place. She wanted to discover the feeling of life, the cool kiss of water. Most of all, she wanted to plunge her face in and drink it. She clenched her jaw, pulling her lips into a thin line. She was not here to touch. Not here to discover.

She was here to deliver.

They had left her standing before the three massive domes built behind Potala Palace. These domes housed all of the Family's business. Su Song, Luópán, and Xīn ran everything from agriculture to education. She let her head fall back and took in the largest dome, sitting proudly front and center. Luópán Hall was a mountain of glass and copper reflecting the greenery around it. She let her eyes rove over it briefly, swallowing down the disdain climbing up her throat. Jule would have fallen to her knees and cried. She would have smashed those glass windows to pieces. But 288 was not a Banjarian. She was a Sepa.

And Sepas do not disobey.

She'd heard plenty of talk about Luópán out in the Banjar. It was the Family's greatest asset. Grumbles of resistance amongst the people always included "Start by taking out Luópán Hall" or "If I could pass as New Bhutanese, I would get a job in Luópán Hall. Then..." The dome was made in a pattern of hexagonal solar panels, glass windows, and plant life. It struck her as too flashy, too big, with its top towering over the palace so the common folk could sneak a glance and wonder what was inside. Everyone in the Banjar knew full well that this was the place where New Bhutan's famous innovations were created and maintained; the water purification systems, the air filters that kept the country safe from the outside, the palm tech used to communicate, the Listener's bugs and transmissions. None of those wonders were on her mind, however, because it was also where they created the Sepas, built to be traders between those within the barrier and those without.

This was where she had been pieced together.

She swallowed tightly, her raw throat protesting as she stepped into the dome.

The entryway of Luópán was less grandiose than she'd imagined, but it hummed with a quiet power. The ceiling, although far out of reach, was still lower than the dome's massive size promised. Cold black marble floors reflected the light from the windows and walls of the same material doubled as running fountains, creating the effect that they were walking within a quietly rushing waterfall. Pathways lifting off the ground curved right, left, up, and down; a tangled tapestry of exits. There were no plants here, no people sitting on benches to chat. People walked by purposefully, following those curving paths out of sight. 288 considered how big this dome was, the largest one by far. If everything was packed this tightly, she marveled at just how much it could contain. More than the Banjarians could have imagined.

Meera San, the SEPA Project Coordinator, was waiting for her just inside. Her white sleeves and billowing pant legs were sliced along the outer seam to allow for airflow. Her clothes seemed designed to withstand the heat, a luxury those outside the barrier couldn't afford. She'd always held a fierce, hard quality about her face as she surveyed their training at the bunkers. At the moment their eyes met, however, Meera's expression was softer. 288 could tell she was holding her breath by the way her chest was raised and her eyes seemed to search hers hungrily. It was only a second. One quick moment in time before she snapped her mouth closed.

She approached with a tense smile and greeted her with warmth. "288. Welcome back."

When she did not respond, Meera looked around and added, "Fai should be up in a moment."

288 stared straight ahead, watching Meera San from the corner of her eye.

"Would you like a glass of water?" Meera asked.

Not glancing over, she bowed her head in assent.

Meera San smiled and brought her palm to her mouth. She asked for water to be delivered to Luópán's foyer.

288's face remained impassive, but her fingers flexed.

In Bengalia, where Jule lived, the ocean sits in pockets here and there throughout the town. The streets squish between your toes with million-year-old bits of stone and a poisoned water that will eventually cause you to lose your skin. The houses are made of ancient driftwood, plants, and crude stone, built over frames of what was there three hundred years ago, before the waves came and destroyed the town; before the poisoned waters killed off most of the people.

When New Bhutan found the Bengalia clan, the Banjarians lived farther inland. They had designated the job of harvesting salt to a few brave leaders in the clan, willing to travel to the shore and risk their health for their community.

The Bhutanese wanted that salt. As their demand for it grew, the Banjarians moved closer and closer to the waters, vying to be the ones who the Sepas traded with. The immediate prize was the trade, but the more time they spent on the waters, the more likely they were to fall ill.

The trade, of course, was for clean water.

Occasionally, storms would pass over the clans of the Banjar, leaving their pots full for a time, but the rains were rare. Generally, every clan in the Banjar depended on New Bhutan to deliver water.

While Banjarians dried out, Meera San was ordering water to be delivered through her palm tech. It came within minutes, and the coordinator pressed it into 288's hands.

We are the water bearers.

She stared at, considering smashing it at the woman's feet and running. Before she could act, the glass was at her lips and she was drinking for her life. It had been a long stay in Bengalia. The water had run low days ago and she refused to take any for herself. Not when she knew that she, and she alone, would soon be brought within New Bhutan's walls.

Within the barrier, there was always water. It was miraculously cold and burned her teeth. She drank anyway. When she lowered the glass, Meera San was frowning at her.

She opened her mouth to speak before a short, disheveled looking man came loping across the foyer and cut her off.

"My apologies, Meera San!" the man called. "My deepest regrets for keeping you waiting."

She waved his apology away. "Did you receive my order for this one?"

He glanced at 288 and his brows raised for a moment. "I did" he said slowly. "I do wonder, Meera—"

"We will speak another time, Fai. We have several Sepas coming in this afternoon. Have 288 escorted back to a recovery room when you are finished."

"Of course."

Meera eased the glass from her hands and nodded goodbye. 288 watched her go for a moment, sure she'd spotted regret in the coordinator's eyes.

Fai gestured for her to follow and she fell into obedient step behind him.

He led her down pathways that circled and stretched, spiraling down and farther down still. After they'd passed through multiple doors where he swiped his palm for access, they entered another foyer. 288 gulped the air as if they'd wandered outside at last. In reality, they must have been at least ten floors below ground. Fai headed straight for a double door flanked by two Quántóu, Potala Palace's guards. He didn't need to scan his palm this time, because one of the Quántóu smiled and opened the door for him.

They came to a balcony that overlooked a deep circular room made up of large red stones and creamy pillars. It felt Old World, but could have been from the very beginning of theirs. A circling path clinging to the wall led them down to the ground floor.

One massive double door, easily fifteen feet tall, stood in the center of the far wall, two smaller doors on either side. She was eyeing the imposing black bolts on the large door with a foreign feeling creeping up her spine. It looked like something one would encounter in a nightmare.

She wondered if this was what fear felt like.

This was it. Behind that door was her fate, and it was emptiness. No Jule's laugh or stories. No ocean waves breaking over the rocks and spraying twenty feet into the sky.

It was time for the Emptying.

She was startled when he sidestepped the nightmare door and opened the one to the right instead. It was a small, cold room built of stone. He walked along the walls, lighting candles that lined a shelf around the entire perimeter. Slowly, the room came into view. There was a cot bed standing near a metallic tub. Tubes stretched from the back of the tub to a machine hanging on the wall directly behind it. There was one shelf, lined with clear and empty glass vials. She waited, eyeing the cot.

He explained the procedure and she couldn't help but wonder how many times he had Emptied her before. Did he recognize her? If he did, he was hiding his familiarity well.

"You may sit, if you prefer," he said. She opted to stand near the tub, looking over a thick, rolling liquid inside.

"You may feel an emptying sensation," he continued, "as the data is removed from your cells. The gel eases the shock."

He took each of her hands, avoiding her gaze and seeming to feel no connection at their touch. Touching was so rare for a Sepa that her entire body felt his gentle grip. He set her palms into the gel surface and instructed her to press until they were wrist deep. She wanted to clench her hands together, each the other's guard, but there they were, and he was binding her wrists with rubber cuffs.

You will feel the emptying.

She wanted to know if that meant she would see Jule drifting away from her memory, like desperately trying to recall a dream. No use asking him. Why waste precious words with questions soon to be answered? She usually had the control, the tricks, to live in the moment. Listening. Waiting.

He opened a cabinet and pulled two thin tubes over to where she stood, tapping at the long needles they led to.

This was what she existed for. She should be proud to deliver her research. Her work. She *was* proud. At this thought, Jule's indignation came screaming into her mind.

Proud?

Suddenly she wondered if she'd been this docile every time. Had there ever been a trip down this path when she'd kicked and screamed? Fought for the memories she was about to lose? Was Jule not enough to fight for?

She clenched her jaw tight, trying to resist the urge to jerk her hands away and run.

A Sepa would never fight.

A Sepa would never run.

When you get to New Bhutan, you can stop this, Jule had said, her fragile hand clasped around 288's.

Her chest started to rise and fall again in that erratic pattern she was so unfamiliar with. Without thinking, she jerked her arms from the pool, easily pulling the buffer cuffs from their cords. She swung around blindly, landing a blow in Fai's stomach. But he was closer than she'd expected. Possibly predicting her rebellion, he'd readied an injection. As the blow landed, so did a needle in her neck.

Fai tsked, shaking his head. "Come now, 288," he said gently, leading her wilting form to the cot, "you know New Bhutan's mantra as well as anyone. *We Break Bread, Not Bones.*"

He laid her down and lifted her hair away, feeling for the spots on either side of her neck that he would need. With careful precision, he inserted each needle at an angle that pushed them straight past the guard of her skull. There was no pain with insertion. They had stunted the nerves around the entry points. Her eyes drooped, and she realized that she'd given up the cuffs in her struggle. The pain was yet to come.

As the needles found their target, she was overcome with memories; flashes of jumping rocks along Bengalia's coastline with the Broken Oceans crashing in the distance. She remembered Jule's freckles mirroring the stars scattered thick across the sky... the memories fading as fast as they'd arrived.

With each disintegrating moment, her body jerked. It wasn't necessarily pain, but something worse; a pulse of grief, of loss, that cut into her very being. The red sunsets and Jule's pained eyes were losing their definition. She clung to them, her screams echoing off the stone walls and bouncing back at her until she wasn't sure who had made the sound. With each shock, the memories became more fragmented, cutting her with sharp seconds that fell farther and farther away until eventually, both past and present faded into nothingness and the little room fell silent.

She was the 288th Sepa, created to spy on the Banjar and bring her memories back for the ruling Family to study. She was trained in physical combat, five Banjarian dialects, negotiation, and, above all, human psychology. As she moved from family to family, clan to clan, she listened. She recorded. She watched. She brought food and water for trade, building relationships with Banjaraians that would give her access to private conversations.

After each mission, her memory pockets needed to be cleared. They checked the data and returned her, clean, to the bunkers. Moments in the Banjar were Emptied from her mind, and all that was left was training. Her life had been training. Training leading to this moment, when she would accept her first mission.

She awoke, ready to start her new life. Trained to trade and spy. She couldn't wait to begin.

How was she to know this would be her eleventh beginning?

PART I

FOXES

1

———

H^{UI}

Hui was on his belly, drawing the finishing touches on the tail of a fox when his door opened with no warning knock. It was too fast to put the drawing away, but he was able to push the book he was referencing under the bed. In fact, he always drew with the book on the floor for that very reason. His maan's eyes found the paper immediately and she walked toward him with head cocked to the side. "What is it?"

"Knocking?" he answered innocently. "It's when you rap your hand against the door to signify—"

"Ha ha." She raised her palm in protest. "The unsettling creation in your notebook."

"It's... well... I'm not sure. It was in my dream last night."

She frowned and gently touched his head. "Well, he does look sad, doesn't he?"

The drawing was made with charcoal, an expensive item traded from the Banjar. It was a special gift he believed she often regretted. The charcoal fox sat amongst billowing black clouds, staring at her solemnly.

"Kind of beautiful though, too, right?" he countered. Not to compliment his work, but the swooping lines of the fox's figure.

Misunderstanding, she replied, "Your art is always beautiful, Hu."

He inclined his head in thanks. "So?"

"I came to ask you to be my companion for the Family dinner tonight. Your faan is unable to attend."

Hui held the eye roll back at the last second. This wasn't an uncommon request, and it commonly ended poorly. The Family dinners were stuffy affairs, royals seeing who can out-royal the others, while Hui inevitably found something interesting to do elsewhere, broke something, caused a scene, and ended the night listening to his faan scold his maan. Hui always willed her to point out that *he* was the one who should be scolded for not going in the first place, but his maan never got the message.

"What's the occasion?" he asked heavily.

"Hmmm. Your Aunt Meera requested a dinner to honor the Sepas. Apparently, her Sepas have only just returned from almost a year long trip. She claims she wants to honor them."

Hui sat up straight in his chair. "The Sepas will be there?" he asked, bewildered.

"Apparently so. Only a select few, of course. Sepas who have outperformed the others. She suggested making it a prize for the highest achievers; give them something to work harder for. You know Meera, always making games."

She trailed off into her own thoughts for a moment before abruptly finding his gaze again. "So, is that a yes?"

"That is an *absolutely*, Maan."

Pleased, she tousled his hair. "You have curious interests, Hu." She cast a lingering glance at the drawing. "Draw me something pretty next time?"

"Yes, Maan."

Once the door clicked behind her, Hui dropped to the ground to retrieve the thick encyclopedia. He lay back on his bed, clutching the book to his chest.

The encyclopedia had been an Eighth Anniversary of Life gift from Aunt Meera; a secret gift. New Bhutan only celebrated three birthdays. The eighth to honor the beginning of individual interests, the thirteenth for the choosing of your art form, and the thirtieth for a celebration of long life. At the eighth, a person receives gifts that may foster their budding talents or broaden their horizons as they move away from the metaphorical nest. Meera's gift had been a cookbook. Her secret gift had been the encyclopedia.

It was contraband, of course. Made of real paper, dated 1991, published in New Jersey (wherever that had been). There were only two ways this could have ended up in Meera's hands: Dorji Tashi himself had gifted it from their limited stores of memorabilia, or it had been smuggled to her through the SEPA Project. Only one of those was remotely likely.

The book seemed to define different important ideas, objects, people, and places that started with the letter F. Hui found the animals the most intriguing—Fox, Ferret, Feline, Frog—but other ideas caught his eye too, such as *frost*. The world outside the barrier, now gone, was coming to life for him one word at a time. The budding interests gift was doing its job, as he had become more and more intrigued by that world with every page.

The animals had not been invited to New Bhutan unless they were absolutely necessary to the founding family. Silkworms for clothing, bees for pollinating, horses for labor, and a few species of fish and insects that happened to live there. The horses had been worked to extinction. The official statement was that they were just unnecessary and disposed of after construction was completed.

The horse was a beautiful creature in Hui's eye, and he often wondered if other creatures as big as the horse had ever existed, or just maybe, still did. The F encyclopedia had taught him that animals came in many different shapes and sizes, and that was only one letter.

The Sepas were the only ones who might know. Traders, spending their days in the Banjar. Adventurers, risking their lives to bring him charcoal and copper. They would have answers, he was sure. He tucked the fox drawing into his book, tucked the book under his bed, and pulled out his dress robes.

Hui was ready to go an hour early. He hadn't cared much to slick his wild hair down or clean the charcoal from his hands but tying his yukata had taken a bit of time. He hoped to slip his encyclopedia in under its folds but it was too thick to stay lodged under the tight pull of fabric. He finally had to give up the notion and decided to smuggle in his sketch journal instead. There was a chance that a Sepa might recognize one of the creatures he'd chosen to draw, but the likelihood was disappointingly slim.

It was still fifteen minutes before their carriage would be leaving that Hui was carefully walking down the steps toward the common room.

"I'm truly sorry to miss this one," his faan was saying ruefully. "At least there will be new blood!"

"I'm nervous," Maan responded. He could tell how close they were standing by their tones, almost touching, or maybe in an embrace.

"The only thing you need to be nervous about is Hui! Are you sure you want to bring him along?"

"I couldn't possibly take it back now! You should have seen his eyes light up when I told him they were going to be there. So strange."

"Come, Mishka, it's not strange. They're different and he's a curious child. I just hope he behaves himself."

"They're... beyond barbaric. They don't even have homes, or names. They're not even fully *human*."

"Well, I suppose now is the time to judge them for yourself. Your sister doesn't seem to mind them."

"My sister..." she laughed a little. "My sister might be as strange as they are."

"Hm. Well, I am sorry to miss this stupendously strange evening, my flower. I'm sure your loveliness will immediately sway each and every one of them into admiration."

"I want you to be there."

"I know."

"How long will you be away this time?"

"A few days, no more."

After that, those disturbingly squishy sounds of kisses and murmurs replaced their conversation, so Hui slipped back to his room and double checked his robes.

It wasn't long before his maan collected him and they were riding the carriage toward the Family's Dining Hall. Hui tapped his foot to release a bit of his excited energy. His maan was staring out the window, thoughts far from the bouncing boy before her. He wanted to ask her about the Sepas, to muse over what may happen tonight, but her words to his faan hushed him.

He didn't like how she felt about them. It wasn't *their* fault they didn't have names. Names were given, like gifts. It was sad they weren't given names, not even lousy ones like *Hui*. He wished he had a more powerful name like Drogo or Talruum. Hui, however, suddenly seemed okay when compared to nothing.

2

____

C ADENCE

CADENCE WAS SITTING at the head of the empty table in the Family
Dining Hall, softly drumming his fingers on the marble tabletop.
Sunlight streamed in from the thirty-foot arches leading onto the
balcony behind him. The view for his guests tonight would feature
him lording over the sweeping city of Lhasa and the lush lands
beyond it. The Eye of New Bhutan, however, would be facing the ten-
foot tall double door, painted blood red and decorated in gold studs
on the opposite side of the room. The door commanded his gaze,
along with the promise of everyone who would soon be walking
through it.

Sai San, his uncle by marriage, would be watching him expectantly. As a Family apprentice and close friend to Tashi, Sai San had
been the acting Eye between the death of Asaka the Just and when
Cadence came of age. He'd laid low, preferring to focus on the acad-
emic side of the Eye's position and neglecting the public. New Bhutan

had been quiet for a few years, bursting back to life with the appointment of Cadence. He'd made speeches, thrown festivals, given interviews. The new Eye had been celebrated by the people. But Cadence wondered if Sai was still disappointed. What would this new Eye do for the Family and the governing of the world? Was he merely a spectacle? This dinner was his first move on actual policy. He would make a clear gesture of support for Meera's shift in focus with the SEPA Project.

He knew that Seldom Chime, his aunt, would smile at him with pride. She would recognize this as his first power move as Eye and want to reassure him that it was a wise choice, no matter what the outcome. She could always be counted on to ease his anxiety, like a maan to a child. Seldom may not have been his real maan, but she'd been playing the part as best she could since he was a child. He glanced around the room, a once favorite play spot. There was a shadow of a maan in his memory, chasing him playfully around the large circular space, but her face was Seldom Chime's, no matter how hard he tried to bring his true maan into focus.

Blood maan or not, she would be proud to see him up here today; the Eye, commanding the table opposite the great Dorji Tashi. He couldn't help but think those words with a bit of malice. His faan and the Heart of New Bhutan, Dorji Tashi was the true leader of the world. That was why he would get the best view at dinner, why the hall was dressed in Dragon Red, and why Cadence, his son, was being forced to marry his favorite apprentice.

His fists clenched on the table.

As if she'd sensed his thoughts, that great red door eased open and Penna herself slipped into the dining hall. He turned his body to the side as she came in, pretending to gaze at a large mural on the left wall. Pretending he didn't sense her every movement. She eased up beside him, her long, pale fingers resting near his on the table.

"Cadence."

He swallowed hard and looked up, gluing the playful smile on his lips he wore so often.

"Penna San. I believe you're a bit early," he joked.

She offered a tight smile. "You've heard the news, I imagine?"

The smile fell from his face. "I have. I'm honored."

"No need to lie to your wife, Cadence."

He laughed. "Tell that to the rest of New Bhutan."

She winced. "Hmm. I'm afraid that joke doesn't bode well for our relationship."

She turned and walked the length of the table. Her backless dress cascaded to her ankles in the teal and gold of a Family apprentice. A long, thick braid of shimmering black hair and gold ribbons bunched under one ear and trailed over her shoulder, nearly reaching her waist. She was graceful, beautiful, and sharply intelligent. He couldn't ask for a better match and had told Tashi that when he'd made the announcement over tea the morning before.

And yet. And yet, there was something about her. A coldness that chilled him whenever she came near. And of course, there was the age difference. While he was just entering adulthood, she must have been... thirty-five? It was difficult to guess. Penna was stunning, no doubt, but it was clear she thought of him as a child. That could be a real issue with her respecting his leadership decisions.

He was also, it was true, slightly miffed by the match. He was the Eye, second in power only to the Heart. He had been born into it and would always be trying to prove his worth to those like Sai and Penna San, who had been chosen for their cunning and intellect. His faan, Dorji Tashi, had reassigned Sai as Cadence's "understudy" on the chance that Cadence met an untimely death. As former Acting Eye, Sai had no need to be an understudy apprentice and was no doubt hired to watch and train Cadence rather than the other way around.

Now Tashi had added Penna to the watch. As his wife, she would be up for any position in the Family, even the Heart. He couldn't help but suspect that Tashi's plan was to hand Penna all the power, and it was through this match that he could justify it.

He watched her back with a scowl. That beauty was deceiving. She was sneaking her way up through the Family with every intent of taking control. And his faan believed that Cadence would let her do it. They were right when they called her Penna Snake, for sure.

As if she'd sensed his thoughts, she turned to face him. Her bright green eyes seemed to ignite in the setting sun rays. "This dinner," she said abruptly. She waved her hand across the table. "I'm certain my sister has some ulterior motive."

"You've come to question my approval? We're not married yet, Penna San."

She smiled. "It's true that when we are matched, I will advise you to say no to all of Meera's plans. She's well known for being deceptive and ill prepared. Terrible combination."

"Sounds like sister drama," he said in a bored voice. "I'm the Eye. My job is to *see*. I discussed the idea of the dinner with Meera myself before it was proposed. How can I oversee our people without ever having met our forces?" He was happy to make it sound like the dinner had been his idea all along. Even if it was a bad idea, at least it was an idea that he had hatched. Cadence, the Accomplisher.

"You could do as the rest of us have and visit the bunkers."

Cadence twisted his mouth. "I'd rather not." Why dirty his robes so close to the Banjar when he could host a party?

Penna rolled her eyes as if hearing his thoughts.

"It's a dangerous idea," she added. "The SEPA Project is built on the Sepas having little to no contact with Lhasa. The experience could be detrimental to their training. Worse yet, they could be *traitors*, dining with their new targets."

Cadence laughed. "Do you think I'm stupid, Penna San? Of course we will be Emptying the memory of this entire trip before they're returned to the Su Song Dome."

Penna let surprise flit across her face for a moment. "Well, what is your purpose? Don't regurgitate Meera's nonsense of a celebration."

He smiled. "I have the same concerns as you, dear wife. Meera San has tasked these particular Sepas with interrogating and stopping Banjarian rebels. I want to get a sense of their loyalty."

He thought he saw a speck of respect dawn in her eyes. Was this what their marriage would be? Always fighting an uphill battle to impress her?

"I've set the seats so a Sepa will be between each Family member, and if you're concerned about safety, rest assured that each will be dressed by attendants. No life-threatening party favors will be slipped in. There will be Quántóu posted along the room throughout dinner, on the chance they're planning a physical attack. I want the Sepas spread out so we can try to coax information out of them. The more they give, the less I trust them."

"Why?" she asked, despite herself. "Wouldn't we want them to be loyal to us?"

"Dorji Tashi is their high commander, and he gave them orders to speak of the Banjar to no one but their direct supervisor, who is Kiro. Kiro is not here. They should remain silent."

Penna was nodding her head. "And if they *do* offer new information, it's still a win for us," she added to herself.

It was his turn for a discreet eye roll. She was playing her own game, the Family be damned. Penna worked for Penna, and that was all.

"I still wonder what Meera is playing at," she murmured.

He shrugged. "She seems to love them, truly. We don't give her enough credit for the work she does for us. She has no title and brings in half our wealth. It really is a shame. I wonder if we could add a member," he joked, raising his brows. "The Feet?"

She stared at him blankly.

He'd almost forgotten who he was talking to. Penna San didn't joke. He cleared his throat. "Well, my point is maybe she's seeking some recognition that is long overdue."

Penna scoffed. "Wouldn't be surprising."

Cadence whistled. "You really dislike her. Did she steal your toys or what?"

"She's chosen her side, and it's not mine."

"What does *that* mean?"

"Haven't you seen how she looks at us? She's as close to a Banjarian as I've met. She doesn't even have a home."

His eyebrows shot up in surprise. That was a low blow, even for Penna. "She left her house when her wife died, Penna San. Surely you understand that grief works in mysterious ways."

"Celio," she spat. "She was even worse. It was her influence that made Meera the way she is, and the death only pushed her further. Before Celio, we were—" she snapped her mouth shut, as if she'd suddenly realized who she was talking to. "Well. She was normal then."

Cadence was at a loss for words. He pulled out his best trick; the trusty casual smile. "Well, why don't we play our own game tonight and try to figure out what she's up to?"

"Sounds like you have a full plate already with your, I'm certain, *thorough* analysis of the Sepa situation," she said sarcastically. Straightening her shoulders, she added a resolute, "I'll keep an eye on my sister."

"So grim!" Cadence laughed. "I, for one, am excited for all this intrigue."

"You're excited about everything," she said with disdain.

"I can think of one thing I'm not excited about," he said sweetly.

She threw him a glare. "That makes two of us."

The sudden glow of Penna's palm distracted her. She glanced down and a bit of her color drained. Regaining her snide air, she glanced at Cadence, flashing her palm to show the word "Meera" scroll by just under her flesh. She tapped her fingers to accept the comm.

He watched her exchange a few sparring comments, wondering about the relationship of siblings. He'd so often daydreamed about having a brother or sister; someone bound by blood to play with him, someone naturally connected, or, at the very least, someone his age living in the palace. The relationship between these two sisters, however, bordered on hatred. That's why he was surprised to hear her inviting Meera to tea.

She disconnected the call and gave Cadence a wry smile. "It appears the game had already begun. I'll take my leave for now."

He stood and gave a low bow. "Wife."

Grimacing, she glided out.

Cadence let out a large breath as if he'd been holding it the entire time. He sat and slumped deep into his chair. If she had come to convince him to cancel the dinner, then he had won that battle. He should've been elated by his victory but just felt exhausted. He looked around the table, imagining it in a few hours, filled with his family and the foreign beings that were Sepas. Not quite Banjarian or Bhutanese, they were not really people at all.

Created in labs and raised to be one entity, they were less than human before the Emptying procedure took away any sentimentality. No name, no family, no past, no craft. They were restricted from the traditional study of the seven arts; an obscenity in New Bhutan. Instead, they were taught the histories, geographies, and dialects of the Banjar clans; something Bhutanese children would never know. They had a lot to learn from each other, if given the chance.

He wondered if that was what Penna had been referring to. Why did she care about the Banjar? As long as it brought in goods and didn't revolt, he didn't see why they should bother with it at all. That burden was on Meera and her SEPA Project.

Cadence had plenty to concern himself with within New Bhutan's border. The Eye position gave Cadence a lot more responsibilities than he was used to.

The original Family of New Bhutan created three branches for their new government: the Heart, the Eye, and the Brain. Each branch had a leader with a team working under them, who in turn had people all over the country working for them. Every person in New Bhutan had a Family member to answer to if they went up high enough.

The Eye sees, listens, records, and analyzes the people. In turn, he is seen by the people. The Eye is the public face of the Family, making all announcements, hosting all events, and hearing all concerns. Any comms to the community at large came from him, so it was lucky that Cadence could be so charismatic. Or maybe that was why he'd been assigned the job.

The lesser-known job of the Eye was to manage the Listener's tapes and Sepa memories. Of course, he had teams in Luópán that collected and analyzed them. Any memory flags would be reported to

Meera San, who worked beneath him. Generally, the full downloads were catalogued by the Library team. These longer and more thorough downloads were used as a record of the collective histories of the Banjar.

One of his assignments was to review the memory reports. The Eye should be a scholar of the history and the present lives of those both inside and outside the barrier. In fact, his early years were spent studying with a Maester and his maan daily. She loved learning alongside him, having never been permitted the content a leader needs in her own lessons. She had been taught the sciences, maths, and invention; never history. History was for politicians. He didn't remember what they had learned, but he did remember being pinned to her lap while she eagerly drank in the Maester's words.

After her death, the maester had stopped coming. In fact, all of Cadence's responsibilities had ceased abruptly. Tashi was most often locked in the Briefing Room, working in the domes, or abroad along the border. Seldom Chime had tried to keep up a normal life for him, but she couldn't control him, and he never sat through a lesson again. Now that he had finally come of age to take on his post, he knew he should really make the time to study. For now, though, he was quite busy being the face of New Bhutan. So many speeches and announcements to do in order to keep the people informed! And, of course, there were events to plan.

For now, he'd assigned Sai to watch over the Memory Library and listen to the reports for him. Sai seemed to find more entertainment from the recordings, anyway. To Cadence, they were highly insufferable. Audio recordings of mostly monotonous and occasionally frantic voices explaining every detail of events in the Banjar. It was at best, boring, and at worst, creepy. Let Sai San handle it if that's what gave him his kicks.

His main concern was events like tonight; keeping tabs on their safety nets, establishing himself as a man of influence, and maybe tonight, seeing if he could arrange a hug-and-make-up moment between two sisters.

Cadence tapped the table as if to approve his efforts. He took one long glance around the room, trying to shake off the feeling that the ghost of his maan was there and disappointed in his thoughts. He sighed and left the room. It wouldn't be long before he would be back, entertaining the lot of them. If Penna San knew how much energy that took, maybe she'd show him more respect.

3

M EERA

MEERA LET herself into the palace after seeing the Sepas safely deposited in Su Song Dome and paused to collect her thoughts. It had been the worst return 288 had suffered yet. She'd been so violent that Meera was forced to administer a sedative at the helio doors. It was necessary, she assured herself. If 288 was going to listen to Meera's plan before the dinner, she would need to be calm. A few hours of undisturbed sleep would only do the girl good.

She slipped down the hall of apprentices, hoping to catch her sister unaware in her apartments. Of course, Penna San would not leave her room without stationing a Quántóu guard. The guard nodded in greeting and respectfully denied her entry. She was silent when Meera asked where her sister might be. Meera bit back the aggressive appeal that jumped to her tongue. It was no use with Quántóu. She sent a silent thanks that she'd decided to forgo her personal servants and commed her sister, shooting the Quántóu one more dirty look. Comming Penna was something she generally avoided; it caused her too much heartache. Memories of their close bond would overtake her mind. This time, though, her thoughts were swirling with too many scenarios that may play out in the very near future to make room for thoughts of the past.

It came as a surprise when Penna actually answered.

"Meera, Meera," Penna said, a hint of amusement in her tone. "We were just discussing you."

"Not surprising," she responded drily.

"How can I be of service to you? I would think that dining with you tonight would be enough for one day..."

"I'm outside your apartments with your Quántóu. I hoped to speak with you before our meal. Can we meet in your common room?"

Meera raised a brow at the Quántóu to make sure she was listening.

Penna was quiet for a moment and she wondered briefly if she'd disconnected.

"I suppose. Have Pa bring us iced tea and meet me on the balcony."

"With pleasure," she responded, throwing a winning smile at the Quántóu. The girl nodded her head and departed.

Meera stepped softly into her sister's home. It was elegant; the sofas of the finest quality, the flowers of the brightest stalk, and completely barren of anything personal. The old tan stone walls had been painted white, and sheer light blue curtains hung still on either side of the towering balcony entrance. The place gave her a chill, and she decided not to linger on her way through the apartment. Penna was a very private person and Meera would respect that. Besides, there was nothing really to see.

Rounding an empty, highly polished table, she found that several guzheng were lined up just inside the balcony archways. Her steps stopped as memories came flooding back. With a tentative hand, she plucked a few strings, letting the sound reverberate off the walls. She closed her eyes and tried to remember the notes. Pluck, pluck, slide... it had been years since she'd heard the sound.

In the Inner Ring, the first ring of community homes a few hours outside of Lhasa, children were all taught the basics of the seven arts: voice, paint, sculpture, prose, theater, dance, and chosen instruments. It was only on the thirteenth birthday that they abandoned study of six to focus on a single art. Meera's choice of instrument had been the guzheng, but she'd never found a talent for it. Much to everyone's horror, Meera never found a knack for any art form at all. Penna, who followed her lead relentlessly, had also chosen the guzheng. Within a moon's turn she could play better than Meera could after two years. She never made Meera feel embarrassed or showed pride in her skill. Instead, she would patiently try to teach her older sister. Penna had always loved to share her skills. She'd found joy in helping people grow.

The thought overwhelmed Meera with grief. She plucked a series of low notes, trying to let the instrument mourn for her. In the end, Meera had given up music in favor of theater. There was no skipping out completely. Not with her connections to the Family. Her education in theater had helped her tremendously in her work with the SEPA Project as she trained them on facial and verbal responses to different situations. Her early theater work, when she was still performing on the side, had brought Celio into her life.

Celio had been an actor full time then. They'd each been barely more than kids. Her and her troupe lived in Yutan but would tour the Rings with performances and occasionally perform at the palace. Meera wasn't taking her art as a career choice and was already working in the nursery at the Sepa bunkers. However, she did, on occasion, perform for the Family.

It was all in good fun then, before Potala had become an unwelcoming place. She'd watched Celio perform a short play in the role of an Old World queen, and Celio watched Meera perform a monologue about returning to earth after death as a single blade of grass.

They'd met after the show, stars of adoration mirrored in each other's eyes.

She danced her fingers across the strings, creating a fast ripple of notes. That was when Penna liked Celio. The three of them had a real time that night. They'd climbed onto one of Potala's many lower roofs and watched the moon progress across the sky, talking about their dreams for the future until the sun rose in the east.

That was nearly twenty years ago now.

"You never could play that," Penna's voice came snidely from behind her.

She pursed her lips, not turning to greet her.

"No, I certainly couldn't. I loved listening to you play it, however. What a beautiful sound it can make in the right hands."

She didn't respond to that, opting to walk past her onto the balcony. Meera followed, plucking her courage.

At the railing, Penna turned, her face utterly expressionless. "To what do I owe the pleasure, Meera?"

Meera had a trick. When Penna's eyes were too cold, that unnatural bite of green ice, Meera would conjure the image of her as a child and place it before this version of her sister. It helped remind her that this was a kind person, encased inside an angry shell. She'd built a thousand brick walls around the person she'd once been, but Meera could imagine that she was speaking right through them.

"I've come to discuss the Sepa dinner."

Penna let out a sharp, quick laugh.

Perplexed, but undeterred, she took a deep breath.

"I brought them for you, Penna."

This got the reaction she was hoping for. A surprise. She was startled but recovered quickly. "You informed the Dragon that you were here to celebrate their, or should I say your, accomplishments. What part do I play in that?"

"The Sepas..." she began, trying to form her words carefully, "are our frontline. They trade for us. They'll fight for us if need be. They give their lives for the betterment of both the Banjar and New Bhutan."

Penna's face was stony. "They cannot give lives they never had in the first place. We give them life to live as we see fit."

"And yet, they are human beings."

She sniffed. "Hardly. Might you get to the point, or are you here to tell me how much you love your little monsters? I should think you've made that perfectly clear already."

Be patient, Meera reminded herself. She went on gently, masking the irritation building inside her. "Just see them, Penna," she urged. "That's all I'm asking. Look into their eyes and tell me they aren't human; that they don't deserve to live as long as we do."

"Speak plainly, for Dragon's sake." In an annoyed whirl, Penna turned to lean on the balcony and look out over the mountains.

Meera came to stand beside her, speaking to the sky.

"I'm alluding to the Banjarguay. This plague takes the Sepa's lives so frequently, we can barely keep up with trades. I'm tired of sending them out to die. They are our soldiers, whether we use the words or not. We should offer them health in return; to our ambassadors at the very least."

Penna had raised her chin high in the air as if to stretch that long neck. She took a deep breath and responded without looking Meera's way. "Their short lifespan is our security, Meera. Dead soldiers don't turn on you."

She smoothed her dress out. "Besides," she added, pretending to be occupied with the folds of her skirt, "Once one group has a cure for the Banjarguay, who is to stop others from wanting them? Soon every clan will be asking."

"Every clan *is* asking."

She met her sister's eyes with a flash of anger. "If we had a cure, we would obviously use it. It would allow us to expand our world beyond the barrier."

Meera's composure broke. "Liar," she spat.

Penna let surprise flit across her face. Meera watched one of those rare moments when her sister's expression revealed the internal war inside her brain. She responded slowly, almost thinking aloud. "New Bhutan has seen a three-hundred-year peace. Not one fight against our family's rule; not one environmental crisis. No crime. Soon, I will be Heart. Expanding our world outside the barrier comes with so many risks. Even without the Banjarguay, the Banjar poses threats. Heat, starvation, dehydration, war... Would you have me be the leader who jeopardized a three-hundred-year peace?"

Meera looked at her sadly. "It always comes back to you. How will you be remembered? You are the heir of Dorji Tashi, even without the bloodline. I thought you might be more like our faan."

Penna looked as though she'd been slapped. "Faan would have wanted me to keep our people safe," she said stiffly.

Meera offered a tight smile. "On who our people are, you two may have disagreed. Just look at them, Penna, that's all I ask. Look into their eyes and consider if they deserve life any less than we do. I know Luópán could make a cure if they tried."

She didn't wait to be dismissed. She turned on her heel and departed, letting her request hang in the air behind her.

She'd been working in the SEPA Project for nearly twenty years now, changing roles several times. She'd still been working in the nurseries when Sepa 288 arrived. She had been inquisitive at five and Meera would always have to redirect her to the task at hand. By eight, she was as fierce as a Banjarian.

These little Sepas were like the children she'd never had. Celio, by then her wife, had refused to bring a child into the world, claiming that she had a more important role to play. Meera couldn't possibly take time off for bearing a child with her role in the Family. Still, it had been difficult, sitting with ten or so bumbling children who reached out to be held, wishing that she could at least have one of her own to comfort. She'd fantasized about slipping 288 into their home in the Inner Ring and raising her up as her own, wildly inventing ways that no one would be none the wiser. Instead, she had continually sent her off on missions, hoping she would return safely.

Counting on it.

When Celio died, her mentality changed. Instead of wasting her time on daydreams, she would put her position and her secrets to good use. Now, so many years later, it was time.

Meera held her head high as she left Penna, heading for Su Song Dome. It was time for 288 to complete her real work. The work Meera had been hoping she could achieve since the moment they met.

4

2^{88}

IT MIGHT HAVE BEEN the most terrifying moment of her life, but, of course, she could never really know. She'd lived among strangers; been dropped from a helio into strange lands countless times. She usually remembered nothing, so she had nothing. So, generally, she feared nothing. Now, however, her chest tightened and a nauseous sweat sprouted across her brow.

It could be because these people controlled the one thing she still had hold of: herself. She was theirs to do with what they would, that was true. But to some degree, she was in charge of her own body. She moved these legs and blinked these eyes. She had her own thoughts, unique to the Sepa beside her. Although raised to be a Sepa in the sense of a thing, same as the Sepa before and behind her, she was thinking what they were not, and that made them each, in some small sense, their own. The Family had the power to take this one thing that was hers and do whatever they wanted with it.

Meera San was nervous too, although she worked hard to only convey excitement. She should have known that attempting to fool the Sepas was pointless. They knew that when her hands were clasped together behind her back, she was excited. When they stood rigid alongside her, she was trying to stifle her fear. And, of course, when they were clasped in front, she was furious. If they didn't know that, they wouldn't be her prized Sepas. Tonight, her arms were straight as arrows.

She had instructed them to glide into the dining hall with heads bowed, circle around the table after her and take each available seat in turn. Every other chair should be empty to allow them to spread out. She wished she would have instructed them on what to do after sitting.

I think it's safe to say I've mastered sitting in a chair, she thought wryly, but conversing with the Family would be completely new. How did you make small talk with people who controlled every part of your existence? She wondered if the Sepas around her were scared. She knew from a rather distressing meeting with Meera San an hour earlier that she, and she alone, had not been emptied of her last mission. The Sepas before and behind her only remembered their training. Did their knees feel like they might go out at any moment, or was it only her, whose body had more and more often reacted to what she was thinking? Her, who only recently realized what it felt like to be scared?

She led them straight through Potala Palace, and 288 resisted the urge to look around. On the third floor, a massive set of red double doors had been thrown open to welcome them. The view struck her immediately. Arches rising two stories high showcased a land glittering with water, radiant with a green-orange sunset. Regretfully, she cast her face downward as instructed, observing the group before her as best she could from the corner of her eye.

She was second in line out of four and was seated between a wisp of a woman and a small child. The child stared at her, wide eyed and open mouthed. She allowed herself a quick glance to the woman beside her but she was keeping a rigid stare straight ahead. Settling into her seat, 288's eyes found their way forward and locked on the greenest eyes she had ever seen.

The woman sitting across from her radiated a venomous energy. Her fury was clenched into her hands and burning from those electric eyes. Her black hair flowed freely around her face, a poor attempt to hide her sharp features. She didn't take her eyes off her. Before 288 could think to be polite and drop her gaze, she found herself ensnared; an unwilling contender in a staring contest. They both held the connection until a young man four seats down broke the heavy silence with a jovial, "Well!"

She felt the boy beside her snap his eyes from her to the man in the front, straighten his back, and close his mouth. She followed suit, breaking contact with the woman.

The young man stood and bowed to the room at large. The room rose in response, (Sepas quickly following suit) bowed back, and sat again. "We have come to this very special event at the creative requests of Meera San. She has dedicated many moons of her life working on the edge, sometimes even venturing beyond it," at this everyone sat up in the seats a little straighter, "to facilitate a program that has gifted us with many luxuries harvested from the Banjar." He smiled around the room, seemingly unaffected by the grim faces that met him. "Let us welcome the Sepas with respect, give them a savory meal, and see them off back to their duties." He turned his attention to the Sepa near him and let his gaze hop to each one. "Sepas, we welcome you to the Family's table. We are honored to meet those who Meera San call her frontline." 288 was still watching him when he glanced back at her. He met her gaze for a second time before quickly turning away.

He was young; much younger than many of the people sitting around the table. Twenty at most. He wore a dark purple kimono unique to any in the room. His carefree tone and posture made her certain that he was born into his role, a child of needs met before they were needed. 288 fixed her face to show respect instead of the resentment she was feeling.

"Allow me to introduce our Family," he continued, "and then, perhaps, Meera San can tell us about your individual achievements."

Everyone seemed to inhale sharply at this, Family and Sepas both. The word "individual" was not used when referring to Sepas. They were one entity. To give them individuality would mean to give them identity, and that, they were not allowed.

She tried to discern if he had expected the reaction or was abashed at his mistake. His quick glance around the room, briefly meeting eyes with several of its occupants, left her unsure. She herself was shocked and intrigued by his words. She snuck a quick glance at the other Sepas at the table. They were each dressed in a new blue toga, as she was, their hair freshly washed and braided. Their skin was deeply tanned compared to the Family and their faces were thinner. It was clear who ate regularly and who didn't. It was their expressions that set them apart from the Family the most. They moved their eyes from one person to the next, sometimes roving features or watching a particular person's movements for longer than was comfortable, all the while keeping their face completely expressionless. They were observers, taking in every detail without developing a single opinion. She wondered what trades they had made to earn a seat at this table. Were they intrigued to find out what they had done? It would surely be news to them as much as it was to the Family.

The man cleared his throat, pulling 288 from her thoughts. "Sepas, I am the Eye of—"

"Sing us a tune, would you Cadence?"

It was a grunt lined with malice, coming from the opposite end of the table. 288 turned to find the largest man she had ever seen. He looked like a small sun, his obscene size wrapped tight in a flaming red kimono with trailing gold tassels.

"Faan?" The one named Cadence responded, glancing uncomfortably around the room. "Surely introductions should take precedent?"

"This meal is depressing enough as it is," he grumbled. "Let's start with a rousing song, yes? Do we agree?" He looked to see many around the table offering hesitant nods in agreement.

"Something merry, Cadence."

Cadence squirmed with uncertainty for a few more moments before a small smile twitched his face. "What an idea!" he exclaimed. "What better way to celebrate than with a song?"

288 couldn't help but feel a bit sorry for him. Every Sepa in the room knew he was mortified. That the man ordering him to sing was feeling extreme pleasure watching him squirm.

Cadence pushed his chair out of the way and stepped a few paces back from the table. She watched his brain cast around for the words. After a moment, his eyes clouded over in memory and he began. His singing voice was quite different from his jovial speaking voice. It was deep and sorrowful, and the song moved it in a slow and steady rise.

"Lo, the river,
    Lo, the rain,
    Earth and stars will meet in the sky again.
    Lo the river, lo the rain,
    Ocean breaks free from the tide again.
    We'll see, we'll see,
    Roots splintered from their trees
    We'll see.
    Grow again my maan, grow again my faan,
    Shade me from this burning sun.
    Wise men will grow, wiser men will fall,
    Quit trying to run before you've learned to crawl."

288 PEEKED around the table to see if the Family was as surprised as she was. The song was anything but merry. It was fierce and angry, drawn out in that impossibly deep voice.

"Lo, the hands that hold,
    the faces turned to stars,

the moon will rise on a new night,
Land, and stars, and sea,
Will lend the people their might.
The bay will rise over stony shore;
The sun will set when the waters roar.
Lo, the river
Lo, the rain
Earth and stars will meet in the sky again
Lo the river, lo the rain,
Ocean breaks free from the tide again."

SEVERAL PEOPLE at the table listened with a somber, passive expression. A few were frowning. The man who had asked him to sing was absolutely sizzling with rage. 288 imagined the heat of it could reach her from across the table.

Cadence let the last note hang in the air for a moment before taking a deep bow. A smattering of reluctant clapping rounded the table. Lifting from his bow, she caught him throwing the man a satisfied smirk.

"Ah, thank you! Thank you. That is a very old tune my resting maan, Kiba Chime, may she grow, would sing to me. I hadn't thought of it for years and it just came to me quite suddenly. Rather haunting, I suppose?" He threw his hands up in helplessness. "Well, Tashi, you can't blame the artist for the whims of their inspiration. Now! On with introductions." He gave a broad sweep with his arm.

"I am named Cadence, son to Dorji Tashi, the Heart, and the Resting Brain, Kiba Chime. To my right is Seldom Chime." As everyone shifted their attention away, she let her attention linger on him for just a moment. The moment when the facade fell and he took a relieved breath, quickly attempting to pull an unwilling lock of hair back into his high bun. She was letting the words of the song sink into her mind when he glanced up and met her gaze again. Hastily, she jerked her eyes away.

Seldom Chime stood up with some difficulty. It seemed that one side of her body didn't work. Her long hair was white and her face covered with gentle wrinkles. She smiled softly and nodded at the Sepa sitting directly across from her.

Seldom took over introductions. "I am Seldom Chime, the Brain, Daughter to Raju, the Resting Heart, sister of the Resting Brain, Kiba Chime, and wife to Sai." Her voice sounded like leaves rustling in the wind. "To my right is Sai." She eased back into her seat gratefully.

Sai smiled easily at Seldom Chime as he stood up as if delivering an inside joke. He cleared his throat. "I am Sai, husband to Seldom Chime, The Brain."

She was quick to notice that Sai offered no lineage or title and he spoke his introductions as if he would rather be doing anything else. Married into the family, apparently. Next in line was the green-eyed woman across from her. He did not, as seemed custom, introduce her.

Penna stood gracefully and gave a thin smile to the room at large. Her face seemed to have paled since she looked her way last. She looked like she might be sick.

"I am Penna, Daughter to the Resting Eye, Asaka the Just, and the Resting Ling." She added no title either. Her voice was hard caramel. Everyone at the table seemed to be entranced by her, including, to her surprise, 288. The woman managed to be sharp as steel but vulnerable at the same time. It was fascinating. "To my right," she continued, "is Dorji Tashi, our Heart."

Everyone let out a held breath as she sat down and turned to face the opposing head of the table from Cadence. That angry heat was still radiating from his expression. His small eyes stared straight at Cadence during his entire introduction, which he said from his chair.

"I am Dorji Tashi, the Dragon, the Heart, the Leader of New Bhutan, Husband to the Resting Kiba, Faan to the young Eye we have before us today. To my right, is Mishka San."

Penna's eyes sought hers. She felt their pull and glanced over. The fire had faded and she simply stared at her. She was shameless. 288's eyes flicked back and forth from her to the speakers. After Dorji

Tashi, they introduced a woman named Mishka, who (shocking to 288) was sister to Penna San and Meera San. She said it quietly and quickly, introducing her son in one rushed breath before sitting down. On 288's left, her son stood proudly and looked each Sepa in the eye.

"My name is Hui, Son of Susu and Mishka." His small voice made everyone but Penna and the Sepas smile. She took a quick inventory of the clothing distinctions. Sai, Penna, Mishka, and Meera were each wearing flowing robes of teal and gold with beautifully stitched floral patterns. The others at the table had a distinct robe: Dorji Tashi with the offensively loud red, Cadence a deep purple, and Seldom Chime a deep blue. Each robe represented a branch of the Family, she imagined. Each, upon closer inspection, had their role stitched into the patterns along the arms.

After Hui was seated, Meera San stood and introduced herself. She lifted her chin bravely before following Cadence's instruction. She referred to them by the numbers implanted into the back of their necks at birth. By the time she'd introduced the second Sepa, her hesitation was gone. This was her work, and she was proud. She generously bragged about each of their accomplishments, from 253's trade for rubies to 272's deal with a community in Kargilik, allowing us to trade sugar cane for salvaged steel. This made Mishka and Sai smile. They were getting the better end of these deals, by far.

The first Sepa to be introduced had kept her face bowed toward the table. 288 was sure she didn't want to be caught looking proud. The others gratefully took her lead. The guests did not clap or say anything at all. Seldom Chime and her husband Sai nodded kindly while Mishka, the woman next to her, held a napkin to her mouth as if the whole discussion was revolting. Cadence, for once seeming calm, watched thoughtfully.

Her gaze kept skipping to take in each of the intriguing personalities around the room. These were the people who controlled everything. These were the people who decided where she went, when, and with how much. These were the people who made decisions that would lead to who lived and who died in the Banjar. 288 felt heat rise to her cheeks and she took a calming breath. Then her eyes met Dorji Tashi's.

She had been sneaking a furtive glance at his ruddy face, wondering if spirits were the cause of his drooping lids, when their eyes connected.

A ripple of fear went up her back, igniting her scalp with tingles that made her whole body twitch. His lip had curled up under the bushy mustache and he was breathing heavily through his mouth. The eyes that met hers were full of fire. She was watching his fingers drum the table when suddenly her number was being spoken.

"288 is one of three Sepas who works exclusively as an ambassador. Her emotion recognition ability has allowed her to intercept three rebels in this last year alone."

Dorji Tashi grunted and slapped his palm on the table. Laboriously, he pulled himself to his feet for the first time. 288 leaned away into her chair without thinking.

"Rebellions?" he asked quietly. "Come, Meera San, what have we to fear from Banjar barbarians? You waste our resources. Keep the Sepas for trading, as was intended." He fell back into his seat. Everyone's heads turned in unison toward a flushed Meera San.

Meera's face lost all color. "Yes, Dorji Tashi," she replied simply, as if his words hadn't sliced her heart open. It was clearly her only option.

288 knew the color had drained from her own face. The ambassador program, directing her to seek out potential rebels, was her ticket to keeping her memories.

Cadence eased to his feet. "It seems we have a disagreement at the table."

He began to stroll the perimeter, casually trailing his hand over chair backs. "Let us have a Family discussion on the matter and put it to a vote." Dorji Tashi glared at him and received a wink in return. "Meera San has selected three of the fifty active Sepas to be ambassadors. These advanced beings," (here he cast a smiling sidelong glance at her) "have the job of rooting out communities who are planning a way to refuse trade with us, to join other communities to form larger governments, and perhaps, even, attack us for our resources. Once they've discovered them, they use their heightened understanding of the human psyche to convince them that this is not, in fact, what they want, and we carry on our merry way. It is no easy feat, I'm sure." Here he paused behind his own chair. "Table?"

Mishka, the woman sitting beside her, was the first to say something, blurting it out as if it had been waiting to dive off her tongue. "What do we care if we lose a trade or have a sad attempt at an attack? We have everything we need, and New Bhutan is impenetrable." Her eyes were small and dark, darting back and forth from Cadence to Dorji Tashi.

Sai quietly disagreed. "It isn't anymore, if you recall, Mishka. That was the only downside to starting the SEPA Project, one which many thought wasn't worth the trade. If the Sepas can get out, the barbarians can get in."

288 bristled at his use of the derogatory slip of *barbarians* to describe Banjarians.

"Yes," Cadence chimed in, "and losing the wrong trade deal could be catastrophic. Our resources have come to depend on items from the Banjar."

It appeared that Dorji Tashi and Meera San were forbidden to speak during the discussion, because both looked like someone had wrapped their mouth with a bit of cloth and they were dying to rip it off.

Seldom Chime slowly stood, causing everyone to give her their full attention. "The likelihood of a rebellion reaching through our stronghold and causing any damage is miniscule. We must ask, however, what harm there is in using a few Sepas to calm them. They are still bringing in the same amount of goods as before Meera San added the ambassador program, are they not?" Her lips turned to the side in a thoughtful gesture. "I hope that others are noticing that we are overlooking a key point in this conversation, which is *why* the Banjar wants to rebel, and *how* the Sepas are able to stop them. I know I for one am interested and concerned to hear about life outside New Bhutan." She swept a challenging glare around the room and returned to her seat.

No one said a word. Meera San was unable to speak, and who else could answer the question? 288 was shocked by the woman's words. She had plucked the thought from her brain and threw it at the Family. Didn't they want to know why the people wanted to rebel? Here, someone did. Seldom Chime was her new hero.

The silence stretched until finally Seldom Chime returned to her standing position. "No seconds? Too afraid to ask, I see. Well, I put my vote for keeping the program. The Sepas and Meera San obviously know more than we do, as we have decided to remain willfully ignorant."

Cadence jumped to his feet. "Come now, Seldom Chime, let's be cordial. Perhaps it is time to put the matter to a vote. All in favor of Dorji Tashi's suggestion of dismantling the ambassador program?"

Penna was staring at her again. She caught 288 in a moment of weakness. Concern had bled across her face, and she quickly bowed her head. With eyes on her lap, she awaited Cadence's announcement of the results. She hadn't needed to. She felt Dorji Tashi's posture shift in his chair, a shift of anger and ultimately, defeat. She breathed a shaky sigh of relief as Cadence announced that the Sepa's ambassador program would remain and that perhaps they should begin dinner. She wondered which way Penna had voted. The last Sepa in attendance to her right was never introduced. Perhaps Cadence thought to continue describing their feats might test Tashi's patience, or perhaps everyone just forgot.

Dinner was served on three large plates across the table, each plate containing piles of mushroom dumplings, red rice, string beans, and spiced red lentils, set carefully on a bed of injera. The Family each murmured *meshu meshu* before reaching out and snatching bits of food with their bare hands, pinching their bites into folds of the injera. Each Sepa tried to catch Meera San's gaze to ask with their eyes if they should follow suit. For 288, she gave a near imperceptible nod. As the Family ate, small conversations broke out across the table, always over or around the Sepas between them. No one seemed to speak to them at all. No one, that is, but Hui.

In the Banjar, children were the only ones brave or ignorant enough to say what they truly felt about New Bhutan in her presence. An integral part of Sepa training was understanding what Kiro, her trainer, called the "human condition" which explained the weaknesses inherent in a real human's emotions. Children were too open, and therefore an easy target for information. She had been grateful to see one, Miracle, on this last assignment because it made the mission easier. What Kiro had failed to tell her was that sometimes, toward the end, it made it harder. Children were often ill, and the parents would hope for aid from her. Aid she did not have to give. When he'd spoken of the human condition, he'd told them of the irrationally strong protective nature of a mother to her child. He did that sometimes; he would craft his words to make it feel like human emotions were a weakness and that the Sepas were almost superior in their lack of them. That was why she'd been so thrown off guard when that same protective tug had pulled at her chest for Miracle. And she certainly hadn't been prepared for the deep bellied devastation that followed.

The child next to her had never wanted for anything. His black hair, although unruly, shined and gave off the luxurious scent of rare oils. His eyes were wide as saucers and his mouth hung slightly ajar as each Sepa's work was announced. He picked at his food now, casting sidelong glances at her. When the guests were well into their dinner, she noticed his hand, tracing letters into the fabric in his lap. She was trying and failing to decipher the invisible letters from his movements.

He gave up and spoke out the side of his mouth, as if he was the spy.

"Hello," was all he said, his cheek full of dumplings.

She swallowed down a smile. Slowly, she raised a hand to the side of the table and traced out the letters, "H-I." He turned his face and looked right at her, a big smile stretched across his face. So much for incognito.

"Ambassador, huh? Crax." He looked at her expectantly.

"Crax," she agreed, picking up on his lingo to mean something appealing. She knew seven dialects fluently and could easily recognize terms she didn't know based on tone and inflection.

"288," he continued thoughtfully. "That's a pretty okay number, I guess. Do you like it?"

She glanced around nervously but no one seemed to have noticed their exchange yet. "It's better than 277," she spoke out the side of her mouth, practically looking the other way.

She looked back to see him concentrating hard and nodding his head in agreement. She had only been joking, but he was trying to decide what she meant by it. She casually made her hands into fists with a curled pointer finger and brushed one on top the other, a gesture for "only kidding." He caught it and his smile returned, larger than ever.

Joking was new. Fun was new. She had picked it up with Miracle and apparently was having a hard time putting it down.

"Hui."

Penna was staring at them, her eyes licking green flames.

"Penna San," Hui responded dutifully.

"Contain yourself."

Hui glanced around the room with uncertainty, his eyes falling last on his maan, Mishka.

Mishka shifted uncomfortably in her seat. "It does seem imprudent to bother the Sepa with your questions, Hui."

Meera San leaned in. "What is a dinner with Sepas for if not to ask questions?"

Penna sneered at her and appealed arched eyebrows to Cadence.

"I must agree with Meera San. These are our guests tonight, as unusual as it may be." Cadence met 288's gaze before skipping his eyes over to his faan.

She was getting the impression that this dinner had not been approved by a family vote.

Everyone was looking at her now, as if now that she had permission, she would speak freely.

She found her gaze dropping to Hui. He smiled at her encouragingly. Her voice sounded like it had only just emerged from her mouth for the very first time. "It is an honor, Hui."

She glanced up and locked eyes with Penna. Perhaps it was the length of time she'd been in the Banjar that gave her the strength, or stupidity, to hold it. It was Penna who looked away first, face somewhat ashen. They didn't meet eyes again.

Halfway through the meal, she realized she had been surveying the group as if on assignment and wondered if the other ambassador Sepas were doing the same. Who here was for us and who was against us? Who had something to be angry about and enough of a following to lead? Observing them, she was surprised at how many secrets there seemed to be to learn.

After eating, Cadence had directed them off the terrace and down the steep steps to a small garden for tea. There were no chairs set out, so guests were expected to stand and sip. She noticed Meera San's slight signals directing the Sepas to move away from her; to mingle. While two attempted a casual approach to Sai San, two others found themselves in conversation with Seldom Chime and Mishka. She was interested in eavesdropping but stayed back, wanting to observe the dynamics of the group. Hui had cleared the way for the Sepas to speak, but they remained relatively quiet.

Leave it to the kid to make change, she thought. He was still tagging along beside her, alternating from asking a string of questions to picking up on her behavior and falling into observation mode. A few questions he asked were:

Do you get to decorate your bedroom?

Are you friends with other Sepas?

Do you have a favorite place in the Banjar?

Have you ever almost been *killed*?

To all of these she replied with a simple "no" while keeping her eyes forward. The only lie was about having a favorite place. Of course she did, but that would require a long and complicated answer. Although, to be fair, how would she know if she'd almost been killed? She only remembered her last assignment.

Hui was quietly watching the guests along with her when he asked in a hushed voice, "What do you see?"

She almost smiled.

"I see... enemies. Desperation. I see sorrow, and loss. I see hope." She threw on that last one for him but refrained from saying that he was where she saw it.

His eyes had gone wide again as he searched the garden for these feelings. In a sidelong whisper, he asked. "Have you ever seen... an animal?" He took in and held a deep breath.

She glanced over at him. It was clear that this was an important question for him. It was also one she didn't know how to answer.

"I don't know *animal*."

He whipped his head to face her and searched her eyes for honesty. Finding it, he looked like he might cry. His face fell to the ground. "Oh."

"Define it."

He looked back at her, trying to put on a brave face. "It's..." his hands turned up helplessly. "It's something alive, but not human. It comes in many types, from the size of your hand to taller than me."

"Is it a plant?"

"No! It's alive like we are... It usually has four legs?" He looked at her as if he was giving her a clue.

"Do they fly?" She was remembering the vultures on Godsmeet Peak.

"Sometimes! The falcon flies! Have you seen one?"

She didn't want to disappoint him. "Maybe. I don't remember."

"Sepas don't forget," he said, smiling and completely certain that she must have.

Mishka was eyeing them nervously.

"Let's go talk to your maan."

"Why?" Hui asked, letting the y drag a few seconds longer than necessary.

"Because she's scared of me. Sometimes just talking to a clan you're scared of can ease your fears."

They slowly made their way over. She didn't mention that now might be the best time, as she was speaking with Sai and Seldom Chime, both defenders of the SEPA Project during dinner.

She approached with a bowed head.

Seldom Chime's smile widened. "Hello, child. We were just discussing what I brought up at dinner, much to everyone's displeasure. Perhaps you could weigh in."

Mishka's eyes hardened, but Sai was unreadable. He simply gazed at her with subdued interest. Perhaps the right comment from her could change that.

She cleared her throat and raised her head, shooting a side glance at Mishka. "It is an honor to speak with you, Seldom Chime. Is it the cause of unrest in the Banjar or the tactics of Sepas you wish me to comment on? You had inquired about both."

She looked at her thoughtfully. "What comes to your mind first?"

"Tactics, of course, as that is my concern." It was a lie that any Sepa would have recognized; her quick and forceful response, the fill-in-the-blank wording. She swallowed down the emotion she felt at being asked to describe the conditions of the Banjar. Speaking of it was against every unspoken rule. She had been testing her, but she was uncertain if Seldom wanted her to pass or fail.

Seldom let a silence fall between them all before responding. "I see. Go ahead."

She took a deep breath, considering how best to describe Sepa ways. "Sepas have been dropped in the same regions for trading purposes for many years. The Banjarians know the Sepa's face and see them as gift bringers. They trust them." She was being very careful to avoid saying "us" or "I" as if they were people. A Sepa is a thing. "An ambassador Sepa is permitted to stay longer than the standard. They may be stationed for several weeks, sometimes months." Grief and anger were climbing like bile up her throat as the memories of those months flooded her. It was a new feeling for her. These uncontrollable waves of emotion were really quite annoying.

"How do you know where to root out rebels if other Bhutan officials are not investigating?" Mishka asked suspiciously. Her hand went to her mouth as if shocked and ashamed that she had spoken to her.

288 wasn't sure where to keep her eyes in this group. She settled on rotating from person to person, finding a moment of solace each time it was Hui's turn. He was simply enthralled.

"A Sepa hardly ever knows for sure. Sometimes a murmur is picked from the last Sepa's Emptying. Most times, they hear it for themselves on regular trade assignments. If they notice something worth staying for, they alert Meera San and she sends a backup Sepa to pick up the trade. They stay under the title of ambassador."

She cleared her throat, mentally preparing an ambivalent tone before continuing. "The people believe we are there to report their concerns or needs to the Family so those needs can be met."

The silence stretches again. How many of them were wondering if those concerns were ever heard? Obviously Seldom Chime, a Family member herself, had never heard them. 288 realized she'd slipped and used the word *we*. It felt a little exhilarating, and with a sense of recklessness, she continued.

"We gain their trust, look out for the ones who are angry rather than hopeless; focused rather than chaotic. Those are the ones who are working toward taking action."

"Do you kill them?" Hui breathed.

She looked down at him. "No."

"What do you do with them?" It was Sai asking. His genuine interest had peeked its head. 288 smirked internally. She might be able to figure him out after all.

She looked him dead in the eye. Reveal nothing. "Convince them they're happy."

"Tell us what it is like in the Banjar."

It was Cadence. He had eased his way between her and Seldom Chime and joined the conversation in one fluid motion.

She shot a glance at Seldom. She was gazing approvingly at Cadence.

"I apologize, but I'm not sure how to proceed. I have delivered all of my memories of the Banjar to the palace."

Cadence laughed. "Surely you remember something?"

"I..." She cast her eyes around for help. Didn't they know that they had been Emptied? Was this a test? She was about to say nothing, nothing at all, when her eyes met Hui's. He was hanging on her silence for something, some hint of the world outside his small one. She found herself saying the only true thing she could. "I only know that they are thirsty. They're always thirsty. That part stays in my dreams, no matter how many times I am Emptied."

The atmosphere was suddenly taut, as if even the bees were holding their wings silent for what would be said next.

"Well," Seldom said decisively. "Your dreams have you to thank for bringing the Banjarians water! Thank you for your time, Sepa." She turned to Cadence. "And how was your visit to Bankhar Market yesterday? Did you find the seeds you were hoping for?"

It wasn't unkind, but still a definite dismissal. She bowed to each in turn (even Hui) and walked away, in search of the comforting presence of Meera San.

Hui trotted along beside her.

"If you don't remember the Banjar, why did you tell me you saw a falcon?" he whispers.

"I didn't."

"You did."

"I said I *may* have."

"Did Dorji Tashi take your memories?"

"No."

"Good thing for you! He's scary."

Her eyes found Dorji Tashi. He was standing under the arches with Penna San. She looked taller standing up, draped in her flowing formal wear. He was shamelessly staring at her while she glared out into the night. A sharp fear twisted in her stomach. The people around her controlled who lived and who died. They were *all* terrifying as far as she was concerned.

The garden seemed to be swarming with secrets. She could almost see them, casting across the stones and snagging on each other. It was in covert glances between Penna and Mishka, Penna and

Sai; nearly imperceptible nods between Seldom Chime and her own Meera San. Dark looks between Dorji Tashi and Sai San.

"How often do you attend these parties, Hui?"

"Almost every moon," he groaned. "Faan is supposed to escort, but he's usually gone on assignment."

"Gone? Where is there to go?"

"New Bhutan is bigger than you might think. There are lots of faraway places inside. Faan is the general of the borderland patrol and is usually gone, circling the perimeter."

"What does the borderland patrol do? There is no way for anyone to cross it."

"Maintenance, I think." Hui's face was scrunched up in an attempt to recall. "I actually don't know," he admitted.

She looked thoughtfully around the garden. "You should count yourself lucky to be invited here often. You get to see and understand the makers of the world." She gave him a sidelong glance. "Maybe even become one someday."

He scoffed. "No way. I'm going to be an explorer. The first New Bhutanese to see every land in the Banjar!"

Her heart swelled painfully. She wanted to thank him for not hating them. For not being afraid of them. She wanted to tell him how much he would love the drums in Tumail, the dancing after a Sepa Feast. But she was keenly aware that the Listeners were monitoring every word.

"Bhutanese tend to stay where they are for safety's sake," she said finally. "Besides, everything you could ever want is right here in New Bhutan."

He nodded, a shadow of sadness flickering over his face.

"What is it?" she asked, watching him.

"I know I should be happy. I have a name. And... I'm not thirsty, like you said. But... I don't think anyone here likes me very much."

"*I* like you," she said, giving him a reassuring smile. "Of course," her tone darkening, "there is a one hundred percent chance that you will be Emptied from my memory."

He looked stricken. "I don't want you to forget me."

She grimaced. "That is the Sepa way."

He frowned at her for a moment before hastily pulling a small notebook from inside his robes. It was no bigger than her hand, bound in a rough fabric casing.

"I like to draw," he explained. "Can I draw you? Then you can draw me. We can keep each other's portraits so we never forget."

She smiled, knowing that the Listeners may pass this recording on as insubordinate behavior and Kiro would no doubt confiscate the drawing. And yet, his expression of earnest accomplishment was too much to deny.

"Okay. Do you have two graphites?"

"Yes." He opened the journal, revealing a variety of drawing utensils resting in small slings on the inside jacket.

He tore two pages out and offered her the journal to use as a solid surface, opting to sit on the ground and rest his paper on his knee. She squatted across from him and they shared a big conspiratorial smile before Hui became lost in his drawing. He didn't see her as a person anymore, but as a collection of shapes and gestures. He bit his lip and squinted his eyes as he worked, making it difficult for her, who had very little experience with drawing, to capture his face at all.

She took a quick glance around the courtyard, but everyone seemed to be engrossed in their own awkward conversations. Returning to her drawing task, she studied Hui carefully. His round face was clinging to baby fat, his lemon wedge eyes twinkling under thick lashes. She was doing her best to copy every detail when her last look at Miracle started puncturing through her vision. Another sweet round face, covered in blood. She put the pencil down, a solid breath suddenly difficult to grasp.

His brow knit in concern. "Are you okay, 288?"

"Yes," she gasped, pulling herself together. "I just..." *I don't want to lose him again.*

"I just hope this works," she said, offering a tight smile. It was then that she realized one thing she could do. It wasn't much, but it was all she had.

5

______

M EERA

MEERA HAD LED her Sepas to their apartments after tea and came straight back to the garden. She eased in gently, hoping to overhear before being heard. Mishka had taken Hui home as Meera was leaving, so the adults would be speaking freely.

She could hear Dorji Tashi speaking as she edged in, the spirit tea adding a slight slur to his words. "He's a smart boy, Penna. Having you wed into the Family eases my path in electing you as Heart. I don't appreciate being questioned."

"Cadence is a *child*, Tashi. Might waiting be more appropriate?"

"He needs good counsel from someone he will listen to. This forsaken dinner is proof enough that he's out of my control."

Meera watched Penna's color drain a bit. "I blame Meera San for this, not the boy."

"I'll gladly take the blame," Meera chimed in, strolling into the room.

"Ah, there's the mischief maker herself."

Dorji Tashi draped an arm over her shoulders, crushing her to his side. He'd been friends with her father, Asaka, and had kept his three daughters close after his death.

"I was remiss to miss out on the chatter following our departure." She looked about the empty room. "Are you the only two gossip bees left?"

"We *were*," Penna sneered.

Meera smiled sweetly up at her. "Did I interrupt?"

She looked up to Dorji, the sharp scent of alcohol overwhelming her senses.

"In truth, I came to speak with you about that vote at dinner, Tashi. I thought you would be pleased to meet our spies and was disappointed to see your disdain for my work."

He dropped his arm and cocked a heavy brow at her. "I admit, they seem well trained, disciplined... more than I can say for my son."

"And?" she pressed.

"And... I can see why you would be proud, Meera. But how will it affect them to see us, I wonder?"

"Nothing affects them. That is the beauty of the project. We empty anything that would affect their trained minds. In fact, they're off to Luópán Hall within the hour."

Tashi frowned. "We only have one man trained to empty in Lhasa. Is that sufficient to keep up with all of them?"

"Plenty, Tashi. Kiro takes care of them at the base if it's urgent and Fai does the yearly empties here. They are both here tonight, working together to empty the dinner completely."

"What a waste of effort and fine food. Cadence doesn't stop to think of the price of his play."

"Perhaps Cadence sees the importance of learning about the ambassador program?" Meera asked irritably.

Penna was watching her with disdain. "You spend too much time at the barrier. I dare say the air is getting to your mind."

"Penna!" Tashi laughed. "I remember a day when you two were thick as thieves, always plotting against poor Mishka."

"Cadence wasn't entertaining Meera's *whim*," Penna snapped. "He agreed to have them here to test their loyalty to the Family before they head off to consort with our enemies." After speaking, she flushed with embarrassment, perhaps realizing she'd come to Cadence's defense.

"And?" Meera asked, eyeing Penna closely. "What did he decide?"

"Well..." Penna hesitated for a moment, just a moment, before haughtily replying "It's obvious those things have no personality at all. How could they be loyal or disloyal? You have to be human to have morality."

Meera couldn't help the small smile flitting across her lips. Penna's hesitation was all she needed. "So true, Penna. So true. They are made to be whatever we want them to be. Well, I will let you two finish your whispers so we can all get some rest."

She began to walk away, turning back at Dorji Tashi's call.

"You are an impressive sergeant, Meera, with well-trained soldiers. The problem is, New Bhutan has no need of them. Careful you don't create a problem where one doesn't exist."

She bowed deeply at that and made her way toward the Su Song Dome.

Meera San had two homes. One in Su Song and one in the Sepa Bunker. Neither were true homes, like Mishka and her communal garden or Penna with her plant filled balconies. Both of her spaces served as spots to rest, recharge, and set out again. Tonight she returned to her city home, just a few floors above where her Sepas slept. She never wanted to be too far away.

The space was bare of personal items. Several copies of her uniform were folded neatly in a small chest in her private room and a modest wall garden covered the wall in the kitchen nook. The common space was only large enough for a small desk and chair, boasting floor to ceiling windows looking out over the mountains behind the palace. No need for chaise lounges or sofas here; no one was invited over. She sat at her desk, lost in thought.

Dorji Tashi had assigned her this apartment after Celio died. Their house in the Inner Ring had been full of life. Celio loved to get creative with the few ingredients issued from the Family, and they would invite the whole honeycomb over for dinner almost weekly. It was Celio who had created the cookbook she gave Hui for his Anniversary of Life gift. She couldn't bear to look at it anymore. Celio had been a painter, too. Where Meera couldn't get a hold on any of the arts, Celio had mastered several. The house was full of beautiful renderings of the garden, the cliffs and mountain sides in Bhutan's center, and (much to Meera's embarrassment) several paintings of Meera herself.

New Bhutanese culture was one of sharing. Most didn't hold on to valuable or sacred items for more than a few years. The people would trade baubles and art so that everyone could have a taste of them. After Celio's death, Meera dropped one painting off at each house in the honeycomb, spread the silks of Celio's robes in the next, and delivered all leftovers to Mishka's community.

Only when the house had been completely emptied did she cry. She'd sat for meditation in the center of the empty common space, hoping to let go of Celio gently and beautifully. Instead, her deep breaths had turned into ugly sobs, the sounds echoing around the empty room and back at her.

The echo of an empty space hadn't left her still, years later. Throwing herself into her work with the SEPA Project had kept her busy. Protecting New Bhutan had given her purpose.

Then, nearly a year ago, 288 came back to her. Seeing Sepa 288 that day, all grown up, had sparked the fire in her. She knew the change would be coming now. Celio had always promised that the time would come. She had told her to be patient.

I wish you were here to share it with me, Meera thought, sitting down for her evening meditations.

Celio had taken the place of everyone else in her life, and Meera had been grateful for the trade. Seeing her family and everything they stood for through Celio's eyes had changed her. They had wanted to be away from Lhasa, to connect with the people in the Outer Ring and learn as much as they could about the Banjar. They saw themselves as fighters for Banjarian rights. They were rebels.

Artists. It was all very exciting until suddenly Celio was gone, and Meera the Adventurer became Meera the Outcast.

She knew that if Celio could see her now, near tears on her mat in Lhasa, she would give her a stern lecture. This isn't about me or you, she would say, it's about everyone. "Think bigger" had been one of her signature phrases. Meera sighed. Imaginary Celio was right. She should be celebrating.

The dinner had gone just as she had hoped. Penna's expression had been proof of that. Having mastered and taught the skills of the Sepa, Meera knew that Penna had changed tonight, if only a little. Her performance after dinner was to be expected. She'd had time to put her guard back up. But she'd been watching her closely during the meal, and for a few moments here and there, she had been vulnerable to change. There had been a crack in that armor; a sliver of uncertainty. That's all that she needed.

Imaginary Celio smiled.

6

---

2 [88]

THE SEPAS WERE PERMITTED to stay the night in the city before heading back to the bunkers. In the past, her evenings had been spent in bed, groggy with a headache from the Emptying. Tonight, as a Quántóu gently closed the door behind her, she took a deep breath and looked around. She was alone, in an apartment three times the size of her bunker, and dizzy with thoughts about the evening.

She put the kettle on to boil and stood at the window, looking out over the lush grounds that led to Potala Palace. Although night had stolen most of the view, lanterns dangled along the path and solar ground lights were appearing in the gardens. Her fists clenched, thinking about how many times she'd stood here, gazing out in wonder, having no idea what they had taken from her. No idea of the truth.

Since 288's last Emptying, she'd been chasing a rebel named Story through the clans, picking up new bits of information at every stop, and even found and stopped two other rebels while in pursuit. She had been to Bengalia, Karjilik, and finally, Tumail. She'd been in the Banjar for ten months straight.

So many of those nights she'd asked the sky to let her remember; whispered the names and lives of everyone she'd met, told herself the story of everything she had seen, promising to never forget; *don't let them make you forget.*

They had finally picked her up and sent her through the barrier to Lhasa. Sailing through the sky on the helio, she'd dwelled on the idea of the previous versions of herself in that very seat, headed to and from the very same fate. She pitied those girls as much as herself now; about to lose people so sacred, experiences so shocking.

It's no wonder Sepas have no individuality, she'd mused, *they steal every experience that builds who we are.*

The water had been boiling for a few minutes now, the steam screaming into the room. She stood still, letting the high-pitched wail fill the space with the anger she was feeling before sighing and turning back to the kitchenette. The rich foods of the dinner had settled into a dull pain in her abdomen, and she hoped to let the tea settle her belly as well as her nerves before retiring. The wall garden was minimal compared to the one she'd seen in Meera's apartments earlier, presumably because no one lived in this guest space. A browning basil plant and a wilted mint were the only plants with any green on them. She rummaged through a shelf of jars housing dried herbs and fruits; peppermint, chamomile flowers, raw garlic, and ginger roots. She found a canvas bag in a drawer for dried goods with a few lemons, obviously stocked for her benefit. Rubbing her aching belly, she crushed a mixture of lemon balm, ginger, and fresh lemon and pulled the water from the heat.

Meera San had collected her from this apartment earlier, half carrying her across the dome to her private space. She'd still been groggy from the shot and felt a pang of shame for her outburst earlier. Meera San expected her to be the best Sepa, and Sepas don't fight back.

Their brief walk was silent, trickling fountains and bright green leaves mocking everything 288 knew to be true about the world. Meera led her into her apartment and closed the door behind them with a decisive click.

Her rooms were similar to the Sepa rooms, really, only slightly larger. 288 had been covered in a thick layer of dust, sweat, and old blood, but Meera had not asked her to wash up. She'd directed her to sit in the only chair in the room.

"You've been gone a long time, 288," she'd begun. "I understand you've successfully calmed a serious threat."

288 only clenched her jaw in response, staring just past her. She'd been thrumming with grief, barely containing the urge to throw Meera to the ground and slit her throat.

"I had hoped that you would capture Story, but the report says you calmed her instead."

Even in her rage, these words caught her off guard. She wanted her to *capture* her? Wasn't that always the last resort? Before she could respond, Meera went on.

"Your memory pockets are nearing their capacity. Anything after this will be misplaced in your permanent memory." It was then that she noticed Meera's hands, twisting into one another nervously. Her eyes raised to Meera's, paying full attention. "But, I feel that it would be a waste of the information and skills you possess to Empty them at this point. You'll need to keep your knowledge of the different actors in Story's rebellion attempt. The more you know about their connections and plans, the better you can root out new adversaries."

She'd swallowed past a lump that formed in her throat. Was Meera San saying she would not be Emptied this time?

Meera waited for her to respond for a moment before adding "Besides, they have certainly communicated about you. It would not serve for them to be ahead of you from the jump." She looked at her expectantly.

288 tried to recall how to speak. "I'm not to be Emptied," she finally whispered.

"No." Meera offered a grim smile. "You're not."

The world swayed around her for a moment, relief stealing her breath.

Miracle, you're staying with me.

For once, she let herself ask a question. "Then...why am I in Lhasa?"

She knew that off-duty Sepas (which were rare) were simply returned for training drills.

"We're inviting the Sepas to a Family dinner," Meera explained, obviously working to keep her tone casual, "To celebrate dismantling the attempted rebellion and keeping the trades coming in."

She was nervous to say it. Meera turned to the window, facing away from her as if she knew 288 was reading her. "You need to understand the importance of your discretion. The dinner guests may ask about your missions and what you know of the Banjar. You are to say nothing, as if you had been Emptied." She turned back to look her in the eye. "Is that clear, 288?"

She'd agreed too easily, she thought now, finally testing a sip of the steaming tea. It had been clear that Meera was hiding something. She should have asked why Meera would host a dinner for the Sepas during such a fragile time in the Banjar. Story had been calmed, but what about everyone Story had riled up? It wouldn't be long before another leader took her place. And why would Meera let her near *anyone* with the memories she had tucked in her pockets? She hadn't asked, though. She'd been too relieved and grateful for the respite of Emptying that she didn't think to say a word.

288 sipped her tea and looked out into the darkness. The dinner was done. Whatever scheme Meera San was growing had been harvested. Her mind was stretched, trying to find meaning between those crisscrossed lines pulled taut between each person at the table. She was thinking of Penna, like someone cornered, metaphorical fists in the air. There were more than a few untold stories behind her fierceness. Seldom Chime seemed to know more than the others, but maybe that was wishful thinking on 288's part. She had shown the most compassion in the group.

There was Dorji Tashi and Cadence, the two men in charge—one simmering with aggression and the other naive and drunk with authority. Those laughing eyes of his came back to her then and a blush rose to her cheeks. His eyes had seen her... and then he'd laughed and turned away. 288 pushed Cadence out of her mind, too. He seemed too foolish to be caught up in anything Meera was looking for. Mishka was nothing more than a cut onion, stinging who she could. 288 scratched her off the list, too. Then there was Sai San. She wondered if Sai was the key. He was obvious in his discretion, trying too hard to be passive. Sai and Seldom Chime married, although she double his age. They acted as maan and son more than husband and wife, as far as she could tell. Of course, Bhutanese marriages may very well be different than those in the Banjar.

The child, Hui, was harmless. A sad smile flitted across her face at the thought of him. His wide-eyed wonder and look of victory when he noticed her secret message. He reminded her so much of Miracle, if Miracle had had a chance at life. She still wasn't sure what had possessed her to write it. What could come of it? What was she risking by including it? It was impossible to guess what kind of punishment she would receive for trying to stay in contact with the child. If Meera had noticed, she might spend a day locked in her bunker as a reminder to be obedient. If Dorji Tashi or Penna San had noticed...well, her imagination was coming up with some gruesome speculations, but there was no way to know if any were close to reality. She had been moved to act on instinct. She wanted to know more about this Family; the rebels in the room and the alliances. She had been swept up on an assignment she hadn't been given and the next logical step in that moment was to create a contact.

Or, she chided herself, *he reminds you of Miracle.*

She frowned and took a scalding sip. Either way, it had been a foolish move. Hui may help her find out more about the Family, which could aid her in her plan, but those were a lot of ifs for such a gamble. Nevertheless, she had made up her mind to fulfill her unspoken promise to Miracle, and the first step was to not let anyone make her forget.

They would never make her forget again.

She stood and went to the window, pressing an open palm to the glass. It was only so many times in a Sepa's life that she was in apartments alone, even rarer to be looking out over a dark green night sky, and never, not even once, that she would be permitted to remember it.

HUI COULDN'T CONTAIN his excitement in the carriage home. His hands itched to grab for his notebook, but he had to settle for drumming the bench seat and filling the silence with chatter.

"Which Sepa was your favorite, Maan?"

"My favorite? I can't tell them apart, Hui. Besides, they didn't say a word. How could I have a favorite?"

"They each accomplished different feats in the great and terrible Banjar!" At this, Hui brandished an invisible sword at her. "They fought off the evil rebels and saved New Bhutan!"

Mishka laughed, swatting away his sword. "Is that what you took from all that? They don't even have weapons. New Bhutan is a military-less state. We break—"

"Bread, not bones. I know." Hui sat back down and looked at his mother thoughtfully. "Isn't that what makes them even better? That they fight with words?"

She smiled tiredly. "What a smart boy I have. Yes, you are right. That does make them more powerful." Her smile faded and her eyes found the window. "That might be the danger in them."

"But they're on our side!"

She shook her thoughts off and found her smile. "Of course they are."

As soon as the carriage locked into its charging cell, Hui was out of it and bounding to his room.

"*Satsriaka!*" she called after him.

"Good night, Maan!"

Slamming his door behind him, Hui pulled out the journal and threw himself onto the bed, brushing through the pages. Quickly enough, he found the picture 288 had drawn for him. After she'd finished his portrait, she'd insisted that he keep both. "Hui, Sepa's don't keep personal items. This portrait would better serve to keep us connected in *your* hands."

But how, he'd wondered. He took the picture from her hands, a decent drawing of a boy that looked very little like Hui. It was clear that Sepas were not trained in rendering. She had taken time to shade around him, layers of dark and light strokes criss crossed over one another.

This was what he focused on now, almost positive he was right in her meaning. Then, he saw it. Barely discernible, formed in variants of the shadow, was the message "B.5.7."

Like words drawn on tablecloths. Hui felt excitement ripple across his skin. B57. A code? A password? He sat on his bed without moving his eyes from the text. B57. Was it a riddle? He thought of words that begin with the letter B that had five letters, or was it five syllables and seven letters? Might it be the fifth month and the seventh day? His mind raced along with possibilities.

Long after the excitement had faded into frustration, he fell into a deep sleep, the journal open across his chest.

The next morning he awoke comfortably under his blankets, the journal set on the bedside table and the lamp turned down. His maan must have been in. He grabbed the journal and tucked it to his chest protectively. Had she taken one last look at the Sepa's art? Had she slowly admired his own or shook her head in concern at his quirks? Most likely she had just set it aside, concerned with him sleeping through the night more than his interests.

The house was still when he came down the steps for mori. His faan would be gone for several days and his maan would take her time leaving their bed chambers. She tended to do her meditations before mori when it was just the two of them. Feeling very grown up, Hui decided to make mori for his maan instead of waiting for her.

The kitchen was a long rectangle, one wall covered in a vertical garden, the other a window facing the rising sun. First light was waking the petals and leaves along the wall, highlighting ripe tomatoes and mint leaves as if in offering. Hui put a kettle on to boil and picked mint and lemon balm for a simple tea, crushing the leaves with the pestle into two ceramic cups. He set to cutting onions, garlic, and beating rice cakes for mori on a long rectangular countertop that almost ran the length of the room. It was used for cooking, eating, writing, and all else.

Although his parents were of high stature, every family in New Bhutan lived within the same means. The house was a kitchen and a small common room on the main floor with two bedrooms and one bath above. Each apartment was connected with eight others, designed to mimic a honeycomb. These honeycomb communities shared all of their resources. Pipes from their shared water solar tower provided hot water to each home and a large garden grew in the center of their properties. The crop provided all of the food for the small community, excluding the weekly deliveries from Yutan. Of course, each family kept a simple vertical garden in the home for their personal stock.

The smell of garlic had lured Mishka from her meditation. She came down stretching her arms high above her head, a soft smile playing on her lips. "Hu! You spoil me this morning."

Pleased with himself, Hui set a steaming plate and cup before her and climbed onto a stool, his legs dangling as he blew on his tea.

"Mmmm. This is good," she sighed. "That was quite an event last night, wasn't it?"

"It was wonderful!" he said around a mouthful, happy that she had brought it up.

"Yes. I wonder..." she trailed off.

He tilted his head at her, cheeks still full of rice cake.

She gave a small laugh before sighing and adding, "I wonder why my sister did it."

"To celebrate! The Sepas are doing better than ever!"

"Yes, that is what she said. But there's usually more to the reason for doing something than the one people offer. Especially my sister." She waved a chopstick at him knowingly. "For example, your decision to make mori this morning. One reason may be because you wanted to do something nice for me. What's the other reason?"

"There is no other reason!"

She cocked a brow at him.

Hui searched his brain. Had there been an ulterior motive? Maybe that he had woken up hungry himself and didn't want to wait.

"I... I wanted to thank you for tucking me in after I fell asleep in my dress clothes last night."

Mishka looked taken aback and her hand stretched across the table to lay over his own. "Hmmm. Either I'm a cynic or you are kinder than this world, Hui. Thank you for mori."

She offered a quick smile before pulling her touch away. After a few quiet bites, she gave him a sidelong glance. "You fell asleep with your journal over your chest. Late night drawing?"

"I was looking at the drawing the Sepa made, thinking about what New Bhutan might look like from the outside."

"I imagine it must look very tempting," she said darkly.

"I dreamed that I was trying to get in," he suddenly remembered. "I was climbing that rocky cliff, but the wall was crumbling under me. I was so thirsty. I couldn't think of anything but the water on the other side. I didn't even think about the crumbling rock or that I might die. I just thought water, water, water; over and over." He scowled at his tea. "It was a terrible dream."

He felt his maan's countenance change and she stood abruptly, taking her barely touched plate to the wash basin.

"You should run along to your meditations before Maester Fre arrives."

Their backs were turned to one another. "Yes, Maan." He slipped off the stool and away to his room.

Meditations were three times a day; once to ready your body and mind for a new day, once to rejuvenate and focus for the afternoon, and once to ready for rest. Mishka let them skip the night meditations when they attended an event, and he must admit, he usually ended up sleeping poorly. Each family member had their own meditation space, with rug, candle, and plant. The soy wax candle was a rarity, and only burned during those three ten-minute intervals.

He was supposed to clear his mind and focus only on the way his body breathed, but his mind had raced ahead to Maester Fre. What would he think of the Sepa dinner? Would he know what B57 meant? Could he ask?

Maan hadn't liked his dream at all.

The intrusive thought interrupted his musings. Her disappointment in him always came fast, hard, and seemingly out of nowhere.

Soon he heard the chime of bells as Maester Fre arrived in the courtyard below.

Children of different ages from the honeycomb came spilling out of their homes and Hui hastily blew out his candle and ran to join them. Besides the garden, the center field housed a small amphitheater, five steps high. The children gathered on the steps before him, organizing themselves into age groups by stair. Hui was one of three children in his age group, eight–thirteen, but the other two were younger girls and had never paid him much mind.

Maester Fre preferred to introduce the children to the lesson with some exciting or harrowing narrative. Today, it was The Legend of Dorji Tashi I. His forces held off the horde of Banjar barbarians as the last layers of the sphere were completed in the Last War. He led the fight himself, going beyond the barrier as it was shut off to him forever. He left a son behind, who would be the first Heart of New

Bhutan. Throughout their history, many leaders had been named after their brave ancestors, but none had had a chance to prove their heroism as the original Tashi had, and hopefully never would.

They were studying the mechanics of the sphere, very loosely related to the story, but it did make it seem like more important work. Hui had questions, but the Maester did not appreciate interruptions. He waited until the lesson, activity, and writing had been completed before approaching him. The other children were at picnic tables strewn throughout the gardens, working on their writing. Hui tended to finish first, although he wasn't sure if that was because he was smarter or less thorough.

"Maester Fre?"

"Hui." He turned from a plant he'd been inspecting and smiled. His eyes were always glittering with laughter, it seemed, the sun's lines warm across his face.

"What is a barbarian?"

He arched an eyebrow. "Someone who doesn't belong to a community. An outcast of sorts, who doesn't understand or believe in the way things should be done."

"But... but if they were trying to get into New Bhutan and we didn't let them, are we sure they didn't believe in how things should be done?"

"Ah, I see. Well, in those days, it was different than the Banjarians we have now. New Bhutan didn't even have a way to prescribe to. Everyone was looking to survive. Some were fortunate and others were not."

"And now? Some are still fortunate and others are not?"

"That is the way of the world, Hui." He offered a solemn nod and smiled.

Hui dug his toe into the dirt. "Well, I don't think we should call the Banjar people barbarians if we haven't given them a chance to learn our ways."

The Maester's smile grew. "Wise boy, Hui. However," he paused, pressing his palms together in thought. "There is a balance that must be found between wisdom, justice, and power if we are to survive. Think on that, child."

He turned back to the plant, crouching to inspect its leaves.

"Maester Fre?"

"Yes?" he murmured, still turned.

"Did you know about the Sepa dinner last night?"

"I had heard, yes."

"And?"

"And what?"

Hui realized that he wasn't sure what he had meant to ask. He just wanted to talk to someone about it and his maan had made it clear that she was not an option. He glanced around at the children scattered throughout the garden. He had been friendly with a few of them over the years, but he was always the last choice if others were unavailable, and soon allegiances had formed around him.

"And... I met them. Maan had me go along because my faan is working the perimeter this week." He crossed his arms, squinting up at him. "Do you think Sepas are less human? They seem human to me."

Maester Fre turned to face him, now holding a few leaves from the plant in his fingertips. "SEPA pockets," he mused. "Do you know what SEPA stands for, Hui?"

He shrugged. "No."

"Sepas have *Severing Emotive Personal Association* pockets. Kiba Chime created a block in their brains that directs memories into these pockets. She called them that because when the memories are stored in the pockets and not integrated into other experiences and emotions, the Sepas lose the ability to connect their emotions to their memories. What *makes* us human might be the question you're really asking. Some would say it's an emotional connection to others."

Hui shuffled his feet, thinking. 288 *had* been all business. But she'd also smiled a few times.

"I think Maan is scared of them."

Maester Fre smiled. "And you are not."

He said it simply, as if he knew what Hui was getting at before he did.

"Should I be?"

"Sepas are no different than the bees buzzing around our heads. Some will pollinate a flower you love and some will sting you. They work for the same hive, but are their own bee nevertheless. It's easy to say that you should or you should not be scared of them as a whole, but at the end of the day, no Sepa is the same."

8

2⁸⁸

MIRACLE'S MAAN was pounding on the door, screaming to be let in.
She wanted to see him one more time. *Let me see my baby*, she wailed.
288 was crouched over Miracle's bed, watching helplessly as blood
erupted from his mouth. She couldn't bring herself to leave him and
let his maan in, not when his eyes clung to her for dear life. The three
of them were suspended in time for what felt like an eternity. The
screams, the blood, and 288's heartbeat. Suddenly, the pounding
stopped and she broke the connection to look behind her. The door
was gone, and in its place stood the winking dome of Luópán Hall.
They were outside in a searing heat. She turned back to find Miracle
gone, replaced by his maan. Story's throat was slit, her eyes wild as
she gurgled a last choke. Black blood covered her and 288 as both
women tried to to stop the bleeding.

288 awoke gasping for breath. She had been choking right along
with Story. Stumbling out of bed, she hurried to the window and held

her palms before the moonlight, looking for blood. Clean. She pressed a hand to the glass to steady herself, trying to shake the vision. The images of Story's throat and Miracle's desperate eyes would not leave her, however, so she went into the dark washroom and used the basin to rinse her eyes. She tried to replace those tortured faces with the ones she had played, worked, and ate alongside for several months.

Conjuring Miracle's face, inches from her own as he whispered in a dialect she had yet to learn, was easy. His baby cheeks were still round and sun-kissed. Starvation never had a chance to steal that away from him. His hands would naturally curl around her blue robes while he spoke. No one ever touches a Sepa, but this child didn't see a Sepa. He saw her. He would look at her with wonder and joy, his eyes glittering brown and gold, hidden behind thick black lashes. The kid saw so much that the adults around him didn't. He was constantly playing games with people who were not there. He'd had a mischievous smile, one that would play on his lips as he inched by on some secret mission, completely unaware that she and Story were watching. He'd been just a week from being six when he died.

Soaking up this image of him to banish her nightmares, she took a few steadying breaths and crawled back under the light sheet they provided for comfort. That violent sun was just beginning to make its ascent over the city center, and she watched it, immersed in memories that were hers to keep.

The people of Tumail were rather tall compared to the Bhutanese, and Story was no exception. At twenty-two years of age, she was a towering six feet. Despite her lanky frame, 288 could see the tight muscles flexing under her clothes. Most Tumailians were strong from mining the Himalayan mountains for copper and iron to trade with New Bhutan. Story was lucky. Her faan had kept her out of the mines as a child, extending her life range by two times. She'd explained this to 288 regretfully, a bitter bite in every word.

They'd been sitting in what might have once been a field along the mountainside but was now another desert, the mountain a sizzling fist punching the sky before them. Miracle was a few paces off, drawing in the dirt. "I'm going to make a mural," he'd declared with solemn determination. He had learned the word only the day before.

"Why does the prospect of a longer life make you sad?" 288 had murmured. Never push.

Story had kept her eyes trained meaningfully on her son. "The longer you live, the more death you see."

288 followed her gaze curiously, wondering why she would rather die than watch the child die.

"I'm glad you're here, Sepa, and that you'll be staying with us," she continued, still looking toward Miracle. "I know you've been tracking me." She met her eyes and smiled knowingly. "Didn't think I knew? The clans have our own means of communication. I'm glad you found me here, where we are from. Tumail is my home, and will be Miracle's home. That's why I invited you to stay with us here."

288 hadn't understood what she meant. Yet.

Staring resolutely away, she added, "It is rumored that the Family has protection from the Banjarguay." It was obvious she was afraid to betray how important this unspoken question was to her. 288 almost felt sorry for her, but didn't.

Not yet.

She kept her eyes on Miracle too. "Sepas live along the barrier. We train and trade and that is all. If we fall ill, we die. If there is aid for illness, I know nothing of it."

Story's lips pursed and she turned away, looking toward the mountain. She didn't speak much, making her a difficult target. Meera San had sent her after Story, claiming the memories had heard her say "Luópán Hall" more than four times and in multiple territories. It was a trigger word. The trading Sepas' pockets kept everything on file. Every conversation within ten yards. They were Emptied and analyzed consistently, but certain combinations of words in the Emptying would trigger a flag for the Listeners. Those phrases included breach, the barrier, Luópán Hall, and Dorji Tashi.

288 had been with Story and Miracle for three days at that time. She had already been in the Banjar for a few months tracking Story

and had heard about her from other clans. She seemed reserved so far, but the clans had talked of her traveling there multiple times, pushing for them to join her in Tumail and plan an attack. To hear them tell it, there were many people amongst her now who had followed her.

She had brought her small child along with her. Miracle's faan had died when he was still in her womb. Some said that his death and the new baby were what drove Story to fight so aggressively for change. Looking at her then, watching her son, she didn't seem so aggressive.

The child had taken to 288 immediately, following her around as she toured the sprawled community. That could be because of all the treats she'd brought along with her in offering. The Tumailians lived all along the mountain, a dry river of sheds snaking along the base of the Himalayas. They used large gongs crafted by Tumailian artists to communicate with one another. Each mile marker had their own set and would start a pattern to announce a message. Each marker following would pick up the beat and spread the word. They had pounded the gongs for her arrival. They had pounded the gongs for Miracle's death.

When a person dies in Tumail, the family carries the body along the cliff's edge path to Godsmeet Peak. The path winds away from the southern point of the community and spreads out into a wide oval plateau before ascending once again. This is where families say goodbye and drop the body over, and the mourning drums begin. Two days later, the family returns with arrows, hunting the vultures who will have started to peck at the dead's flesh.

Those closest to the dead feast on bird meat in a ceremonial meal, so the body of their lost one will live on in their bellies. If the bird sits well in their stomach, the loved one is happy with them in death. If they become ill, the dead wants one more thing from them. If they become so sick as to die, the community knows they wronged the dead terribly in life and would now pay the price.

288 hadn't waited to eat the bird of Miracle. She'd left Bhutan

with his blood still on her hands and a certainty of what he'd want from her. She didn't need the bird to feel sick.

It was good fortune to have met Hui, the Bhutanese child. If Hui read between the lines, they could start an alliance. It may be a dead end toward fulfilling her unspoken promise to Miracle, but at least it was a start.

She was cataloging the possible benefits of this alliance when Meera San entered her apartments. She had changed from the elaborate robes she generally wore in Lhasa to her unbleached shorts and tank, the uniform of the Sepa bunkers. She had come straight into the private quarters without a knock, saying "288?" as she opened the door.

She stopped short when she saw that she was still in bed, as if she'd never imagined that Sepas sleep at all. Her face immediately flushed and she took a step back. "I'm sorry to intrude," she muttered.

288 jumped out of bed and stood at attention, head slightly bowed. She was stark naked, having laid her blue robes over the basin the night before. She thought about pulling the sheet around her but decided that would it make her look weak. She was not weak.

She heard Meera step closer, closing the door behind her. No Quántóu had followed. 288's heart set to beating at a faster rate. Would they be Emptying her after all?

Instead of coming to her side, Meera walked past her to the washroom and returned holding the Sepa robe. She wrapped it around 288 tenderly, tying the knot over her shoulder. Finally, she took a finger under 288's chin and pulled her face up so their gazes met.

An ache settled in her chest at the gesture. Unable to help herself, she asked quietly, "Is it time?"

Meera San looked at her thoughtfully. "The other Sepas were Emptied last night. It's unwise to show them our way of life before sending them back to the Banjar."

288's throat constricted with anger. "Then why bring us here in the first place?"

"I have my reasons," she said lightly, and set herself down at the foot of the bed. She gestured for 288 to follow.

She sat, careful to keep her expression blank. She wanted to ask if it was her turn now. Wanted to know how Meera could give and take so many experiences from them with such ease.

Meera was rubbing her face, oblivious to 288's thoughts. "Whew. I am exhausted! I've been up all night." She offered her a small smile. "I was thinking about you, actually."

288 swallowed and worked to keep her expression blank. Reveal nothing.

"I gave you that number on your neck."

Her hand acted of its own accord, reaching back to skim fingers along the scar tissue. What did it feel like to insert numbers into a child's flesh? Why did she say it so tenderly?

She dropped her eyes to the sheet, waiting.

"Sepas don't have names, but they do have numbers. It's necessary to keep track of who is where. When you were a baby, we, well, I... I called you by a real name sometimes, when we were alone."

288's eyes had lifted to Meera's. Her heart began to pound at such a rate that she wondered if Meera could hear it.

Meera shifted uncomfortably. "You see, I suspected then what I'm almost certain of now. You're different, 288. You're highly capable, and because of that, you will have to face more danger than the others. Now that you will be keeping your memories, I will be speaking with you directly to hear reports. We will be in contact much more frequently. And we will have to trust each other."

She tried to put a hand over hers but 288 snatched it back. No one touched a Sepa. Her hand had reacted before her brain had a chance to consider.

Meera grimaced and pulled her hand back. "I don't blame you. That's why I want to start off a new relationship with you today. Between us, when we're alone, I would like to call you by your true name."

At first, there was only suspicion. Why would Meer give her a name? Then, looking at her earnest expression and seeing authenticity there, there was a delirious hope. The world swam before her in a fit of dizziness, like reality had been tampered with. And yet, her face remained blank as a doll's. Reveal nothing.

Completely unaware of 288's inner chaos, Meera continued. "It's Sepora. We, well, I, have called you that since you were made." She reached her hand out again, this time much more tentatively. "Is it okay if I call you Sepora?"

288 watched Meera's hand on the bed, reaching toward her with palm up.

What was Meera hiding? What did she want from her that she would go to the extent of letting her keep her memories and gifting her with a name? Who was the "we" she kept slipping? Doubts swirled around her mind, but none strong enough to cloud the elation that was ballooning in her chest at the thought of having a name all her own.

She slowly put her own hand out and set it lightly on top of Meera's, letting their palms touch.

"Sepora," she agreed softly, the notes of the word dancing in her mouth. She finally raised her eyes to Meera's and found that, for the first time that she could remember, her own had filled with tears.

9
____

C ADENCE

HE WAS TAKING his evening walk through the northeastern corner of the Family Gardens. The center courtyard was laid out in a glass mosaic meant to look like the starry nights of the Old World. New Bhutan's sky was dotted with the moon and a single pulsing star, but according to legend, art installations such as this patio were an accurate portrayal of the sky as it had been; a sky filled with stars, endless little lights scattered to form drawings in the sky. When he was younger, he would look straight down at this mosaic and pretend he was looking straight up. He had often daydreamed about the Old World when he was younger, but Seldom had always countered his games with cautionary tales, filling his young mind with the horrors of the old ways. Eventually he stopped sharing his daydreams, and a few years after that, he stopped having them.

In the center of that stone night sky crouched the water dragon fountain he'd nicknamed Hépíng. The fountain's pool walls were made of the tail, wrapping itself into a circle. The tail led up and out of the water as it grew into the body, its thick legs submerged in water and the head reaching twice Cadence's height. Although intimidating, the water dragon's expression was calm, its face looking off to the north. Water sprouted from the small fins along his body as well as its mouth. He much preferred Hépíng to the second dragon fountain in the center of Potala; a fierce fire dragon with water spewing fast from its nostrils. Cadence nodded a greeting to the creature and walked on, headed to the Polar Garden.

The first Family had created the gardens, which stretched over a mile wide, when they made the barrier, bringing in as many plant varieties as possible to keep alive for their descendants. It made sense to create a garden on the grounds of Potala Palace. The palace was the center of creation, built in the seventh century, it was said. Why not have it be the home of the last ruling family, the last garden, where people and plants alike would sprout in a new world?

This museum of life was created by building four temperature regulated domes, each housing its own climate. The Polar Garden, Temperate, Subtropical, and Tropical housed their own types of plant life. Some species had been lost throughout the years due to over-harvesting or disregard by different Hearts, but most of the plants still thrived.

Most Family members or visiting elites spent their time near the fountain, enjoying the many flowers in the Temperate Garden or basking in the rich plant life and warm weather of the Subtropics. Cadence preferred the Polar Garden. For one, he knew for certain that he would be alone there.

He closed the door gently behind him, pulling the purple cloak closer over his shoulders as he adjusted to the temperature. The temperature, however, was the other reason the Polar Garden was his favorite. Nowhere in the world was it this cold anymore. Only here did his breath plume out before him and only here would intricate ice patterns form along the glass. Only here, in this little garden, could these one-of-a-kind plants exist. Long ago, this city was named the Land of Snow. The histories explained that it was one of the last places on Earth to have clean water in the ground; one of the last places to see a rushing river. They said this was the reason it was chosen as the center of the new world. He let his hand graze over the lichen and mosses as he passed, doing a lap through to warm up. He loved to imagine the palace being covered in ice and hoped an hour in the garden would ease his heart, which had been pumping double-time since the dinner.

Of all the scenarios he had entertained, none came close to the reality of how the Sepa dinner played out. Dorji Tashi throwing Meera and Cadence out for slaughter was his first surprise. Why he was surprised, he wasn't sure, now that he thought about it. Of course Tashi would wait to voice an objection until everyone was around. What a perfect way to make Cadence look weak. It wasn't the first time his faan's instincts had been to humiliate or undermine him. He wondered if Penna and he had hatched the plan together. Making him sing was the tipoff that Tashi was in the mood to play with him. He'd been using that trick since Cadence had been fool enough to choose voice as his art form. Tashi had beat him mercilessly for choosing such a weak art and had made him sing for crowds as a way to publicly humiliate him ever since.

Cadence sighed in frustration and reminded himself that he had won that round, singing a song that undercut Tashi's authority. The look on his faan's face was prize enough for Cadence. Besides, his faan and wife-to-be aside, the night had gone well. The Family had voted in his favor. The Sepas had proven their loyalty, staying relatively silent no matter how many questions he threw at them. He'd asked them leading questions such as *if you could change something about New Bhutan, what would it be?* Or *What would you rather do than be a Sepa?* They always said the right thing, with short nods and one sentence claims of allegiance. They were very observant and polite. In truth, he'd never really thought much about what Sepas might be like. Not once had he cared. He had his life to lead and they had theirs, as far as he'd been concerned.

Still, he'd had a certain vision of what they were. He had been wrong. For some reason, he'd pictured them with shaved heads, identical in cloth and countenance. He'd pictured them moving as one, marching and turning heads in step like different pieces of one machine.

Instead... the girl's face came to his mind, not for the first time that morning. In fact, her gaze had been popping into his mind at least once every hour since the dinner. She wasn't bald at all, but had thick black hair, pulled to the side and left loose to tumble down over her shoulder. Her skin was deeply tanned and slightly freckled, with eyes that seemed to see right through him. She'd watched everyone that way. While every Sepa there was clearly taking in every detail of the people and place around them, it was only this one that seemed to have an opinion about what she was seeing. He'd felt more self-conscious than he had in his entire life, his whole world being judged and analyzed by this... this *creature*.

Even thinking it was a lie. And that, truly, was the most surprising and troubling turn of events. She wasn't a creature at all. She was a young woman. Cadence cupped the yellow blooms of the arctic poppy. A young woman that would soon die from the Banjarguay, as they all did after twenty or so years.

This was only half true, he reminded himself. She'd been *created* in Luópán Hall. A young woman was hardly the right description for a machine. He'd realized at the dinner that he'd never looked into the process of making a Sepa. How much of what he was seeing was natural and how much was engineered? He knew they were created through human donations and only modified to be what they were in synthetic wombs, so really, to say she was *not* human was just as incorrect as calling her human. The Family could not have crafted the expressions of bewilderment, fear, or anger that flitted across her face. In the gardens, he'd had an urge to say something silly to her; try to make her smile. But the sudden realization that after making her smile he would be sending her off to death paused him. That smile would have haunted him for life.

Damn you, Meera, he thought now. *Is this what you wanted?* The girl's face floated back into his daydream. She was finally smiling, holding a bouquet of the arctic poppy. He fell so quickly and deeply into this fantasy that he did not hear the door to the Polar Garden creak open.

"Cadence?"

He flushed with embarrassment as if she could read his thoughts.

"Seldom. What a lovely surprise." He strode back to meet her at the door. "We don't usually see many visitors in the Polar Garden."

She smiled knowingly. "I apologize for intruding on your solitude, Cadence. I was working in the Temperate Gardens and saw you pass. Your mind must have been quite occupied to have missed me!"

He sighed. "You know me well. What were you working on? I thought the botanists had taken over all maintenance."

"Yes. But you know how the task soothes me."

"Just like it did for Maan," he said, taking Seldom's weathered hands in his.

"Yes."

"Did you garden together?"

"Of course. With you always between us."

He smiled sadly to himself, wishing he could remember.

"You know," he said conspiratorially, "I've often wished that botany could be considered one of the seven arts instead of a science. If only my art could have been arranging plants!"

"I believe those were florists, not botanists, in the Old World. Unfortunately, there are not enough flowers in the world to have a demand for every seventh citizen. Some make it a hobby, however. Including one of my medics in Luópán, in fact. Besides," she scoffed, "what would the Family do without your lovely voice to carry the anthem?"

"True, true," he joked, wondering if Seldom knew the weight he bore around his voice.

"I was quite surprised to hear you sing 'A New Night' at dinner."

"I would argue that everyone was," he replied, a mischievous grin lighting up his face.

"Well, some say the song is a call for rebellion. Tashi forbade your maan to sing it to you when you were a child."

"I know."

She shook her head at him ruefully. "Would you pause your brooding for a walk?" she asked.

"I would be happy to." He closed the door behind him, cutting off that refreshing cold bite of frosted air. "Lead the way," he added.

"I would assume it is the dinner that turns your thoughts?" she asked, leading him back toward the center patio.

"You would be correct," he said with a smile.

"You didn't let Dorji get to you?"

"It can't always be helped."

"It can. How do you suppose I've lived so many moons alongside him? We have the power to master our minds and our hearts against gut reactions."

"That sounds like an unpleasant life," he said lightly.

"And you sound like a spoiled child, Cadence. Life is not necessarily meant to be *pleasant*."

He paused his steps and turned to look at her. "What is it meant to be, then?"

She smiled. "A timeless question that has yet to be answered."

"Ah-ha," he wagged a finger at her. "So it *could* be about seeking pleasure; finding peace."

"Peace and pleasure are quite different! Pleasure is luxury, whereas peace is found within our hearts."

"I see. And this garden, then?" He gestured at the walls of bright blooms that now surrounded them as they passed into the center courtyard, the water dragon happily gurgling by their side. "This garden gives me peace, and yet, it is also a physical luxury that most cannot access. It brings me pleasure as well as peace."

She looked around thoughtfully. "Does it bring you peace to think only few may share in this pleasure?"

His mind immediately went to 288. He imagined the look of wonder that would light up her face. "No," he said firmly. "In fact, I'll admit it was more that thought than my faan's antics clouding my mind when you found me."

She nodded. "The Sepas?"

He inclined his head in assent, hoping she wouldn't disapprove.

"You know that your maan was Brain before me," she said slowly. "I was her apprentice, even though we were nearly the same age. In fact, I was a bit older. Age didn't matter when Raju chose the next Brain. It was intelligence. Kiba had genius in a way that comes once in a century."

She found her way to a bench and eased down to sit, using his hand for support. "Of course, the experiments started with the Brain before her, but at that time, we were playing with creating babies with tech. They didn't have the memory receptors yet. The Family had been working with memory for a long time, but Kiba was the one who connected it to the Sepas. She was the one who created the memory pockets for storage and removal. Brilliant."

Cadence wasn't sure where she was going with this story but was nevertheless intrigued. His faan had never once mentioned his resting wife, and it was extremely rare for Seldom to mention her either.

"She was using them as test subjects for a greater idea," she said, eyes inward on a memory. "The plan to use their memories to spy on the Banjar was not, at the time, to look for rebels. We had no thought of rebels or threat in our mind. Rebels were what we found, though. We'd always assumed the Banjarians had mostly died out."

"What was her original idea?"

She glanced at him as if only just realizing he was there before yawning loudly. "My dear, we might need to continue this discussion another time. My body aches and it is near nightfall. It takes me longer than you would care to imagine to shuffle to my quarters with this broken body."

He smiled to hide his disappointment. "May I escort you, Seldom?"

"No, no. My two Quántóu are waiting at the garden gates." She stood, turning to him. "My point, Cadence San, is that your faan never earned his place as Heart for his leadership, as your maan earned her place. When she was chosen, Tashi immediately began to court her, hoping a marriage would land him his position as Heart. It did. Connections are everything here, as you well know."

She laid a hand over his heart. "I don't know why we have these lives, but I'll tell you one truth that I have observed in my years. Life is meant to be meaningful. Peace can be found in life when you believe in something and work hard to help create it. Your maan did that. You can do that, too. She changed who the Sepas are and what they do, bettering the lives of Banjarians and New Bhutanese alike. As Eye, you have the power to make changes just as great."

She smiled and turned to walk away. He watched her for a few moments as she inched her way down the exit path.

"Seldom!" he called out.

She turned back to face him, eyebrows raised.

"Do you know that Tashi intends for me to marry Penna?"

She sighed. "Yes, my child." A shadow flickered across her face. "The Brain knows everything that happens in Potala."

10

———

S EPORA

Two days after the dinner, Sepora was picked up from the Sepa Bunkers by a Quántóu pilot and dropped in Tumail. Just like any other drop. Except this time, she was returning with her memories.

Like coming home.

She was realizing, however, that while remembering was better than she'd ever imagined, it certainly had its downfalls as well. Sepora had never felt so human as she walked into Tumail, nodding hello to familiar faces as she made her way down familiar paths on her way to Story's small home.

If she hadn't been coming to betray them all, it would have been an incredible feeling. As it was, her stomach twisted with guilt.

During her last mission to Tumail, Sepora had spent months building Story's trust, and had just begun to convince her that the Family was doing everything in their power to help Tumail. After Miracle's sudden death, she'd reported that Story was too far gone with grief to be a threat. It was only a half lie. Maybe it was Sepora herself who had felt too broken to do anything.

What do you do with them? She remembered Sai asking her at the dinner. She was about to know the answer.

After Meera gave her the gifts of memory and a name, she'd given her orders.

"Sepora," Meera had begun, "I'm asking a lot of you now and I know it." She'd gripped her hand. "I want you to go against orders. Can you do that?"

Sepora's eyes had flickered nervously to the ceiling.

Meera smiled. "Don't worry, I've silenced this room."

Wondering how in New Bhutan she'd done that, she nodded slowly. "I take my orders from you, Meera San."

"Good," she smiled thinly. "That's good. There is another base I need you to investigate. Your missions to the Banjar have all gone very well, but for the Sepas who have failed..." She paused to brush a runaway hair back from her face. "Tashi ordered that we report all failed missions and leave the Sepas at their station. He said a Family helio would pick them up. I've asked as many questions as I dare, but he refuses to share more." She lifted her brow mockingly and added, "*It's not your branch's concern.* We've been observing the areas, however. I've found that after a mission fails, the rebel disappears. I don't know what happens to them. All I know is that the Sepa fails to calm them, and I never hear of them again."

Sepora's jaw tightened, thinking about Story and what could have happened to her if she had failed. "A prison base?" she asked.

"That's the assumption. The problem is, New Bhutan has never had a prison. Offenders are generally put to work in Midland or trained as low rank Quántóu. If there's a prison, there should be a discussion on the sentence. It seems as though it is only Tashi's will that decides."

"What happens to the Sepas?"

"They disappear along with them for a time before being dropped back at the Sepa Bunker."

"Why don't you ask them about the base?"

"That's the issue. There must be an Emptier there. My Sepas return with no memory of picking up the rebel at all."

Sepora's stomach dropped.

Meera was going to ask her to go to the base.

There's an Emptier at the base.

"I would go, but the location is kept under tight security. I've requested to deliver a rebel myself but was turned down. More of that 'none of your branch's concern' business."

Sepora remained silent, her heart pounding.

"I want to know what the base is like. Is there another dome, are they returning to a hidden location within New Bhutan, or, worse case, are they left to die in the Banjar?" She took a deep breath, apparently hesitant to share this last bit of information with her. Sepora steeled herself for the worst of it. "You see, in the last few years, we've noticed people in New Bhutan disappearing as well. After they've been flagged by Listeners for speaking ill of the Family or committing theft, they're just... gone."

The fear constricting her chest gave way to utter shock. "You think Bhutanese are being sent to the Banjar?"

"It seems like the only explanation. I want you to record a full report on the base. How many prisoners are there? What are they doing? Who's running it?"

Sepora couldn't help but feel a sense of injustice begin to form in the pit of her belly. Sepas and Banjarians *lived* in the Banjar, but for the sake of these missing Bhutanese, Meera would defy Family orders.

She tried to remind herself that this was the woman who let her keep her memories. The woman who had gifted her with a name. She was thinking about how Meera had always been kind when her next words slashed her goodwill with a sharp blade.

She told her that she would be bringing Story to the base.

"She's no longer a threat," Sepora immediately responded.

"I heard your report," she said simply.

"But, Meera San—"

"We need a ruse to get you into the base, Sepora. She's been a threat for a long time. It will work."

Sepora's mouth had turned to ash. Her mind filled with Story's eyes emptying, like watching a person turn into a ghost before your eyes. They had lost Miracle together. Now she would be returning to take her to a prison at best. At worst... she had no idea what they were capable of.

Meera noted her stricken face and put a hand on her shoulder, misinterpreting her grief for fear. "I know you're anxious to keep your memories, and we're going to get you out intact. That's why I'm sending my best Sepa in for the job. I must admit, I had hoped you would fail to begin with. This will be better, though, you see? Now we can plan openly."

She gave a small nod, swallowing her anger. Meera had hoped she would fail last time without a care of what would happen to Story, or to her. "How am I going to avoid being Emptied?"

Meera offered a small smile. "Do you know how Sepas are made?"

She gave a small shake of her head. She had a general idea, but the topic always made her squeamish.

"Kiba Chime, the Resting Brain, was able to map the mind, charting how our thoughts and memories are created and stored; how they collide, grow, change, and disappear. She was able to create pockets to catch and store them in different places depending on the type of memory. For example, any recent, daily norm memories, such as eating your mori this morning, will be stored here." She raised a tentative hand and pressed behind Sepora's left ear. "If your mori suddenly grew a mouth and started screaming at you, the memory would be triggering, as it triggers a change in who you are permanently. Then, the memory would be stored here." She pressed behind the right ear. "Sepas have extra space in these pockets, so that every detail can be recalled from long trips, no matter how mundane. I can pull out the color of the sky on a certain morning, or the clothes of a man passing by. I can see everything. In a normal person, those memories would disappear."

Sepora raised her brows in question and waited. Meera hadn't answered her question.

"So," Meera went on, "I know that they will pull from the left pockets when you're finished. They'll assume that nothing fazes you or could be a trigger memory, because you're—" She cut herself off, biting her lip.

"Because I'm not truly human," Sepora finished for her. She cleared her throat.

"That's just it, Sepora," Meera said tightly, "A Sepa doesn't connect with the people around them. Nothing could faze them enough to be stored as a permanent memory. The only time we take permanent memories from a Sepa is when we perform a full Emptying in Luópán. They have a standby Emptier at the base, I'm sure of it. There isn't the equipment available for a full Emptying. What they don't know is that you, Sepora, are different. You have memories and connections; *you* have a name."

Sepora was feeling a little sick to her stomach. Had her gift of memories been part of the plan to prepare her for this task? Was she being groomed for a mission when Meera San gave her a name? Maybe the name had only been made up recently as part of her scheme. Sepora, a name so similar to Sepa that it could have been created in the moment she was saying it.

"You are more human than they think," Meera continued. "When you're there, think on what could change you. Do your best to connect with someone... try to do something important before they take you."

She was thinking about Miracle again, and how that connection had changed her. How many other times had she met someone who changed her, but they had been Emptied in Luópán Hall? How were they sure Sepas wouldn't be changed by their experience at the base?

"And if that doesn't work," Meera was continuing, "just kill the Emptier and run as fast as you can. You are my best fighter. Watch the route on your way in. Look for landmarks and find your way back to Tumail or the bunkers. I'll send a helio out for you the very next day."

Meera had patted her hand and left without waiting for Sepora to agree, saying she would be round to pick her up in an hour and to make sure she had eaten.

Sepora had let out a long-held breath as the door clicked closed behind her, looking around the empty space without seeing any of it. She had hoped to return to the Sepa base. She had hoped that Hui would find her and she could learn more about Luópán. Instead, she would return to the Banjar and betray Miracle's maan for the second time. Her fists clenched around the sheet.

A Sepa doesn't disobey.

A few days later, she'd been climbing into the helio from the bunkers. Meera had clutched her hand, her eyes suddenly wild with fear. "Sepora, I have to tell you. Sometimes, the Sepas don't come back. I don't know why." She tightened her grip. "Come back. Make sure you come back."

Sometimes, the Sepas don't come back.

Sepora had swallowed and nodded, pushing down her anger, her fear, and that strange sense of betrayal. She'd returned to Tumail and found Story in her home, sleeping in a ball on Miracle's bed. It wasn't hard to get close enough to knock her out. Story barely moved when she saw her and didn't say a word. She just reached out one long arm as if to ask Sepora to lie beside her. She obliged, curling her legs up in front and facing her, their hands entwined.

The room was only big enough for the small mat, made of sacks from food deliveries stuffed with sand. The winds would blow sand through the cracks in the shanty walls, but Tumailians didn't mind a clean breeze. The mountain kept the homes in the shade for most of the day. Still, the temperature could spike to 130. A sandy breeze across your bed was welcome. There was no breeze that morning, and sitting so close to Story, Sepora's face had begun to sweat.

Story stared at her for a minute before bringing her thumb up to Sepora's face and pressing it between her brows. She let the thumb move slowly down her nose. Sepora swallowed down the emotion this gesture of love brought to her throat and returned the movement on Story's face.

A small smile lifted the side of Story's mouth when she was

finished. She untangled her other hand from Sepora's and brought both to Sepora's face, squishing her cheeks together toward her mouth.

"Miracle loved making you look funny," she whispered. "He was the only one who could make you smile, wasn't he?"

She released her face, her smile fading.

Taking a deep breath and silently asking for forgiveness, Sepora brought her own hands up to wrap around Story's jawline. Story's eyes had clouded over with grief and she didn't even notice her touch until Sepora began to put pressure on her. Her eyes found her in a moment of realization before she passed out.

Methodically, Sepora stood and retrieved her bag. She pulled out the cuff ropes and gag and waited for the Family helio, as instructed.

As if watching someone else, she had done everything she'd been told to do, and now here they were, on their way to the base. The Family helio was different from the helios used to drop Sepas. Its back end was walled off from the driver seats, creating a small room for the two back seats. The driver had lifted her palm and scanned. her identity without a word, gesturing for her to load her prisoner and get in the back herself. He shut and locked the door behind them and they were lifted into the air. Being put in the back gave her a sense of foreboding. The Quántóu who worked as Sepa delivery drivers were never talkative or even cordial, but they at least allowed her to sit in front. She glanced warily around the small space, eyes falling on the inert figure across from her.

Attacking Story had been the hardest thing she'd ever done. She felt connected to her in their grief, in their shared memories of Miracle. She wondered if this was how people felt about friends. She glanced over at the gagged and bound figure before her and shook her head. *Nice*, she thought to herself, *your first friendship is going fantastic.*

Out the window, Sepora caught a glimpse of their destination. A small mountain range was creating a half circle around a patch of dark green. She'd never seen the color green outside New Bhutan, where plants grew in abundance. In the Banjar, all lands were wastelands. But here, a crescent moon of green hugging the mountain, and beyond that, a sparkling stretch of blue. Sepora shot to her feet, nearly hitting her head on the ceiling. She cupped the glass and pressed her face in, squinting to see clearly. There were no lakes left, no rivers. All water other than the Broken Oceans came from New Bhutan.

Sepora's heart was racing as the water came closer and closer. Beautiful. A miracle. The water stretched for maybe six miles. Its surface rippled in a breeze, turning silver, green, blue, grey; mesmerizing. They had a real lake. Her hand covered her mouth. *No wonder they erase our memories*, she thought bitterly. *They want the lake for themselves.* Meera was wrong. They must have been doing full Emptying at the base. The sight of this lake would change anyone.

She slammed her fist against the glass.

Behind her, Story moaned. It snapped something in Sepora. She needed to focus and get through this. She could not forget. She could not disappear.

Their next steps would have to wait until she arrived, but she couldn't wait. She needed to do something now. She clutched Story's shoulders and gave her a rough shake, but she merely moaned. Sepora gritted her teeth and slapped her.

Story's eyes opened. Quickly, Sepora pressed one hand over Story's gag and one over her own mouth. She nodded with eyebrows raised and pointed to the ceiling. *They can hear us. Do you understand?*

Although her eyes were full of mistrust, she gave a slight nod. Wrapping an arm under her body, Sepora half carried, half dragged Story to the window.

She let out a cry behind the gag.

Sepora had seen the ponds of water in New Bhutan, the moat that had once been a great river, but they were nothing like this.

The only water Story had ever known, on the other hand, was delivered once a week by the Family's Sepas. They were given just enough to survive and keep working. She wondered if Story assumed she knew where she was going. If she thought Sepora had known about the lake. She put her hand on the window in reverence, hoping Story would understand that they were on this journey together.

They stared out the window in silence. After a few moments, she gently took Story's chin and turned it to face her. She didn't really know what she would have said if she could say anything. *I want to help you* or *will you help me*, or just *what the hell are we going to do?*

She tried to say it all in her eyes and with a fierce kiss to Story's forehead. It was the first kiss Sepora ever gave. She'd seen Story give them to Miracle, including the day he died. She pulled away to see Story's eyes fill with tears. The look that passed between them said so much. They were united in their helplessness. In their bondage.

The helio began making its descent, and as one, they both turned back to the window.

Nestled between young trees and lush plants were buildings, built in the traditional imperial style of open walls and sweeping roofs that curled up on either end. Stone statues of strange creatures stood as sentries around the landing site. Some had curled tails while others had hair hanging from their entire body. Another had large horns protruding from its face. *Animals*, Sepora thought, suddenly thinking of Hui. She'd have to return and tell him that yes, she had seen animals in the Banjar.

They landed in a series of concentric circles laid in red stone. Sepora quickly pushed Story back to her chair and sat in her own, staring straight ahead as if the view meant nothing to her. The door opened and two men in New Bhutanese civilian robes pulled them out. One offered a helping hand to Sepora while the other carelessly threw Story over his shoulder. Story went one way, fighting with all she could, and Sepora was led another. It took all her strength not to look back.

Use your skills, Meera had told her. She let her eyes slide to the side, carefully studying the man leading her. His robes were clean enough but wrinkled. He had no partner to press it in the morning and didn't care to do it himself. His hair was just an inch too long and his cheeks were a shade darker red than his round face. *He was drinking spirits last night*, she thought. *Did he spend the night here?*

She looked around. There were men dressed in fine robes scattered around the gardens he was leading her through, laughing and talking. It felt more like New Bhutan than a labor prison. Who were these men who lived outside the barrier? Most seemed past thirty, even forty. She squinted up at the sky. Had they flown through an aerial barrier door? Was there a second dome over this lake?

She turned to the man. "I have delivered the rebel, Sir San. May I receive my next assignment and be on my way?"

He let out a bark of a laugh and stopped, looking her over from head to toe. Then, without warning, he threw a backhanded slap across her face. Her knees threatened to buckle from the surprise, but she remained upright, slowly turning her face back to stare at him, impassive.

"It's my understanding that Sepas don't speak," he said, and continued walking.

Sepora swallowed the blood that was pooling in her mouth and walked alongside him. *He's a weak man, deathly afraid of being incompetent. He uses physical strength to prove himself, even if it's only over the weaker.* She almost smiled. *He thinks I'm weaker than him.*

She decided to play the part. She pulled in an audibly deep, shaky breath and slowed her steps. When he noticed her pace, he turned back and grabbed her elbow.

"We'll take all afternoon at this rate," he grumbled. She saw that his eyes were puffy, as if he'd had little sleep. She considered taking him out at that moment. It would be easy. Just a quick swipe at his throat with her free hand and he would be down. She glanced around. They were making their way to a large building about forty paces ahead. As they neared, the collection of loiterers grew. They were emerging from the building dressed in morning robes, sipping tea, and murmuring amongst themselves. It was no time to fight her way out.

As he led her up the steps, the men turned to look at her in the appreciative way some men in the Banjar had. One man on the deck who they passed at close range reached out and grabbed at her chest.

"Wait one second with this one, Kao San. I think she likes me." He smiled at her and squeezed her nipple. The shock and pain made her cry out.

The man named Koa San put a palm up in helplessness. "She's yours if the boss says so, Tyroshi, and no sooner," and he continued to pull her forward.

Sepora tried to quell her fear. Fear, like worry, was pointless. Focus, she reminded herself. Koa San led her into the building, decorated in shining gold statues and thick red carpets. The symbol of the dragon was everywhere. He led her up and up, passing two floors lined with numbered doors.

On the northern wall, a three-story painting continued around the steps. It was of three women, obviously Banjarian, lying with arms and legs entwined in the nude. Around them, smaller figures of Bhutanese women fanned them with intricate fans and offered them fruit. Sepora couldn't help staring at it as they passed. On the third floor, they came through a huge two door entry. This room's exterior wall was a massive balcony overlooking the lake. There were three men sitting in armchairs around a small table, drinking tea.

At their entry, the largest of the three turned.

"Koa! What an early morning delivery. How many?"

"One Sepa delivered one traitor, Sir San, from Tumail."

"Is she in the training center already?"

"Yes, sir. I had Niche take her right away."

"Hmm. I do like to see them first." To his friends, he added, "I like to see the fight in them before I take it away, eh?"

He eased his large bulk from the chair and turned toward them. Sepora swallowed a gasp of shock. It was Dorji Tashi himself. His mustache hung down long enough to meet with his beard and be tied under the chin and his robes were emblazoned with the dragon. She wondered if he would recognize her from the dinner less than a week before.

"You've done your job well, Sepa," he said, smiling. "What do you think of Qinghai Lake?"

She glanced with feigned nervousness at her captor, who had

ordered her to be silent. He smiled. "She knows to keep her mouth shut around me, Sir."

"Well then, I suppose you better excuse yourself so we can talk."

Koa San let shock flit across his face before bowing humbly. "Sir." And with that, he left her.

Her new captor smiled. "That one," he said conspiratorially. "Would you like some tea, Sepa?"

"Please," she murmured. She was dismayed at losing such an easy target. Dorji Tashi would not be so easily manipulated. His calm and kindness were deceiving and his bite would no doubt be deeper.

He led her to the table, where two men appraised her. One with a forked beard eyed her hungrily. The other was Sai San, the mystery man at the dinner. He grimaced at the sight of her and turned his eyes back to the view.

When offered tea, she tipped the cup to her lips but didn't drink. Who could say when they intended to knock her out?

"Tell us about your captive," he said, settling back in his chair.

"Her name is Story. Tumailian. Kitchen worker." She kept her eyes at his chest level, staring into the eyes of the fire breathing dragon stitched into his robes.

"And?"

"She wanted medical attention for the ill." Her eyes flashed to his. "Her son, in particular." At his raised eyebrows, she went on. "She had a group of fifty-five or so followers, planning on traveling East to look for another clan that would refuse trade with New Bhutan until we gave them what they wanted. They had already made contact with two clans."

"Why didn't they just deny us goods in Tumail?" He smiled at the notion. He knew exactly why.

She forced a smile as well. "Tumail wouldn't last a day without our water. She hoped somewhere else could."

He clapped his hands together. "Ah! And she would have been seriously disappointed. Lucky for her, now, she gets all the water she could dream of." He gestured toward the sparkling lake. "Fate is a mysterious thing, isn't it gentlemen?"

The forked beard man nodded and laughed, but the other just stared out the window as if he wasn't there at all. His attitude didn't phase Dorji Tashi a bit.

"So!" he said abruptly. "Did Meera San send you on this mission, or Kiro?"

"Meera San, Sir."

"Mmm-hmm. And what did she say?"

Sepora's heart began to race.

"She said that I failed in my first attempt to calm Story. That it was time for me to proceed in a phase two interruption. I've never failed before, Sir San." She bowed her head as if in deep shame.

"Never failed, eh?" He stroked his beard for a moment, eyeing her. "Were you at that dinner at the Family Hall last week?" He cocked his head. "I believe you were, talking to Hui."

"I...I don't recall, Sir San."

"Ha! Of course, of course. " He let his gaze roam over her for a moment before adding, "Well, aren't you a well-traveled Sepa. Do you like my lake?" he asked again.

She glanced at it and then met his eyes. "I'm sure I prefer the ponds of New Bhutan, Sir."

Dorji Tashi snort laughed.

Sai San looked up, his eyes doing a quick scan over her.

"This one is a snapdragon, Sir," the bearded man laughed.

"She knows what she's doing," Tashi added. "Maybe too much. Tell me, Sepa, what did Meera San tell you to do after capturing our Story?"

"Wait for a Family helio. She said that others would take it from there, and they did. The rebel has been delivered and my mission accomplished." She took a steadying breath. "I wonder if I could return for my next mission, Sir."

"I see why you got that mark on your face within five minutes of being here," Tashi replied sharply. "Saucy, isn't she?"

"I think, Sir San, with the right training of course, she could make a valuable addition as a Rue." It was the forked beard.

Sai turned, finally taking an interest in the conversation. "Dorji, with due respect, if this Sepa was at the dinner, Meera knows her number. She is not one that we can pick off like a common Banjarian. If she doesn't return, you will hear of it."

"Good counsel!" He slapped his hands to his chair arms. "Let us keep her for a few days, just a small treat for a few good men, then send her back."

The forked man rubbed his hands together. "Wise decision, Sir San."

Dorji picked up a bell and let a sweet tinkle fill the air. The man who had hit her returned immediately.

"Take her to Palace in the Blossom House, and see that she gets a quick training. She'll only be with us for a short time."

"Gladly, Sir San."

Dorji Tashi leaned into her. "That's for being *too* smart, Sepa."

Koa San grabbed her elbow again and took her back down the stairs and out the door. They walked past where the helio had landed and back the way they'd taken Story. Sepora was silent and compliant, using the walk to think. Dorji Tashi himself was here, outside the barrier. It didn't make any sense.

And the comments from the men... the painting... she must find a way out before she became a *small treat*.

They came to a building similar to the last. This one was a floor shorter and longer. Koa San walked across a deep porch and rang the large bell hanging near the door. A woman almost as old as Tashi answered.

"Koa San. Wish I could say it's a pleasure." Her face was deeply tanned by the sun as only a Banjarian's would be. There were lines etched across her face and her eyelids drooped over her eyes.

Koa San ignored the slight. "Palace," he greeted, inclining his head. "Tashi wants this one finished soon. She'll only be with us for a few days." He shoved her across the threshold, forcing Palace to step back. She grabbed Sepora by the shoulder and looked her over.

"A Sepa, huh?" She smiled grimly. "Well, at least they're obedient." She pulled her back and shut the door in Koa San's face. She turned and started to walk up the steps, only turning back when she realized Sepora wasn't following.

"Come on now, hon."

Sepora was thinking fast. There hadn't been any men outside and this was an elderly woman. It was a good time to make an escape. Had she seen enough to satisfy Meera? Surely the information that Tashi was here, that they were collecting prisoners, and that they had a real lake would be enough.

What about Story? The question appeared in her mind unbidden and refused to go away. Meera's plan had not included Story beyond being a ticket inside. 'Find out as much as you can and return safely.' *What about Story, Meera?* Sepora knew that Meera wouldn't have spared a thought for Story's fate. Get in, get out.

A Sepa doesn't disobey.

She was gritting her teeth, fighting the internal battle to either attack Palace now or wait for a chance to save Story when Palace interrupted her thoughts.

The woman stepped back and put a hand on her shoulder. She smiled up at her knowingly. "No need to run, soldier. They'll shoot you with a stunning arrow and you'll be right back here, but with a headache. We've all tried it more times than we're proud of."

"I didn't see anyone," she said stubbornly.

"Oh, they're there. They have guards on watch from the trees around the clock. This house holds their prize possessions." She turned again and headed up. Sepora followed behind, slightly relieved to have a reason to stay.

"What is this place?" she asked at the woman's back. She seemed forthcoming enough. It couldn't hurt to ask.

"This place is Blossom House," the woman grunted as she climbed the stairs, "and the lake is Dorji's paradise." They had reached the second floor and the woman led Sepora to a view of the lake. "See there?" She pointed to a line of low dwellings along the opposite side of the lake. "That's where they play, night after night. Betting, stealing, drinking, fighting, you name it. And see over there?"

She pointed back to where Sepora had just been. "That's where they get to play with you, and all the other rebels."

"I'm not a rebel," she replied thickly.

"Perhaps not, but you are theirs. Isn't that so?"

Palace said her deepest fears so flippantly, it made her stomach turn. She was theirs; had always been. She leaned out the window, staring hard into the distance. "Is the lake protected by a new barrier? Only some are invited?"

The woman raised a bushy brow at her. "Can't you tell the difference between real and synthesized wind? A cloud? The Sepas usually figure it out right away. They're the only ones who have experienced the difference. Banjarians come in believing they've finally penetrated New Bhutan!" She coughed a laugh. "This is the Banjar, with its broiling sun and gusty winds, morning dew, and thunder clouds."

"How?" was all she could say. How could Dorji Tashi himself risk being out here? "The Banjarguay...?"

Palace laughed in earnest, slapping her leg.

"Oh, you poor thing. Take a deep breath, sweetling. The air is fine."

Sepora stared at Palace until her eyes began to burn. Blinking, she turned and looked out at the lake. She walked to the window as if in a trance, staring at the buildings dotting the other side. She followed Palace's advice and took a deep breath.

The air is fine. The words were echoing through her brain and over.

But... but how?

She turned back to Palace, who was seated on a cushioned bench, stitching a bright teal costume.

Her voice came out in a whisper. "I've seen people die. I've watched the Banjarguay take people's bodies and tear them apart." She turned back to the window and squinted up at the sky. "They must have built a second dome."

Palace's voice came thoughtful behind her. "I don't remember what it was like out there, you know. They emptied every bit of it. For a long time, I believed that I had been born here, but after watching so many be Emptied, I would be a fool not to believe I had been, too."

Sepora turned back and looked at her thoughtfully. "You would have a number on your neck if you'd been a Sepa. I would guess by the look of you that you're Tumailian."

"You will have your number to remind you, at least."

Sepora's eyes narrowed. "I am not planning on being Emptied."

The woman chuckled softly. "Is anyone? You are fierce, aren't you?"

Sepora found herself coming to sit next to her. "Why would you help them when you could help take this place down? Who knows what they stole from you?"

"Ah," she smiled knowingly and patted Sepora's hands. "Plotting time. Next it's bargaining, then it's fighting, and then..." she snapped her fingers. "It's over." She nodded and reached for a cord hanging from a large bell behind her.

"Don't," Sepora begged. "Just for a moment."

The woman's hand stilled, but she didn't put it down.

"Tell me if there's a barrier. If I'm going to be Emptied, it doesn't matter what you say, does it?"

The woman smiled sadly and pulled the rope.

In the chimes, she began to sing softly to herself, "Breaking bread, not bones, we thrive, New Bhutan, will stay alive..."

"Palace..." Sepora hated the begging tone in her voice.

"I'm sorry, child. This isn't a place we escape, or win. We simply survive."

"What does 'training' mean?" she asked frantically, terrified that any moment the door would open and she would be gone.

The woman stood up and tucked a strand of hair behind Sepora's ear. "When they Empty you," she said softly, "they'll add a new memory. A wonderful memory full of love and desire for those you now belong to. Then, you'll be anxious to please them. You'll be trained."

Sepora was still staring into the old woman's eyes when the door opened.

She thought it would be Koa San, but the firm grasp that wrapped around her arm from behind was another's. He wore a simple black toga robe and returned her terrified glance with a distant stare; as if he was looking right through her.

Palace patted her on the shoulder. "Soon you'll be a happy woman, Sepa. You'll see." She leaned in as if to kiss her cheek and whispered, "Mind the trees."

She nodded to the robed man and he turned and marched her out.

Sepora wasn't running on strategy anymore. She was fighting for her life. She kicked, pulled, and scratched until he threw her onto the ground and pinned her wrists together. He used a cord to bind them, cutting into her skin so quickly that blood immediately began to flow down her wrists. He hauled her up with one arm and pushed her along.

Palace's words came back to her: conspire, bargain, beg, fight, lose. She was on her last step. The man was marching them behind the Blossom House, further out from the landing site. He hadn't said one word. A silent and strong soldier in a thin black robe. She remembered Meera's advice to use her skills, but this man didn't seem to have a weakness. He had nothing; was nothing but strength. Meera had told her to make her move for escape at the Emptying. This is where there would be wiggle room, and it would be her last chance.

She glanced up at the trees, trying to spot these hidden guards. She saw nothing, but admittedly, couldn't see very far into their folds. Mind the trees. Don't forget.

She could see their destination now and tried to case it as best she could. One single wide door in the front, painted a dark blue. The Brain's colors, which signified a science building. No windows. The door was facing East, toward the main lodge where they'd come from.

The lake opened up along the northern edge of the building. Twenty paces or so to the south, the trees began to get thick. She knew that through that forest was the route to New Bhutan. Mind the trees.

Somehow in her struggle, her mouth had begun to bleed. She

could feel the slow salty pool forming around her tongue. The voiceless man pulled a large key from an inner fold of his robes and unlocked the blue door. It let out a loud creak as it swung open. She noticed that its hinges were rusted and the door weathered. This building didn't see much of the Dragon, she thought. He liked everything to be beautiful.

The thought sent a shiver down her spine. Did he think she was beautiful?

The door opened onto a thin hallway with three doors on either side and one at the far end. He walked her straight to the far door and opened it to reveal a staircase. The staircase went down twenty-two steps, each one bringing a sharper stench of mud and rot. Here there was another hall of doors. He took her to the second door, opened it, and unceremoniously shoved her in, shutting the door behind her. She immediately jumped to her feet and tried to open it, but he was locking it from the outside. She rested her forehead against the door, trying to think.

"Sepa?"

Sepora whipped around at her voice.

Story, she wanted to say.

Instead, she strode to where the woman was sitting and cupped her hand to her face.

"Come to save me?" she asked.

Sepora smiled sadly.

"He'll be on his way now. Shouldn't be long." Story heaved a deep sigh. "That Palace woman said they told them when we arrived. Should take an hour or so. There's no sun down here to tell the time, but I'm sure it's been over an hour."

Sepora scanned the room, thinking fast. There was nothing. Just an empty square with no windows. No weapons, but a lot of space for fighting. If she could get whoever it was on the opposite side of the room, they might be able to bar him in. Story kept speaking like she didn't notice that Sepora hadn't responded, as if she wasn't really talking to her at all. She glanced back at her with concern. Story was lying on her back, staring up at the rotting beams of the ceiling.

"They're going to take Miracle from me. They're going to make him disappear from the world. From my mind. From my heart. I didn't think they could take him from me again." And then, the woman who had thrown her son's body off the cliff at Godsmeet Peak without so much as a tear, who faced his death with the determined glare of someone who sought vengeance, broke into sobs.

Sepora remembered her terror at the thought of losing her memory of Miracle, the only human in the world she had ever loved. She watched Story cry, realizing that she couldn't fathom the pain his maan must feel at the same thought.

Conspire, bargain, beg, fight, lose. Story had lost, but Sepora was going to keep fighting.

As if they'd sensed her thoughts, someone above them opened the blue door with a rusty scream. She grabbed Story and pulled her to the left of where the door would open, and she backed up to the right, planning to be blocked by the door.

Her heart was beating frantically in her chest as feet descended the stairs and the door unlocked. He opened it cautiously, finding Story slumped along the wall on the left. Sepora inched her face around the door to see him bending over her. She thanked dragons it wasn't the same man in black, but a man of a smaller frame in a white robe.

She almost smiled, and then raised her leg and kicked him in the back of the neck. He fell forward with a cry, landing on Story. She raised a foot and stomped on the side of his face, spitting the blood in her mouth across his cheeks. She didn't have a logical reason to have done so. She'd just wanted to. Confused at herself, she quickly reached into his robes and fished out the key.

She hauled Story up from the ground and pulled her out of the room, closing it, and with a shaking hand, locked him in. Story had been jostled out of her stupor. She ran up the steps of her own accord, forcing Sepora to follow. She wanted her to move cautiously, but it was too late. Story ran up the steps and out into the main hall, straight into the arms of the voiceless man.

He had wrapped his arm around her neck and pulled her close to him in the seconds it took for Sepora to catch up. She was fighting him with all the strength in her wiry body, her eyes wild.

Sepora knew how to get out of this situation. How many times had they run through it in the bunkers? She ran at him at full force, diving feet first into a kick to his shins. He doubled over, losing his grip on Story. She wrenched away and brought a knee up to his face, breaking his nose and sending blood flying across the hallway.

Sepora grabbed her hand and pulled her toward the door. At the door, she leaned into Story and whispered frantically. "Run to the lake. Follow the shoreline west. At the western edge, move southwest toward Tumail... she has Listener bugs in Tumail's outskirts. Say 'Meera' for as long as you can. Meera will help you."

The man was getting up behind them. She looked at her one more time. "Stay away from the trees." With that, she pushed Story out the door and toward the lake.

Once the girl was out of sight, Sepora ran toward the trees, making as much a spectacle of herself as possible. She waved her arms wildly and screamed "Help me!" as loud as she could.

She made it about eighty feet.

11

———

P ENNA

PENNA FOUND herself plucking her guzheng more and more in the past weeks. Like a nervous tick, her hand would absently find the strings. When she called on Dorji Tashi for her studies and found him unavailable, the strings would come second. When her palms itched to call her sister Meera, they would seek the instrument instead. Sai, too, was often missing from Lhasa these days, apparently hard at work for her husband-to-be. Playing, playing, playing. Her mind could lose itself in those deep, resonating low beats that would swiftly cascade into teardrop high notes. It reminded her of the Broken Oceans. The deep sucking of the waves followed by the gentle crashing of foam and spray. Back and forth. In the music, she would find some respite from her thoughts.

When the last note faded, her treacherous mind would immediately return to the Sepa dinner. The fight she'd had with Meera just an hour before she'd strolled in with her pack of feral beings, parading her loyalties before the entire Family.

"Just see them, Penna," Meera had urged. "Look into their eyes and tell me they aren't human; that they don't deserve to live as long as we do." Penna needn't have worried about discovering Meera's purpose. She'd come right out and told her.

Meera had grown attached to her monsters. She wanted Penna to use Luópán Hall's resources to provide them with a vaccine for the Banjarguay, the plague that made the lifespan of all Banjarians and Sepas so short. She wanted Penna to hand over a cure.

Penna *had* looked into their eyes. She couldn't help it. She'd looked directly at the one sitting across from her. The more she looked, the more she couldn't deny what she saw. Thinking about it now, her hands started itching to call her sister. *Meera, Meera, tell me what you know.*

Penna stood up abruptly, clenching her fists to keep from connecting thumb to pinky. She couldn't ask. Couldn't demand. Saying it, even thinking it, gave the idea substance. She caught her reflection in the looking glass.

The great Penna San, the next Heart of New Bhutan. Mishka had always complained that it was Penna's unique face that had given her so much sway with Dorji Tashi and even their faan before that, while Mishka and Meera would be married off for the connections. Penna did look different. Her skin would freckle in the sun, something she found horrifyingly grotesque, but others observed with something bordering on reverence. Her eyes, too, were unique. Although skin came in all shades, eye color in New Bhutan did not; just a variety of browns. A limited few who lived there originally had green or blue eyes, but most of those genes had faded out over the last three hundred years. A dormant gene, her father had boasted as he bounced her on his lap.

Some said her eyes were what made her so cold. She wasn't oblivious to her nickname of Penna Snake instead of the traditional honorific of San. She thought of it as a badge of honor. The snake had been a sacred creature. It had the power to eat its enemies whole.

Her fingers found the strings and she played her fiercest song, "Sun Quan The Emperor," staring into the reflection of those snake's eyes in the mirror. She would live up to her name when she took her place as Heart.

After the song's last note faded across the room, she looked around the empty space and sighed. Her private quarters faced the mountain behind the palace, the worst views being reserved for the apprentices. Still, the stone ceilings arching in rounded domes kept the rooms relatively cool. Once she knew she'd secured a spot as one of Tashi's favorites, she'd requested a few trickling fountains to be added to the space. There were wide leafed palms at either end of a white fainting couch, a rounded dining table she never used, and several guzhengs of different sizes and models. Other than these, the large space was empty. She'd always enjoyed the quiet serenity of an austere palette, but lately it was growing to be more and more claustrophobic. It was too quiet.

Maybe she'd pay young Cadence a visit. Her training with Dorji Tashi had dwindled down to nothing, as he was consistently occupied. She had not been given access to the Dragon's workplace, the Xīn Dome, and any attempts to enter had been stayed by Zeesha, the Xīn Quántóu standing guard. Her young groom, however, was annoyingly available. He wasn't her first choice for company, but anything was better than sitting here wondering about her sister.

She left her private quarters and climbed the path to his, Pa following close behind. As the Eye, his apartments were second to the top. His doors were open and she took the liberty of walking through, the Quántóu stationing herself outside. Cadence had the second-best apartments in Potala Palace. His floor to ceiling views looked to the southeast, featuring lush lands and mountains in the distance. His décor was all done in the Eye's purple and gold. Penna tried to imagine what it would be like to live here with him as she passed through his common spaces and center garden, with its indulgent amount of flowers. Where would she hide away to have some peace? Was there more than one private room, so she could sleep on her own? The thought of sharing a room with this cocky adolescent made her stomach turn.

She found him reading over the next week's seven daily papers in the sunroom, using a green ink to mark stories he approved of and a purple one for what he wanted removed. She noticed a likeness of him with a purple X over it.

"Not your best angle?" she asked over his shoulder.

"Ah," he exclaimed, turning. "Wife!" It was a new game he liked to play. He knew the word was jagged glass on her nerves.

"Husband," she murmured.

"To what do I owe the pleasure?"

"I'm wondering if you picked up anything in the Outer Ring yesterday."

He raised an eyebrow. "Are you on a case of some sort or just making small talk?"

"Does it matter?"

He put that stupid smile on his face. "I'll take that as small talk."

This had been a mistake. She turned to leave.

"Penna San! Wait," he said cheerfully. "You know, I don't have any interesting tidbits from the Outer Ring this week, as usual, if you want to know the truth," he said with a wink, "but the Listeners *did* pick up something from the northern border. It came in from the border team early this morning. I was planning on passing it on to Sai's team after finishing the paper check, but we can look at it first."

She raised her brow skeptically. "I thought Sai runs the Library team for Sepa downloads, not Listening flags." She barely caught herself from adding *you lazy baka*.

Cadence leaned back casually, flipping a wave of silken black bang from his face. "Sai asked if he can be in charge of all recordings, for training purposes."

She rolled her eyes. "He doesn't need training, *Husband*. He's been working for Tashi for thirty years."

Cadence shrugged and held his hands up helplessly. "He asked! What can I do? I may be his trainer, but he's still my elder."

He's playing you, she realized with a jolt. She wondered what Sai was up to without telling her. She thought they told each other every-thing, but he hadn't mentioned being interested in the recordings at all. He *had* mentioned that her fiancé was a lazy baka a few times, though.

"What did the flag say?"

"Murmurs in a place there shouldn't be. He couldn't quite make out the words, but there was definitely a voice along the northern border, miles from any community. Probably some young explorer dreaming of traveling the entire barrier, but we should check all the same. You never know," he whispered dramatically, "it could be a Banjarian dug a hole and is coming at us this very minute." He wiggled his eyebrows. He looked so ridiculous that she almost, almost smiled. She covered it by pursing her lips into a grimace.

"Well, what are we waiting for, then?" she asked, annoyed, "The painter to return and make you prettier?"

He laughed as if she was joking around with him. Her annoyance deepened. He set the paper down and stood, offering his arm to her. "My lady?"

With a flip of her hair, she turned and walked out, ignoring the arm.

His sigh and footsteps followed.

The Family shared a hall in the center of Potala Palace for private quarters. It was spacious enough that it felt as though they each had their own apartments. Some members kept a honeycomb space in the Inner Ring, but they rarely stayed long; the luxury of the Family Hall was hard to leave behind. Each apartment had a misting room; rooms that opened up to the city in large glassless windows and were equipped with misting sprinklers in the ceiling. It was, in Penna's opinion, the only way to enjoy the city. The floors were made of the coldest stone, cool to the touch no matter how high the temperature spiked. Quántóu brought fresh fruit and coffee every morning. The coffee bean crop had proven difficult within the barrier, along with so many others. It was a small harvest reserved for the Family. And of course, the view from the steep rise of the palace was impossible to beat.

Her faan had been one of the exceptions. Asaka the Just had been the last Eye of New Bhutan before Sai took over as intermediary. He had chosen to live in the Inner Ring exclusively, traveling to Potala only to work for the day before returning home. He had wanted to live alongside the people to better understand their needs. She remembered living in that small honeycomb house with two sisters and her faan. It had been cramped, to say the least. A strict rule of New Bhutan was a two-child limit, and each living quarter was only made with two private rooms; one for the aans and one for the children. Most women were clipped after their second birth, but the procedure done on her maan after her birth must have been defective, because Penna, Ling's third child, was born two years after Mishka.

Usually, a third child would be given to a barren family or honored as a Quántóu, but because her maan had died shortly after Penna's birth, Tashi had taken pity on Asaka and let him keep her. And so it was that three girls shared a room in a house with a grieving faan. Meera was eldest by two years, so she was given her own bunk, stacked on top of a slightly larger bed for Penna and Mishka to share. By the time Penna was six, she and Meera had a strong bond and they decided to give Mishka the top bunk. The thought of herself and Meera hiding under a blanket to tell secrets made her heart twitch. She shook the image away.

She left Cadence's apartment, with him trailing a few steps behind. Once they'd entered the main balcony, both of their Quántóu appeared from their waiting place along the walls, following silently behind. They headed down the great stone spiral walkway, past Sai and Seldom Chime's quarters and finally past her own quarters, set alongside the other understudies on the ground floor.

Outside, the sun hit them like a wave of fire. Penna slowed her steps and looked down, trying to blink away the red stars that had exploded across her vision. The pathways from one hall to the next were set in ancient brick from before the divide, dusted with diamond so it winked in the sunlight. Once her eyes adjusted, she raised her head to see Luópán Hall towering to their left.

Cadence's Listening team was in Luópán Hall, a few floors above Sai's Library team. She wondered if they would run into him. Catching a glimpse of him was always a gift. Their public interactions were always carefully watched by Dorji Tashi. Occasionally, on the day following one of these interactions, Sai would have bruises along his face. He'd never said, but she knew that Tashi punished him for speaking to her. He was protective of his sister Seldom, she assumed, and didn't appreciate Sai giving Penna extra attention. Still, they risked being together now and then. It couldn't be helped. He was the only one she could talk to openly. She let her guard down around him because he loved her unconditionally. His dark eyes were always watching her, giving her a thrill of excitement and making her feel protected. He was her warrior.

Maybe once or twice a moon did they find themselves alone together, and only dared stay for a few minutes. Those minutes were mostly silent. The Listeners were everywhere. They used their bodies to talk, his hands in her hair and his lips dancing across her neck, occasionally breathing a soft word in her ear. She thought about her future husband. What would he do if he found a revealing recording? His wife to be and his uncle by marriage. She knew that Seldom Chime, Sai's wife, had been more like a mother than an aunt to Cadence after his maan passed. He would most likely want to report them to her. He might even see it as a way to disgrace her out of her role as Heart and steal it for himself.

She glanced his way. He was strolling alongside her, seemingly without a care in the world, smiling at every person they passed. Or maybe he would never listen to the recordings, anyway. Is that why Sai wanted control of the Eye? So he could be the first filter of what people heard? She shook the ridiculous thought away. His moves were never motivated by her, as much as she daydreamed they might be.

Once they were in Luópán Hall, the people parted for them. These were Potala workers from the Inner Ring. They looked at her with flickers of shock, but it was Cadence they bowed to. Everyone seemed honored to see their supervisor, and she wondered how often he made it over here at all. Watching him, though, she had to admit that he made a great Eye. His easy smile seemed contagious here, and yet he was managing to exude a regal authority as well. He stopped to say a kind word or share a smile with every three people or so, as if he shared an inside joke with each of them.

They loved him.

She suddenly realized what a great team they would make as Heart and Eye. She would run the country and he would entertain it. Dorji Tashi was no fool.

Every dome was built with the swirling paths in place of stairs, and much to her disappointment, they passed the hall that led to the Library uneventfully. Luópán Hall's paths went higher up and deeper down than the others. She knew there were countless floors below them, an underground hive of ingenuity, where the Family's deepest secrets and valuable projects were kept. Seldom Chime, the Brain, was the overseer of those projects and Penna could only speculate what was down there. As Heart, someday, she would be able to ask any branch of the Family anything she wanted. She would have complete control of the Xīn Dome and full access to the others. She smiled to herself. All secrets would be revealed in time.

At the entrance to Listener Hall, Cadence paused their Quántóu. They would not be invited to enter. Listener Hall was a quiet place, with high rise ceilings and stacked balconies. It looked like a library might have, but the shelves were stacked with tapes, labelled with years and locations. The room was organized by area: Inner Ring, Outer Ring, Midland, Paro, Yutan, East, North, West, and South barriers lands, Bunkers, and Barrier Ring. Penna pulled a tape from a shelf near her. The case had a description on it: "Honeycomb 389, Quarter 7, 2/4/2400, 9:30am. Kim discusses the ineffectiveness of Dorji Tashi the Second."

She took another glance around the room. No section for Potala Palace. No place for a tape with her name on it. She tried to decide if that was a good sign or not. "Why do you keep all of these?" she asked Cadence.

He looked back at her as if he'd forgotten she was even there. "We don't." He stopped and fingered one of the tapes. "We listen and catalogue anything suspicious. If there's a second flag on the same house, it gets investigated in person. Then we keep both tapes until that person has been interrupted or died of their own accord." He put the tape back and smiled at her. "At that point, we recycle them." He laughed. "If we kept all the tapes, we would fill up every dome in Lhasa."

"What does 'interrupted' mean?" She was feeling a little ill. Why did this child know ways of the Family that she did not?

He looked surprised. "That's Dorji Tashi's department. I thought you would know."

She tried to hide her embarrassment. "I'm obviously not cleared for that information yet."

"Oh. Well, I don't know either. We just pass the name on to Tashi's team in the Xīn Dome and the recordings from that dwelling change."

"Change how?"

"They're silent for a few weeks. Eventually a new family takes up residence."

She raised her brows at him.

"What?"

She let out a frustrated sigh. "Doesn't that bother you?"

"Tashi knows what he's doing. Who am I to question him?"

Well, that was something they could agree on, at least. He didn't have a right to question anyone.

"Where is the mystery tape of today?" she asked, tucking those thoughts away for later.

"Right this way. Active Listeners are in the balconies." He led her up to a third balcony, saying a quiet hello to every Listener on the way.

"Cadence San!" a young man jumped to his feet when he saw them approaching. "I'm relieved to see you. It's a very tempting tape!"

Cadence laughed softly. "Well thank you for waiting for me." He leaned into Penna conspiratorially. "They can't run the Flags through a second time without my key. Luckily for me, flags are rare."

His breath smelled of spearmint. It wasn't unpleasant, but the fact that she could smell it made her cringe. She inched away from him. The young Listener pulled a tape from his machine and walked through a small door behind the desk. Cadence gestured for her to follow him. Using the identification chip embedded in his palm, Cadence swiped at the door and it opened. The room beyond the door was another world from the refined library environment. *This is where the work is really done,* she thought. It looked like the room circled the entire library, full of whirring machines, cords, and speakers.

He carefully slipped the tape into a machine the size of him, covered in hundreds of knobs, dials, and switches. Cadence picked up a pair of headphones and held them out to her.

"Care to do the honors?"

She accepted them with an eye roll, putting them on and wondering how bored one could actually get without dying.

"I don't hear anything."

He was nodding and saying something to the boy. Cadence flicked a switch and the sound magnified. Suddenly she could hear that a conversation was happening, but the voices were muddled to the point that she couldn't understand.

She shook her head and pulled it off. "I hear voices. Two. But I can't understand a word. It's crackling too much." She was wondering why she'd agreed to come in the first place.

Cadence smiled at her and turned back to the board, twisting knobs and flipping switches with ease. She watched him for a moment, amazed that he was capable of doing something after all. When she put the headphones back on, the voice came to her clear as day. So clear, she turned around to see if he'd come in through the door behind them.

It was Sai.

PART II

SNAKES

12

HUI

HUI WAS WATCHING his faan too much. Susu kept feeling his gaze and glancing up as he lifted chopsticks to his mouth.

"Yes?" he asked.

"I apologize, Faan," Hui responded, dropping his eyes. He sighed. His plan of nonchalance had failed miserably. The new plan to grow up to be a Sepa ambassador seemed pretty unlikely if he couldn't even keep his cool around his own faan.

Susu had been gone for three weeks; longer than ever before. He looked gaunt and sun-stained. Hui had asked Maester Fre about just how long it would take to cover the perimeter of New Bhutan, but he only replied with "Depends on who is making the journey. One man might care for the sick, visit the old, play with the young; while another marches straight through."

If he knew, he wasn't telling.

Maan was flitting about the rooms still, trying to make every corner look perfect for her husband. He had surprised her early this morning after weeks of his prolonged absence filling the house with tension.

"You look different, is all."

His faan looked up from the plate and met his eye.

"It's not an easy job out there, Hui. How has Mishka been?"

Hui looked down awkwardly. He would not speak of his maan's erratic behavior; her angry outbursts, stony silences, or the days she wouldn't leave her private quarters at all.

"She was worried about you."

"Yes," he said quietly.

"We haven't seen you since the night of the Sepa dinner."

"I know the last time, Hui." He was pointing a chopstick at him as if it was his fault. He heaved a heavy sigh. "Don't you have lessons to get to?"

"Yes." Hui jumped from his seat and just as quickly cleared the plate and went to his room. He didn't have lessons today, in truth. It was the day of rest. He knew a dismissal when he heard one, though, and was happy to leave his faan to brooding.

In truth, Hui and Susu had never been close. He was always coming and going, leaving his mother's moods to swirl in response. Susu's arrival used to excite Hui. It was like a holiday because his maan would prepare an extra savory meal and wear her best clothes. She would dress Hui in special robes as well. After so many years of the excitement ending with Susu walking into the house and straight to his private quarters, however, the thrum of excitement had turned to anxiety. Susu never brought gifts or hugs. Half of his returns would be full of affection for Mishka, but those returns would lead to both parents sweeping into the private quarters, leaving Hui dressed in his best for no one.

He went back to his room and pulled out the encyclopedia, his most constant companion. Little slips of paper marked the most beloved pages: feline, fawn, fairy, ferret, fox, falcon, frost, fireplace, fowl. His walls were covered with sketches of them all: his dreams, as far as Mishka knew. His maan would peer at them with mistrust, but

Faan knew nothing about them. He never came into Hui's private quarters.

In the center of it all was 288's drawing of Hui. It had been weeks since they'd met, just as long as his faan had been gone. He wondered where she was, and if she was waiting for him to figure out the message. B-5-7. He murmured the code almost reverently, as if the words would make his friend appear.

Sighing, he pulled his sketchbook down from its shelf and settled in at the desk. He would try the fox again, but this time imagine what it might look like facing the other way. Sometimes he would try imagining how the animals moved and draw them in action. He flipped through the encyclopedia to the word, tracing a loving finger over the description.

Soon he was deep in thought, sketching and erasing the outline of the body, twisting and turning it to find the right angle. The art of drawing was similar to meditation. It cleared his mind as his hands moved as if of their own accord. He wondered at the muscles under those legs, or if there were muscles in the tail that bloomed out behind them. Was it just hair, or an additional leg? He wondered where the fox lived, what it ate, what it sounded like. These thoughts soon led to where the book might have come from and what the world was like then. He paused, flexing his drawing hand, and sat back in his chair.

He had discovered many secrets of the Old Word from this book, and it was only one letter. He imagined a place where falcons flew through the sky all day, maybe traveling with their wives and children as humans do. He had learned about Fenway Park, a place where people would gather to play games. The adults would play, with families cheering in the crowd. There were no games for adults in New Bhutan. He tried to imagine his faan playing a game but could not. His stern face chastised him for even trying to conjure the image. There was too much work to be done.

One of his favorite people in the book was listed for his creation of the Falling Water House. His name was Frank Lloyd Wright and he had been an artist too, drawing places for people to live that worked with nature. He was what Hui thought of as an Old World good guy. He had known then that people should be building along with the beautiful natural world around them, but apparently, no one listened. The Falling Water House was built above a waterfall, which was a body of water that poured out over a cliffside. One of his favorite fantasies was to imagine living in that place, where clean water snaked its way through the land. Sometimes, he imagined that he rescued 288 from the Sepa Bunkers and ran away, finding the Falling Water House and never thinking about his faan again. He imagined jumping from the Rail in the dark of night and sneaking along the base. He would jump from bunker to bunker until he found—

Hui's eyes widened and he sat straight up. How would he know which bunker was 288's? The Sepa had written B57 in the drawing. His eyes found it again on the wall, as if just to make sure. The honeycombs Bhutanese lived in were numbered with an H for Honeycomb. He lived in H272.

B57. It was her room number, he was positive. 288 wanted him to find her at the bunkers! His heart soared at the thought.

He itched to contact Meera San right away, but before his feet found the hall, he remembered what waited outside. Too young to have his own palmpad, children relied on the adults to make contact with one another. He considered his options. His maan would be too agitated to help him contact his aunt. Faan might be a better bet.

He inched past her private quarters, where the doors were unexpectedly open. She was not, as he had assumed, cleaning. She was seated in a prayer position on the floor, tears stealing out of her closed eyes to roll silently down her cheeks. Hui stopped and watched her for a moment, breath held so as not to disturb her. He was used to his maan crying, but it was always when Susu was gone. With a puzzled frown, he headed downstairs to find his faan. Susu was seated in the common room, staring out the window into the garden.

Hui came up alongside him and sat in the chair to the left. He didn't look over.

"Susu San?" Hui asked, using his faan's name.

The man moved his eyes to him, expressionless.

"Maan seems sad."

He looked back out toward the garden.

"Maybe it would be best if I spent the night with Aunt Meera, so you two could talk."

He might have said it too casually, too practiced, but it caused Susu to raise his eyes again. After a moment, he nodded. "You know much, Hui," he said, and a ghost of a smile passed his lips. He pressed his thumb to pinky. "Meera San," he said softly into his palm. He had never had that tone of voice before. So flat; so broken. Hui's eyebrows knit in concern for him as well.

"You seem sad, too," he blurted.

Susu looked at him as the connection from palm to palm synced with his Aunt Meera. Suddenly her voice came through his wrist.

"Susu. Hello." She sounded surprised.

"Meera San. I've just returned from a long trip and am hoping that you can take Hui for the evening. Mishka and I have much to discuss and Hui is hoping to have a visit with you."

There was a long pause on the line. "I *am* in the city at the moment."

Susu glanced at him. "But?"

Another pause. "But nothing. I'll be there shortly."

Susu pressed his thumb to pinky pad once more and returned his stony stare to the garden, as if Hui and the conversation had never happened. After a few moments Hui's fingertips lightly touched his shoulder. "Thank you, Faan," he whispered, and hurried off back to his room.

He packed his encyclopedia first, then unhooked the Sepa's drawing from the wall and carefully placed it on top. He also added a few drawings of different animals, including two foxes. His journal went in, too. After that, he chose his sharpest green shorts and cleanest white shirt. He also packed his pencils, his map of New Bhutan (operatives need maps, right?) and his dinner kimono. He glanced around the space, wondering what else an operative might need. This was his first mission, so he better be prepared. His eye caught on a small, framed painting of his maan. She was younger then, not yet twelve. She sat smiling demurely between her sisters, Meera and Penna. Even Penna looked happy here. Hui had always loved the painting because the sisters feeling happy together seemed so sacred. He had slipped it into his room years ago and Mishka had never mentioned the move.

He considered bringing the painting but thought he might leave it for her. Maybe it would cheer her up if she ended up sleeping in his quarters. On nights when his faan was feeling particularly moody, she had often sought his room for a bit of comfort.

Meera didn't arrive for another two hours. In that time, Hui stayed in his room, pretending not to hear his maan leave her meditations and try to speak with Faan. He plugged his ears to ignore her pleading with him, when the pleading turned to screaming, and when the screaming turned to glass breaking.

"I don't understand," she was saying over and over.

Hui ignored that, too.

"It's time, Mishka. For me, it's time. This has gone on too long," his faan was saying, crying himself. Sobbing.

Hui ignored that.

"We'll always be together, won't we?" she asked.

"We grow from the same ground, Mishka. That's all I know. That's all I know."

He ignored their kisses and their sobs, until they had returned to their room and quieted.

Finally, the chime of the bell out front sounded. As Hui ran out to greet her, he saw both his aans in meditation position, sitting side by side with eyes closed.

Meera met him in the common room and offered an easy smile. "Ready to go, I see," she said, noting his traveling case. She glanced around for her sister or brother-in-law.

"They're busy," he said, grabbing her hand to turn her away and out.

"Come, Hui! I should at least let them know we're leaving."

"They *know*, Auntie."

At his tone, she stopped trying to look around him and met his gaze with a heavy sigh.

"Okay. Let's go, then."

With one last look back into the empty room, she walked out the door. She strapped him into her two seater cruiser, jaw clenched tight. Hui could feel his heart beating in his chest as the silence of a sunny day settled over the front grounds. He fingered the grips of the cruiser. It was nicer than his maan's. Three horizontal wheels swirled under a carriage, hovering just above the ground. This carriage had no top and the seats were built for straddling rather than the benches his maan had, almost like a bicycle. Most Bhutanese traveled by bicycle, but Aunt Meera was very important.

This cruiser was meant to go fast. Each seat was equipped with its own handles, but only the first one could steer. The other was for holding on. Hui quickly strapped his case onto the rack behind him.

Meera threw her leg over the cruiser and started it in one fluid motion. They shot forward without a word.

Hui couldn't help but smile. This cruiser was *much* faster than Maan's. They flew through the Inner Ring, toward Lhasa, and turned off at the Rail Station. She swung into a charging station and cut the power. She turned back to look over her shoulder at him.

"Feel like an adventure, Hu?"

Hui's hair was blown up and out from the wind whipped journey. He started to laugh.

"Yes!"

"Good."

She helped him off the cruiser and slipped her bag from a compartment under her seat.

The Rail Station wasn't particularly busy. Most people living in the Inner Ring were either working in the domes of Lhasa, gardening, or busy with their chosen art form. The Outer Ring was a stop away and those people weren't coming this direction. They would head farther out, toward the rice patties or farmlands in Midland.

The Rail was a series of pods docked on a rail that arched high above the ground. The tracks shot out like spindles all the way to the border in eight different directions, its course traveling from Lhasa to both the Inner and Outer Ring, Midland, Yutan, and even beyond those to the barrier lands. Of course, the pod would only take you to locations your identification chip allowed for. His Aunt Meera, he knew, was authorized to go anywhere.

She flashed her wrist across a small panel on a parked pod and the door slid open. Hui had only been past the Inner Ring's borders twice in his life. Once to visit the ancient grounds of Paro on a family vacation, and once to visit a cousin in the Outer Ring.

They settled in on benches facing one another, surrounded by the small glass dome over their heads, and Meera pressed a code into a small pad along the window. "Off we go," she said quietly. It looked like whatever anger had taken her as she threw herself onto the cruiser earlier had deflated.

Hui wanted to ask why she was upset, so he did. It was like that with his aunt. He could say what he wanted and she wouldn't mind.

She sighed heavily. "Mishka and Susu are fighting some dark demons and trying to love each other at the same time. It's hard to watch."

"What demons?" Hui asked, bewildered.

She gave a soft laugh. "Not real demons, Hu. Scary thoughts that crowd into their brains and hearts and make them sick."

"Oh." Hui nodded sagely. He knew those demons of his maan's well. He felt sorry for his aans. It wasn't their fault the demons were inside their heads. His eyes welled with tears but he stubbornly looked out the window and blinked them back.

Meera clapped her hands to her legs. "Guess where we're going?" she said brightly.

He whipped his head back toward her, tears gone. "Paro?" His vacation there had been a highlight in his life, although terrifying. It was said that the ancient dwellings there were full of magic from Old World priests. Celio had told him all kinds of stories, but Meera and Mishka had agreed that Celio was just teasing.

"No. When Susu connected, I was preparing to head back to

work. After disconnecting, I made sure there would be a bunk available for you."

Hui was speechless. She was taking him to the bunkers. He had hoped to somehow ask her about the living quarter numbers without revealing his paper conversation with the Sepa, but now he could simply see for himself. Comming her had worked out far better than he would have dreamed.

"Your mouth is open, Hu."

He shook himself. "Thank you, Meera San!" He jumped off the bench and hugged her.

She laughed. "I wouldn't thank me until you see what we're up to. We're going to work today!"

He sat back with a smile. "Hui San, at your service!"

She eyed him curiously. "Why is it that you enjoy the Sepas so much?"

"They know about the world in the encyclopedia."

The silence stretched between them and Hui wished he could take back the words. It was the first time they had spoken about the secret gift she had passed to him a little over a year ago.

She gripped her jaw and was rubbing her cheeks thoughtfully. "Hu..."

"Yes?"

"You saw the date in the book, didn't you?"

"Yes. It's from before the Divide. It's very old. I've taken very special care of it." He pushed the image of the book falling off his bed a few times out of his mind.

"That's good and it is very old, but—but what I mean to say is, you know that those are the old ways. That book contains items and ideas from the Old World. That world is dead. It's a relic. The Sepas... they don't know that world any more than you do." It was obvious she felt terrible delivering this news, but he just laughed.

"So we think! They are the only ones who know for sure." He sat back with a satisfied smirk.

She laughed. "Okay."

"Did you read it?"

"I read some," she nodded. "It is a pretty fascinating history that we're not taught."

"Why don't they teach us?"

She shrugged. "Why teach people about things they can never have but would surely want? It's better to keep them satisfied with what they have and keep the dome over their dreams, so to speak."

Hui frowned. "Then why would you give it to me?"

She smiled at him. "Do you remember Auntie Celio?"

"A little." He remembered her more from likenesses and stories than life. She had died when he was only five.

In the Last War, survivors from all over the globe had fought to get inside New Bhutan before the barrier closed. Nevertheless, most of the people in New Bhutan still ended up having similar physical traits because of the people who already lived there. Celio was one of the exceptions. She had been tall with large brown eyes that she would dress in charcoal. Her skin had been darker than most and her hair grew out in a circle around her head instead of down her shoulders. She was an actor and in all portraits had a small, mischievous smile on her lips.

"The encyclopedia was hers. Her family kept it hidden away and well cared for, sealed against the elements; dust, rot, temperature. Did you see the bottle of sealant it came with? You should paint the pages once a year."

Hui was not sure where it had got to, but yes, he'd seen it.

"Celio loved that book. She loved the histories and would paint the animals in it. Those were her most treasured paintings, but we of course weren't allowed to share them. Even if Celio was allowed to paint, Dorji Tashi doesn't want people daydreaming about what was or could be, and the book, of course, had to be kept a secret."

Hui felt his drawings in the case pulling at him. Should he show them to Aunt Meera or would she be upset that he, too, had risked the discovery of the book? Were his "dreams" a clever enough ruse?

"Do you still have her animal paintings?" he asked.

"Of course. They are my favorite treasures."

"Can we see them in the bunker?"

"Hmm. Most are in my apartments in Lhasa, but yes, there is one at the bunker."

He hoped it was the fox.

"But I thought Celio was an actor?" he asked.

"She was. That is why the paintings had to remain a secret. Celio was such an artistic soul, she wanted to keep doing many forms of art. In her later years, she became more and more keen to paint over act, but it was too late."

Hui thought about the choice he would be making in two years. He knew without a doubt that he would be studying painting. He could barely bring himself to practice his instrument and prose bored him to tears. Singing, though, was enjoyable. What if he changed his mind later?

"Couldn't she ask Tashi to be reassigned?" he asked.

"Oh, no. You must stay dedicated to your chosen art. Endurance and dedication are highly valued. If you were to switch, it would be seen as giving up and you would be cast as a failure. It's very shameful. She wouldn't want to bring that shame on Kiro." She shrugged. "To answer your question, Hui, I passed the book to you because I knew you would treasure it as much as she did. You remind me so much of her."

His chest swelled with pride. He knew Celio had been loved by all who knew her, even if he didn't remember much.

"But, Meera, what happened to her?"

Meera grimaced, and Hui immediately apologized for asking.

"It's alright. Celio ran the production and distribution of the southern farms in Yutan. She would be gone a week and then come home for a week. That's why she had so much time for painting," she smiled. "One week she left for work and two days later, she died. They say she became violently ill, probably from catching a virus more common to the people in the field lands."

Hui made a mental note to never travel past the mountain range that divided the Rings and Lhasa from the southern half of New Bhutan. He wiggled in his seat uncomfortably and decided to change the subject. "What will we do at the bunker?"

Meera shook her memories away, leaning back in her chair. "I receive reports from the trainers on new Sepas, review recordings flagged by our resident Listeners, sign off on proposed trade deals. Just a lot of managerial duties."

It all sounded kind of boring to Hui besides the flagged recordings. "Do the recordings tell you where the traitors are?"

"Sometimes."

"And what happens then?"

"We send an operative out with a trade."

"And then what happens?"

She laughed. "Didn't you get the full scoop from the Sepa you befriended at dinner?"

Hui shifted in his chair. "Well, she's not supposed to talk about the Banjar."

"That's true. They are our soldiers in a sense. You know, you're probably the first person in New Bhutan she's ever had a conversation with."

"She's the first Sepa I've ever had a conversation with. That's why we're friends, maybe."

She smiled. "Maybe."

"Maan would be upset if she knew you were taking me to the edge."

"I know. Can you keep it between us?" she smiled conspiratorially.

"Yes. What are the demons saying to Faan, do you think?"

She sighed. "I don't know."

They were quiet then, both deep in thought. Hui watched the view change as they passed through the Outer Ring. The honeycomb houses were just the same on this ring as they were on the Inner Ring, but there were gardens in the front as well as the back. He knew that the Outer Ring received less food in their monthly delivery, because most of the occupants were farmers. They had the space to grow more than the people who worked in Lhasa. This ring seemed more full of life than the Inner Ring. Faans were chasing around their sons with smiles on their faces and children were playing games in the streets. Hui started to feel a little jealous, as his ring was very controlled by proper behavior. The children played during the break from lessons, but the aans were always busy in Potala. Playing with your children was not appropriate behavior in the Inner Ring.

After the Outer Ring, they rode through the tunnels in the mountain range for what felt like hours before Hui's eyes drifted closed.

When he awoke, they were just curving past the last of the old Bhutan cliffs. He jumped from his chair and pressed a hand to the window to steady himself. The Bhutan cliffs were a sacred place. The ancient dwellings along the cliffside had been preserved in recognition of the sacrifice of the original Bhutanese people. Hui tried to remember his lessons. "The Bhutanese invited the surrounding nations to use their water and land as refuge in exchange for protection against the West. Is that right, Auntie?" He glanced over at her.

She had been dozing. "Hmmm? Ah, yes. Something like that. Bhutan became the center of the world in one swoop, but it grew quite a bit. Most of New Bhutan was once Southern China."

"And did the countries protect them as promised?"

"I should think so. They appointed a Bhutanese woman and man to be part of the original Family. The whole family was descended from Bhutan for a long while, but that had to change over time. But look. Look the other way."

Hui turned and saw the rail leading into a cave in a hillside. He could see the tops of buildings beyond it.

"We're here."

With the proximity of really seeing her again, Hui had the sudden realization that Sepa 288 would probably be in the Banjar. He was flooded with disappointment.

"Well don't look too excited about it," Meera teased.

"I am! I just... I was hoping to see Sepa 288. Will she be there?"

Meera's smile faded. "I don't know. She's on a long assignment." She looked out the window for a silent stretch of minutes.

"Why don't they get real names?" Hui asked, breaking the silence.

She blinked as if he'd just woken her up.

"What?"

"The Sepas! If they can get their own number, why can't they get their own name?"

Meera looked thoughtful. "Well, names have meaning, and meanings have power. It may not decide your fate, but a name does have some influence over it."

"And?"

"And a Sepa's fate is no different than another Sepa's. They are one."

"Then why give them a number at all?"

Meera waved her hand dismissively. "Tracking purposes."

Hui leaned back on his bench. "Well," he said, crossing his arms. "I think 288 *is* different from the other Sepas, name or no name."

Meera's eyes snapped to his. After a few moments of eyeing him, she softened, sighing heavily. "I think you're right, Hu. Can you keep a secret?"

"Another one?"

"Yes."

"Definitely!"

"You are right about 288. She is, in fact, the only Sepa who does have a real name." She wiggled her brows and a real smile lit her face. "A *secret* name."

Hui's eyebrows had shot up too. "What is it?" he breathed.

"Her name is Sepora."

He leaned back, looking thoughtful. "But that sounds just like a Sepa."

She grimaced. "As I said, names don't decide your fate, but they certainly influence it."

13

———

P ENNA

Penna was sitting on a bench with her head level with Cadence's torso, trying to think fast. It was Sai. Sai and Susu, her leech of a brother-in-law. Sai was saying goodbye. Penna put her hands over the earpieces and ducked her head. She didn't want Cadence watching her face.

"You deserve a break," Sai was saying. "You will be missed out here, of course."

"Don't give me that shit," Susu spat back. The aggressive voice in her ears made her jump. Her eyes caught Cadence's but she quickly dipped back down as if she couldn't hear. "I'm not a fool, Sai San, as much as Tashi would have everyone believe."

It was quiet for a moment, and then Sai spoke again. "Go see your family, Susu. Sleep. Tashi knows you're not well, that is all. We both know you weren't making sense. We just want to see you rested."

Susu let out a grunt of anger and there were sounds of a scuffle. Penna jumped to her feet as if to defend the invisible Sai.

"You know damn well, I'm right, you snake," Susu panted. "You're all snakes."

Penna heard the sounds of a helio. The recording was about to end. She started thinking fast. What did Susu know? How much damage would this recording do if Cadence got hold of it? How could Sai be so stupid as to be caught on a recording?

Before any of her questions could form into answers, Cadence was lifting the band off of her head.

"Looked pretty intense," he said, looking at her quizzically. He threw the headphones on himself.

She watched helplessly as he listened with head cocked to the side. She considered ripping them off his head or hitting the machine that played it, but what would that do but make her look guilty? Guilty of what, she wasn't even sure.

Cadence glanced at her in surprise, but quickly averted his gaze to the floor, listening intently. She wondered if he, too, was wondering how to react in her presence. When the tape ended, he pulled the band off and clicked a few buttons, ejecting the tape. Facing away from them, his shoulders began to shake. She thought he might be crying.

He turned around, laughing, and Penna thought she might hit him.

"Wow!" he said, clapping the young Listener on the back. "I can see why our Lady Penna San looked shocked." He leaned in near the man's ear and whispered audibly. "A couple made it out to the edge to...." he bit his lip and smiled. "To have some fun, shall we say. I'm sorry you didn't get to hear that one, Wile, I'm sure it would have been a story to tell the other Listeners. I think I'm still blushing! With Penna San here, I obviously can't condone sharing this vulgar recording. I'll dispose of it myself. You're dismissed, Wile."

He clapped him on the back and offered a second chuckle. The young man smiled ruefully at Cadence and bowed deeply to Penna before making his exit.

Cadence shut the door after him, standing at the closed door for nearly a full minute before turning back to her.

"Well," he said.

She was staring at him, and he was avoiding her gaze. He sat opposite her, flipping the tape over and over in his hand.

"Well?" she came back.

"That was a surprise." He cocked his head. "Know anything about it?"

As if I would tell you if I did, she thought. "I know that my brother-in-law has been gone, working along the barrier, for over a week longer than expected. Mishka's been sick with worry."

Cadence rubbed his chin thoughtfully. "Well, sounds like he's on his way home by now."

Penna rolled her eyes. "Apparently so."

"You'll be missed out here... What do you think he meant by that?"

"How would I have any idea?"

Cadence raised his eyebrows. "It's no secret that you and Sai San are close, Penna. Does he work along the barrier as well? I've never sent him out that way, but he's only been under my employ for a year."

She was still caught on his casual mention of their relationship. *A close friendship must be all he's referring to*, she assured herself. "He hasn't mentioned it," she said flatly.

Cadence shrugged and walked to the far side of the room. She watched in surprise as what looked like wall space turned out to be a series of filing cabinets that could glide open at the passing of his wrist. He opened one and gingerly set the tape inside.

"What is that?" she asked, walking over to have a peek inside. She was just close enough to see several tapes stacked along the side.

"Sai's file."

"You've flagged him?" she asked, incredulous.

He just laughed. "No. As you said, Sai has been in the Family longer than me. That's his filing cabinet."

She looked back and forth from the cabinet to him. "He owns

those tapes?"

Cadence was nodding. "He wasn't too pleased when I became the Eye and gained access to every cabinet. He doesn't mind as much now, though, knowing that I don't meddle in his affairs."

"So, you haven't listened to his tapes?"

"No."

"And you're not going to inquire after that one?"

"Nope."

At her puzzled expression, he added, "Sai is my elder and my uncle by law. I have no place questioning him."

Penna wasn't sure if she was furious or relieved. She watched him close the door and swipe his wrist across the seemingly seamless wall. *He locks it too*, she thought. Her eyes swept across the twenty-foot-long wall containing who knew how many locket cabinets. So many secrets.

Cadence elbowed her playfully. "Always so serious, Penna San. Want to get out of here? Maybe head down to Bankhar Market?" He was already gently guiding her out the door. They passed the young man who bowed respectfully and wound their way down and out. She was silent, looking curiously toward Sai's Library.

The Memory Library. The words sent a chill down her spine. She shook the feeling away and looked up at Cadence strolling casually beside her. "I *am* feeling a little claustrophobic here," she said in acceptance.

He covered his shock at her acceptance within seconds and played it cool. Was it so strange for her to be social? She sighed. Yes. She'd always been a worker bee, trotting along in Dorji Tashi's footsteps, happily at his beck and call. *He just isn't becking or calling these days*, she thought wryly.

She shook her head at herself. She was even working now, in a way. The markets were on the way to her sister and Susu's house. She intended on heading there as soon as possible, and if Cadence could escort her halfway, so be it. He may not be curious as to what the two men were up to, but she was. She would be the Heart soon, and it was her duty to know what everyone was up to.

14

MEERA

Meera was kicking herself. And her damned brother-in-law, Susu. Every day since Sepora had left for the mysterious base, she'd been waiting on pins and needles. She had been waiting for too long, nearly two weeks without a whisper. She'd sent her Quántóu out in the helio to Tumail, hoping for word. Nothing. The girl did not return. *What's your move, Meera? Grab your ten-year-old nephew!* She gritted her teeth and glared out the window of the rail. *Damn Susu.*

What could she have done? She knew what he meant when he asked her to pick up Hui. He'd only ever commed her once before since they'd met over twelve years ago, and it was when Mishka had tried to take her own life. She was terrified when she got the comm, only to find out they were fighting again. Their relationship was like a simmering pot; always warm but on the verge of boiling over. She didn't want Hui to get burned.

She glanced over at his sleeping face. He was the closest thing to family she had in this world. Her two sisters despised her and her Sepas could never know how much they meant to her. Besides, Hui reminded her so much of her faan. He loved unconditionally and saw beauty in everything. She shook her head at herself. Maybe she'd picked him up for her benefit, come to think of it. She was hurting for a friend.

It wasn't long before Hui woke up and started asking questions about Sepa 288. Maybe it was because Sepora's life was at risk and she was more human to Meera now than ever before, but she couldn't stand hearing her called 288. She confided in Hui that the girl's name was Sepora. She held back why, thank the moon. What was troubling her now was his response to the news. Instead of being satisfied with 288 having a name, he wanted to understand the very nature of name giving.

"You said all Sepas serve the same purpose and therefore don't need individuality. Does that mean Sepora has her own purpose, then?" he'd asked.

Smart kid, she thought, annoyed at herself. Of course, the answer to that question was yes, although she wasn't about to discuss that. She'd obviously said quite enough.

"And when I become a Sepa," he continued, "will my name be taken away from me?"

"You will not become a Sepa," she'd replied, relieved to have something to say.

"If not a Sepa, then, what if I never find my path? What if I don't have a purpose? Will my name be taken?"

"No one's name will be taken. A Sepa is not a human as you are. It's different, Hui."

"How?"

"It just is."

"Was Sepora happy when she got her name?"

She'd sighed heavily at that. "Yes."

They'd arrived at the Sepa Bunkers at the highest heat of the day. The sun beat mercilessly on the sandstone walkways, making everything shine. Hui looked around in wonder, clutching his case against his chest. His head whipped down every aisle, searching for sights. On the Rail, she had told him that Sepora was on assignment but should be returning by evening. She hoped she hadn't been lying.

"Let's set our stuff down in my bunker and eat before heading to meet Kiro."

"Yes, please!" Hui said, skipping alongside her.

Meera smiled. Hui was a bright child, too often swallowed by the shadows that clung to her sister. And yet, his joy remained, natural and infectious.

His sense of justice was also infectious.

How is it different, Meera? he'd asked.

Her answer kept swirling around her head.

It just is.

She was leading Hui to her own bunker when Hui's jaw dropped. He stopped in his tracks, squeezing Meera's hand.

She followed his gaze to the tag built into the door. B57.

"She's not here, Hui."

"Can we look inside?" he asked breathlessly.

She sighed but slid her wrist along the door all the same. It opened with a loud clank. Hui peered in. He frowned, probably taking in the size of the room. It had a single cot along one wall, the top and bottom of which hit each end of the space. There was a thin counter running along the other side, with just enough room to stand in between. Really, it couldn't have been more than seven feet wide.

"They're barely here," she said abruptly. "It's really just a place for them to sleep between missions."

Hui nodded, stepping into the room.

She heard him utter a small gasp and watched as he crouched and ran his hand along the wall.

She frowned, confused. She stepped in behind him and her brows shot up in surprise. Sepora had stayed here a few days between the Family dinner and her mission to turn over Story. In that short time, the girl had been busy.

The wall on the opposite side of the counter, hidden from view from the outside, was covered with amateur drawings. It was clear that Sepas were not taught the seven arts. Several unrecognizable Banjarians, Meera, Penna, and even Hui were depicted. There was a large and ugly beast as well, with a large, sharp mouth and black eyes.

"I knew she'd seen an animal," he breathed.

He glanced back at her, his eyes full of triumph.

"I slipped her a graphite."

15

———

P ENNA

They called the markets Bankhar. It was to honor the ancient street surrounding the Jokhang Temple long ago. The Jokhang Temple had been one of many sacred places destroyed in the disasters that plagued Earth before the barrier was constructed. In fact, its loss was what had spurred China to make the Alliance Treaty in the first place.

Potala Palace had once kneeled at the shore of a great river, but the river was long gone before the Last War. All the rivers were. After the first Dragon settled into his reign, he had ordered a small moat to be built around the palace, in homage to the river they had lost. Now, centuries later, it served as a reminder of the Family's grandeur. On the opposite shore of the pond was the ring of markets, Bankhar, and then the Inner Ring began. Many Bhutanese traveled to see the sight of the pond and palace beyond. They would spend their day in the markets, trading wares, and gaze out across the moat, wondering what it might be like inside the palace.

Penna knew Cadence made the trip often, seeing it as his duty to "mingle with his people," or feel important was more like it. Meera made the trip, too. She'd never been scared to do anything. Mishka, though, would send attendants to pick up what was needed. She knew too that Tashi had never set foot in the market. She couldn't imagine Sai there, either.

The place made her uncomfortable. Everyone seemed to stare at her. She'd changed into a casual dark blue kimono with pink and white dogwood flowers, but she knew it did little to help her blend in. She glanced from the people to Cadence. She was just... different. She was taller than most. Her hair was pulled back in a bun at the base of a long neck, maybe revealing too much of her green eyes.

A toddler came by with his mother, arms up, and Cadence casually swung the boy up to rest on his hip.

"My apologies, my Eye," the woman said anxiously. "A painting of your likeness is in the common room. He thinks he knows you."

Cadence laughed. "I would like to see this painting someday. Tell me, did they include this mole? I hope not." He pointed to the small brown circle on his cheek she knew he hated.

The woman smiled and nodded, opting not to say one way or the other. He put the boy down and clapped him gently on the back before smoothly walking past them.

"A painting?" Penna mocked. "How lovely."

"What do they do in the Inner Ring but paint and garden? I'll bet there are several paintings of you for trade in this very market. Perhaps I'll buy one and hang it in the common room when we are wed."

Penna swallowed hard. The crowd was getting thicker as they went further from the bridge and into the web of walkways. "Has Dorji mentioned when that might be?" She snuck a glance over to him.

He seemed preoccupied, scouting about to find a path for them. "I'm to have dinner with him tonight." Suddenly his hand grasped her own. She tensed until she realized he was merely trying to lead her to the left. "I believe he will tell me then. I don't know why else he would want to see me." He glanced back at her. "I haven't seen him once since the dinner with Meera San. Have you?"

She hadn't, but she didn't want to tell him that. "He has been preoccupied," is all she would say. People were all around her, their shoulders often grazing her own. Finally, Cadence pulled her out to an open space near a wide, open tent. Inside, pillows and rugs were strewn about for resting and, she assumed, trading. Block tables were set up along the edges of the tent, and Cadence kept her hand, urging her to a table in the back.

The block was hollow, acting as an open case for the seller's goods. Inside were necklace pendants, stones, gems, and ancient style ornaments featuring old Tibetan gods. In the next case were more modern wares, such as stone carvings of Potala Palace and several different versions of the Dragon and the Family Seal set in a variety of colors. The Seal was a map of New Bhutan, in a sense; the Inner and Outer Rings, the eight rails, and in the city center, the emblem of Heart, Brain, and Eye, combined. Cadence dropped her hand to pick up a green version the size of his palm. He held it to her chest. "What do you think?"

She swatted it away. "I believe I have enough of that design, thank you."

He laughed and nodded a thank you to the seller, moving on. "Let's find our painting." Penna dreaded going back to the path, but followed close, hoping he wouldn't take her hand again. She followed for a few minutes before an elderly woman stopped right in front of her, glaring at her. "I know you," her voice graveled out. "I know those eyes. You're the Snake!"

She pointed a gnarled finger at her. A man near her age looked their way and also stopped. "Penna San!" he cried, falling to his knees right in the middle of the pulsing crowd. A few others followed his lead, but most pressed on, walking around and sometimes on his fingers.

"I should be on my way," is all she could seem to get out. The air felt thick with heat and incense. *They shouldn't be burning that*, came randomly into her head. It's restricted to meditations. People started noticing and reaching their hands out to touch her; petting her hair and face, grabbing at her hands. Her throat felt like it was closing up. Someone grabbed her hand from behind and she cried out, spinning around in fright. It was Cadence's face she found, tight with concern. He must have come back around on the side to get to her. "Come on," he urged, and pulled her back the way they had come.

They walked along the outer edge of the market, diving into tents when it got too busy. Cadence kept a tight hand on hers and didn't say anything. After many long, silent minutes, a tent full of flowers caught Cadence's attention and he stopped, finally letting go of her. His tense demeanor melted as he inspected each and every bloom in the place.

He touched a stem with oversized curling leaves and tendrils with a lavender bloom. And smiled at the seller. "Nianzu! Kita has you working the tent again?"

The seller smiled. "You know I am here whenever I can be, Cadence San. Kita's the one who should be angry, having to stay home!"

Cadence smiled easily at him and turned to Penna. "Nianzu works in Luópán's hospital. He's one of our doctors, in fact. But, much like me, finds the flower business irresistible."

The man bowed his head respectfully. "My wife grows the flowers on our plot in the Outer Rim, Penna San. We trade them when we can."

Cadence picked up the flower and reached toward her face. She flinched away, causing his hand to pause. They met eyes and he tried again. He tucked the bloom into her hair expertly, better than her Quántóu might. "This color suits your kimono, Penna San," he said softly. He looked at her again. "I apologize for leaving you in the streets. I—" he sighed. "I didn't think about how they would respond to you. I feel very safe here, but you're..."

"Different?" She couldn't help the bitter word from spitting out her mouth.

"Yes." He cocked his head at her. "You know...well, never mind."

She wasn't in the mood to press him. In fact, all of this close contact was making her very uncomfortable. She eased away on the pretense of looking at a basket of blooms to their right.

He followed her, picking one up tenderly. "Plumeria Rubra. One of my favorites. This one... its yellow blooms would do well near sun kissed skin, don't you agree?" He turned to the merchant. "I'll take the basket. And the Impatiens for the Lady San."

"What do you need a basket of flowers for?" she asked incredulously. "You have the whole world's garden."

He shrugged.

"He's a regular," Nianzu smiled. Then he started asking Cadence questions about the Dragon Garden. Penna realized they could be there for a while, so she wandered to a pile of pillows near the edge of the tent and eased to a comfortable resting position. She closed her eyes and let the sounds and smells of the market wash over her. It wasn't so bad with her eyes closed, away from the touch of the crowd. The conversation between her husband-to-be and the doctor came to her in waves.

Cadence seemed to know more about flowers than the trader did. *Full of surprises*, she thought. They spoke at length, as if Cadence had invited the man over for tea. *He treats them the same as he treats everyone else*, she thought. Then his words snapped her eyes open.

"Would you know what, if any, flowers bloom in the Banjar?" He had lowered his voice a bit, as if to hide his question from her.

"Impossible to say, Sir Eye San," the man replied, obviously perplexed by the question. "The Banjar doesn't keep water, so I would venture a guess that a few plants may still grow, but even that is unlikely."

Penna kept her eyes nearly closed in an attempt to watch Cadence without him realizing it. He was looking at the basket of yellow blooms with a sad expression on his face.

Finally, he swallowed hard and looked back at the man, suddenly all smiles. "It's a shame, isn't it? The world should be full of flowers."

The man squirmed uncomfortably. "This is the world, Sir Eye San."

He laughed. "Right. Of course." He turned to her. "Penna San, are you ready to move on?"

"I think I give up on finding my painting, Cadence. Can you escort me to the Rail?"

"The Rail?"

"I think I will visit my sister Mishka for the remainder of the day."

"Oh. Of course."

Penna tucked her legs under her so as to rise gracefully from the ground while he haggled with the seller on a trade. She watched him pull a priceless bracelet off his arm and pass it over.

This time, she grabbed his hand as they left the tent.

He threw a quick bow back to the florist. "Goodbye for now, Nianzu!"

"Be well, Eye San. And please, visit me in Luópán sometime!"

He turned a conspiratorial tone toward her. "He wants me to take him to the Dragon Gardens."

"Why isn't he at work?" she asked, perplexed.

"Flowers are his art form. His wife cuts the crop in the Inner Ring while he works and he spends his off hours here. The man loves flowers."

"I didn't realize flowers were one of the seven arts."

"They're not. But it didn't stop him." Cadence sighed.

"I didn't realize you were so interested in flowers, either" she said teasingly. After a few steps, she added, "or the Banjar."

He flashed a sideways glance at her. "I've always loved the gardens. The Banjar may be a more recent obsession."

She raised a brow at him, although inside she was irritated. *Let me guess*, she thought. "The dinner, I presume?"

He laughed. "Maybe."

"Meera got what she wanted, didn't she?"

He laughed again. "Our game! Did you figure out what she wanted after all, then?"

Penna looked at his smiling eyes, wondering why in New Bhutan she was smiling back.

"I did," she said grudgingly. "She was hoping we might offer a cure for the Banjarguay to the Sepas, in recognition of all they do for us. As if we have that to give!"

And perhaps to show me the girl, she thought, before pushing the thought from her mind.

"A cure? That would be something! I'm sure Seldom Chime has been trying to create that since we opened the barrier."

She murmured her agreement.

"A cure," he repeated wistfully to himself. "Do you think the cure could help people at any stage?"

"I think there is no cure, so no."

"But if there was?" he pressed.

"I don't play "what if" games."

He fell back with a glum expression. "Do you remember..." he said hesitantly.

She threw him a raised eyebrow.

"Do you remember the Sepa who spoke with Hui?"

Penna almost tripped. She coughed. "Not particularly."

"She was sitting next to him," he pressed. "She drew that picture in his journal."

She coughed again. "Yes, that rings a bell. Why?"

Cadence didn't answer, but his fingers found the petals of the yellow blooms in his basket.

Oh my Dragon, she thought. She almost laughed. "Tell me my husband-to-be is not telling me he's attracted to a Sepa!"

He blushed crimson. "Of course not. Well, I certainly don't mean to offend, Penna San. It's only... well you're easy to talk to... and, well, I think we both know that there will be no romance between us, wedded or not." After a moment's pause, he added "I have grown strangely fond of you in the last few weeks, though."

She was shocked at his forthrightness. And, if she was being honest, relieved.

If only it had been someone else he was interested in.

"Thank you for your truth, Cadence," she said stiffly. "It will ease our conversations to know where we both stand with the marriage contract. But..." she paused in her steps and turned to face him, "if you have no interest in me, why agree to the marriage?"

He laughed. "Why would you think I had a choice?"

She bit her lip and looked around at all the people; their people. "Everyone has a choice, Cadence. It's what you're willing to risk in making the choice that matters."

"Trying to convince me to say no for you?"

She laughed. "Me? I need this marriage. Look around you."

They had made their way up a few steps toward the Rail station and had a vantage point over the market. The people milled about, shouting trade offers and resting large woven baskets on their heads, clothing bright with a rainbow of color. "These people don't know me," she said quietly. "They don't love me. I know that my value begins and ends in strategy and policy. Your value is here, amongst the people. We would rule this land together; the Heart and the Eye. What else could I ask for?"

He was still looking out along Bankhar Street when she squeezed his hand softly. "Thank you for the market day, Cadence San. I needed it." With that, she turned and hurried up to a Rail Car, flashing her wrist and easing into the opening doorway before he could respond.

The Rail ride to the Inner Ring Station was over an hour and she still had to check out a carriage after that to continue to Meera's honeycomb, but the time passed quickly. Her mind was running the entire time.

Why did the girl keep coming back to her? Those eyes, sizing her up. Cadence had noticed them, too, apparently. Again, her hand itched to comm Meera. She wanted answers, and, as always, she wanted her childhood friend back.

She remembered when they'd first received their palmpads. Meera had waited to get hers until Penna came of age so they could go together. Three whole years, she'd waited! Even when Mishka, born between them, got hers, Meera still waited. They ran around the gardens, talking to one another through their palms (usually about how to avoid Mishka's pursuit). Every secret, every hurt, every first crush, all heard through these fingertips. She studied her hand as the carriage glided along. She wondered what Meera would say about Cadence's proposal for an honest friendship. A sham marriage where they could gossip about their true loves! Sai and Seldom popped into her mind. It wouldn't be the first marriage of its kind in this family. At least he wasn't expecting her to share his bed. Her arms instinctively moved to circle her belly at the thought.

There had been times when Sai and her stolen kisses had made her wonder about what it might be like to go to bed with him. She imagined it to be just as satisfying as his kiss. If he ever tried to pull her gently toward his quarters, however, she always froze, suddenly afraid. They'll hear us, she would gesture silently to the ceiling. They'll know.

In truth, it wasn't the Listeners she feared. She didn't know what it was. At the move toward a bed her whole body would just freeze like a block of ice and suddenly his warm touch would feel scalding.

Maybe her body knew he was a liar, she thought, circling back to her reason for being on this journey in the first place. She played the recording over in her mind again.

You deserve a break. You will be missed out here, of course.

Don't give me that shit. I'm not a fool, Sai San, as much as Tashi would have everyone believe.

Go see your family, Susu. Sleep. Tashi knows that you're not well, that is all. We both know that you weren't making sense. We just want to see you rested.

You know damn well I'm right, you snake. You're all snakes.

Susu would have been home for almost twenty-four hours by now. She wasn't looking forward to seeing him. He was certainly not her favorite person. Mishka would have been married off to Cadence if her faan hadn't died. Instead, she was free to choose her own husband and she'd chosen the first man who gave her any attention. He was handsome enough and had a distant relation to the Family line. Still, though, Penna didn't think their father would have approved. Susu was arrogant when he shouldn't be and whiny other-wise. He'd been given a job under Dorji Tashi as a favor to Mishka, but Tashi had made sure to send him along the barrier rather than working close at hand.

You're right, Susu, she thought. *We do think you're a fool.* She wondered for the hundredth time that day about what they could possibly have been doing out there. She shook her head.

Mishka's honeycomb was a twenty-minute ride from the Rail stop. She arrived as the sun was starting to turn down. She paused to take in the view of the mountains and take a few calming breaths. It had been a very long day. She had got what she asked for, she thought ruefully. One minute she was clawing at her own walls, itching for something to do to keep her from coming to her sister's. Ironic that her diversion had led her here, to her other sister's home. She took another deep breath and pulled the bell strings.

She straightened her shoulders and tucked a loose strand of hair behind her ear.

She looked out at the view, shifting from one leg to the other and back.

She rang the bells again.

After another minute, she gave a heavy sigh and let herself in.

In the late afternoon, Mishka's living quarters were getting dark. The combs were designed to stay as cool as possible so were set back from the light with curved overhangs. Everything was in perfect order, and the house was still. She popped her head into the small kitchen, just in case. Empty.

Penna sighed, angry at herself. She had thought that a surprise attack would be best but hadn't thought that she might travel all the way out here for them to not be home. Mishka and Susu weren't known for having an active social life.

Maybe they were celebrating his return. She put a pot on to boil, deciding she would at least help herself to some tea while she waited. What about Hui? She was sure that they wouldn't have taken her nephew with them if they were celebrating. Their relationship tended to ride on passionate love or a passionate hate, both of which left Hui out. The child was left with no discipline, as far as she was concerned.

Maybe he was in his resting quarters? What time did children go to sleep? She poured the water over the tea and blew gently over the steaming cup, judging her own ignorance about children.

It was worth looking upstairs. Maybe Mishka herself had already retired. She left the kitchen and climbed the short staircase. Hui's room was first. His bed was perfectly made, but the room was empty. As she was passing, a frame caught her eye, propped up on a small desk near his bed. She walked into Hui's room and picked it up.

It was a small painting of her and her sisters. She remembered sitting for this painting well. Their father had painted it, just months before he died. He had asked for them to hold hands, and their palms had become so sweaty that they'd started wiping the sweat on one another's faces when he looked away to mix a color. One of those rare times that the game wasn't Penna and Meera against Mishka, but all of them playing with each other equally. Penna smiled softly. So long ago.

She set the frame back down and stepped softly to her sister's resting quarters. The door was open. As she came closer, she could see the bed, where both Susu and Mishka were lying, side by side.

Side by side, toes pointed straight up. Her heart jumped to her throat as she quickened her last few steps around the corner, before stopping abruptly.

She stood there for a long time, making no sound. No cry. No plea. Just standing there, holding her steaming tea, looking at their bodies, their necks ceremoniously sliced, a dagger resting in each slack hand, one on the other's body.

Damn you, Mishka. Everyone knows you're weak.

She took a sip of her tea, eyes never leaving her sister's face. Then her hand must have forgotten it was holding anything and the cup crashed to the floor. The shatter reverberated through the house, provoking her feet to start moving. She stepped through the shards and to her sister's side. There was a sheet thrown across a chair next to the bed. She picked it up and tucked her sister in tight, covering the slash across her neck.

She looked at Susu, wondering if he deserved to be covered. The knife lay loose in his left hand, stretched over to fall between him and Mishka. The knife that had taken her sister's life. She had a sudden urge to take it and plunge it deep into his chest. She sucked in a sudden, jagged breath, realizing she'd been holding it. His right hand was on his chest, clutching a scrap of paper. She glanced back at her sister's face before reaching over her and pulling the paper from his grasp.

It was curled into a scroll. She unfurled it and read it. She read it a thousand times. As night fell, she sat there, eyes glued to the page. Where else could she look? What else could she do?

When all the light was gone, and they shared the darkness, her voice came out and repeated the words.

"Breaking bread,

not bones,

we thrive,

New Bhutan,

will stay alive."

16

C ADENCE

CADENCE'S LEGS were sore and he wanted nothing more than to retire to his private quarters when he returned to Potala that evening, but Tashi had other plans for him. After seeing Penna off, he'd wandered the market with ease, stopping to speak with merchants, stooping to play with children. The people of New Bhutan would hear his voice projected everywhere, see his likeness drawn into their papers. Speaking with him, however, they could see that he was a just and kind man, and his rule as the Eye would be just as well. He wanted to be remembered as a peaceful ruler; a hero. If he was being completely honest, he wanted even more.

The New Bhutanese were not religious people. The worship of gods had died with the Old World. But in his studies, he had found in the ancient days in China, great leaders had been deified after their death and said to watch over and give good fortune in whichever strength they possessed. They still kept the likeness of those gods hanging in the common rooms of Potala Palace. In the Thinking Room, where he was headed now, hung the portrait of Shang-ti, or The Jade Emperor. He watched over the order, justice, and creation of men. Ironically, he also watched over the seasons. *He lost one job*, Cadence thought. The planet was one broiling summer now, and New Bhutan kept a steady one hundred degrees at all times (the coolest they could manage).

He had dreamed up a name for himself to be remembered by, on the off chance they might deify him: "Cadence, God of Laughter." Or at least, if not deified, Cadence the Kind. If he was loved throughout his rule, he might plant the idea in a few farmers' heads and see if it stuck.

The worship of Penna had scared her, but for himself, he enjoyed it thoroughly. Of course, he thought, the worship of her was different, because she was so different. He realized with a touch of annoyance that if anyone would be deified it would probably be her, with her unusual appearance and ethereal demeanor. He would be the one to make them happy, though. He had big plans for New Bhutan under his rule, although he wasn't quite sure what they were yet.

He sighed as he climbed the last few steps, suddenly feeling incredibly weary. He tried to stick the image of the people's smiling faces in his mind before entering the Thinking Room. Facing his faan usually came with a hot bath of shame, so he needed all the pride he could muster.

The Thinking Room was in the center hall of the palace on the top floor. It had no windows, but the walls were draped in different tapestries stitched with the gods or former leaders (mostly The Dragon) and one portrait of the original Dragon, hung here at the beginning of their time.

As he came in, his eyes were drawn to the portrait, as it hung above his faan. The first Dorji Tashi of his name had sacrificed himself to save the barrier, leading the last charge against the Old World as the barrier was secured. The man in the portrait had a fierce expression and intricate costume robes on, but at his feet sat fat, smiling children.

Cadence swallowed hard and plastered his own smile on.

"*Satsriaka*, Faan," he tuned and bowed deeply. "Sai San."

Sai, Dorji Tashi, and himself were set to have these secret meetings once a month. They were used to express concerns, give reports, offer ideas, and discuss the movement of other lower-level family members such as Penna, Susu, or Seldom. That meeting wasn't scheduled for another week, however.

He jumped into a reclined position in his chair, playfully throwing his feet up on the table. "To what do I owe the pleasure?"

Tashi threw a disapproving glance at his feet before pursing his lips and saying reluctantly, "I have a gift for you."

Cadence looked back and forth between them as if he hadn't heard right. Sai offered a tight smile. He let his feet fall to the floor as he sat upright in his chair.

"For what?"

"It's a wedding gift," Sai said softly. "A tradition, passed down from the last two Dragons."

"When am I to be married?"

"As soon as we return."

"Return? Are we leaving?" They were being very vague, and it was starting to grate his nerves. He wished for a window.

"We are." Dorji Tashi clapped his hands together and rubbed them, which Cadence had learned was his version of smiling.

"My son," he began, "New Bhutan is a beautiful place, and its people live simply and happily. We provide them with just enough to feel satisfied and give them just enough work to let them feel useful. It's a perfect balance. But we in the palace are the leaders. Our work is much more difficult. We deserve benefits, do we not?"

He looked back and forth between them, waiting for affirmation. Cadence was frowning. He was well aware that they had benefits others did not.

"We do," Sai agreed after a moment.

Tashi stood up, rubbing his hands together again. "I've been wanting to take you for a while now, Cadence. We need some time, faan and son."

Cadence's eyes widened. He could think of zero times his faan had spent any time with him. It had always been his maan, and then Seldom, and then, as he grew older, no one.

"The great minds of Potala need time to relax if they are to spend so much time in the dreary tombs of Luópán Hall."

Tombs? Cadence thought skeptically. *The place where we've created our survival. The very center of life.*

"There is a lake, just north, discovered by Druk Tshering. I use it as a retreat. A getaway of sorts for a bit of relaxation."

Cadence stared hard at his faan. "A lake? In New Bhutan?" He knew every inch of the landscape, or at least, his worker bees did.

"It is within a second orb, north of the barrier."

North of the barrier?

He opened his mouth to speak, but no words came to mind.

Tashi gave him a moment to process.

"A second orb? Built... two Hearts past?" His mind was spinning. That was nearly a hundred and thirty years ago.

"I don't enjoy people repeating my words back in question form, Cadence."

"No one knows. The people don't know?"

"Those who attend know. My most trusted Family members. People who have earned it and can keep the secret from their wives and children. You have to understand that the lake is a sacred place. The only lake in the world." He watched his own fingers drum softly on the table, adding, "It is only for the greatest of men to enjoy. If common knowledge, it would too quickly become overused and destroyed."

"Our people would want to see it," Cadence snapped back. He was feeling protective of his citizens.

His father let out a scornful laugh. "You need to think bigger than what the people would want if you are going to run the world, Little Eye. Luxury equals currency. Currency equals war. The people get what they need from us; no more, no less. We distribute what they need and they work for all they get. It's a system that's always worked and it will continue to work." He said it in a rush, lightly hitting the tabletop with his fist.

"But *you* get luxury." He met his father's eyes angrily but immediately dropped them.

Silence filled the room until Sai gently broke it. "Cadence, the Family has ways that are time tested to keep New Bhutan safe. Don't forget, *We Break Bread, Not Bones*. We are not here to fight, and our people are not here to fight. Let's not give them a reason to."

"There's a lake," he repeated, mystified. "And a second orb." He raked his hands through his hair. "I'm sorry, Faan, you just doubled the size of the world."

Sai reached over and patted his shoulder. "We know it's a lot to take in. Go pack and rest, and we'll show you this other world tomorrow."

Tashi rubbed his hands again, the tension forgotten. "My son and I!"

It was early the next morning that the two of them were off in the northbound Rail, Sai having departed the night before. The Rail stopped at a place between the second to last and final scheduled stops. They were in the middle of nowhere, jammed between two rising mountains. A helio was parked so close to their rail car that they could step off from one to another, silently shifting from one vehicle to the next and then off into the sky. Cadence thought of the tape he and Penna had found. This must be where they had fought, making the mistake of stepping away for a moment. His Listeners were everywhere.

What had they said? Something about Susu being a fool and Sai being a snake. Cadence bristled at the thought of Susu knowing about the Domed Lake (as he had dubbed it) before he did. No one liked him. He wasn't a great man.

He looked across the helio at his father, the Heart. The Dragon.

It was only weeks ago that Cadence would have done anything to please him; had thought everything his faan did was always right and that he, Cadence, was always wrong. The Sepa's gaze floated before him again, replaced by those elderly merchant men bartering with a smile and the young children playing at his feet in simple white toga cloth. A bubbling of mixed emotions turned over his gut.

He shook his head, cursing Meera once more for good measure. Then he cursed himself. If the approval of a pretty girl, damn near a Banjarian pretty girl, for that matter, could make him question his entire way of life, what kind of leader would he be? His faan was right. If everyone could visit the lake, the lake would be destroyed. Isn't that what happened to the Old World? Luxury for all? As for Potala Palace, the Family needed that space to run the world. What would his people expect? They understood that he kept them safe and fed. He racked his brain for a rationale for the luxury of his elaborate clothing. Finding none, he smiled to himself and shrugged. He looked handsome in paintings. Wasn't that enough?

The thought flew from his mind as the helio shot through a gate in the barrier wall and the arching sky of the Banjar opened up before him. His stomach dropped as if he'd just been thrown off a building. The world spun out around him, the sky open to a forever that he couldn't quite grasp. Feeling like he might retch, he turned away from the view and faced Tashi.

He realized that this was one of the few times he'd been alone with the man in his whole life.

His faan looked different than he remembered. More like a man than the god he had always seen him as. The Sepa had seen his faan for a person; had sized him up and seen something lacking. Cadence had followed her gaze around the room all night, and through her, had seemed to be seeing them all for the first time. Compared to the simple dress of the Sepas, Cadence's gloriously stitched and flowing purple robes had started to feel tight around the collar. His faan, in his flaming dragon robes, had seemed obscene and clownish. It could be that his people looked at them that way, high up in Potala Palace, wearing ridiculous clothing and wasting hours of working light, basking in the beauty of winter flowers in private gardens.

Scowling at himself, he glanced back out the window. His mouth fell in shock. The Domed Lake suddenly came into view. He understood his faan's words. *The lake is a sacred place.*

He was so riveted by the shifting blues and greens as they descended that he barely had time to inspect the barrier entrance. They flew through a stone archway that shot seventy feet or so into the sky. Other than the arch, however, Cadence detected no skeletal structure to keep the dome connected. The barrier of New Bhutan was also made of a clear material, but every forty feet a thin rail of white metal crisscrossed across the sky to create a net for the dome. Here, he saw nothing. *The tech must have improved a great deal*, he thought in wonder. *We could make more of these.* Suddenly he was lost in a full-blown fantasy of his legacy, Cadence, Lake Bringer, Dome Builder. When he and Penna ruled, he would expand the world.

When they landed, Cadence was distracted from the beautiful landscape by the men who loitered around the patios. Men he didn't recognize. Who were these "great" men? Why were there so many? There were four enjoying morning tea on a stone patio halfway from the house to the lake, two more reclining on a porch swing, and he could count five men meditating at the shoreline. *The best kept secret seems to be no secret*, Cadence thought. He wondered if Raju, his faan's predecessor, had been more careful and it was Dorji's lack of impulse control that had led him to invite all of these nobodies. All of these nobodies before his own son.

He shook his head and his mind again slipped to his own rule. *And Penna's*, he reminded himself. He didn't like to think that she would have more power than him. As husband and wife, he hoped they would share responsibilities and decision making. Snake though she was, he'd become more open to their partnership. Her cunning could be an invaluable asset. Besides, it was fun to push her buttons.

They stepped into the house and Cadence was taken aback by the three-story painting along the far wall depicting naked women... tending to one another. He had never seen a naked woman before. Never a painting of one, either. His faan clapped him on the back and he realized that his feet had stopped moving; that his jaw was hanging open. They looked so... *different.*

"Beautiful, isn't it?" Dorji said, hand sweeping over the painting.

"I had that done my second year as Heart. What a drab wall it was before!"

He laughed and led Cadence up the stairs. When they reached the top floor, Cadence was happy to spot a familiar face sitting on the balcony.

"Sai San!"

Sai stood gracefully and offered a smile and a bow. "Cadence San! The Eye, come to Qinghai Lake for the first time. What an honor to be present for the occasion."

Cadence looked past him at the view of the lake, shimmering across the entire view. "It is something, isn't it?" he murmured.

"I was about to enjoy a morning dip," Sai said. "Would you care to join, Cadence? I know Tashi won't accompany me," he jabbed playfully.

Dorji laughed. "True. I always take an hour of rest and rejuvenation when I arrive. We'll get you yours soon enough, Cadence." With that, he clapped Cadence on the back once more and descended back down the stairs.

Sai smiled and turned to him. "Shall we?"

Cadence looked to the lake eagerly, but he was also afraid. How deep was it? Water didn't go past your waist anywhere in New Bhutan or anywhere else in the world, as far as he'd known. He had never read up on the art of staying afloat in water.

As if reading his thoughts, Sai added, "There are planks made to float. You can rest on it and paddle your way around or hold it with your arms and let your body hang in the water. It's quite safe."

It did feel hotter than usual, Cadence realized suddenly. The lake looked even more promising because of it. He nodded his assent and Sai led him down and out to the shore. Without ceremony, Sai untied his robes and walked into the lake, his sagging buttocks catching Cadence off guard. He laughed nervously as Sai disappeared under the water.

The sun was really beating down today. He would look into their temperature control software as soon as he was finished here. He clapped his hands together, knowing that it was past time he followed

Sai's lead. He could see the floatation planks ready and waiting on the sand. Instead, he sat down.

This didn't feel sacred. Watching Sai's butt dive into water didn't feel holy. It felt... crass. Walking into this lake for the first time should be a ceremony. His faan should be here, and a song should be sung; a candle lit. One person at a time should be allowed in for a private experience.

A deep sadness filled him. This glorious place had become a playground for his faan. How could he make it right? He filled his hands with the warm grains and let himself sink into a meditation, watching the ripples of the water and feeling the sun bake his body.

Just when a peace was stretching across his mind, two men came traipsing from behind him and jumped in, splashing Cadence and jerking him back to reality. He sighed. His divine moment with the lake would have to wait. Standing up and grabbing a plank, he stepped into the water. Suddenly Sai hooted his encouragement. He'd been watching him from the side but now paddled out toward him, having procured his own plank at some point.

"Let me show you how to use that thing," he said as he approached. The two boisterous men were laughing and splashing each other nearby.

"I think I can handle it," Cadence snapped, feeling like a child.

"I think I would rather you *know* you can handle it," Sai answered back, gently taking the plank from him. "Drowning isn't what we have planned for you, Little Eye."

Cadence grimaced. Little Eye again? Had he already earned a nickname and hadn't known?

Sai spent over twenty minutes explaining how to use the plank, what to do if you lost hold of it and what to do if you realized you had drifted too far. He taught him how to kick with his legs to stay afloat and they practiced. Once Sai was satisfied, Cadence positioned himself on the plank and drifted away, feeling more like a child than ever. The men seemed to be laughing at him, although it was impossible to know for sure.

He was lying on his stomach so his arms could trail along in the water and paddle him forward if he so inclined. He was only too eager to get away. He paddled as Sai had taught him, one arm and then the next, arching over his body and pushing the water behind him, keeping his core flexed and centered to remain evenly on the plank.

Cadence felt a wave of joy wash over him. The rhythm! The movement as his arms propelled him forward. The way the water glittered, at one moment clear and the next deep blue, how it was heavy and weightless all at once. It was intoxicating. He felt that he wanted to go as fast as he possibly could, to fly across the lake, his body and the water working together. He lost all track of time and space around him. It was just him and the lake. Finally, his energy was spent and he slowed, his arms taking strides at a gentler rate, like a dying clock's final ticks. Finally, he let them trail in the cool water behind him as he floated, now so far out that a light breeze rocked the water and his plank moseyed along on its own accord.

His head was laid to the side, the sun warming the drops of spray covering his face and lighting up his closed eyelids with an orange glow. *It feels sacred now*, he thought. He could float here forever, resting between two worlds, half his body in the cool watery depths and the other facing the fiery sun. He might make a painting of it, he thought sleepily.

He must have dozed, because he woke with a start that nearly jostled him off his plank. He lifted his arms out of the water and set them crossed before him, allowing his head to come up comfortably so he could have a look around. He had gone far. The shore he had launched from was almost out of view, as the lake began to curve. The shore was lined with trees, but he could see from here that they didn't last long. Only five hundred feet or so of green and then the desert took over again. There were grandiose Dynasty era houses dotted about along the shoreline, he could see from here. Who had planted the trees? Who had made the lake? He wanted to know everything. He found himself feeling annoyed that Sai had not kept pace with him so he could ask his questions now. He wondered petulantly if the old man was watching him now to make sure he didn't drown or if he'd wandered away after his own pursuits.

I sound like a child. Annoyed with himself, Cadence squinted across the shining waters to the nearest shore, thinking he might go ashore and investigate one of the smaller houses. And not just to prove that he didn't need Sai babysitting. The nearest shore was where the lake began to curve. He would lose sight of where he'd come from if he reached it, he realized, but he could find his way back.

He set off slowly, waking his arms up. A few feet further out and a bit of beach was revealed on the other side. Cadence stopped and craned his neck and strained his eyes. There was a line of small, identical shacks, stretched along the shore for a mile. Behind them were taller buildings. He couldn't place what they might be used for.

Curiosity grabbing him, he set out again at a faster pace.

At twenty yards from the shore, Cadence was startled to see a contraption glide across his path, with Sai in it. He held what looked like a giant spoon and was sitting on top of the water.

"Care for a lift?" Sai asked, smiling.

"What is it?" Cadence asked.

"It's a canoe. Or at least, our best shot at it. It's an Old World design."

Obviously, Cadence thought.

"Paddle alongside it and I'll help you in. You've been out here for a long while. Your body is probably craving some iced tea and shade."

This was true enough. He did as he was asked and was soon awkwardly catching his balance in the canoe. Sai explained the paddle as well as the physics of the canoe. Soon they were flying across that water, back the way he had come. A smile broke across Cadence's face. This canoe was almost as exciting as his plank. He took a deep breath and pushed his face up to the sun. *This might be the best day of my life,* he thought. For some reason Penna came to his mind. He would have liked to take her on this canoe. She would have been scared and too proud, but then delighted in the spray. He wondered if she would be an exception to the rule of "great men" only.

He turned to Sai. "Has Seldom Chime been here?"

"She has not," he grunted between strokes of the paddle.

It's a shame, he thought. Suddenly he remembered the rows of buildings around the bend. "What was all that around the corner? Looked like bunkers. Does this dome have a Sepa outpost I was unaware of?"

Sai worked through a few more strokes before replying. "Those are the factories and worker houses."

"Factories for what?"

Sai laughed. "For everything we don't grow. Rail parts, carriages, this canoe, water boilers, paints, honeycomb housing parts... everything."

"But I thought—"

"That everything we have is made in the depths of Luópán Hall?"

Suddenly the idea seemed absurd. "Some of it, surely..."

"We do make many wonderful things down there, but common construction pieces are not among them."

"Are the men at the shore the factory workers?" he asked, thinking he might be putting it all together.

Sai smiled. "Not really, no. They own the factories."

"They *own* the factories?" Cadence was confused. No one owned anything in New Bhutan, save for the Family, who owned and distributed everything fairly. Oh sure, a family may grow an extra garden in their kitchen, or paint a picture, but even those were seen as communal. Shared. Extra products such as these were traded in the common market. He realized that this might be why he was invited to the lake before his wedding. He needed to learn how Tashi was running things.

"Your faan can't run everything, Cadence," Sai was saying.

Cadence rolled his eyes and sat back, not thinking to offer to help row the canoe as Sai pushed them along.

"Who works the factories, then?" he asked, eyes closed. After waiting a few moments, Cadence opened one eye.

Sai was scowling across the lake, but after a particularly brutal swing of the oar, he said, "Banjarians."

Cadence wasn't sure if he'd heard right. "Banjarans? Here, in our dome?" He felt an urge to tuck his body lower in the canoe. They might be out there now, watching him from the trees. "Has Faan lost his mind?" he blurted. "They will kill us all in our sleep."

Sai smiled. "I doubt it. They like it here. Much better than in the Banjar. They are fed, safe, and healthy. What more could they ask for?"

Cadence looked around and thought about that and was suddenly quite jealous of the Banjarians. Why was it that Banjarian beasts were allowed to live near this lake, enjoy its splendor daily, while his people didn't even know of its existence? When he hadn't?

"Banjarians get to live here, but my people can't even see it?" He voiced, sitting up.

Sai looked at him thoughtfully. "I think that is a question for Tashi himself. He commed a few minutes ago and asked that we return. That's why I picked you up. He has your wedding gift prepared."

Cadence's interest was piqued, despite himself. He'd thought the lake was his gift. He imagined an oversized portrait for his common room. It might be of Cadence standing before the Eye symbol. If he was the painter, he would add a laughing Penna to it. *She would hate that painting*, he thought with a smile.

It wasn't until the canoe pulled into shore that he thought again of his and Sai's nudity. They'd been talking as if it was any other day, not that they didn't have a stitch of clothing on and were sailing across the only lake in the world. He laughed aloud at the thought as they climbed out and he awkwardly put his robes back on.

Other men nodded at them as they made their way to the main house, where Dorji Tashi stood waiting for them with a grin on his face.

"My son!" he said, which almost made Cadence trip. He never called him that.

Cadence bowed back. "Tashi," he murmured.

Tashi clapped him on the back. "How did you like our lake?"

Cadence shook his head in wonder and laughed. "I have no words."

"Good, because you don't have time to talk," Tashi said playfully. "I have your gift waiting." He nodded a goodbye to Sai and led Cadence into the house and up the steps. "Everyone wanted this one! Everyone! I said, no, no, we'll save this one for my son. He'll be here soon. Almost two weeks I've had to keep her hidden away from them with Palace on guard!" He leaned in and whispered conspiratorially. "She's still brand new."

They had left the steps on the second floor and he'd been leading him back into the house, along a long hall of large, blood-red doors. They stopped at the last door. "This is the second-best room, too," Tashi whispered proudly. "I get the best, of course." Then, his faan, the Great Dragon, smacked him on the behind and opened the door. After he stepped through, Tashi closed it, leaving him alone.

The room was exquisite. Its floor to ceiling windows faced the forest, and those paintings of women dressed every wall, but here the women were riding the sky dragon or wrapped tight in the long body of a sea dragon. He was crossing the room to inspect one when he heard a voice, making him jump.

"It's you," she said softly.

He turned slowly and his jaw dropped. Those eyes. He'd never thought he'd see those eyes again. How had his faan known? How had he found her?

"The Eye has come to see me at last," she said coyly. She was wearing a loose silk kimono, and at her words, it slipped open. She stepped closer. Her voice sounded different. Lustful. That sharp, observant air was gone.

Cadence found himself stepping backward.

"Sepa?" his voice came out uncertain.

She walked slowly toward him, her eyes full of a fierce hunger. She picked up his hand and led it under her robe.

"Dragons!" he cried out in surprise, snatching his hand back. "What are you doing?"

She bit her lip and tried to ease up against him, her hand reaching toward the hem of his own robes.

Without thinking, he turned and ran out the door, shutting it and leaning up against it. The hall was abandoned, thank dragons. What would his faan have said if he'd seen him running out of the room like a child? *What* will *he do, you mean*, he thought. He had to return.

He took a deep breath and opened the door again. She was gone. He walked through the room and peeked through the door she had come through. It was a private quarters room, with only a bed and no windows. This bed was larger than any he'd ever seen, even in Potala Palace. Candles were lit on little shelves that seemed to grow out from every foot or so of the wall. Bathed in the flickering light, 288 was lying on her back, robe falling open, rubbing her feet together and languidly dragging a finger across her naked belly.

Cadence reminded himself to breathe and keep his eyes on hers, but they kept slipping down despite himself. He'd never seen anything so beautiful. Not even the lake.

She was looking at him with a soft, inviting expression, the fierceness gone.

"288?" His voice came out as a croak.

"What can I give you, my Eye?"

It was still the same husky voice, rarely used and blackened from Banjar dust.

He found his legs walking him toward the bed. She was close enough to reach out and touch. Her skin had been oiled, he could see now. It gleamed in the dance of flame and shadow. She reached out one hand, palm open for him.

His hand reached out, too.

"What are you doing here?" he whispered, watching their hands entwine.

"I'm here for you," she replied.

"For me?" He didn't understand. "How did Tashi know to bring you?"

"Bring me?" Confusion briefly clouded her eyes. "I've always been here. Waiting for you."

Cadence had been rubbing his thumb along her beautiful hand, but her words stilled him.

"You live here? How would Meera know you? She doesn't know about the lake."

"Who is Meera?" she asked, as carelessly as flicking at a fly, "All I know is Cadence, the Eye."

Cadence dropped her hand and took a few steps back. "You... you don't know anyone else?"

"Why would I want to?" she smiled and reached her hand out again, but he didn't move to take it.

"What about the dinner?"

"Do you want to have dinner now? I have a feast to feed you if that is what you wish, Cadence San." She had pulled herself up to sit on her knees, completely naked now.

He was getting lightheaded and wished that this room had some natural lighting. Somewhere in his brain he remembered that outside, it was only late morning.

"I am hungry, yes. Yes. I would like to go to the patio and eat something." Anything to get out of this room.

She stood up in one graceful motion and slipped her silk back on, walking out the door.

Cadence followed slowly, trying to piece together what was going on. She led him past the common room and out to a small, private garden. He drew a grateful breath of fresh air.

"288?" he asked her back, but she did not respond. Suddenly he had a thought. "What is your name?"

She turned to look at him, then. "Ocean."

He let out a rattled breath. "Do you want to make me happy, Ocean?"

She was bringing a skewered chunk of juicy pineapple to his lips. "Yes," she murmured.

He pushed her hand away. "What would make me happy is if we sat out here and you told me what you've been doing, and why you're here." He didn't mean his voice to sound harsh, but it did. He was growing more and more frightened at the possibilities with every passing second.

She immediately sat down. Her voice sounded hesitant. "I... I live with Palace and the other girls in the Blossom House down the path, along the lake. Palace keeps us groomed and ready for when we are chosen. The Mighty Dragon led me here to meet you because men were trying to steal me away. He protected me until I could be here, waiting for you. I've been here all morning, waiting for you." Her voice turned into longing and her free hand reached out to lay on his chest. She leaned in close and took her own small bite of the pineapple. He could smell the juices as they pooled on her lips, so close to his.

He coughed and pulled away. "I see. Thank you 28—Ocean." He tried to think. Her mind had been tampered with, obviously. Could they do that? He knew they could empty... but... could they fill as well?

He thought he might be sick. The smell of the pineapple became overpowering. He sat down on the ground, gently pushing her away. "Ocean," he said wearily, "Do you think you could take me to your house?"

"If that is what you want."

He grimaced, thinking about all the things the men here might ask her to do.

She's brand new, his faan had said.

He intended to keep her that way.

17

HUI WAS ENJOYING what was arguably the second-best night of his life (second, of course, to the night he met 288). Meera had exaggerated their workload and they'd been finished for hours. They were curled up on the couch in the Briefing Room, a space Hui was wildly impressed with. An ancient map of the whole world stretched across one wall. It had obviously come from the Old World, as it was done in fine lines and colors that no human could have drawn. The land was divided by harsh lines and filled with hundreds of names. Over the old map were pins and lines drawn all along it, new names and circles written in hibiscus and bone inks. New Bhutan and the known lands of the Banjar were shockingly small compared to the rest of the planet. There were only five names in the Banjar, clustered around the dome. Bengalia, on the Southwestern coast, Tumail, a mountain post to the West, Kargilik, on the rim of the Taklamakan desert, and the Dredger posts, Karachi and Aizawl.

On another wall, a bank of windows boasted views of the rocky cliffs leading to the Banjar. He hurried to it, gazing at the desert beyond with his heart pounding.

The Banjar. It was beautiful and terrifying. He had clutched his suitcase to his chest and asked Meera if they could look at the encyclopedia together.

He had never shared these pages with anyone, and soon they were on the sofa, fawning over every word and trying to imagine what these things had been; stuff like freezing rain and fighter planes. Meera knew some that he didn't. She said working on the barrier had its advantages. They learned a lot from the Dredger clans. The firearm, for instance, was one she recognized. She'd traded one before, even though they didn't have the material for ammunition.

Meera stood and beckoned Hui to the map. "You see," she said, pointing, "these are the two Dredger communities." She pointed to Aizawl, and one where, she explained, a great city had once stood. Aizawl was destroyed by heavy bombing in The Great War, leaving mountains of discarded relics from the Old World to be found underground. Karachi was drowned out in one of the thousands of tsunamis that hit the coasts as the climate rebelled and changed. Karachi's Dredgers sifted through miles of muddy lakes, looking for the right relic to please the Family.

"The Dredgers bring all types of items to the Sepas, trying to trade. It's always a puzzle trying to figure out what they are."

"Like what?"

"Like... well, let me show you." She knelt down and used her palmpad to unlock the drawers of an oversized table stationed in the center of the room. After rummaging around, she pulled out a large bound book, even larger than the encyclopedia. "You're going to love this," she said happily.

She set the book down on the desk and opened to the first page. Hui bent over the pages and read.

Trading Log, 327AB

Every page was organized into four columns. The first column was the widest and was full of small renderings of strange objects.

The next column said what they believed its purpose was. The following columns explained where it came from, what was traded for it, and where it ended up. Most columns were missing at least one of these boxes.

"Old World things," he said to himself.

"Yes. Everything we bring in is in this book."

"And it looks like everything we get goes to Dorji Tashi!" He was scanning the last column that documented where everything went.

"At least at first, yes. He tends to trade items eventually. It's hard to say where these items landed in the end."

"Have we ever tried making them?"

Meera shook her head. "These items are mostly made of materials that hurt the Earth when they made them, used them, and disposed of them. They don't become earth again, ever."

"Ever?" Hui's eyes were wide again. She loved when he made that face.

"That's why they are still here. And that's why we won't make them again."

Hui was nodding and turning the pages, wondering what each item had been used for that had been worth so great a cost to the Old World people. Most were missing descriptions.

"There are several of these books, only touched by a couple pairs of hands." Meera was smiling down at him, happy that he could be one of them.

"Do you want to see my favorite word in our book?" he asked.

"Of course," she smiled.

He leaned across the Trading Log and flipped the pages of his own beloved relic until he found the fox page. There were three pictured, but it explained that there were many different types of fox. She looked closely and smiled. "This one looks familiar," she said.

His eyes shot to hers in surprise.

"Not that I've seen one in person," she added hastily. "I believe Celio was taken by this image, too."

Hui's disappointment left as quickly as it had come. "Is there a painting?" he asked eagerly.

"There may be," she teased.

"There is," he said with satisfaction. "Is that how Celio got the encyclopedia? Did she take it from the Dredgers?"

"She thinks it was passed down in her family since the divide, but I always guessed her aans had traded the Dredgers for it, somehow."

Hui looked over the map. "Where do you think Sepa 288 is now?"

His abrupt change of topic made his aunt tense up. "It's... it's hard to say, Hui. I—"

Before she could finish her thought, her palmpad glowed red and Kiro's name flashed across it. She pressed her thumb to pinky.

"Kiro?"

"Permission to bring you a tape, Meera San. I believe it's urgent."

Her eyes met Hui's. "Permission granted."

Kiro strode in immediately, tape in hand, but stopped short when he saw Hui. Hui also froze. Kiro's muscular form seemed to barely fit in the room. His only clothing was a loose undyed pant, and his dark chest was oiled, reflecting the evening sun rays. Having only seen people in full robes before in his life, Hui blushed furiously. Meera didn't seem to notice.

She was immediately on her feet. "Is it her?"

"I—I'm not sure," he said, his voice deep and uncertain. "But it's from the outskirts."

"Play it!" she said urgently. Kiro glanced at Hui again, but his aunt seemed to have forgotten he was there.

She rushed over to the Listening tech along the left wall, watching him push in the tape and press the button to begin.

"Meera!... Meera!... Meera!" The voice was alternating between a strong shout and a desperate cry. Sometimes it would come out as a whisper, other times a scream. Over and over, she cried. "Meera." The cry filled the room in an ominous echo.

Meera was watching the machine as if she could see the person. After minutes, she leaned over and stopped the tape. Still staring at it, she said "It's not her."

"Why—" Kiro began, but he was cut off.

"She sent someone else. Or it's a trap to see if I'm a traitor." She exchanged a worried glance with Kiro. Hui, meanwhile, felt his head might fall off from all the turning back and forth between them.

"It's too risky," Kiro said. "It could be anyone."

Hui couldn't help himself. "You have to help her! She... she must be so thirsty." Hui was thinking about his nightmare of trying to climb into New Bhutan.

Meera looked at him hard before turning to Kiro. "Where was it coming from?"

Kiro came to the map and pointed to a spot beyond the barrier, in the northeastern deserts just west of Tumail.

"Dragons," Meera breathed. She clapped her hands decisively. "Hui, I need you to pack up your things and get on the Rail. You will follow it all the way to the Su Song Dome and use my apartment for the night. I'll be meeting you there in a few hours. I might even get there before you. Kiro? Can you see that my nephew makes it safely to my apartments?"

He was looking at her with worry spread across his wide face. "And where will you be?"

She threw a quick smile to both of them and looked at Hui. "See you tonight, okay?" And with that, she slipped out the door.

Kiro looked doubtfully at Hui, who was already packing his book into his traveling case.

The man remained stoic on their journey, only speaking to give Hui a direction. Hui's questions kept popping out of his mouth involuntarily, despite the man's stony silence.

"Why would anyone think Meera is a traitor?" he asked as they walked down to the tunnel. Kiro was silent.

"How is Meera going to find the voice in the Banjar?" he asked while they were loading onto the Rail. Silence.

"Meera said she would see me tonight in her apartments. Will the girl on the tape be with her?" he wondered as they cruised along. Silence.

Hui stared at him pointedly, hoping to goad him into responding, but the man just stared out the window. He was taller than most people Hui had seen before, and broader. His hands were folded into each other on his lap, but one thumb was mindlessly rubbing at the top of the opposite hand.

"You're nervous," Hui said, looking out the window himself. "Sepora taught me that at the dinner. She pointed out who was nervous, who was angry... she could tell it all by the way they moved their bodies. Your thumb," he offered a general nod toward Kiro's hands. "That shows you're nervous."

Kiro looked down at his hands, looked at Hui, and turned back to the window.

Hui sighed. "I wonder if Meera meant Sepora when she said it's not her. I think she might be missing. Meera said she wasn't sure when she'd be back." He turned to Kiro, "Do you know Sepora? Or —" Hui flushed red. Maybe he didn't know her secret name. "288?"

Kiro closed his eyes and pretended to doze. Hui sighed again, deciding he would get out his sketchbook and try to draw the mystery objects he had seen in the Trading Log. It wasn't until he was filling out the rough sketch with some shading that he felt Kiro's eyes on him. He glanced up. He was glaring at the drawing.

"Where did you see one of those?" he barked.

Hui put his graphite down, not sure what Meera would want him to say. "Potala Palace?" he suggested.

Kiro's eyes went wide briefly. His fingers started tapping on his leg. "Do you know what it does?" he asked, a little softer this time.

"No." Hui was relieved to offer an honest answer. "Do you?"

Kiro returned his gaze to the window in response.

Hui looked down at his drawing. It was one of the more haunting images he had spotted. It looked like a human head, almost, with two large round eyes made of glass and a long snout made with what might be fabric. At the end of the nose was a large metallic looking circle with a wide hose attached to it. The hose circled around and went behind the face. He thought it might be a mask, or a new creature.

He darkened the eyes and thought about adding a reflection of himself staring back at it. The drawing started to give him the creeps and he thought about his maan. She would really hate this one.

Kiro kept stealing glances at it as well. Finally he turned back to Hui and said "I'm going to have to take that drawing from you."

"Why?"

Hui didn't mind, really. He didn't like the drawing anyway. Besides, he could always draw another one if he really wanted to.

"That's not an image we would like made public. That, or any other images you saw while in the bunker." He didn't say it to challenge Hui's lie. He said it as if Hui had never lied at all. He didn't need to challenge him, because he was so certain of the truth. Hui had forgotten that Kiro was second in command at the Sepa Bunker. *He can probably read my mind*, he thought uneasily.

He tore the page out of his journal and handed it to him. Kiro stared at the picture in his lap, and Hui's graphite found the page again, this time taking inspiration from what was right in front of him. His hands retold Kiro's rounded shoulders and pained expression. He tipped his journal up so Kiro couldn't see it. This picture, he would want to keep.

The rest of the trip went by in silence. Kiro had folded the paper into a small, neat square and tucked it into a pouch he kept tied to his waistband. Shortly after, he'd rested his head on the window and fallen asleep. Hui spent the rest of the time drawing him. He drew him from different angles, studying the curves and lines of his face and his hands, especially.

As if an alarm was built into his brain, Kiro's eyes snapped open just as they were pulling into Lhasa. He sat straight up without yawning or rubbing his eyes, as if he'd been awake the whole time. "You'll want to pack that up," he said, nodding to the closed journal in Hui's lap.

Hui nodded and quickly put his things back together. The Rail station ended at the Bankhar Street Market, across the bridge from Potala Palace. It was well past midnight now, and the market streets were abandoned. Every trader packed up their tent and took it home in the evenings, and the streets were wide and warm, the heat of the day still rising from the ground. As they crossed the bridge, Hui looked down and saw the ripples of dark water folding over one another and felt a shiver of fear. Kiro was using his palmpad to disengage the locked gate. Hui had never seen Potala Palace and the domes bathed in moonlight before. They were hauntingly beautiful, with the creamy white walls of the palace dashed with bright red trim and the glass and gold wiring twinkling along the windows of the domes.

Hui felt like a spy. He pretended he was Sepora, on a mission to a new place, looking for her target. He began to tiptoe along the edge of the street in a crouched position, taking in everything he could.

Kiro ignored him until Hui whispered, "Target found," into his wrist.

"What are you doing?" he demanded, sounding just as frightened as he was angry.

Hui stood up straight and looked at Kiro, finding a real, wild concern in his eyes. Hui suddenly realized that this was no game.

"I was only playing. I don't even have a palmpad." He came to Kiro and put his palms up as proof. The man grabbed his wrists and pressed them, although Hui could see that he felt foolish for checking.

"Your aunt's apartments are this way," he whispered. "Stay close to me now, and don't say another word."

Hui obeyed, treading lightly.

Su Song's lobby was full of shadows, the only sound the tinkling of fountains. Hui followed close as they passed through and rode the elevator to Meera's floor. At the door, Kiro paused and looked down at him.

"Meera San needs your loyalty, young man. Will you give it to her?"

Hui nodded his head.

"Even if it means lying to the people you love?"

Hui considered. "I don't think I love anyone more than Aunt Meera."

Kiro nodded slowly and then awkwardly set a hand on his shoulder. "Good boy."

He slid his palm across the door pad and it slid open. The lights were off.

"She's not here yet," Kiro said, obviously concerned. He looked down at Hui. "My orders were to see you safely here, but I believe I need to go back to the bunkers. If you can..." he hesitated.

"I'm sure I can, whatever it is," Hui offered, wanting to be helpful.

Kiro nodded. "If you think to let me know that she's made it back safely, that would be appreciated."

"I don't have a pad yet, but I'll ask her to let you know. I promise!"

Kiro nodded and abruptly turned and left.

Hui turned back to the dark apartment. He heard the elevator door open and close, and in the leftover silence was suddenly quite afraid.

He stepped through the dark to the candle nook, a fixture just inside the door of every house for evening entries. He felt for the match and shakily lit the candle.

Hui yelped and threw himself against the wall. Someone was sitting in the single chair in the room, facing the window. He could just see the top of someone's head. The person didn't react to his cry, or the candlelight. Hui felt the hairs on his arms rise and found he couldn't take a breath. He stayed there, frozen in fear, until his curiosity started to inch his feet along the wall toward the window. He couldn't seem to leave the steady support of the wall, but he inched along it until he could see the profile of the stranger. Thoughts were crashing around his head as he went; visions of corpses or villains with no eyeballs. He thought wildly that that would make a very terrifying drawing. In his last few steps, recognition made his heart start to slow. The lustrous hair, the sharp profile, the jeweled hands. It was his Aunt Penna.

He took a huge breath, realizing that he'd been holding it this whole time, and walked across the room to her. She was staring out the window, unmoving.

"Penna San?" he asked timidly.

After a few beats, her head slowly turned to look at him. Her face looked ashen, but there was no recognition behind her eyes.

"Are you alright?" he asked.

She didn't respond but dropped her eyes to her lap.

"Auntie Meera will be here soon," he said. "Or have you seen her?"

Penna's eyes snapped back up to his. "Meera." she said. Her voice came out as a hoarse whisper, as if she hadn't spoken in years. "I need to see Meera."

She jerked to her feet and walked around the room, away from Hui. "I need to see Meera," she muttered to herself.

"She should be here any minute," Hui repeated reassuringly.

Penna gave a shaky sigh, looking at him and then looking away. She sat back down in the chair and looked back out into the night.

Hui glanced around the small place. It may be that his aunt had a game around the house somewhere that could distract them while they waited. He usually didn't care much for his haughty Aunt Penna at all, but this version of her was worse. It scared him.

He left the small common room and went to the kitchenette to put some water on to boil. "I'm going to make some tea," he said.

She didn't move. Once the water was heating, Hui continued to look around. There was nothing. The apartment had a chair, a small table, the stove, and a bed in the private quarters. No shelves, no statues, no paintings... and then Hui remembered that Meera had promised to show him Celio' paintings once they were back at her apartments. Celio's paintings were here! He glanced around doubtfully. The space was so small that he'd covered every inch in under a minute.

The water started to hiss and spit, so Hui rushed to the counter and steeped the tea. He looked on the shelves for a snack, suddenly realizing how hungry he was. These apartments didn't have ice boxes in them. Similar to the honeycombs, each apartment shared a cellar where the ice boxes were kept cooler. In the kitchen, Hui found a basket of bananas and a few wrapped bao zi. He found trays and made one for both he and Penna, taking care to arrange the items to look more appealing, peeling and chopping the banana into small rounds and adding a sprig of mint from the garden wall to the tea. Last, he pulled a stem of the rosemary plant near the door and garnished Penna's plate with it. He carefully carried his tray out and set it on the ground near her, then left and returned with her tray, setting it at her feet. He sat down cross legged and started shoving banana rounds in his mouth two at a time. He was starving. He looked up to see her watching him. Ashamed, he swallowed and sat back. She hadn't touched her plate.

He frowned. Something was wrong. He was reminded of his faan the last time he'd seen him. They had that same vacant expression. Hui stood slowly before really thinking about what he was doing. He picked up her tea and placed it between her hands, carefully wrapping each of her palms around it. She watched his face while he did it. When he was certain she had a firm grasp, he stepped away. Penna slowly looked down at the cup and stared at it for a full minute. Then, without warning, she threw the cup across the room. Blistering tea splashed them both but the wall bore most of the damage. Shattered bits of porcelain littered the floor. Hui turned back to Penna, eyes wide and mouth open.

"I don't want any tea," she said quietly. She was staring at the wall where the tea was dripping down in brown streaks.

Hui sat back down slowly and took another bite of his banana, watching his aunt. He had never seen her look so disheveled. Her blue kimono was wrinkled and dirty. It looked smeared with dark stains around her lap, and even her hands looked dirty. Her hair had all but fallen from its bun completely, wisps of it sticking every which way. He glanced back at the mess she'd made on the floor and sighed.

He stood up and inched around the opposite side of the chair into the small hall that connected the community space to the private room. There was a sliding closet door there. Just like at his house, the closet contained a small broom and other cleaning supplies. He bent down to look for a dustpan on the ground. Finding it, he reached in and pulled it out, only to reveal a handle in the wall behind a pair of gardening boots. He glanced back at his aunt, but she hadn't moved.

He grasped the handle and pulled, realizing that the handle lifted up and out. The whole back wall of the closet was a door. He stood up and pushed those dresses Meera reserved for family dinners across the rack and out of the way. He pulled the door open. "Dragons," he whispered, and a smile burst across his face. It was the paintings.

He looked back over his shoulder and decided to clean up the mess first. He closed the closet and returned to Penna with broom and dustpan in hand. He couldn't help glancing at her as he swept.

"Why are you all dirty?" he asked before immediately dropping his eyes.

He saw her hands turn over in her lap, palms up. They were filthy with a reddish-brown stain.

After a stretch of silence, Hui collected the full dustpan and stood. "Auntie Meera should be here soon," he said again before walking away. He dumped the glass into a recycling bin and went back to the opened secret closet. The secret room was really a tall, thin slit in the wall, crammed with canvases. Hui carefully pulled one from the tight stack. They were covered in dust and sent him into a coughing fit. Recovering, he was finally able to inspect the painting. He placed it up against the wall behind him. It was a painting of his Aunt Meera, with flowers in her hair. The flowers had bees in them, he could see, but Meera didn't seem to mind. She had a relaxed smile on her face. The painting made Hui smile. He thought it might make Penna smile, too.

Careful to touch only the back and sides, he moved the painting into the common space. It was up to his waist and the frame was rather heavy. He huffed it over and set it over where the tea had stained the wall. He glanced back at Penna, hoping she didn't have anything else to throw. She was staring at the painting, and it looked like she might cry. Hui stepped back and studied it himself.

Celio had used white and yellow paint and a lot of oil to make it look like sunlight was streaming across his aunt's face. He wondered if his maan would ever buy him oils and paints, or if he would only work with graphite until he was of age to trade. He shrugged to himself and hurried back to the closet. He wanted to pull every painting out into the common room, where the lighting was better. Without inspecting them first, he heaved one painting after another into the common room, lining them up along the wall, sometimes covering others partially because he ran out of room. He was looking for the fox.

It was the sixth painting in the stack. After he found it, he forced himself to keep pulling them out without stopping. He wanted to see all of them at once. When he finished, he settled near Penna's feet cross legged and took them all in. There were several smaller ones of Meera, two where she was laughing with the bees and one where she was sleeping in the sky without any clothes on (Hui immediately stood up and covered that one up with a different painting). There was a long rectangular painting of five Sepas standing shoulder to shoulder in the desert, with the center Sepa holding an eye in one hand and cupping a brain in the other. Her chest was open to reveal her enlarged heart.

The rest of the pieces were even stranger, featuring desert landscapes with strange objects floating in the sky and foreign animals on the ground. The fox painting, his favorite, featured a white fox standing before what looked like a blurred Potala Palace. The ground and sky were painted a gauzy white. The painting was so white that you barely made out the outline of the fox, his yellow-green eyes drawing Hui's attention. It was a beautiful painting; one that should be up on a wall, not hidden away in a closet. He wondered if Meera would consider trading him for it.

He looked back at Penna. "Aren't they beautiful? My Aunt Celio painted them."

Penna was staring at a different desert painting, her brow knit in concentration. The piece had a pile of human skeletons in the center, but each skeleton still had a red, pulsing heart inside it. A thin red string snaked its way out of the pile and into the pointed mouth of a large animal. The animals surrounded the pile in a semicircle, their heads pointed away as they tried to pull the string. They were half covered in feathers and half skin with sharp, curled, knife-like mouths.

He turned back to Penna. "That one is pretty scary, huh? I wonder what kind of animal they are."

Tears brimmed in Penna's eyes again.

"They're called vultures," she whispered.

Hui looked at her in astonishment. "How do you know that?"

She looked at him with red rimmed eyes, a look of childlike vulnerability on her beautiful face.

"I don't know."

The front door opened quietly then and Meera came in, using a spare arm to support a young woman who was leaning on her heavily. "Hui," Meera huffed, "Help me get her to the bed."

Then she looked up and stopped dead as she took in the scene; her sister Penna with tear and dirt-stained face and all of Celio's paintings set out along the wall.

"Oh my," she breathed. "Here, Hui, help your aunt."

Hui hurried over and tried to support the woman's other side, but he was a little too short. They got her to the bed and laid her down. The woman made a soft groan.

"Who is she?" Hui whispered.

"Come help now, and get some tea for her."

"Yes, San."

When he came back into the common room, Penna was standing up. "Meera," she was saying into her palm, speaking the name over and over again with rising panic. "Meera!" The sound echoed from Meera's palm down the hall.

Meera came running out of the bedroom. With one look at Penna, she rushed to take her sister in her arms, holding her close.

Meera was still petting Penna's hair in bewildered silence when Hui's water was finished and he took the tea into the private room.

The room was dark, with just one candle lit on the small bedside table.

"I have some tea for you," he said hesitantly.

The woman opened her eyes and reached a weak hand out for the cup.

"You'll have to sit up if you want to take a sip. Can you do that?"

She pushed herself halfway to a sitting position, revealing a mass of curly black hair. Her face had the yellow tinge of an old bruise along her cheek. Hui gingerly took her hand in his and helped her hold the cup, just as he had done with his aunt. This time, he helped her lift it to her lips as well, then set it on the table. The woman was staring at him.

"I knew you would be thirsty," he whispered. "I had a dream about how thirsty you would be."

"Come," she said simply. Her voice was hoarse, but a sad smile tipped the side of her mouth. Hui climbed onto the bed and sat next to her.

"My name's Hui."

She coughed and smiled again. "My name's Story."

"Are you a Banjarian?"

She cocked a brow at him. "I'm a Tumailian."

18

———

C ADENCE

A WOMAN CLAD in nothing but a thin strip of silk brought them a tray of coffee the next morning, a very rare treat, even for the Family. Cadence had stopped speaking about an hour before, lost in thought, and 288 was sitting on a patio chaise lounge, staring at nothing.

"The Dragon says good day," the woman said in a chipper voice, "and that he expects you and your Rue to be quite finished within the hour. He would like you to join him for a late mori on the balcony." She bowed deeply and began to leave.

"What's a Rue?" he called after her.

"We are, of course," she said, gesturing toward 288.

He nodded slowly. "And what's your name?"

She looked confused for a moment, and then said with a bright smile, "Pond."

"I see. Pond? Can you send my father a message back?"

"Yes, Sir San."

"Give him thanks for the coffee," he smiled, "but I will have to catch up with him later. The lovely Ocean has filled me up to bursting and I was just going to take her for a walk along the lake to digest. I will find him after."

"I will deliver the message. Enjoy your swim," she said warmly. She bowed again and left. The smile fell off Cadence's face.

As the door clicked closed behind her, he sighed heavily and looked at 288. He still had zero clue as to what he should do. He wanted to take her back to her house so none of the brutes that surrounded the place would take her now that he was presumably finished. Once she was back where the girls lived, then what? Tell his father he wants to keep her? He had entertained that idea for a minute before realizing that he was about to marry Penna San. Neither his faan nor his wife would be too happy with that request. He also thought he might ask that she be returned to Meera San now. She was, after all, their best soldier. Or at least, she *had* been. He looked doubtfully over at 288. Her eyes were unfocused and she hummed softly to herself.

The first step was to see if they could fix her. He wanted to find her memories and see if they could give them back to her. He would figure out what to say to Tashi later.

"Ocean?" he asked softly.

She looked at him as if surprised to see him there. "Cadence," she said lovingly. "What can I do for you?"

"I would like to take a walk along the lake. Will you accompany me?"

"Of course."

He shuddered and reminded himself to stop giving her requests. Every time she responded that way it made him a little sick.

They stood up together and left the candle apartments behind. Cadence's heart was smashing into his chest as they made their way down the steps. If they could just get to the lake without running into his faan, he would be able to get 288 safely back. He wrapped her arm in his and pulled her close to his side as they left the main house, surrounded by men playing at cards. Some were already visibly intoxicated.

A few of them called after them as they passed, asking for her name or to get a look at those eyes.

He ignored them, pulling her along to the lake.

"You see?" 288 said. "They want to steal me away from you." She tucked her head into his shoulder like a frightened child.

The sun was beating down in earnest and the lake's shimmer looked more beautiful than ever. "Let's walk with our feet in the water," he suggested.

Just as he took his first step and smiled a genuine smile at 288, a shadow fell across her face. He turned around to see Sai joining them.

"Cadence," he greeted. "We saw you heading out from the deck. Your faan is disappointed you won't join him. We expected to see you at cards last night, but, apparently, the gift was more than we bargained for." At this he offered a tight smile that didn't quite reach his eyes.

Cadence turned and waved a hello toward the balcony, unable to see what exactly he was waving at. "Well," he said cheerfully to Sai, "it is my wedding present. I would like to enjoy it as long as I can."

Sai looked at 288 for a long minute. "Well," Sai said, falling into step with them along the beach, "I am sorry to say that this girl will not be with us long. She works for Meera, and I believe that it would not be worth the trouble we would hear from her if we kept her."

"Where will she go?"

"Back to her post as a Sepa Operative."

Relief flooded Cadence. "So, you will change her back?"

Sai smiled softly. "Want to keep her the way she is, eh?"

Cadence forced a laugh. "Who wouldn't?"

Ocean smiled, too.

"There are plenty of lovely girls for you here, with new ones always arriving."

Cadence looked at his uncle. He had said the words so casually, as if this situation was completely normal. Where do they come from? he wanted to ask.

Cadence dropped 288's arm and opted to hold her hand. He looked out across the lake, trying to breathe and think clearly. Here he was, walking along the most beautiful place in the world with the girl he hadn't been able to stop thinking about, and she would do anything to please him. It was a dream come true for him. And yet, Ocean wasn't 288.

Maybe Ocean is better, a small voice whispered in his head before he could stop it. Maybe 288 wouldn't have smiled at you and held your hand. She looked at you and everything you are with disdain, remember?

He looked over at her, trying to forget her number and try her name. Ocean. It was a pretty name. She batted her eyelashes at him and smiled coyly. He smiled back, appreciating the way her silks had fallen off one shoulder and her bare skin shone in the sunlight.

She would be sent home soon and be safe. Maybe she could come back just when he was here. Tashi wouldn't let him take her home, but she might let him bring her here when he came. Penna didn't need to know and probably wouldn't care.

His body was feeling a mixture of shame and arousal at the thought.

"Let me escort your lady back to her cabin, Cadence, so you can take a swim before joining your faan. It's so hot and she needs some rest."

"She couldn't take a swim with me?"

"The lake is a sacred place, Cadence, the only one in the world. We can't let just *anyone* swim in it. Besides, Ocean needs to rest and get ready."

Relief swept through him. Here he had thought he would have to find a way to get her safe and headed home in secret, but Sai was already planning to get her ready to go as early as today.

He stopped and picked up both her hands, taking a long look at her beautiful face.

"Do you think I'll see her again?" He was looking at Ocean but talking to Sai. There was no need to talk to her anymore. She would only say what he wanted her to.

"Not unless you become a Sepa or a rebel," Sai joked, "but like I said, she's only a fraction of what we have here."

Cadence dropped her hands. "I don't think I need a swim. I want to go eat with my faan, after all. You will see her to the cabin personally?"

"Of course." Sai bowed and took the crook of Ocean's arm. She looked back at him wildly, fear clouding her eyes.

"Cadence? He's taking me away from you. He's stealing me away from you." Her voice was rising in a kind of hysteria.

He looked on helplessly, not sure what to do. As she began to repeat it, at an even higher volume, Sai's hand flew across her cheek. She fell to the ground, crying softly.

Sai smiled apologetically at him. "Sorry about that, Cadence. We haven't figured out how to turn off their enhanced attraction without going through the Emptying at the resting cabin."

He grabbed her arm and jerked her to her feet. "I'll catch up with you later," he said brightly, and turned, leading the girl along with him.

Cadence watched them go. Sai kept a firm grip on her, as she kept trying to look back at him. Their eyes met, and he thought he saw betrayal. He wanted to go after her and be the hero she thought he was, but sternly reminded himself that she didn't really think that. She wasn't really hoping for him to save her. It was all a trick, crafted to make the men here feel wanted, him included. He felt a little sick again. Without her hand in his and her easy smile, the illusion cracked and split before his eyes. The lake's glimmer seemed blinding. And yet, he thought, he wanted to have her back with him. And he could. Wasn't that an intoxicating notion?

They were bending around the side of the lake now, headed toward the place she had described. Satisfied that she was safe, he turned and headed back to face his faan, trying to find the words for what he had to say.

He found Dorji Tashi on the front deck, playing cards with two men in bed robes.

He was clad in silks, stained a deep brick red with black tassels hanging from the sleeves and dragon talons stitched on either lapel. He smiled at Cadence as he walked up and threw his cards down.

"Li, Chen, meet my son, Cadence." The two men stood up, one's robe falling open. Cadence blushed crimson and kept his eyes trained on the man's face as he shook hands. None of the men seemed to care one bit.

He nodded a greeting and turned to his faan. "Are you available for mori now or should I return later?"

Tashi rubbed his belly. "Let's take a walk. It spurs my appetite." He turned to the two men, now seated. "I fold, gentlemen, but demand a rematch tonight."

The men laughed and agreed as Tashi walked away, steering Cadence toward the lake and in the opposite direction he'd just sent Ocean and Sai.

Cadence didn't hesitate. "Did you know I liked her? At the dinner?"

Tashi cast him a sideward glance. "No. I had my own concerns to deal with that night." He smiled. "The Listeners gave me the tape from your shopping trip with Penna in the markets."

Cadence almost tripped at the words. He immediately started running over that entire afternoon in the market in his head. To his embarrassment, he'd sounded petulant while Penna sounded wise. He was sure his father saw that, too. She had spoken of ruling together, and he'd spoken of a pretty girl.

He gritted his teeth. Wasn't he the Eye, in charge of Listening? "And here I thought I was the Eye," he said with a forced smile.

"The Heart pumps blood into the entire body."

They walked in silence for a moment as Tashi let his words sink in.

"So," Cadence said with forced brevity, "you listened to Penna and I in the market to see what I might want for a wedding gift?"

Tashi offered a cold smile. "Something like that."

The hair on his neck rose, despite the heat. Why had his faan been spying on him? *Or her*, he thought. He considered that. That would make more sense, really. She was to take over his role. Maybe he was always keeping eyes on her.

Tashi brought him back to the present. "She's a beautiful girl, but unfortunately not ours to keep. It's rare that I'll take one I can't keep, but," he stopped speaking to smile and chuckle at the memory. "She was so full of fire. Unafraid, ungrateful, obviously trying to manipulate us. I couldn't resist the satisfaction of snuffing that light out and reigniting it with love for me." He sighed contentedly. "How was she?"

The color had drained from Cadence's face, but at the casual question it flooded back red. "Good!" he coughed out, but realizing that probably wasn't a satisfactory answer, he added "Incredible." Her face came into his mind as he said it, but it wasn't Ocean's face. It was 288's, staring down his faan across the dinner table.

"Meera thinks she controls everything," Tashi continued. "True, I was fond of her as a child and her faan was a dear friend, almost a brother to me; Asaka the Just, they called him. But, she believes the Sepas are hers to control. She has to realize that it is only the Heart, the Eye, and the Brain who make final decisions. We have to keep the power balance intact, Cadence, I want you to understand that."

Cadence wasn't sure he was understanding a word.

Tashi clapped him on the back conspiratorially, "We could always relay the tragic news of her death. Sometimes a little lie keeps the power where it needs to be without a struggle."

"288's death?"

"Isn't 288 dead already? Ocean, rising like a phoenix from her ashes? Let's let the new girl live. I want to see her fire, too." He winked at him and kept walking, closing his eyes to enjoy the midday sun.

Cadence's throat was so constricted he could barely breathe. He took shallow breaths and looked out over the water, trying to gain some control.

"Sai wouldn't be pleased," Tashi continued, oblivious to Cadence's pain. "He's always trying to keep everyone calm, Meera included. That whole show at Meera's dinner. I could have throttled him right there at the table. Where is he?" He looked around as if he might be sitting on a nearby stone.

Cadence cleared his throat, hoping his voice would come out calm. "He's escorting Ocean back to her resting cabin."

Tashi nodded. "My most trusted advisor! I want you to keep him as yours."

"Wouldn't he be Penna's advisor, Tashi San?"

"Ah! And now we can get to the grit. Have you read your histories?"

"Most," Cadence said, suddenly feeling an ashamed child. "Which time periods?"

"Before the Divide."

"Little," he admitted.

Tashi didn't seem to mind. "It is known that rulers before the Divide would pass their rule on to their children, and that this would often end in a bloody, unsuccessful rule. It is unlucky to be so greedy that you would try to rule twice through your children. That is why in New Bhutan, we must never choose our children to rule."

"I know that much," Cadence muttered.

"Well, your faan is a greedy man." He patted his belly and smiled. "Look around you! This full belly is mine. This lake is mine. Your Ocean beauty will be mine. It looks like greed hasn't hurt me any."

Cadence swallowed away that thought. "So, you would name me Heart anyway? The people will be terrified; they'll believe my reign cursed."

"No, no, of course not. You will be the Eye, Sai your understudy, and Penna will be the Heart. And when you sire a son, he will be Seldom's understudy."

"I'm sorry, Faan, but you're not making much sense to me."

"Penna!" he glanced at his son. "Penna is the key. She's my little snake turned dove, just like your Ocean."

Cadence's feet stopped. He looked at his faan with a confused frown.

Dorji stopped, too. "Penna is the strongest woman I've ever met, almost like a man. I saw it in her when she was a child. She would make a great ruler, I said to Asaka. We were always watching her lead those two sisters around. She always had the ideas, the plans to execute them, the voice to lead them. She had too much heart in her, though. Too much empathy to rule effectively. There has to be balance, yes?"

"Yes," Cadence murmured, hardly knowing what he was agreeing to.

"Penna will make a perfect ruler, with you as her Eye. She has a good mind for strategy if it's needed, a mind for detail, beautiful, and," and here his face broke into a satisfied smile, "a complete lack of empathy." He laughed and resumed walking.

After a moment he threw his arms wide, almost smacking Cadence across the chest. "Who says we can't be Gods, eh?"

Understanding was flooding over Cadence like a wave of molten lava, flooding him with a hot rage. He took a moment to assure that his voice would come out passive.

"You emptied her."

Tashi looked back at him. "Several times. This is the gift I am giving you, my son. Penna, Ocean; any of them. Penna may be the Heart, but you get to decide what she wants and what she remembers." He almost stumbled over to Cadence and whispered loudly in his ear, "Who needs to play Heart when you can be a God?"

Cadence's eyes were wide when he met his faan's.

Cadence the Generous. Cadence the Mighty.

Cadence, the God.

19

————

MEERA

THE LAST TWO candles were almost out. Meera was sitting on the ground in front of Celio's painting, surrounded by candle holders, petting Penna's hair. She had fallen asleep there, in Meera's lap. The house was so still now. Three people who had never set foot in her apartments, each having lost something, asleep. Meera wondered what nightmares might plague their rest; what dreams may start their morning with a painful hope.

She was grateful that Hui had set out Celio's paintings. It made her feel a little less alone. It was just her and Celio now, up late into the night, discussing their next move.

"What are we going to do now?" she whispered.

She tried to imagine what Celio would say.

"Take care of that baby, there," she would have said, eyebrow raised. *Which one?* she thought, glancing down at her sister.

"Take some time to mourn yourself. She was your sister, too,

Meera." Yes. Meera conjured the image of her younger sister in her mind. Mishka. Try as she might, grief did not chill her skin and tears did not prick at her eyes. She felt angry. She wanted to know what Susu had done to convince her to die with him. She had always been a follower, and would have followed Susu anywhere.

"You better find out what happened to her, even if it takes going to the edge of the world," Celio would have said. She always fancied them to be vigilantes.

"And while you're at it, Meera," she whispered, "find out what happened to me."

Just then the candle's flame flickered out, and Meera was left in the dark. She didn't know where that thought had come from. The hair on her arms rose as the request swirled in her brain. What would Celio have said? She knew she would say all of those things. The last thought felt like a natural progression. Find out what happened to Sepora. Find out what happened to your sister. And then find out what happened to me.

Dragons. Why had she never wondered that before? Had she been so blinded by grief as to not even consider the possibility of foul play? Why would she have? It was just her wife; just an actor and a farmer. *And a rebel*, she thought. A vigilante. And maybe, she thought wildly, her sister and Susus had also been killed, and it only appeared to be a gishiki shinju.

The note. Susu's scroll said only New Bhutan's famous maxim "We break bread, not bones." Was it a warning? A threat? A confession? Was it planted? No, no, they'd both been falling apart for a while now. It made sense that something could influence them to leap into the dark together. But what?

Her head was spinning in circles and her legs were starting to cramp. She gently lifted Penna's head off her lap and set it on the ground. Free to move around, she leaned over the candles and poured the liquid wax from the last candle into her palm. Rubbing her palm with her fingers, she used the other hand to light a match on the stone block nearby and reignite the candle. The painting before her sprang to life; a beauty of the palace covered in white.

In this light, she could barely make out the fox Hui loved so much. She thought she might give him the painting. She might give him anything at this point, as long as she didn't have to tell him that both his aans were gone. If not her, though, who else?

She thought about the process she would start as soon as she notified someone that they were there. Penna had just left them there, without notifying anyone. The Stone Men from the Samsara Center picked up the bodies of the dead to be recycled. In its place, they would leave a small stone with an etching of a plant. The belief was that keeping the stone kept the person near you as their body grew into the new plant. As soon as the stone holder saw the same plant flourishing, it was time to throw the rock back into nature, because the person you loved had moved on. It would be nice to know that the Stone Men had taken the bodies and let their journey to a new life begin, instead of knowing that they were still there in the dark apartment, their blood soaking through the floorboards.

She looked over at her little sister, her face finally wiped of worry in sleep. If Penna had been able to comm for the Samsara, then at least that wouldn't be Meera's job. How could she begin the business of death (something she'd done only too recently), let a child know that he had been orphaned, find a place to hide a Banjarian fugitive, and rescue Sepora all in one day? It was all too much to consider. She returned her gaze to the fox, prowling the castle.

"What would it take for a fox to conquer a dragon?" Celio whispered.

She nodded to herself, thinking. Wit.

Eyes trained on the fox, she set her palm close to her lips, and croaked out a call.

"Samsara."

"Stone Men, here," a gravelly voice issued back through her palm.

"Mishka San and Susu San of the Family are dead, it appears by gishiki shinju." Her voice sounded sharp and too loud in the candle-light. "They are in Honeycomb seventeen, south side, Inner Ring. Due to distress, we have left them there. Please comm me, Meera San, when you have completed the trade."

"Is there anything we should document that you found on arrival? A forced entry? A note?"

She swallowed. "Nothing."

"We'll notify you when the stones have been planted."

At least Hui would find only stones.

Meera signed off and laid back, stretching out on the floor and then curling into a tight ball, her face pointed toward the flickering flame.

Her sister was dead and Sepora most likely dead also.

Story hadn't said much before falling asleep. She wasn't well. Meera had tracked the girl's voice to a spot less than a mile from Tumail. The town was in sight from where she touched down, so she knew that Story would have seen it, too. She could have made a break for freedom.

Instead, the girl was lying in a ball on the ground. She wondered if this was an ambush, or some plot to take Meera as a hostage. And yet, she'd known Sepora's instructions. This was enough for her to take a chance. She landed and pulled Story up from the ground, lifting her into the helio. It was clear that the girl was truly dehydrated. She took down the water from the flask Meera passed her, coughing most of it right back up.

"Where's 288?" Meera had asked, eyeing her warily. "Who are you?" Her voice was muffled behind the thick scarves she'd wrapped around the lower half of her face. She cast a nervous glance around her, as if the Banjarguay could be spotted on its way to infect her.

The girl leaned forward to cough, her tangle of black curls cascading over to obscure her face. "She's still there, I would think," she said weakly.

"Still where?"

She looked up, fixing one angry eye on Meera. "Wherever you told her to take me."

Meera swallowed hard. So this was Story. She'd assumed it would be a prisoner from the base, but she hadn't imagined it would be the rebel she'd been tracking for over a year. She seemed so... young.

"You don't know if she's there?"

"That was half a moon ago."

"How did you escape without her? And where have you been all this time? Don't tell me you survived this desert for two weeks!"

Story was eyeing the water flask again. Meera handed it over impatiently.

After taking a long pull from it, she smacked her lips and laid her head back, sighing. "Are we going to the great and wondrous New Bhutan?" she asked, her eyes closed.

Meera gritted her teeth. "I asked you a question."

"You asked me two questions," Story drawled, "but I thought maybe we should talk when we're in safer territory." She opened her eyes, fixing her gaze on Meera. "The Sepa said you would take me to New Bhutan when she helped me escape. That you would protect me. I plan on doing one more, if you'll help me. I plan on getting her out of there, too."

Meera felt her breath catch. At that moment, it was trust or don't. She nodded stiffly and rose the helio into the air.

The conversation had taken all the girl's strength and she immediately fell asleep. They entered the barrier at the northern border. She was trying to figure out how she could possibly slip an unconscious Banjarian into her quarters in Potala when Kiro commed.

He'd waited for her arrival in the lobby of the Su Song Dome. He said he'd been worried about Hui being left alone, but she knew that it was her he was concerned for. Since Celio's death, he'd been increasingly overprotective of her.

She thanked dragons for it and asked that he help escort her from the landing pad to her rooms. She would dress Story up in the clothes she'd brought from the bunker and they could escort her up together, arm in arm. Seeing them safely to the door, he'd reluctantly left her, headed back to the bunkers.

After their safe arrival to her rooms, the unexpected appearance of Penna and her news, told in alternating gasps, whispers, and dry sobs, Story and Sepora had been driven from her mind. All she knew for now was that Sepora had helped the Banjarian escape, possibly at the cost of her own safety.

I thought I told you to use your training, Meera thought. A Sepa doesn't sacrifice herself for the trade. She makes the trade to her advantage.

Meera looked toward the door to her private chambers, where Story and Hui were sleeping. Maybe Sepora had made a trade, Story's safety for hers, but the advantage was still unclear. A hint of hope fluttered in Meera's chest. Maybe the battle wasn't over.

Celio, what should I do now? she thought.

"Get some sleep, my love. You have a big day tomorrow."

Meera nodded to herself and curled up next to her sister, letting Penna's sweet face be the last thing she saw before sleep.

Sepora was still missing.

And Mishka was dead.

But at least there was this to be grateful for.

At least Penna had come back to her.

PART III

VULTURES

20

———

C ADENCE

THE DRESSING ROOM in Cadence's private quarters was, to say the least, more lavish than he cared to admit. Purple velvet chaise lounges bordered walls dressed in gold silks and oversized mirrors. There was a small circular platform in the center so he could see himself slightly elevated. What did it look like when he looked down at the people? He had wanted to know. This gave him a slightly more accurate vantage point.

Tonight, he would be addressing the people of New Bhutan as they gathered in the market for the celebration of the engagement. He and Tashi would make the announcement together. Tashi usually preferred to stay invisible and let the Eye stand before crowds, but an engagement (or any sort of celebratory event) caught his attention.

He turned to the left and right, fluffing his robe out and smoothing it down again. This was a new piece, made to celebrate the union. The tailor had sewn eyes flipped onto their sides, running the length of either side of the robe. They had long lashes that swept to the hem, creating thin black lines striping the purple folds. It was an impressively symmetrical piece. Cadence frowned, turning to the side to see if the imagery still made sense at any angle.

The tailor was in the dressing room, watching anxiously from the corner as his work was assessed. Cadence hated the way he watched; so eager to hear positive feedback.

"It will serve. Leave me."

The man bowed and hurried out. Cadence grimaced after him, sure that he must be one of Dorji's puppets. He felt suffocated by them. Every man since his return had smiled at him adoringly. How many felt it, truly? How could one ever know who was genuinely anxious to please you and who had simply been filled to be?

He'd asked his faan that when they'd shared mori.

"Does it matter?" he'd responded, a Rue rubbing his feet.

"Yes, it does" he'd responded angrily. "What if Sai was filled, or Seldom? Don't you want to know that your closest friends are truly that?"

"Don't be hysterical. Emptying is only done here, for these criminals."

"Except when you empty our new Heart." He eyed the girl warily. She was nearly orgasmic as she rubbed his faan's thick feet.

He grunted and took a loud slurp of his coffee. "You will make difficult decisions as a leader. Some people are made to be leaders, and others are not. Alone, you and Penna are not. Together, you are. Penna would have been lost to her passions if I had not intervened. New Bhutan is safe in your hands."

"How can I know where your meddling ends?"

He looked at him thoughtfully. "You're worried your people won't truly love you. They will. You can't empty the country. We only have two technicians!" He laughed and pulled the girl into his lap.

"You will come to trust the process and the necessary pleasures of Qinghai Lake will win you over. New Bhutan is full of people who need your leadership." He leaned back and sighed as the girl in his lap played with his loose hair. "Leading takes a toll on your mental health. You'll see. The lake serves as a rest and rejuvenation space for great minds. You can't perform at your best for the real people, the people of New Bhutan, without it. What is this?" Here he squeezed the Rou's butt cheek and smiled. "This is just a filthy Banjarian rebel." He threw Cadence a quick wink and returned his smile to her. "Why waste perfectly good flesh out in the desert? It's like throwing away good food."

The Rue smiled back at him.

He'd thought about Sepa 288 then, just as he couldn't help thinking about her now. She wasn't from the Banjar. The Sepas were the creation of New Bhutan, created to trade, built to keep extra memories, survive extreme heat, and trained to fight for Lhasa.

It was with a sudden drop in his gut that he'd realized Sepas were not normally used as Rou's. It was only because of his desire for her that 288 had been snatched away to the lake. His Faan had brought him a present.

"I would have preferred a Banjarian Rue to the Sepa," he'd said thickly.

Tashi laughed. "Not this one!" he joked, pulling his companion closer.

"You will send 288 back to her work as a Sepa?"

"Tomorrow, yes, or Meera will have my eyes." Tashi was waving him away like a fly, becoming more immersed in the company before him.

Cadence had left Tashi's balcony and walked through the tables of men at cards.

He would also be leaving tomorrow. Maybe they would fly out on the same helio. He scoffed at his own stupidity. The Dragon would never fly with a Sepa or a Rou. And yet, he mused, he would take one to bed. In what ways were Banjarians nonhuman, and in which were they human? Rou. The old word for flesh. They were still flesh, yes. Was it their minds or their spirit that wasn't enough?

In all the stories Seldom told him as a child, the Banjarians were monsters creeping along the barrier, waiting to steal little children who misbehaved and eat them. Food was scarce, the stories told, and the Banjarians had become cannibals. As a young man, his studies had taught him of the fighting between clans that had caused the Great War in the first place. The people's greed had driven them to use up and waste the planet. They had created devices that could kill a man from sixty feet away with just a click. They could drop one ball from the sky and it would send a wave of fire that killed over one hundred thousand. When the earth couldn't take their fire anymore, they created airborne illnesses that could drop from the air and kill a country. They thought airborne disease would kill the people without any further damage to the Earth, but the illness had spread out of their control.

Refugees swarmed New Bhutan as the barrier was being built, but New Bhutan was victorious in the Last War, as they called it. A small number of survivors were left to bang at the walls of New Bhutan, and the ancestors of those survivors still roamed, sick from the poisoned earth that was left for them. He had always imagined them disfigured, with sagging eyes and gnarled hands. Now, thinking back on the ladies giggling on men's laps, he had to again marvel at his ignorance. They were beautiful. Their skin had a ruddy, reddish hue, probably due to living outside the protection of the barrier. The Earth's temperature outside the barrier averaged a hundred and fifteen to a hundred and thirty-five degrees, whereas inside the barrier it remained a steady one hundred. They seemed taller, too, with strong, hard bodies. Their eyes were shaded in all different colors. They were different, yes, but didn't seem any less human than him.

Cadence sighed heavily and began to carefully strip the robe off. He called the tailor in for assistance.

The man scurried in, bowing, and began to undo pins along the left side of Cadence's back.

Cadence turned toward him. "What's your name?"

The man looked up in surprise. "Hoa."

"Hoa... and do you have a family, Hoa?"

The man suddenly looked frightened, and Cadence wondered if that had sounded threatening.

"Yes," he said quietly, dropping his eyes.

Cadence sagged with relief. This was no puppet of Tashi's. He wondered if he'd always be suspicious. "I would like to send them a gift, in thanks for this beautiful robe."

The man looked back up, smiling. "Thank you, Eye San! You are most generous!" He finished and carefully sank the robes around his ankles. Cadence stepped out and slipped into a simple white pant hanging on the wall.

"Leave your honeycomb number on the receipt for the robe, and I'll see to it. Thank you for the exquisite work, Hoa San." He bowed to the man, and he bowed back.

Civilized. Kind. Generous.

I will be a better leader than Dorji Tashi.

Both men left the dressing room together, Cadence heading to the balcony. He sat in the late morning sun, trying to rest a wrought mind.

Tashi always made him feel like a child. *You'll have to excuse my son, here. Cadence's vision is so limited. He was left with the women for too long, I regret to say.*

He could conjure the image of Tashi and Sai's condescending smirks easier than he could their smiles. What was he missing this time? Why couldn't he feel at ease with this way of life they had been living for so long and were ready to pass on to him? He tried to get inside Penna's mind, the one that his faan so admired but didn't mind tweaking. Penna would get down to the bare bones of it. She would raise her brow and ask, "What, Cadence, is your actual complaint? More importantly, what's your alternative?"

His alternative... he threw his head back and tried to find those thin lines of the barrier's framework in the sky.

How was he to know? According to his faan and Sai, the Banjarian laborers made most of New Bhutan's amenities: the rail, the honeycombs, the helios. It was only the palmpads, memory tech, and Sepas they made in Luópán. So what was his alternative? Release them into the wild where they may starve to death and let New Bhutan make their own tech (most likely destroying the environment they had fought so hard to protect)? Cadence, the Disrupter. Or if it went worse, Cadence, the Decimator.

Or, he could open transportation from New Bhutan to Qinghai Lake and let the laborers be a mixture of citizens, allowing the Banjarians to take residence in New Bhutan in return for their willing service in the barracks, same as any other citizen.

Still, the idea of them living amongst them sent a small chill along his arms. They were still the monsters under the bed and he wondered how many Bhutanese believed that as well. How many saw them as nonhuman? Cadence, the Monster Bringer.

He wished he could speak to Penna about this. He knew that she would offer wise counsel. During the helio ride home, however, Tashi had made it very clear to him who could be informed about the lake and who could not.

"A woman is made for raising a babe into a man, Cadence. Their hearts are double the size of men. Big enough to bring people into the world but too big to manage them. That is why they raise men to be strong in mind and body until they have the strength to manage even their mothers. The Earth gave us these skills for these reasons. We must keep to them. The lake is for men only. No matter how high a woman rises, she does not earn the right to the lake. It wouldn't be right, and the secret would certainly be revealed. A woman can't keep her tongue."

Sai was nodding his head sagely.

"But, even your wife...?" Cadence appealed to Sai.

"A political marriage, just like yours to Penna."

Cadence had put that thought aside, all too much to consider.

"So... how do I know which men know and which don't?"

"I have better advice than to worry about who to speak to. Speak to no one. The only time the lake should be mentioned is between the three of us when we plan to go there. Is that understood?"

"Yes," Cadence had said, but now it seemed like too much to ask. It wasn't just discussing a vacation. It was a way of life; a way that New Bhutan depended on. As a ruler, he needed to seek council outside his faan and uncle. Didn't he? He considered speaking to

Seldom anyway, who had raised him. Surely she would be a sympathetic ear? But then he remembered his faan's disdainful words about women and their gossiping tongues. If he couldn't keep his, what would his faan think of him?

Cadence rubbed his face with both palms. He clicked his palmpad with thumb to pinky and said "Penna San." Even if they couldn't speak of the lake, he would rather her surly company now than this constant loop in his brain. He had been assured by his fann that Penna would never be filled. He wouldn't have to worry about her emotions being fake. They had only emptied a few memories here and there to allow her analytical side to flourish. He could still trust that her actions were her own.

Only silence met him. He scowled at his hand. He had already commed twice and even checked for her in her apartments that morning, only to find her Quántóu asleep near the door. She'd woken with a start and blocked his entry. After much persuasion, she finally admitted that Penna San was not in her rooms, anyway. Where was she?

He remembered with a jolt the last time they had spoken, when she had asked about the disappearing families after a second flag was recorded at the residence.

Don't you care where they go? she'd asked.

Now he had a better idea. Those disappearing citizens must be the ones who left to live at the Lake, those gambling men who had abandoned their families for luxury. He knew more than Penna, then, giving him the upper hand. It was comforting in a strange way. He didn't have to prove himself to her anymore. She didn't know half of what they were up to. She was no one, really; just a beautiful snake without a clue about what was really going on.

He pressed his palmpad once more and called the palace host.

"Hello, Arjun. Can you locate Penna San and advise her to call Cadence immediately, please?" He disconnected without waiting for a reply. He knew the host would be doing a scan on the palace to locate her chip and connect a mic in that room.

It was only a minute later that he commed back.

Cadence frowned and answered, already knowing what response he would be getting.

"I must apologize, Cadence San, but Penna San is not on grounds. From my readings, she hasn't been here for two days." Cadence could feel the man's concerned frown through the connection. Fearing a leak of bad publicity, Cadence shifted to a light-hearted tone.

"That's right! Penna is vacationing at her sister's. How could I have forgotten? Thank you, Arjun." He hoped that would be enough to quell gossip, but after the announcement of their wedding later tonight, a missing Penna San story would become quite a bit juicier.

He had sent her off to her sister's two days ago. Had something happened to her and no one was the wiser because they'd been off gallivanting at the lake? He swore to himself and commed Susu instead, hoping to inquire if Penna was still visiting.

A recording made by a slightly robotic female voice filled the room. "This comm address has been disconnected." The phrase repeated over and over until Cadence came to his senses and cut the connection. He sat in shock. The only way a comm was disconnected was death or amputation. The device was linked into a person's palm from their thirteenth year until their death. Numbly, he commed Mishka. Surely Penna was mourning the loss alongside her sister.

"This comm address has been discon—" This time Cadence slammed his hand shut, cutting the connection himself. It wasn't possible. His mind started to spin. Had they cut their hands off and run away? He thought of Penna, headed there just days ago for her first visit in probably years. Maybe she killed them, he thought wildly.

Don't you wonder when people just disappear? she'd asked.

No, not really.

21

P ENNA

THEY HAD MADE QUITE A SIGHT, sneaking along the streets of the Bankhar Market in the early morning. Penna was still unsure why she was going with them in the first place. Maybe her life had become too quiet up there with only the dull company of Cadence, she thought as she glanced back at Potala Palace. She would return soon. Of course, she felt like she should be there for Mishka's stone retrieval. And, she admitted grudgingly, she didn't want to leave her remaining sister quite yet.

Meera had dressed Story in Sepa robes and was traveling with her a few paces ahead. Penna was dressed in one of Meera's old Inner Ring outfits, traveling alongside Hui as if they were mother and son. The outfit was a little small for her, as Meera was quite a bit shorter. Hui was clutching her hand tightly.

She looked down at the top of his head, black hair pushed askew, his traveling case clutched in the opposite hand. She had stayed next to her sister as Meera told Hui the truth that morning. He was humming as he snacked on mori, going from seated to lying on his belly to his back. He kept getting up and inspecting the paintings between bites. Meera and Penna were staring at him, unsure where to begin.

"Hu?" Meera had finally called.

He came to her side immediately, casting a wary glance at Penna.

"Last night, when you found that Penna was here and very upset —well, I'm sorry you had to see that. But, she had some very bad news yesterday."

Meera met Penna's eyes briefly for support.

Hui was eyeing her again.

"Hu, Penna went to visit your maan. When she got there, well, she found two stones."

Hui's eyes shot to Meera's face in disbelief.

"Two stones?"

"Yes. Do you know what that means?"

He nodded, his eyes welling with tears. "Faan. Faan, too?"

Meera nearly lost her voice. "Yes," she said faintly, "I'm so very sorry."

Hui's mouth was twisting around, trying to gain some control for a few minutes.

"But how?" he finally squeaked out. Once the words were out, the floodgate was opened, and he started to sob. Instead of curling into Meera's lap as she'd expected, he turned behind him to Story, who was sitting on the only chair in the room. He buried his face in her belly and cried. As natural as can be, she scooped him up into her lap and rubbed his hair, murmuring her support.

Meera looked at Penna with a frown. They used to do this all the time as kids; communicate with a glance. In that look they agreed that neither woman trusted this Banjarian for a second. They also agreed that she obviously knew much more about children than they did, as Hui had not left her side since she'd arrived.

Penna returned her gaze to Hui, relieved that he was able to cry.

Crying was supposed to help the pain flow out of you, leaving you cleansed. She'd never been able to cry, at least that she could remember. Her feelings stayed inside of her, heavy as lead.

They were headed to drop Story off at Meera's old Inner Ring quarters to hide out while they took Hui to pick up his parent's stones. From there, Meera would pick Story back up and take her to the Sepa bunker. It was there that Meera hoped to hatch a plan to save Sepora. Penna would take Hui back to the palace and explain the tragic ends of Susu and Mishka.

All of this had been organized by Meera, who had stepped up when Penna seemed to fall apart. She was angry at herself for being so helpless. What kind of leader would she be if she fell apart at... the images of her sister's sliced throat burst into life before her and she shook them away, trying to slow her racing heart with a jagged breath. Meera glanced back at her, as if sensing her pain.

She gave a small smile of reassurance. Her heart ached for Meera's friendship as her sister turned back, leading the group through the empty streets. She was marveling at how easily they could fall into their routine of big and little sisters if she let them.

Big and little sister. No middle.

Penna suddenly wished she could go straight back to the palace. She had no desire to return to that blood-soaked room where she'd found Mishka. The thought threatened to throw her into panic. Secondly, the Banjarian woman gave her the creeps. The Banjarians were wild creatures, and Story was no exception. Her curly mass of hair was matted into thick piles around her head and her skin was coarse and patchy. Her eyes were bright blue, shining out of her stone red face like ice fire. She stared at Penna too often, until she wanted to ask her to stop. The Penna of yesterday would have told her to keep her filthy eyes off her. The Penna of yesterday would have commed Tashi immediately to report Meera bringing a Banjarian within the barrier.

Two events had put that version of herself on pause. Everything she was certain of was now uncertain. The first was her faith in Dorji. Susu's note had clearly implied that he blamed New Bhutan for their deaths. Why else would he write their motto as a suicide note? Were she and Dorji somehow to blame? She remembered Susu's words in the recording like a whisper all night.

You know damn well I'm right, you snake. You're all snakes.

What had she done?

It was the first time her nickname as Snake truly cut her.

The second truth to be shaken for Penna was her history, and it happened because of those godforsaken vultures. Those watchful birds with black heart faces, stretching their wings to soak up the sun, crying out when... the images would blur and fade, but they were there. She knew how they moved and how they sounded. How? Had she seen them in a dream? Was she some kind of prophet? She wanted to ask how Celio had painted them. How had she known about them? Maybe her and Celio had been in the same class as children. But that couldn't be right. Celio was from Yutan. She had tried to leave the thought alone, but every time she closed her eyes she either saw Mishka's hollowed face or those watchful vulture eyes.

Hui squeezed her hand. She glanced over to see him looking up at her with the grim determination he'd had on his face since they left. After crying for a while, he had turned to Penna and looked her right in the eye. "What happened to them?" he'd said quietly.

Penna had looked to Meera but Meera only stared at Hui sadly. It was Penna's turn. "I don't know," she'd said. "Something convinced them to die together." She could barely let the words out around the lump in her throat.

Hui had nodded as if he already knew. He'd marched into the private quarters and come out a few minutes later with his packed traveling case. He set it before Meera.

"Let's go find out what it was."

Meera was nodding with fresh tears in her eyes. She ruffled his hair. "Sepa Hui, reporting for duty?" she asked thickly.

He gave a curt nod, his dry eyes staring determinedly but his trembling mouth giving him away.

Penna had never understood the draw of sticky, crying children, but Hui's expression in that moment made everything clear. She wanted to scoop him up herself.

Now here he was, ready to uncover the truth. She offered a small smile, the best she could do. He squeezed her hand and returned his gaze to the road before him.

They were almost to Meera's old honeycomb.

Meera had made the plan quickly and they had set out immediately, one of the biggest rules being no speaking. They didn't want the Listeners picking up on a band of people making their way across the market at four am. If she could have, Penna would have asked why they were taking the Banjarian to Meera's old home. Hadn't she given it up to another family? Could she trust them with this secret? It would take one comm to send the woman back where she came from, which from what little Penna knew, wasn't a good place.

Her nerves were raw by the time they reached the door. Instead of ringing the bell, Meera pulled a device from her robes and stuck it in a small hole in the door, turning it and pulling the door open. Penna's eyes went wide but she remained silent, as instructed. Once everyone was inside, Meera shut the door. "We're free to speak in here."

"What was that?" Penna asked immediately.

Meera looked at her with confusion for a moment and then gave a tired smile. "The key. It's an Old World mechanism. We learn a lot about Old World ways at the bunkers. When Penna was still looking at her for explanation, Meera sighed and continued. "I couldn't keep my palmpad tied to the residence. When Celio died, I wasn't permitted to live here anymore. A single can't keep a family comb. But I couldn't bring myself to let it go. Besides, a house off the grid has its advantages." She nodded toward the communal space that Hui and Story were already inspecting. Penna followed her gaze and gasped. It looked like a museum, full of strange items set on tables with tags near each. They were stacked on the floor and hung on the walls.

Meera was still talking, but Penna wasn't really listening. "...a friend in Luópán helped me rig the system so it looked like the home is under repair indefinitely. It can't be assigned, and the Listeners don't need to monitor it."

Penna had followed Hui and Story to inspect the items. They were obviously Banjarian, probably traded at some point. Some of the tags explained the items functions and purpose, while others only listed where they had come from and when.

She was trailing her fingers along the items as she walked, reading every word on the cards. They were mostly machines, made to create items. They were all worthless without the Old World's sources of power. Here and there were items that could still serve; a ring or a metal box. There were two books in glass cases that Hui was standing stock still in front of, his fingertips on the corners of the case in reverence.

She approached curiously. "What have you found there?"

He looked up at her in astonishment. "It's letters B and N."

Penna just twisted her face into a question mark.

"The encyclopedias! Meera!" He looked past her at her sister.

Meera walked slowly over, a small smile on her lips. "I thought you might find those."

"This whole time you've had two more letters?"

Story had wandered back to them at all the commotion and was leaning over Hui's shoulder.

Meera knelt down and looked Hui in the eye.

"These need to be protected, Hui, including the one you have. Are you willing to store the F in this case if I allow you to borrow a new letter?"

Hui looked from the case to his traveling case with uncertainty.

"But the fox..."

"Close your eyes." Meera commanded.

Hui obeyed.

"Is the fox there, in your mind?"

He nodded.

"Then you don't need the book anymore. It's inside your head now."

He opened his eyes and jumped onto Meera, hugging her tightly.

Penna still had no idea what these books were, but Hui's smile left something stirring in her chest.

Meera told Hui to go grab his traveling case and they would make the switch. It was then, with a smile on her lips, that Penna looked up behind her, following Hui's movements. The smile fell off her face. On the wall behind her was a painting of a stretch of land done in dark reds and browns; an oppressive grey bank of clouds hanging low in the sky. In the center was a pile of human bones and in the foreground on either side of it perched two vultures.

It felt like someone had sucked all the air from the room and punched her in the belly at the same time. Her knees buckled, and it was Story who dove over to catch her. She frowned at her in concern and then followed her eyes to the painting.

"Godsmeet Peak," she said quietly. "Not a pleasant place, is it?" Her voice was deep and scratchy.

Penna looked at her weakly. "It's a place you know?"

Story looked back at that pile of bones. "It's where the dead leave their bodies in Tumail." She swallowed, adding quietly "It's where I left my Miracle."

Hui was inspecting the painting, but Meera was watching her. She could feel her eyes and turned to meet them.

Meera's eyes were dark with grief and guilt, and it filled Penna with her old venom. All the anger and hurt she felt around her sister welled up inside her. Why had she chosen Celio over their way of life? Why was she always looking at her with such disappointment? Why did she bring that Sepa into her life? What did she know? There were so many secrets Meera was always keeping from her. She wanted to scream every question until the balloon of anger finally deflated, but instead, she simply brushed Story's helping hands away and stood up on shaky legs.

In a voice that was colder than the Polar gardens, she demanded "What is it, Meera?"

Meera sucked her lip in but remained silent.

"Meera!" she screeched. She stalked up to her with a full intention of striking her, but a wave of nausea hit her and she instead fell to her knees in front of her sister. Instead of hitting, Penna found herself wrapping her arms around her sister's legs.

"Tell me," she whispered, her eyes closed. "It's damn time for you to tell me."

"Okay," her sister was murmuring. "Okay."

22

S EPORA

Sepora was staring out at the lake unseeingly, eyes turned inward in a memory. This was a daily ritual for her. Turn inward and reflect on every moment she could, from the moment she started remembering until now, carefully sorting what were her memories and what were someone else's.

It was Miracle who always came first, showing off his missing front teeth with an eager grin. His face always turned to bone before her eyes, and that's how she knew it was hers. It came with connections and pain; there were layers. The ones that were not hers were like dreams; sometimes they came with sharp stabs of emotion, but it was all surface level and one never connected to the other. She sighed and focused her eyes on the lake. There was a rumor that she was being sent back to the bunker today, but Palace had told her not to count on it. Tashi was impulsive and his actions couldn't be predicted, even if he had said the words himself.

Just as she was thinking of her, Palace slipped into the room and sat on the bench beside her. "Hmmm, I love when Tashi leaves. The shore is so quiet. Everyone has returned to work, and we are all safe." She patted Sepora's leg and leaned back, closing her eyes contentedly.

Sepora studied her, trying to memorize her face. In the last two weeks, this woman had become the closest thing she had to family. The thought made her think of Story and wonder for the thousandth time if it had all been worth it - if she had found her way to Meera.

"Tell me the story, Sepora," Palace murmured, her eyes still closed.

Sepora smiled and closed her eyes, too, trying to pull the memories out of their tangles in her mind. "You are leading a charge of three clans, two from Bangalia and one Dredger from Kargilik. You're headed to Tumail. You're scared that you will lead your people to death but know that this is no life anyway. They know it, too. What they don't know is that you have a babe inside your belly, and your fire for their plight has been tamed by the fear for your child. You're wondering if your lover will return to you. If he will even be able to find you."

Palace sat up. "Can you feel it?"

"What?"

"The love for him?"

Sepora squirmed in her seat. "If I focus on him, yes, I can feel it."

"And?"

"And it feels like I would do anything to see him again."

"Even betray your people?"

Sepora hesitated. "Is that what you think you did?"

Palace shrugged. "Haven't I?"

"You were forced here. They stole your memories."

"If what you say is true, I was the fiercest rebel the Banjar had ever seen. Now I work in this Harem, erasing my people's memories and making slaves out of them."

"You didn't do that to me."

Palace scowled at her. "You're different."

"Why?"

"I don't know why, Sepora! You just are."

She'd said this before, when Sepora first realized that Palace had saved her. When Sepora was led to that awful building to be emptied, Palace had felt compelled to follow. She wanted to be there. She'd made the excuse to herself that she was just coming to aid the lake's emptier, Kinsu San, but had admitted that it was something about Sepora that made her feel different. She had helped Kinsu many times over the years and had become a sort of unofficial emptier. She knew where everything was kept and how the procedure worked. Kinsu and she had developed a friendship of sorts. He was a lonely man and she was a lonely woman.

When Sepora had attacked him, Palace had been in a back room on the opposite side of the basement, the Emptying room, prepping Kinsu's station for him. When she heard the scuffle, she'd raced out and found him passed out on the floor. It was at that moment, she'd told Sepora, that her body started moving without her mind. She ran back into the Emptying room and grabbed all the cases off of the shelves two at a time and brought them to his side, using his wrist to unlock every single one and then putting them back on the shelves, only slightly ajar. Her heart had been lodged in her throat the whole time, she'd recalled. By the time he awoke, almost all the cases were open. She pretended to be trying to help him up and hid the case she had been bringing behind her. It wasn't until he ran after Sepora that she was able to return and read the labels of the vials she now had access to. Skimming through, she recognized a few names here and there of more recent Rous. Most of their real names had been forgotten. She wondered if she would even know her own name if she saw it.

And then she had her answer. She saw it printed in faded ink, one of the oldest vials on the shelves: Ruby. Her eyes filled with tears and she had felt a wave of nausea take her over. She'd stumbled out of the room to compose herself before Kinsu returned.

Sepora had been caught and quickly thrown back into the basement room. Palace had stood like an obedient soldier, ready to do what was asked, trying to blink away her dizziness before Kinsu noticed. They had shot Sepora with sleeping darts, so he easily tossed her onto the ground. Even though she was clearly out, Kinsu kicked her in the gut three times. "The whore broke my nose!" he cried angrily.

Palace rushed to his side and set a calming hand on his arm. "You are bleeding quite badly, Kinsu San. Maybe you should go back to Blossom House and have one of my ladies tend to your wounds. Tashi need never know. She isn't going anywhere."

He had eyed the girl angrily and argued that Tashi wanted her trained immediately. "Come now," Palace had cooed, "When is Tashi ever on time?"

He had smiled at her reluctantly. "You're right, as always, Palace. Will you ready the solution? I'll return within an hour."

Palace had got to work immediately with her own plans, having no clue where these ideas were coming from.

"They came from Ruby," Sepora insisted when Palace recalled the tale. "She's still there," she added, pointing to Palace's head.

Palace knew how the Rue transformation was done. A memory of desire for the men of Qinghai Lake was inserted into the base of the neck. This memory was so powerful, it would take over any day-to-day memories a person might have tucked in different parts of the brain.

"How do they know it will block out all of them?" Sepora had asked.

"Think of it like an obsession; a thought that can take over your mind and drive it to constantly return to that one idea. Or if you notice a bothersome sound and then it's all you can hear and you feel as if you'll go crazy. The brain still has the other memories inside it, but these intense memories force it to be hyper focused on just them. There may be brief moments of clarity when a Rue remembers something, but it is quickly swallowed away again by obsession."

"And do you have this in you?"

"No," Palace snorted. "They take it out once you get too old for anyone to want you. Now I'm just empty. They did a complete

Emptying on me several years ago, I'm sure of it. What they don't consider is that a person makes new memories, even here. They haven't tampered with me for years."

That's why she had known exactly what Kinsu would do and had been in charge of readying the serums. The deepest, emotional memories in the human body were kept in memory receptors along the left pockets. These memories could not be overpowered by the obsession serum and had to be extracted first if a fill was going to be effective. Her fast plan was to extract Sepora's left pockets herself and immediately inject it into the receptors in her right. They might feel a little different, but at least she'd have them.

Then, she filled the left side with one of the vials of a forgotten Rue. That way, Kinsu would only be stealing memories that didn't belong there anyway.

Instead of the Rue serum, and with shaking hands, Palace readied the memories from the vial labeled "Ruby". She could have tucked the Ruby vial away for safekeeping and given Sepora something else. It was a survival instinct that made her choose her own. In that moment, the opportunity to learn about her true life had arisen, and she had taken it.

Once everything was ready, she'd gone to work slapping Sepora until she awoke.

She'd fought her until Palace said, "I'm here to help you, stupid girl!"

Sepora was suddenly hit with those unknown girl's memories that Palace had just injected into her mind. She began to sob.

"Listen to me! When the man injects the serum into your neck, you are immediately to offer yourself to him. He'll expect you to desire him. Do you understand?"

She shook her head that she didn't.

"Your mind is going to be flooded with memories that are not your own, making yours feel distant. If you don't think you can fake desire, act sick. If he thinks you're going to puke, he'll send you to Blossom House to rest. There I will teach you how to pretend." She had grabbed Sepora's chin. "I'm not going to let them empty you, okay?"

Finally, Sepora was fully focused. She nodded and tried to push back the flow of emotion from the Rue's life. She was being hit with a deep mourning for a father that she was being torn away from. The grief and terror had sent Sepora's body into uncontrollable shakes.

A few moments later, Kinsu had returned and emptied those memories from her body, filling her with someone else's.

They were Ruby the Warrior's, and it was years of emotion slamming through her veins. She had doubled over involuntarily and forced herself to vomit on Kinsu's shoes. In truth, the vomiting had been easy; tumbling from one life to another was making her sick.

"Someday soon we'll return these memories to you," Sepora said now.

Palace sighed. "Now that Dorji's gone, our chances will be better. But we still have to wait for Kinsu to come back for another girl."

"Or to take me."

"They won't. They never undo a Rue."

"They will. I'm their highest ranking Sepa. Meera won't leave me here."

She said this with an arrogance she did not feel. Would she leave her there? Would Meera be proud of her, fooling all of them and staying safe until she could return, memories intact? Was she on her way to help her as they spoke?

"We need to have a plan if they come to take me back. We need to at least consider it."

"What plan do we need?" Palace scoffed. "You go with them and get back home. Seems pretty simple."

"I'm not leaving you here," Sepora said quietly.

Palace laughed. "What would be better for me than this? I have my own house, can care for all the little girls that come here, and no man would touch my old flesh. Seems that I'm right where I should be."

"There's more for you, Palace." Sepora swallowed. "I know."

"You know nothing," Palace waved her off.

"Ask me to tell you about your family."

"What family? The man? The baby?" she scoffed.

"Yes."

Palace tensed. After a moment of heavy silence, she responded begrudgingly "What about them, then?"

Sepora had been trying to figure out how to tell Palace this for weeks. If she was going to be taken back today, it was now or never. She took a deep breath. "He came back for you when you were campaigning in Tumail." Sepora felt a flutter of excitement that was not hers at the thought. "Your daughter was nearly a year old by then. You loved her so much. Asaka loved her, too. You two fought, a terrible fight. He wanted to smuggle her into New Bhutan where she would be safe. He knew you would either be captured, killed, or catch the Banjarguay soon, and you refused to stop fighting."

Palace let that sink in, looking out on the water. "Did I let her go?" she asked quietly.

"You did... and the pain of that moment is almost more than I can bear. That's why you can't stay here. She's still out there, waiting for you in New Bhutan."

Palace turned to look at her in surprise. "You know her?"

Sepora nodded, hardly knowing how to say it. "She's about to become the Heart of the country."

"The Heart!" Palace cried. She started to laugh. "This Asaka must have been one hell of a smuggler. Well? Is she a good girl?"

Sepora hesitated. "She's... she's just as fierce as her mother was, but she fights for the opposite side."

"Ah. I see." Palace glared at her. "Do you see me as a secret weapon, then? Is that why you want me along?"

"I want you along because you both deserve to know the truth. And yes," Sepora admitted, "she might feel differently about the Banjar if she met you. Sometimes it takes knowing and loving to stop fear and all the irrational hatred that comes with it."

Palace was pinching her nose as if a headache was coming on. "You know, I couldn't care less about the girl. Isn't that the sad part? You could tell me she's about to be burned alive if I don't get there soon, and I would wonder if I could take a nap first. They stole that from me, didn't they?"

Sepora slipped off the couch onto her knees so she could hold Palace's hands in her lap. "Palace... *Ruby*. I can tell you that the love for Penna I feel inside me is so overwhelming I can barely breathe. I want to see her and touch her face and tell her I'll never leave her again."

Palace had tensed again.

"Penna, you say? That's the baby's name?"

"Yes." Sepora smiled. "You named her after the feathers of the vulture. You wanted her to be strong in the face of death. It's not a name you hear in New Bhutan."

Palace cleared her throat, her eyes glazing over as if she *did* remember.

Sepora fell into her own thoughts as well and they sat in silence for a long time. She was thinking about Penna San; her proud and haughty expression, her disdain at the mention of Banjarians. How could she be the daughter of Ruby the Warrior? Was this one of the many secrets that had been swirling around the garden that night at the palace? Who knew? How did she rise so high in rank? Sepora would have assumed it was a different baby by the same name, except for that Ruby's lover's name, Asaka, had been spoken at the Family dinner as well. Faan to Penna, Mishka, and Meera. Were they all daughters to Ruby and she only remembered one? Who was Asaka the Just?

Penna had seemed so cruel at the dinner, but there had been moments where she seemed a little fragile as well. When her face would pale at their eye contact... she knew that Ruby's memories and emotions were toying with her own. Her memories of the dinner were different now. She wanted to reach across the table and comfort Penna, a feeling she knew had not been there originally.

Sepora pulled them both from their thoughts with a sigh. "I have to keep reminding myself that these are your feelings. There's so much love and pain in my body right now. Honestly, I'm scared that when I let yours go, I'll just be empty."

Palace came out of her reverie with blazing eyes and put a hand to Sepora's face. "You won't be empty, girl. Your people are in there, too. Story and Meera... they are all still there. Those two little boys you're always on about. Oh. And of course, there's Cadence in there, too." She winked and tweaked Sepora's nose.

Sepora swatted her away. "Cadence San is not in there," she huffed, turning away from Palace to rest her back against the sofa.

"Please, you've sounded like you were made a Rue for him after all with the way you've gone on. "

"I was only telling you what happened. And yes, I was relieved and... well, in wonder that he didn't do what he was told. Every time I asked him to touch me my heart would stop in fear, but he never did."

"Uh-huh. Quite the hero."

"I'm not saying he's a hero. I'm saying he's not a monster."

They were quiet for a few moments.

Sepora was thinking about the moment on the lake when Sai San was taking her away from Cadence. Palace had taught her to be frantic at the thought of separating from her supposed obsession, but it turned out that she hadn't needed to fake being scared. Cadence had seemed so determined to help her; so horrified by the situation. And he was the Eye, after all. She'd let the hope that maybe he would protect her slip into her heart. When he passed her off to Sai and she was being dragged away, she watched her hope of a savior get smaller and smaller along the shore.

"Isn't Cadence San about to marry the new Heart?" Ruby asked suddenly.

Sepora sighed heavily. "Yes."

She didn't know what it meant to care for someone. She wasn't sure if what she felt was relief or affection. All she knew was that Ruby had been right when she'd compared her to a Rue, if a Rue couldn't keep control of where her mind went. Sepora found herself going right back to the morning when they had sat on the porch together. She could see him sitting there, trying to decide how to save her, how he curled into a ball while he slept the night before, crying out in his sleep like a child. She thought about their walk around the lake, hands entwined, and how he lied to Sai San; his reluctant face as Sai led her away. She had believed that he would come to steal her away that night and take her to safety. She imagined herself telling him the truth; that she had never been made a Rue after all but had been willing to sacrifice her body to keep her memories.

This morning, though, a day later, he flew off in a helio with his faan, and she was still right here.

HIS AANS WERE DEAD. This was a fact, but Hui still didn't quite believe it. He kept thinking back to his faan's face the last time he spoke to him, asking if he could visit Meera. He had been so intent on finding Sepora that he hadn't cared to wonder much on why his faan was acting so strangely. Broken, he remembered thinking. His faan had looked broken, and Maan had been crying in their private quarters. He remembered he'd just wanted to be away from them.

Waves of guilt would wash over him, constricting his throat. He wasn't sure what he should be thinking or feeling. He tried to conjure happy memories of his aans to honor them; a vision of his smiling maan or laughing faan, but he couldn't. He heard their muffled cries as they fought and their stony silences afterward. Searching his memories, the small, framed painting of Mishka laughing with her two sisters popped up, and he leaned over to peek through the doorway at Penna and Auntie Meera. They had known Maan when she was a happy person. He wondered how they were feeling about losing her.

Right now, he didn't think they were thinking about his maan at all. After Penna San collapsed, Meera had taken her to the kitchen and put some tea on. They were speaking in hushed whispers.

Auntie Meera had asked if Story could maybe help him identify some of the items in the room while she talked with Penna, but it hadn't lasted long. Story couldn't recognize items from the Old World any better than he could.

"Most these were pulled from the earth by Dredgers," she'd said in her gravelly voice. Her accent had a musical lilt to it, but her grammar would have disappointed Maester Fre.

"It's okay," he replied. "I think they just don't want us in there." He'd nodded toward the kitchen.

She'd smiled. "You sure know your way around. How old are you?"

"I'm ten."

"Ten! My, my!" Her eyes went wide with astonishment. "You're a big boy, then."

He gave a little smile back. "I guess so."

Her smile faded a bit. "Miracle would be turning five soon, if he'd stayed."

"Where did he go?"

She nodded up at the vulture painting.

"Oh." Hui looked at the pile of bones for a long moment. "I wonder where my aans went."

Story didn't respond, but she put a hand on his head for a moment and sighed.

"What are you on about with that there?" she asked, nodding toward the B encyclopedia that was clutched in his hands.

"It's an encyclopedia. This one is for the letter B."

She raised her brows at him. "You think I know what you mean?"

He laughed a little. "There's a book for each letter. All the words that start with that letter are in it. Well, not all of them, but words they thought were important. Also people and things that happened that started with the letter, too. They're from the Old World."

"My papa said there used to be all kinds of letters and kinds of talking. Is this the one we know?"

It took him a moment to figure out what she was trying to say. "Oh! Oh, yes. The other languages died out long before the Last War. Maester Fre said our language didn't even begin here. Some bits are still different, though, left over from old languages. You can tell they're different."

"Like what?"

Hui's face lost some color. "Like gishiki shinju," he said quietly. The phrase was a ceremony that meant something like a double death. Maester Fre had talked about the people doing it so much in the first fifty years of the barrier that it earned its own name. He wondered suddenly if Maester Fre had taught Susu and Mishka about it when they were his students.

"Who is Maester Fre?" Story asked, bringing him back to the present.

Hui took a steadying breath and tried to push his aans from his mind. "My teacher. He's very educated. All he does is study, and he's very old."

"In Tumail, there are three Readers. You're chosen if you're smart. Not much to read around, so it's most to teach us speaking. Miracle would have been a Reader. He was real quick. Taught Sepa a word or two, even."

"Sepora knew Miracle?"

He wasn't positive who Miracle was, but he was guessing he might have been Story's son.

"She did. They had a bond, a real one."

Hui picked at his shorts. "How did he die?"

He knew that wasn't something you should ask. His maan would have told him to hush, he thought suddenly. But his maan wasn't here anymore.

"The Banjarguay," she replied quietly. He watched her face grow hard. "We're always fighting against the sickness and drying out. It's usually one or the other that gets us."

"Drying out? Like, being thirsty?"

When she nodded, he added, "I dreamed you were thirsty."

She looked back at him, some of the anger fading. "I know, child. That's why Meera come get me and Sepa didn't get me out for nothing. I have you to thank for that."

"Why doesn't the Banjarguay happen here?"

She sighed. "It's from the Old Wars. Sickness still drifting around Earth, riding on a bad wind. Never know when it's coming for you, but you know it's coming. You don't have the wind here, do you?"

Hui swallowed hard. It sounded terrifying. "Sometimes, but it's from machines."

Story nodded. "I was coming for you all, though, you know? I'd been workin' for years, getting clans together. We going to come in and live in one of these here." She looked around the honeycomb space disdainfully. "We live deep in caves when the sun gets going on, and out along the mountainside otherwise. Our houses made of stones and sand. Sepa come take all that work away when she took me down."

"Are you mad at her?" he asked, hoping she wasn't.

"Sepa? Nah. She's sorry for what she did, and look now, she got me here inside, talking 'longside a Bhutanese," she slapped her leg in wonder and then squinted at him. "I hope we get her out, too."

"We will. Meera and I won't let her down." Neither Meera nor Story had told him anything about what kind of trouble Sepora was in. It had never quite seemed the right time. First Penna was sick, then Story. They told him about his aans and then told him to be silent as they made their way across the city. There hadn't been much time for anything, really. All he knew was that Sepora had saved Story, like the real hero he knew she was. He couldn't wait to help her and become a hero himself. In fact, he'd been thinking more about saving Sepora than about Mishka and Susu, even though he had only met her once.

That's because Sepora is alive, he thought, *and my aans are already dead.* The thought should have brought him to tears. It didn't. He couldn't really wrap his mind around the idea or the emotion. He just wanted to know why more than anything. Like a puzzle to solve, he wanted to know what had made his faan look so sad that day. Why had his maan become more and more upset with every trip he took away? He wanted to know why someone had taken Sepora and why Story had to be thirsty all the time and live in a cave.

Hui didn't know how to say any of this, so instead, he said "Sepora was going to teach me to be a Sepa so I could explore the Banjar. Maybe I could come visit you in Tumail?"

She looked at him hard for a minute and then softened. "You come and visit anytime. Now then, tell me something about the letter B."

He smiled and opened his new book.

It was then that Penna started screaming.

24

———

S EPORA

SEPORA WAS AVOIDING THE GIRLS' bunk rooms as much as possible. There were around twenty women in there. They didn't lounge on the porch or take swims when off duty. They didn't braid each other's hair or gossip. They sat in their own beds, wringing their hands together anxiously. They were lovesick. Full of passion with no one to give it to. Their eyes stayed inward, imagining the pleasure of being in the men's company again. Occasionally one would groan in discomfort, clutching their belly. Sometimes, they tried to ease the pressure themselves, right there in front of everyone. Palace explained that it was her job to keep them exercising. Make sure they weren't too consumed to a point where they forgot to eat or use the restroom. She would lead them down to the main common room for meals and chat to them as if they were listening, but they never were.

She wondered if the men had considered how the Rue serum affected them when left alone. She wondered how Palace could stand talking to herself year after year in a room full of women who weren't able to listen.

She was watching from the kitchen as Palace led a girl from the bathroom back to the bunk. She was gone for a few minutes and Sepora could hear a brief conversation taking place. She returned, looking paler than before.

"Sai is on his way to take you back."

She said it so calmly, anyone else would have believed that she didn't care a bit. Sepora, though, rose to her feet and walked across the room to take Palace into a hard embrace.

"I didn't think they'd take you," Palace said softly into Sepora's shoulder. She pulled away and looked into her eyes. "I should be happy that you're getting out of this place, but I'm not."

"Come with me," Sepora urged. "We can find a way."

"He'll be here in five minutes. He will empty all the memories he believes you have, including everything having to do with me. How much do you think you'll be fighting for my escape after that?"

Sepora felt like she'd been punched in the gut. "I thought we needed an emptier for that." "Kinsu's in tow," she replied dully.

"This isn't the end, Ruby," Sepora replied feverishly, grabbing her arms. In five minutes, she could either come up with a plan or forget about the lake, Ruby, and Cadence all in one draining. She had been trying to come up with an escape route for her and Ruby when the time came, but so far, she'd come up with nothing.

Palace stared at her. "Ruby's gone, child. This here is just Palace, a sad old woman making Rues for her own kidnappers."

Sepora gritted her teeth. "You know how to perform the Emptying procedure."

"I've trained plenty girls, yes. Not sure how they'll empty you, though. It's a different procedure that takes a lot more training. Besides, I don't know what they plan to fill you with."

Sepora swallowed.

"Nothing."

She knew that all too well. How many days of her life had already been stripped away? How many people had she loved? She could remember so many days of living with nothing in her heart. They didn't want a Sepa feeling anything, and so would leave her with nothing to mourn. She wondered if Meera had been right; that memories as deep as these would stay. She didn't believe it. No Sepa would have forgotten the lake.

"You better put on your Rue face, girl. They'll be coming through the door any second. Don't want you giving us away, now." She sat heavily on the sofa they had talked on so many times, and looked away from her, gazing out on the lake in resignation.

As predicted, the key turned and the men walked in. Sepora slid her face into a demure smile, but inside, her resolve strengthened. She would rather die than forget.

She stepped lightly to Sai's side, tracing a hand up his length from thigh to shoulder, just as Palace had taught her to do. "Sai San. What a pleasure," she murmured.

He turned to study her face. "Sepa 288." He had forgone her Rue name, Ocean, and it almost threw off her act. She worked to keep her expression clueless and loving. His hand raised to her face, touching her jaw. "You are special, aren't you?"

She felt Palace's head turn in their direction.

"I could be," she said coyly. She let her hand trace the top of his pants line. Sai San was wearing cream linen wrapped around his waist and legs in a loose pant. A gold robe hung loose and open, revealing a bare chest that was strong despite his age, the skin a dark olive tan. He had sharp eyes so brown that they almost seemed black.

"Sai," Palace said sweetly. "Do enjoy my latest Rue before you take your leave. I have rooms available for special guests upstairs."

Sepora swallowed. Palace was formulating a plan. Her eyes darted over to her but Palace was looking squarely at Sai, a smile on her face.

Sai San looked back and forth between the two of them. "This Rue is not for me. She's a Sepa," he replied curtly.

He grabbed Sepora roughly by the arm, as if to prove that he would take her where she needed to go. Palace stepped over to his side and whispered in his ear. "No one needs to know but us, Sai. Our discretion is a courtesy of the Blossom House. Look at her. When will you again meet such a beauty?"

Sai San returned his stare to Sepora's face. She did as Palace instructed and tilted her face down, looking up at him to accentuate her large eyes. She made her lip tremble with vulnerability. She hoped it was enough for whatever Palace was planning.

Sai took a heavy breath and exhaled through his nose. "Just an hour," he grunted, pulling her arm roughly and ascending the stairs without waiting for Palace's direction.

She heard Palace say kindly. "Come Kinsu, have some tea with an old woman."

Her heart was starting to thrum in her chest. Was Palace planning on charging in or had she just sent her new friend to slaughter? Sepora ran a side eye along Sai's frame. Could she fight him if it came to that? And if she won? Then what?

As they ascended the next floor, it was clear that Sai had used the complimentary rooms of the Blossom House before. He knew to pass the bunk rooms where the girls all stayed together. He led her straight to a small stairwell at the end of the hall. This stair led to the only third floor room. It was more an attic than anything, dressed in silks and rugs to cover the dust. It was oppressively hot, but the view was better than the others. The large bay window was the only light source in the room and Sai didn't bother lighting a candle. He closed the door firmly behind them and brought her into the window's light. There, he took her face again, this time gently gripping her chin and pointing it toward the light. She could see him better now as well. In the sun, his eyes weren't black after all. They had flecks of a deep rusty gold along the rim. They were sad as they looked at her.

"Look what they've done to you," he said quietly. "I thought... I thought you would be something great at least, to make this all worth it."

Sepora stayed silent, keeping her eyes dulled. She wasn't about to continue seducing him now that Palace had what she wanted and that Sepora was in danger of actually going through with anything. She wanted to know what he meant but dared not ask. *No point in asking questions*, she remembered. *They will tell you if you're quiet long enough.*

"When I saw you at the Sepa dinner, Meera's prize negotiator, I thought, yes. This is it. She keeps the country safe from traitors, just as we do here. She's a warrior. Of course she is." He laughed bitterly. "But then Tashi brings you here. Reducing you to a common Rue whore. Of course he did. He would take you, too, knowing no better, if I hadn't stopped him. The fool can't even see who you are."

He picked up her hands. "I might have killed him if he touched you," he said quietly.

Sepora's heart was hammering in her chest. What did he mean?

"He has to have everyone. He had her. I know he did. That's why she can't touch me. He would have had you too, the bastard. I wouldn't let him do that to you, you hear me?" He had grabbed her face again, and this time was looking deep into her eyes.

Suddenly he jumped back.

Sepora knew why. She'd let her guard down; let her gaze be true. It was time to try seducing him again, as a Rue would, but she found that she couldn't do it. She just stood there, heart pounding.

Sai stepped closer, eyeing her carefully. "Tell me your name," he commanded. She could feel the fear in his voice.

She said nothing, giving him answer enough.

To her astonishment, he barked a laugh and his eyes filled with tears. He strode back to her side and wrapped her in a tight embrace. With his head nestled in her hair, he whispered, "My warrior. My warrior."

He pulled back and looked at her with wonder. At her determined stare, his brow began to knit. His arms dropped away, and he looked down, defeated. "You can't go back now, Sepora."

Her jaw dropped for a moment before she snapped it shut. He knew her name.

He knew her name.

He turned and paced the room before her. "What can be done now?"

He was wringing his hands, muttering to himself. Sepora stayed still as stone, waiting.

Finally, he stopped abruptly and turned those dark eyes on her. He stared at her for a long moment. "It will have to be done. It's the only way."

He moved to step toward her and she stepped back.

He sighed. "You need to work for Tashi, but how could you after being here? The only option is to empty you." He pursed his lips regretfully. "No tricking us this time, little warrior."

Sepora took another step backward, stealing a quick glance at the door.

"You're safe as a Sepa. I've kept you safe in the Banjar, even." He was still talking more to himself than her. She took another inch.

His sharp eyes caught her movements and he quickly closed the space between them, grabbing both of her arms. "What would you do? Run outside and get shot with a stunning dart? I'm trying to protect you, Sepora." He gave a desperate laugh. "What am I supposed to do?"

Sepora took a shaky breath. "Why do you call me Sepora?" she asked quietly.

He laughed and let the laugh fade into a sad smile.

"I couldn't think of you as a number. And... and if my thoughts yearned for you, I wanted to always be reminded of your fate; to be reminded that I could not undo what has been done. You would always be a Sepa, so I named you Sepora."

Sepora's jaw dropped. But Meera said...

"You named me? But... Meera set the numbers in Luópán." She would not give Meera away, even now.

"Darling. You were never in Luópán Hall. Meera agreed to help me protect you by slipping you into the Sepa nurseries."

"Where else could I have gone?"

He swallowed thickly, stepping closer. "Nowhere. Isn't that the point? I had to protect you, just as I have to protect you now."

She took a step back, pressing her back into the wall behind them. "What are you protecting me from by Emptying me?"

"Yourself. The less you know, the safer you are."

"From who?"

"Don't be a fool, Sepora!" he cried, punching the brick wall just past her head. "Dorji Tashi."

Sepora stared at the bloody fist as he pulled it back.

"You struck me," she recalled. "On the lake."

Sai looked at her and sighed. "Tashi was watching us from the balcony. I needed to prove you were just any other Rue to me, in case he suspected."

Sepora gritted her teeth. "And every other Rue can be struck?"

He came beside her again, eyes fierce and wild. "Do you think to compare yourself with Banjarians? Don't you dare."

"Why? How is a Sepa any better than a Banjarian to you? At least they're human."

Only when saying the words aloud did she realize the envy she'd carried with her for the Banjarians. She wanted to be like Story; to love like they loved, to be free as they were.

Sai cupped her face gently. "You are human, my darling." The fire in his eyes had faded and he was gazing at her with sorrow.

She waited, holding her breath.

A Sepa can wait for a person to reveal themselves. She had never wanted to ask so badly.

"You're my human," he finally whispered.

The thought floated into her mind like a cloud. She could feel her heart hammering in her chest in the silence.

His hand reached up to pet her hair. "Yes. Yes, Sepora. You're my fierce warrior. My daughter." He smiled ruefully. "Dorji was right to want you dead, but for the wrong reasons. He killed you out of spite, not because he thought you posed a threat."

Dorji wanted me dead.

"Do I pose a threat?" she asked thickly.

He smiled. "Here you are, supposedly dead. A living, breathing secret that is smart enough to survive Qinghai Lake with memories intact, steal the heart of our new Eye, and somehow manage to convince me to spill my secrets. I would say you pose a threat."

Sai San was talking in pockets, leaving out details that would connect all of the scraps of information he was tossing her. Why did Dorji Tashi try to kill her? Why was she a living, breathing secret? Was she born?

He was mumbling to himself, hands clenched in her hair. "I would do anything for her. Anything."

"Sai San?" Sepora interrupted. "If you can't let me return with my memories, don't let me return at all. Drop me deep in Tumail with Palace. You can tell Tashi we caught the Banjarguay."

She said it with a pang, thinking of how Meera would react to the news of her death.

Sai's eyes hardened. "Don't try to fool me. I'm no Tashi. You're a sympathizer, it's obvious. Just like Meera. You won't stop fighting for them until you forget about them. In fighting for them, you will lose. They all do. You are safer as a Sepa."

There were a handful of memories that she refused to forget. The first was Miracle's face, both alive and dead. He was the first person she'd ever loved, and the first person she remembered losing. The second was the night Meera gifted her with a name. The third was seeing the lake for the first time, Story's expression of wonder mirroring her own. Now this.

The moment Sai San told her that she wasn't crafted by technology. She was different for a reason; and not because she was smarter or faster. It was because she was human.

She had a faan.

She had a faan and he wanted to protect her.

It was unfortunate that given this news, one of them was still going to kill the other before this discussion was over. She would rather die than forget.

"Why would I release you into the wild just to let you become a rebel?" he was saying.

Sepora decided that stalling, for now, was her best course of action.

"You're my faan?" she asked slowly, "And... and you want to protect me by stealing my free will away?"

"Your free will points you in the wrong direction, Sepora. You have no idea what you're talking about."

"I've spent more time in the Banjar than you, I would venture to guess."

"Oh, I'm sure you developed a relationship with some beasts here and there. We all have at the lake. But this isn't personal. You have no idea how much we depend on our system with them to keep New Bhutan alive. If the system breaks, New Bhutan falls. Sympathizers threaten that system."

"Have you thought about creating a new system?"

"We are the only people that matter." He fingered the tips of her hair. "You look so much like her," he whispered. "I wonder if she knew, in some way."

"Who—"

The door was kicked open, causing Sai San to drop her hair and whip his head toward the door. It was Palace, carrying a tray with both hands. "Sorry about the kick," she said cheerfully. "I heard you two talking and thought I might bring up a cup of iced tea. I know how hot it gets going on up here. I figure since you're talking, you're probably not doing anything else. Besides, the walls weren't creaking and this is an old building." She winked at Sai and set the tray down, handing him a tall glass.

He scowled at her. "I expected to be undisturbed. If we were thirsty, we would ring for you."

"Ringer's broke," Sepora chimed in. "Blossom House doesn't get much in the way of repair. I am thirsty, though. Thank you, Palace."

Palace bowed slightly but turned her tray to serve Sai first.

"Well, I suppose now it's here." He took the glass from Palace's hand and shooed her out with the other. "Get out now, Palace. We aren't finished."

"Yes, San," she said brightly, turning to leave without offering any to Sepora.

Sai scowled after her and took a sip. As he lowered the glass from his lips, his black eyes met Sepora's for a moment, then rolled back into his head. He crumpled to the floor, the glass shattering next to him. Sepora yelped in surprise.

"Palace! What was it?" she cried, falling to her knees to check his pulse.

Palace came back to her side, smiling widely. "Same junk they put in the tranquilizer dart. Sure works fast, doesn't it?"

She looked up at her in shock. "How...?"

She laughed. "Remember when you got yourself shot by no less than three darts, trying to escape?"

"I was trying to get caught." Sepora immediately corrected. "To distract—"

Palace brushed her words away. "Uh-huh. You had broken Kinsu's nose and he was no more kind to you when he found you. He picked you up, covering you in his snotty blood, and threw you on my floor untouched. So, I had three tranquilizer darts to take care of. Two of them were empty, they got you good, but the third had caught on a tie in your robe and was full. So..."

"So?" Sepora prompted.

"So, I kept it in a spice jar next to the tea, just in case it might come in handy."

Sepora suddenly looked toward the door. "Kinsu...?"

"Out cold!" she said cheerfully.

Sepora barked a laugh. "And she said Ruby was gone."

Palace shrugged. "All I know is this ain't over. They're sleeping like little babies, but we're still trapped in here."

Sepora put a hand to Sai San's face. She was relieved that she didn't have to kill him. He was the only family member she'd ever had. She tried to commit his face to her memory. That done, she looked around thoughtfully.

"If we follow the water south, we may be able to leave unnoticed. There doesn't seem to be any construction on that side. That's what I told Story to do."

Palace was eyeing her skeptically.

"Have a better idea? Besides, I haven't seen Story around, have you? She must have escaped that way."

"And died in the Banjar," she muttered. "What if we filled these boys up with the memories they were going to give you?"

"I told you, they weren't going to fill me with anything. They were going to empty me."

"Well, should we do that? He would never know that he met his daughter, and we could slip away without them looking after us."

Sepora's brows raised in surprise.

"I could hear what you two were on about."

An irrational urge to protect Sai San's memory clawed at her chest. She tried to will it away. The fact that she had only just found her faan, that he knew her name, he'd called her his warrior... those things didn't matter, she reminded herself sternly. A Sepa wouldn't take those emotional ties into account.

But you weren't born a Sepa, a voice whispered inside her. Yes, but... and then she realized why a Sepa wouldn't want to erase him either.

Sai San had said that in his mind, they were the only people who mattered. If she was forgotten, then he would be only the one who matters. Taking his love for her away might be the last straw to making Sai San completely heartless.

"You don't know how to make the filler, do you?" Sepora asked. It would be very handy to fill one of them up with a strong desire to take them back to the Sepa bunker.

Palace was shaking her head. "I have no idea. Kinsu does, though. Should we wake him up?"

"Maybe. We don't know if he would cooperate." Suddenly, she had an idea. "How strong is the tranquilizer?"

"Very."

"If they felt extreme pain, would they wake up?"

Palace looked at her uneasily. "Probably sooner than they would otherwise... but no, not right away."

"Get me your sharpest knife and the medical kit," she ordered, moving to unlace her faan's sandals and pulling them off.

"Sepora..."

"Now, Palace! We need to hurry."

Palace shuffled away, muttering to herself.

The only guaranteed way of getting home was to ride a helio, but all locks and ignitions were operated by palmpad registrations. Here were two officials' palmpads, at their disposal. They just had to get them out without killing them.

Sepora lifted her faan's hand, turning and inspecting it with uncertainty. She knew that slices in the wrong place could be fatal. She went through what she knew of the palmpads, trying to guess where the tech might be. Thumb to pinky was to comm. Four fingertips to the palm to disconnect. The top of the palm held a small screen for text just below the skin. She'd watched Meera gain clearance for different doors and Rail cars by waving her palm in front of it, so it could be anywhere. She pressed different parts of his hand, trying to feel for a difference in density. It was just along the ridge of the palm extending from the thumb that she thought she felt a strip of something hard, like a metal bar.

She felt her own hand and found nothing. Sepas didn't have clearance identifiers. "Got it!" she cried. Palace hadn't come back yet so she ran down the stairs to find her, running smack into a Rue named Brook. She stumbled back.

"Are you alright, Ocean?" she asked in a dreamy voice.

Sepora realized then that she had two unconscious men strewn about the house for whom most of the girls would do anything.

"Brook," Sepora said, thinking fast, "Sai San is here and he has asked for complete silence. He's meditating. Can you tell the other girls to stay in the bunk room?"

Brook's eyes widened and she nodded her head fervently. "Yes, of course! Do you think he'll come see us afterward?"

"We can only hope." The girl walked away and Sepora rolled her eyes. It was only after she watched the girl's steps quicken in her haste to be obedient that she realized how cruel it was to leave all these women here. These unknowing slaves were all women like her and Palace, only they had been stripped of their own free will to think and feel for themselves. She stood frozen in the hall, unsure of what she could do.

Palace called to her from the common quarters, causing a wave of "shhhh" to erupt from the bunk room. Sepora shook her head and went to find Palace, promising herself that she would figure out a way to help all of these women, eventually.

Palace was on her knees next to Kinsu, knife in hand. "What's the plan?"

"The first part is to get him upstairs with Sai San. We can't have a bleeding man lying unconscious in the common room."

Palace looked at her with uncertainty.

"I got it," she reassured her. "Just hold the feet and I'll drag the weight from the shoulders."

Kinsu may have suffered a few hits to the head on the way, but they managed to pull him up with little incident. After dragging him to lie side by side with Sai San, Sepora and Palace worked at taking off their robes and sandals.

"Can I ask why they need to be naked?"

"We're going to use their tech to get in a helio, but how can we get to a helio with the men in the trees?"

Palace smiled. "Two men walked in. Two men will walk out."

"Exactly. Okay, do you have tweezers in that kit?"

Palace rummaged through a small bag and pulled them out, smiling victoriously.

"I'm going to slice along this line, and you are going to reach in and pull out whatever looks like a foreign object. It's long and thin, tucked alongside this pad of flesh here."

Palace's smile dropped and she swallowed, nodding determinedly. "What do I do when they're out?"

"Do you have a little cloth we can wrap them in?"

"I have a bandage."

"Perfect. Oh, yeah, let's get bandages ready to wrap them up right away. I don't know how much this is going to bleed."

Holding her breath, Sepora let the knife slide along the line of Kinsu's palm. The first pass wasn't deep enough, so she had to do it again. *A sharper blade would have been helpful,* she thought, blowing a few strands of hair from her eyes. Finally, she had a deep enough cut and used the knife to hold back the pad of flesh, making room for

Palace's tweezers. Sepora glanced at her and saw that her eyes were squeezed shut. "Palace! You need your eyes for this."

"They are open... kind of." She widened her eyes to prove it but her mouth remained in a disgusted twist. "I think I got it!" she cried, pulling out a silver bar as thin as a strand of hair. Blood was gushing out over Sepora's hands.

"Yes!" Sepora cried. "Okay, put it on the extra bandage and let's get him wrapped up." She glanced at Kinsu's face, expecting him to jump awake at any moment.

They repeated the process with Sai San, this time with a little more ease.

With it done, both women were standing over them, clutching their own identification strip. The men looked dead; naked and spattered with blood, lying side by side so ceremoniously.

"They'll be okay." Palace said. "They should wake up in a few hours."

"Let's get out of here, then."

They put on the robes, Palace using the finer gold robes of Sai San and Sepora opting for Kinsu's faded blue. They threw the shading hoods over their heads and looked at one another, both bursting into smiles.

"We're going to make it," Sepora said, "and once we're back, I'll find a way to give you your memories."

Palace's smile faded and she opened her mouth to speak, but nothing came out.

Sepora spoke instead. "It's time. Lock the door behind us. It could give us more time."

Leaving Blossom House, Palace looked back once before whipping her head forward and down. Both of them were keenly aware of the eyes above them, watching their progress from Blossom to the helio landing field. There were usually one or two parked in the fields. She knew that Cadence had taken one away the day before, but she also knew that Kinsu had only just arrived. The chance of at least one helio being there was pretty high. They just needed to get through the forest without being shot and find the helio without being stopped. Also, it was only a hope that the identification strip would work outside the palm. She pushed that thought aside.

These were all concerns flying through Sepora's head as they made their way straight through the forest and into the field. Sepora found herself releasing a held breath. There was the helio, parked right in the center, and not one person in sight.

"Dragons be," Palace breathed.

"Come on," Sepora replied, taking a steady step into the field. She didn't want her feet to rush, to look unsure, but they were so close that all she wanted to do was break into a run. Wait. Wait. She kept telling herself. One calm step after another, sure that someone would be flying or walking into the field any minute. Outside the shade of the trees, the sun blazed down with a vengeance. Sepora's brow was instantly dripping with sweat, and she cursed herself for not thinking of bringing a supply of water from the Blossom House's stores. Who was to say if they would be stranded in the desert without water?

The helios were designed to look like mosquitos, the body consisting of a glass front and a back made entirely of solar paneling. One hour in the intense heat was enough to power an hour of flight. The lock pad was to the right of the door and Sepora waved Sai's tech before it. There was a small click and a panel of glass slid straight upward. She ushered Palace in first, giving her a hand up, and followed behind. The door slid shut behind them

Palace laughed. "Oh my, we're doing this." Then she eyed Sepa, who was staring at the controls. "You know how to fly this, don't you?"

"Theoretically." Sepora glanced at her. "I've read the manual."

She recognized the cyclic bar used to steer. The helio's solar panels should have been charging the power into a bank somewhere, and a switch should be able to access the power and lift them into the air.

There were switches on either side of the yoke, presumably to take the power from one side or the other. Not sure if she needed both or if one was for reserves, she started by flipping the switch on her side. The helio started to hum, and the dash lit up. "There!" she cried triumphantly. There were light icons with ears, speakers, and maps. She ignored all of those, wishing she knew if pressing the ear would turn off recordings or turn them on. She flipped the second switch, and the helio eased straight up into the air.

"Oh my! We're going! Okay," Palace was muttering in fear, pressing her back as far as it would go into her chair.

"I can do this, Ruby."

The woman gave her a meaningful smile and took a calming breath.

"Is it okay to call you Ruby?"

"Don't ever call me Palace again," she breathed.

Sepora nodded, pleased.

"You should fly through that archway over there," Ruby pointed.

Sepora threw a glance at her. "Where else would I? It's the only exit."

She rolled her eyes. "It's all an exit, Sepora, remember? But that's the way they leave to make it look like there's a barrier."

Sepora glanced uneasily at her and then cast her eyes at the sky, looking for a clue that she was wrong. Seeing nothing, she pursed her lips in frustration. "I just don't understand it. Why would Tashi and his men spend so much time in the Banjar without protection?"

"The Banjar isn't all bad, it would seem. The lake seems to be a big attraction."

Sepora humphed. "That lake is like nothing on the planet. I thought for sure they created it in their new dome to make a show of how much power they have."

"They say it's a natural spring. Some say it's been around for decades. Others say it appeared the day Dorji Tashi became the Heart," she said disdainfully.

They were about to fly through the archways and Sepora held her breath, glancing at Ruby with a smile. They were about to be free.

"Well, I'm happy to leave it behind," she said, flying through and on to the other side. The trees ended abruptly and they were once again in an endless desert. She noticed Ruby bend her neck around to take one last peek of the lake, but Sepora didn't care to look back. She tried to remember the direction they had come and how that was related to Bhutan. She was sure there was tech on the helio that would guide them straight to where they wanted to go but had a feeling that it could also track them for others. She kept the navigation tools turned off.

"When we get to the bunker docking station, we'll ask Kiro to speak to Meera directly. I'll tell him that the operation went wrong and I had to bring a hostage. Once we get to Meera, she'll know what to do. If-"

"Sepora," Ruby interrupted. "I'm not going to New Bhutan with you. I want to go home. I want to be with my people again before I go."

Silence fell between them as Sepora tried to understand what she had just heard. Tightly, she finally responded, "You won't remember your people unless we get help transferring them at the bunkers."

"You will tell me the story one more time, and I'll keep them in my new memories."

Sepora kept her eyes on the sky. "I thought we were going to fight this together."

She couldn't describe what she was feeling. Her stomach had dropped and her mind was swirling in dizzying circles. She didn't want to lose Ruby. Every time she started to care about someone, they disappeared from her life.

Ruby smiled and patted her shoulder. "I didn't say I was finished fighting, girlie. I just want to do it alongside my people again. You just do me a favor and don't let any Sepas come take me back."

That is exactly what Sepora was afraid of. They would be after them once Kinsu and Sai woke up. It would make sense to look for them in Tumail.

"I don't think it's safe," she said stubbornly.

"And going inside New Bhutan is?"

She couldn't argue with that. It was just as likely that someone would arrest them immediately as it was that Meera would be there to help them.

Slowly, Sepora changed the course of the helio to Tumail.

Ruby smiled gratefully and sat back in her seat. "You can stay with me there, you know."

"I need to report to Meera."

She sat back up and pointed a gnarled finger at her. "You don't have to be her slave anymore. You know that?"

Sepora shifted uncomfortably. She wasn't her slave.

Was she?

"Meera needs to know about Qinghai Lake. She asked me to find out what I could so she can do something to stop it."

"At the possible price of your life."

"Fighting something like this takes risk."

"And what if you had said no? Did you have a choice?"

Sepora was silent.

She'd never had a choice in her life.

25
———

P ENNA

PENNA WAS SITTING on the floor in Meera and Celio's kitchen. She vaguely remembered being here the morning of their marriage ceremony, and that memory brought the thought of her upcoming marriage to slice through her mind like a knife. She wondered if Cadence was wondering where she was. She couldn't recall the last time she had been home but knew she'd missed a few comms from him already. His name had flashed across her palm several times. All of these thoughts whipped through her mind as her eyes glazed over and she waited for Meera to pour her a glass of water.

She didn't want to think about what she was hearing. She didn't want to know.

Meera came back and sat opposite her, touching her knees to Penna's.

"Do you remember the morning of your marriage?" Penna asked softly.

"Of course I do," Meera responded with a soft smile, passing her the small ceramic cup. "You braided my hair right over there." She pointed to the small dining bar. "I've missed you so much, you know."

"I thought we were as close as two people could be," Penna added. "The whole time," she continued, her tone turning bitter. "The whole time, you were keeping this from me."

Meera leaned back on her arms, eyeing Penna calmly. "Would you rather me risk your very life by telling? Break my last promise to my faan?"

"Risk my life? What life? This life as a... as a fraud?"

Meera sat forward and put a hand on her arm. "You're no fraud, Penna. You were meant to be the Heart. You're the child of Asaka the Just and a Banjarian rebel. What better child to unite the Banjar and New Bhutan?"

Penna swatted her hand away and stood up. "I'm just a pawn for you, aren't I? This has never had anything to do with me." Penna ignored her wounded look. "Did Celio cook this idea up? It sounds like something she would come up with. Tell Penna she's Banjarian trash. Tell her she was chosen by her faan and she'll eat it up."

"Penna, that is absolutely—"

"Everyone always calls me the Snake, Meera, but you're the snake! Always twisting around people's lives to get what you want."

Meera grabbed her by both arms and spoke fiercely into her face.

"I can prove it to you, Penna. But I'm disappointed I have to. I've dreamed of the moment I could tell you the truth a thousand times, and it never ended with you not believing me." She swallowed hard, loosening her grip. "Faan brought an emptier he could trust to our house once you started talking. He knew you could let something slip and find yourself in danger. You were too young to know how to lie. He stored the vial in a case only two palmpads could open in Luópán Hall. His, and when you came of age to have one of your own, yours."

Penna didn't want to believe her, but she could see it happening. But...

"But I'm not a Sepa. How could he empty me?"

Meera's lips twisted in regret. "He didn't have a choice, Penna. It broke his heart to do it. He going to return it once—"

"No, I don't mean emotionally. How could he *physically* do it? Are you telling me anyone can be emptied?"

"Oh. Well, technically, yes. It's different, though. All of the emotions were real and fully connected to the rest of your brain, so it can sever you in a way that Sepas don't experience."

Penna started to shake. It started as a trembling and steadily got worse and worse until Meera had to grasp her in a tight embrace.

Emptied. Anyone could be emptied. The implications swelled behind her eyelids even as she squeezed them closed.

The images were forming in her mind and she knew that Meera was telling the truth. Still, she had to see it for herself. "Faan put my memories in Luópán Hall?"

"Yes."

"Then I have to go." She moved to stand, but Meera grabbed her again.

"Penna! I need you to take Hui so Story and I can get back to the bunker and find—"

"I don't care about your Banjarian rebels, and I don't care about your Sepas!" She was screaming. Her chest was hammering, and she felt like she couldn't breathe.

Meera looked disappointed. "I thought..."

"What?" she spit, feeling defensive.

"I thought once you knew..."

"I would care? Well I don't, Meera, and I have to get back to Lhasa. Cadence and I are announcing our engagement tonight. I'm about to become the Heart, and I have a country to run."

"A world," Meera corrected quietly.

"A country."

Suddenly a timid voice interrupted from the doorway. "Penna San?"

Both women whipped around to face Hui.

"You will still come to get the stones with us, though, won't you?"

Penna took a shaky breath. Somehow she already knew that

Meera was telling the truth, but she still wanted (desperately needed, in fact) to see it for herself. But it would have to wait. She had to complete the burial ritual for her sister with her family.

She glanced back at Meera, whose eyes were trained on Hui.

She sighed. "Yes. Of course I will."

Hui stepped into the room and hugged her around the legs. "Story says it is very hard to survive in the Banjar. Your maan must have been very strong."

She tensed in his embrace, clenching her jaw. She didn't remember either of her maans. Penna wondered how much of her time had been spent in the Banjar, and how much of it she had spent with her new maan, Asaks's wife.

She looked over Hui at her sister. "Didn't Maan mind, me being the daughter of a Banjarian?"

Meera gave a slight shrug. "I don't think so. They didn't really follow the New Bhutan's norms of marriage. Maan said that Asaka was two men trapped in one body; a Banjarian and a Bhutanese. They tended to follow Banjarian ways as much as they could."

"They did?" she asked meekly, trying to remember. Had Asaka loved the Banjar that much? Why didn't she remember?

"They did," Meera replied.

She nodded, wishing she knew more. She gently pulled away from Hui. "We should head to your house, Hui," she said tightly. He released her and looked up solemnly. She could tell going home was the last thing he wanted to do but was trying to be brave.

She would have to be brave, too.

He scampered back into the common room and Penna turned to her sister. "I apologize," she said reluctantly.

Meera smiled softly at her. "They're not monsters, Penna, and neither are you."

Penna just nodded and turned away. "Let's pick up our sister and her godforsaken husband."

They left Story tucked away amongst the Old World relics. Meera thought there was a likely chance that Family officials were already at

Mishka's honeycomb and didn't want to risk the chance of anyone finding Story with them.

Penna avoided her gaze as Hui gave her a tight hug goodbye. But as they were leaving, Story called to her.

Reluctantly, Penna turned and traced back the few steps to stand before her. Story smiled and pressed a thumb gently to the bridge between Penna's brows, then dragged it down along her nose. She turned and walked back into the honeycomb before Penna could react. She swallowed hard and turned away herself, following Meera and Hui out into the morning.

The walk from Meera's to Mishka's was a good hour around the ring. Celio and her had not wanted to live too close to the sour couple. Penna didn't think any of them minded the walk. Hui had given up his case to Meera so he could hold both of their hands, and the three of them walked quietly, letting the morning sun kiss their faces. This was a nice time of day in New Bhutan. When the sun was just rising, it sometimes inched lower than one hundred degrees. In the Banjar, she thought she remembered learning, it was never this cool. It was maybe a hundred and twenty at its coolest. Was that right? Her thoughts kept drifting back to Story and her stupid thumb. At first, when her hand had raised, Penna had flinched. She did not like being touched, particularly by a filthy barbarian. But when her thumb rested gently in that space, their eyes met, and Penna felt... soothed. Comforted. Story was smiling so gently, and the soft pressure in that space was so reassuring, Penna had almost closed her eyes. It felt like a blessing or a hug. It had been a long time since she'd been held by anyone. She glanced at her sister, remembering fierce hugs between the two of them as children, and even as young women. She thought she might remember Meera holding her the night before when she'd been in shock, but she couldn't be sure.

Her thoughts drifted to Sai. The only other person in the world who had ever held her. What would he think of her being a Banjarian? Would he ever look at her the same? She realized with a jolt that he might already know. He did run the Library of Memories. If he uncovered a vial with her name on it, wouldn't he be curious to know what it contained?

She tried to shake away thoughts of Sai. For all she knew, he could be responsible for her sister's death. The conversation between Sai and Susu rang in her ears.

You're all snakes.

Hui's palms were getting sweaty, the slime squishing between their hands. Meera must have noticed too, because she paused their walk with just a few blocks to go and crouched down to speak to him.

"Do you know what to do when we get there?" she asked.

Hui nodded.

"Tell me."

Hui took a steadying breath. "I pick up their stones and say their names, then explain where they are now." Hui's mouth turned again. "What if I don't recognize the plant?"

Meera smiled softly. "You will. You're Maester Fre's best pupil; he told me so himself."

Hui nodded, still unconvinced. "I hold the stone to my heart and wish them water and growth in their new form." Hui was choking back his tears.

Penna found her own eyes misting. She blinked rapidly, wondering where on New Bhutan that had come from. She was certain she'd never cried in her life. She tried to remember a time. The only time she had come close was at the Sepa dinner. She had felt a rush of heat and felt dizzy when she'd met the girl's eyes, her own inexplicably watering.

She almost laughed at the thought. She'd been so obsessed with keeping that thought out of her mind, and now that she had been with Meera for a full sun, she hadn't thought of her once. She glanced at her sister, who was still hugging Hui. She could ask her. What were you playing at during that dinner? What did you want me to see? She exhaled deeply, realizing she'd been holding her breath. She couldn't ask now. She already knew too much. How much could a person take?

PART IV

DRAGONS

26

H^{UI}

T HE HOUSE FELT as alive as it ever had. He had envisioned a dark, shadowy common room and a heavy silence. Instead, the sun was just reaching the point in the day when it hit their personal garden plot, just outside the glass wall that stretched along the back. Of course, the honeycombs were designed to keep direct sunlight out of the house at all times, so this was as bright and cheery as the house could get. The windows and doors had been left open, leaving the hum of the bees to welcome him home.

Hui suddenly felt sure that this was all a mistake. His maan was at her meditations and Faan was sitting in the kitchen, enjoying mori. He ran to the kitchen first. It was empty. A few leaves from the wall garden had fallen to the floor. He swallowed and slowly picked up each of them. Maan didn't tolerate a mess. He clutched the leaves in his hand until they turned to dust.

They had asked how he would like to complete the ceremony.

He'd wanted to bring his aunts with him but realized at the last moment that he wanted to go it alone. They were waiting for him out front, and he was standing still as a statue in the kitchen, creating a mess of crumbled herbs. He glanced out back. Maybe he would go out into the garden for a bit as well. His maan had never loved the outdoors, but he remembered that Faan would often sit at the window, staring at the green plants. He would comment on the beautiful job they were doing while he was away. Hui never mentioned that it really wasn't Maan or himself keeping up the community garden. Now he took a vow that he would care more. He would grow the best garden in Lhasa.

The first plants he would grow would be the ones on the stones. His aans deserved to leave limbo and grow into their next life as soon as possible, he thought resolutely. With a jolt, he realized he didn't know where he would be growing anything. Meera hadn't said anything about where he would live now that both his aans were gone. He thought about Meera's apartments in Potala. There was no garden there. The Potala buildings had their food delivered from the Outer Ring.

He'd never met or heard of an orphan before. Was there a place they were sent to live? Before he had finished the thought, another loomed up before him. The SEPA Project. Were the unwanted and extra children sent to be Sepas? He'd fantasized about being a Sepa for as long as he could remember, but the reality was a different story. Maan's words were ringing in his head now. *They're barely human. They're disgusting.* He was remembering those closet sized bunkers and the bathing tubs. He was remembering Story, explaining that they were always waiting to catch the Banjarguay or dry out. He was remembering his dream.

His mind cast about for comfort, and the image of Sepora's hesitant smile appeared. Sepora wouldn't let anything happen to him. She would be happy to have him work alongside her. They made a great team. As a Sepa, he would have to return his personal possessions to the Family. With this thought, his feet started moving toward the stairs. They led him to his own bedroom, the first door on the left.

Coming into his own room, his eyes filled with tears. He'd never been so happy to see it and at the same time knew it may be the last time he would be here. He sank onto his bed, trying to remember how many days it had been since he'd been here. Two? Three? It was hard to tell. So much had happened that it felt like weeks. He let his eyes take in every detail of the room. His old drawings, tacked to the wall above his desk. A map of New Bhutan. A picture of—it was then that he realized the painting of his maan and two aunts was missing. He frowned at the spot, wondering if maybe his maan had brought it into her room after he'd gone. The day he left came flooding back into his memory. The muffled fighting in the bedroom, his faan's bloodless face. He knew that his faan had convinced her to die with him. She would have done anything for him.

"You can't leave me here alone," he remembered her saying. He had thought she meant on another work trip; had been angry with her for forgetting that she wouldn't be alone. He was here, too. Now, he thought the desperation in her voice might have meant something different. His frustration came back painfully: *I was here, too.*

What had made his faan want to leave so desperately? If Hui had stayed and tried to speak with him more, maybe he would have felt better. That thought had been rolling around in his mind all day, and it came full force now. He wanted to tell him how sorry he was. The thought brought him back to his feet. He cast a last glance around his bedroom and left, shutting the door behind him. The door to his aan's room was open. Both windows were open, too, but the smell of blood was still a foreign object in the room. The floors had been scrubbed clean, but rounded stains still darkened the floorboards on either side of the bed.

The covers were laid immaculately. No wrinkles or creases, with two recently fluffed pillows stacked at the top. On each pillow rested a palm sized stone. Instead of walking to the side and picking one up, he fell to his knees at the foot of the bed.

"I'm so sorry, Faan," he whispered. "I should have asked what was wrong. I should have asked where you'd been." He clutched at the bedspread as tears welled in his eyes. "I'm sorry Maan. I was different." He paused and took a deep breath, pain choking his words. "I... I was strange." His voice cracked and his tears spilled hot down his round cheeks. "I'm sorry I wasn't what you needed me to be." He tucked his sobs into the blanket, ruining the perfectly clean lines.

He was grieving for strangers, for the loss of ever knowing who they really were. Both of them had been so quiet, so far away. They would shake their head at him when he asked too many questions. So many nights had been spent alone, with his faan away and his maan hidden away in this very room. *What were you doing in here, Maan?* he wondered now, as his sobs continued to shake the edge of the bed and his snot ran onto the floor. *Were you hiding from me?* He suddenly remembered a time when he was younger, six or seven, that he had come into their room without permission.

His faan had arrived the night before and it was midday. Neither had come down for mori and he was hungry. Tiptoeing, he'd eased open the door to find his maan sitting up in bed, his faan stretched out across it, outside the covers. His head was in her lap and she was braiding his long hair, unbraiding it, and braiding it again. She was humming, and he would ever so often emit a soft sound of pleasure.

When she finally glanced up and caught him staring, he flinched, sure she would send him away. Instead, she smiled softly and invited him to join them. His faan had rolled over to pick him up and held him high over their heads. His maan was giggling, flushed in the cheeks. For a moment, they were happy together.

His sobs had quieted to slow tears as he soaked in this memory. Finally, he took a shaky breath and stood up, knowing with certainty that it was time. He went to his maan's side of the bed first and picked up the stone.

To his relief, he recognized the plant, but quickly realized that his maan's journey back to life would be difficult. She had been given the Chrysanthemum, a flower that bloomed in cold weather and hadn't been seen in decades.

His hand reached out and tenderly picked the stone up. "Mishka," he began, his child's voice wet with recent tears, "once a woman, a mother, a sister, now will grow and bloom as the chrysanthemum."

His fingers closed over the stone and he brought it to his heart. It felt like he was clutching his maan for the last time. "I wish you water and speedy growth in your new form, Mishka, and will let your stone rest when you bloom."

He remembered that this flower represented joy. The thought made his heart a little lighter. His maan had seen so little joy in her life, but in her next life, she would embody it. It made sense that it would take some time for her to get there. He mentally gave her one last well-wishing for her journey.

He put the stone in the deep pockets of his robes and walked around to his faan's side of the bed. He picked up the stone and gasped, almost dropping it back onto the pillow. It was the Lotus, one of the most treasured plants in New Bhutan. It represented innocence and purity. His faan would grow back into the world as innocence. He wondered what it could mean but put the thought aside and said the words.

He put the stone in the opposite pocket, somewhat comforted that his faan would be returning soon in the form of such a common plant.

There was a strong chance that the Sepa bunkers had a garden that he could plant in. How else did they eat?

He walked back down the stairs, clutching the stones in either pocket, and walked out the door of his house without looking back. Meera and Penna were sitting on the ground outside, holding hands. Both looked up anxiously as he came out.

His voice came out stronger than he expected. "I'm ready to go to the bunkers."

Meera and Penna exchanged a glance.

"I thought you might go to Potala Palace with Penna, Hui. You should check in with Dorji Tashi about—"

"The Dragon isn't my family," he interrupted, sounding harsher than he had intended. "I'm an orphan."

Meera frowned. "But Penna is your aunt, and she will be the Heart soon. I'm sure they can arrange something for you there."

Hui shifted uncomfortably, looking at Penna. Would he live with her in Potala Palace? The thought hadn't crossed his mind. Penna the Snake? He shook his head. "I'm not going to the palace until we find out what happened to my aans and rescue Sepora."

Meera sighed and said quietly "What if we can never do those things?"

"Then let me be your new best Sepa until I find her."

Meera glanced at Penna again.

"Okay, Hui," she said decisively. "You can come with me while Penna asks what we should do on your behalf. That will give us some time at the bunkers to try and find some answers. But once Tashi approves it, and I believe he will, you will be going back to Potala. I'm sorry, Hui, but being a Sepa is not what you think it is."

Hui's jaw clenched. It was clear that his aunt didn't think he was cut out to be a Sepa.

"Let's go, then," he said with determination. He started to walk past them down the street.

"Wait, Hui," Penna called. "What will she become?"

Hui stopped and turned, clutching the stone deep in his pockets.

"Nothing," he said flatly. "She got the Chrysanthemum."

27

Penna

PENNA CAUGHT the Rail straight to Potala, looking down through the window at the bustling Bankhar Market. The people were happily trading wares, playing music, painting, and some were even dancing. It looked like a celebration from up here, not an oppressive wave of bodies as it had felt when she'd pushed through with Cadence.

At the thought of Cadence, her eyes widened. It *was* a celebration. They were to announce their engagement to the country tonight, and the people from both Rings had been invited to music and food, courtesy of the Family. She looked closer and saw that indeed, there were banks of food tables and stages set up along the water, and the deep red and purple banners of both Heart and Eye were stretched across the hanging poles.

Penna sat back in her chair nervously. She wished she didn't know. As Asaka's daughter, she had felt proud to take her place as Heart, but now... she wasn't sure if she belonged there. Would she keep the secret forever, or eventually confide in her husband? *Never*, she thought. He would probably turn her over to Tashi and take her place. A Banjarian born acting as a member of the Family? They weren't even allowed in the country, much less the palace. Tashi would probably have her executed as a traitor. Or worse, she thought suddenly, she might just disappear. She shook the thought away, reminding herself that this could all be for nothing. Celio could have made all of this up to convince her to turn her allegiance toward the Banjarians. She needed to look in Luópán Hall herself.

As her railcar docked beyond the palace walls, her hand lit up with a comm. It was of course Cadence, having tracked her palmpad and seen that she had returned. She clenched her fingers closed to dismiss the connection. She had to ignore it all for now or else be swept up in preparations. She needed to seek out her memories unnoticed. For the first time in her life, she resented the tech in her hand and how it could be used to track her.

The station was out front, offering a commanding view of Potala Palace and the glittering domes behind it. She knew that the balconies facing her were the private quarters of Family members, and one may be watching her disembark. Tucking her head down, she quickly made her way to the shade of the building, curling around the stone paths that led beyond the palace and to the dome courtyard.

The courtyard itself was a series of alternating paths and plants to create a starburst design. The paths led to the different domes, the gardens, and different entrances to the palace itself. In the center, the fire dragon gurgled water noisily. She paused for a moment to take it in, really noticing the beauty of it for the first time. Flowers were in full bloom and a player was seated on a bench opposite her, strumming a mandolin. Players from the Inner Ring were paid to play in the courtyard throughout the day. She'd always found the endless noise to be annoying, but this song seemed so peaceful. She took a deep breath and again reassured herself that this was all a hoax. This was where she belonged.

Setting her sights on the towering Luópán Hall, she resolutely made her way. This dome was the most striking of them all, partly because of its mammoth size and also because of the contrasts of its parts. Most of the octagon shapes were black and blue solar panels, but every three or so was a ceiling garden. These bits of roof were made of buckets set into the structure and planted with oxygen yielding plants. Every month or so, the plants would bloom, creating a circus of color dotting the dome. Rich green ferns dripped down the sides year-round.

People were coming in and out, bowing to her as she passed. She offered a tight smile, rushing past them as her palmpad lit again with a comm. Ignoring it, she entered the hushed shade inside Luópán Hall and began the winding path that would lead to Sai's Library of Memories. Finding the arching entryway unguarded, she set her chin high and attempted to march through the walkway.

A few feet in, however, was a large, closed door. She swiped her palmpad along the lock device, but nothing happened, signifying that she did not have clearance to enter here. She bit her lip and glanced around for someone who may be convinced to let her in. No one seemed to be headed to the Library.

Her palmpad lit up again. Sighing heavily, she tapped thumb to pinky.

"Wife! Are you alright?"

His attempt at flippancy died out in the last two words and Penna realized with a start that he had been genuinely worried about her.

"I'm alive," she muttered.

"We learned about your sister today... I'm so sorry."

She swallowed hard. "Yes, thank you. We completed the ceremony this morning."

"May they grow."

"May they grow," she replied. "Cadence... can you meet me in Luópán Hall?"

Cadence was silent for a moment. "I'm getting dressed for the ceremony tonight, as you should be."

Penna rolled her eyes. Of course he was. "I will. I just need your help with something first. It's important."

Something in her voice must have pulled him because he agreed with no questions. She waited for him in the lobby of the building, her mind wandering around all the places and things she had seen in the last few days. It wasn't a pleasant fifteen minutes.

Cadence seemed to arrive in slow motion, treading carefully in a long and heavy dress robe.

Penna would have laughed aloud if she was in better spirits. As it was, she merely grimaced.

Cadence must have felt quite sorry about her sister, because he took her hands in his and bowed, a sign of deep respect.

"I missed you, wife," he said, smiling softly at her.

She scowled back, unsure how to handle this new Cadence.

"I need to get into the Library but I'm not cleared to go through. Will you be my escort?"

The smile slid off Cadence's face. He shifted his feet uncomfortably.

"Tashi hasn't cleared you for the Library yet."

Penna gritted her teeth. "I'm aware. But as my husband, I thought you might escort and supervise me."

"Escort and supervise are words. So are aiding and abetting." He said it as kindly as he could.

"You think I'm committing a crime? I'll be The Heart and have access within the month."

"Why do you need it?"

Penna bit her tongue. "I don't know why that's any of your concern."

"Yes you do."

She swallowed, weighing her options. Could she trust Cadence with this? Did she have a choice? But she couldn't very well tell Cadence that she needed to know if she was Banjarian born. She looked over his glamorous robes, affirming that he would never speak to her again if he knew.

"I have reason to believe that something was stolen from me, and that it is in that room." She stood up, stretching toher full height. "I deserve to know if it's true."

His face was twisted in torment. "What will you do if you find something you don't like?"

She caught his eye. His big brown eyes were full of worry, and she realized that he knew something already. Her stomach dropped. "Cadence," she found herself speaking in a whisper. "We all deserve to know the truth about our own lives."

He was nodding slowly, biting his lip.

He took a quick glance around the foyer and quickly led her through the door. She exhaled with relief, casting a sidelong glance her way. There was a chance she was Banjarian, and yet, he was helping her. Did he know her faan's secret?

His palmpad was rewarded with a soft click and the heavy doors swung open. Penna paused in surprise at the size of the place. They entered onto a balcony that looked over a small circular room that dipped three floors down. Like the Listening Room, this room had a spiraling pathway to different landings, each landing having a door that led to further rooms

He took her hand and led her along. They went all the way to the bottom of the stairs and crossed the landing at the bottom. There were five doors here. The door in the center was twice as large as the others, carved with an intricate circular pattern and painted black. Cadence passed them all, leading her through a narrow hallway under the stairs. They entered a sort of tunnel that went on for several minutes before opening up into Cadence's own Listening Room, the same room she had listened to Sai and Susu fighting on the recording.

"Why are we *here*?" she asked impatiently. She had clearance to come in here on her own.

He ignored her and led her to that blank wall she had eyed so suspiciously that day, the one with Sai's tapes in it. Cadence paused and grimaced.

"I don't know what the Memory Vault will have for you. We can look after this. I know, though, that this drawer has a vial with your name on it." He swiped his wrist along the wall and a drawer slid open. He didn't move to touch anything but watched her instead.

She swallowed, looking from him to the drawer. "You knew there was a memory of mine in here? This whole time?"

"I thought... you and Sai... I thought you might have asked him to empty it. It's none of my business, what happens between the two of you." His neck had flushed red.

Her anger was a hot knife twisting in her belly.

Sai?

Sai had Emptied her? Her one and only true confidant? The knife wasn't anger, really, it was a sickening combination of betrayal and loss. She found herself staring at the drawer like it might come to life and attack her. Sai had betrayed her. Moments of his smile and touch were flashing through her mind at dizzying speeds and she felt the cold threat of vomit skip across her skin.

She realized she'd been silent for several minutes when she glanced up to see Cadence looking at her with concern.

Without Sai there to rage at, she turned her anger on Cadence. "So you knew that the Family could empty anyone? Not just the Sepas?"

"Well, yes. Every Heart is emptied before they die to preserve their knowledge. I never would have thought they would do it to people who are still living their lives until I became Eye."

"So why are you helping me now?" she asked shakily. Even though she was furious with him for not telling her immediately, she had the sudden realization that if the roles had been reversed, she wouldn't have said a word either. So many secrets in this Family.

He took a deep breath, blowing a strand of unruly hair from his face on the exhale. "You're my friend, Penna. Like it or not." He offered her a quick lopsided grin. "Go ahead and take it. I don't know how long this place will stay empty."

She nodded, glancing around nervously before plunging both hands into the drawer's contents. It had several recordings in it, a few ID chips, some tech she didn't recognize, and two vials. The first one she picked up said "Kiba." Her eyes flew to Cadence's. He was staring at it with his jaw clenched tightly. "But this... this is your maan's?"

He nodded slowly.

"And you've never taken it to see what it is?"

"Sai told me what's on it," he said grimly. "She asked him to take it from her... it was a troubling memory of my faan, "behaving poorly" as he described it. She wanted to be rid of it so she could continue serving him as a happy bride. Sai didn't want Tashi to know, so he kept it hidden here. It was our secret." He glanced at her. "I've always felt a little more connected to her with it here, knowing that I'm still keeping her secret for her."

Penna let out a held breath. "I see. Did he ever tell you what's in mine?"

"No."

She had never seen him look so serious and wondered if he truly believed Sai's story. If she found a memory of her maan alive before she'd died, she wouldn't hesitate to see it. She lifted another tape to find the second vial underneath, *Penna* scrawled in a hurried hand across the label. Seeing her name there took the wind out of her. A piece of her she hadn't known to be missing, tucked inside a wall in Luópán Hall; the man she loved hiding it from her. The reality and the weight of the violation was hitting her all at once. She couldn't bring herself to touch it, as if the vial itself might burn her.

"Will you take it?" she whispered.

"Yes." Seeming to understand completely, he snatched the vial and closed the drawer.

He was leading her away when she stopped him. "Cadence? Meera said that Asaka kept a drawer that only he and I could open. Could that drawer be here?"

"Asaka?" he asked, surprise making his brows shoot up. So no, then, that wasn't what he knew.

He didn't know what she was.

"I'm sure it *would* be. He created this wall. It's one piece of the palace Tashi knows nothing about."

She looked at the wall, an impossible smooth slate big enough to carry hundreds of drawers.

Raising her chin with determination, she raised her arm as high as it would go and began to run her palms along the wall from left to right, then from right to left, a little lower. She would find Asaka's drawer if it took her all evening, the party be damned.

Cadence just watched, occasionally glancing nervously at the doors.

As it turned out, Asaka's drawer was in the very center. It slid open without a sound, and Penna's breath caught in her throat. Cadence came beside her and they both peered into the box.

It was empty.

They met eyes with mirrored astonishment.

"How...?" he began.

Penna looked back at the drawer as if her eyes had deceived her. And then, she realized they had. This drawer was significantly shallower than it should have been. She let her fingers run along the edges inside the drawer, looking for a trick. Her heart began to pound when she found one; a little divot in the metal that allowed something thin as a fingernail to lift out the bottom of the drawer. The secret compartment, however, did not contain the vial she had been expecting. Instead, a tiny scroll was tucked inside.

Without looking at Cadence, she picked it up and unfurled it.

WE'LL SEE, we'll see,
　　Roots splintered from their trees
　　We'll see.

GROW AGAIN MY MAAN, grow again my faan,
　　shade me from this burning sun.
　　Wise men will grow, wiser men will fall;
　　quit trying to run before you've learned to crawl.

THE MOON WILL RISE on a new night,
　　land, and stars, and sea,
　　will lend the people their might.

. . .

THE BAY WILL RISE over stony shore;
    The sun will set when the waters roar.

LO, the river
    Lo, the rain
    Earth and stars will meet in the sky again.
    Lo the river, lo the rain,
    Ocean breaks free from the tide again.

PENNA SAGGED WITH DISAPPOINTMENT. She had thought it might be a letter from her faan, or some directions on where to go next. It was his handwriting, the careful lines and swooping s's. He had written this and tucked it away for her to find. But...it was just a song. A chopped version of the song Cadence had sang at the Sepa dinner.

She handed it over to Cadence wordlessly.

Cadence read it over and let out a "whoa" that caused Penna to look at him sharply. "What?"

"You know this song, don't you?"

She shrugged. Kind of. No. She heard Cadence sing it that one time, but that was it.

"There was an organized Banjarian resistance against the Family before my faan's rule. It was brief, and didn't amount to more than ideas, but it happened. This was their anthem. The story goes that some prophet or "wise man" from the Banjar wrote it, and it came here with the first Sepa's memory drops. It created a stir. My maan, Kiba, loved the tune and would sing it to me all the time before Tashi... before he punished her for it."

Penna was spinning. "So... my faan left me a message of resistance against the Family?"

"Not necessarily against the Family," Cadence said, pointing to the words. "Against the barrier."

The barrier?

She read the lyrics through a few more times, trying to find a way to deny what Cadence was telling her.

"Penna?"

"Hmmm?" she murmured impatiently.

"We need to keep moving. We have two more places to go and need to hurry if no one is going to notice we're missing."

This made her look up at him. "Where else? The drawer was empty."

He shifted uncomfortably. "The Family has an official vault in the Memory Library."

She raised a brow at him.

His eyes glimmered with sympathy. "I have a feeling that there might be another vial with your name on it there, from my faan."

Her eyes unfocused until Cadence was a blur before her. Asaka. Sai. Tashi. Picking pieces from her mind like…

…like vultures.

She grabbed Cadence's arm to keep herself steady and let him lead her away back the way they had come. They returned to the bottom floor of the Memory Library, with its row of doors. He passed two and swiped his wrist at the third.

Craning her neck to glance back, she asked "What's beyond the black door?"

Cadence just shrugged a shoulder and led her inside, where a narrow staircase led them down two more flights of stairs. The room at the bottom was lit in an eerie purple. The glow came from clear cases set along the wall, full of labeled vials.

"The Family Vault?" Penna muttered.

"The Heart's memories. As I said, before a Heart dies, they empty them of every memory they can and store them here. The cool temperature and shorter wavelength lighting retains the memories better than upstairs. This is where we store the greatest wisdom. I imagine, too, that it would be where they keep their secrets."

The way Cadence said "their" made her heart feel a little less alone.

It reaffirmed that he was on her team, not theirs. She was willing to put aside for the moment how or when he came to know she might have memories here. The fact that he was helping her was apology enough. She nodded and turned away from him, inspecting the vials in each case. She couldn't help but marvel at what she was seeing. Several Dragons' lives, stored here for them to learn from. She wondered how many vials Tashi had injected into his body and then pulled out. How much had he learned?

"Penna."

She turned. Cadence was standing away from her, stock-still.

She walked to his side and looked down. He had opened a cabinet at his waist level. Inside were two vials with the word "Penna" written across them.

"There are two."

She took a shaky breath.

He looked up at her, mouth slightly open.

"Three times," she whispered.

It didn't matter what was in the vials at that moment. It mattered that someone had taken her into an Emptying station and stolen her memories not once, but three times.

Four, she realized with a jolt. Her faan's missing vial, then Sai's, and now these two from the Dragon himself.

She looked into Cadence's regretful face. "Do you know how to put them back?"

"I was told once, but..."

"But you weren't paying attention?" she snapped.

"How was I to know I would need to do a filling someday? That's an emptier's job."

"What do you remember?"

He swallowed. "There's a room beyond the last door on the right for Emptying. Once I see the tools, I... it might jog my memory."

"Let's hope it jogs mine," she muttered.

"Was that a joke, Penna San?" he asked with a small smile.

She glared at him before carefully pulling the vials out. "Lead the way."

When they came back to the main landing and crossed toward the farthest room, she couldn't help gazing up at the massive black door, wondering what the room beyond might contain. The sound of a man clearing his throat made her jump an inch. She turned to find that they were no longer alone. A technician watched them curiously. The hairs on Penna's neck rose. They needed to hurry.

"Should we be worried about Listeners?" she whispered.

She couldn't see his face but felt the smile in his voice when he replied. "Consider me King of the Listeners. I think I can handle covering our tracks."

Let's hope so, she thought.

When he led her into the Emptying room, a strong wave of nausea overtook her. It was a small square space with what looked like a chest high tub in the center. Tubes emerged from a machine on the wall and arched over the tub, winding around hooks in front of it.

Before the tub was a tall gurney, equipped with thick strapped belts to hold a person still. The tub itself was filled with a rolling blue gel, lit up from a light below.

"It's heated by the lamp," Cadence said. "It makes it less painful, I'm told."

Penna leaned up against the wall for support. "How generous."

Cadence was eyeing the belts as well, glancing back and forth from the bed to her.

"We need to hurry," she urged. "The sooner we get out of here, the less likely they'll ever know we came."

Cadence nodded and turned back to inspect the machine. "Okay... can you come sit on the bed?"

"Not in a thousand years," she breathed, her eyes closed.

"Just sit on it like a bench, facing the tub. You need to put your hands in the gel."

Reluctantly, Penna inched around the bed and to the tub, opting to stand in front of it.

She handed him the vials gingerly.

"Injections go here... I'm almost positive." He was looking at a latch on the machine that opened up to a pipe. He looked at her for permission before pouring the vials in. If they did it wrong, she would never know. If they didn't hurry, she would never know and they could both be in danger. "Just do it," she said.

"The most powerful of our emotional memories are kept on the right," he was muttering to himself. "Sepas keep extra receptor banks in both. Empty the left for mission memories... catalogue them for study... right for emotional impact, store them in the Library. The neck... pull the day to day from the back for a complete Emptying..."

"Cadence."

"Okay! I just want to make sure I remember right. We don't know what we're working with, so it's difficult. What do you remember?"

She raised her brows at him. "Seriously? I remember my whole life as far as I know."

"Really? Try to think back. Are there any parts that are fuzzy? I need to know what kind of memories these might be."

Penna took a deep breath and closed her eyes. She thought back as far as she could and found that she didn't remember anything before age five. Isn't that how everyone's memory worked, though? She went forward, remembering her childhood and flitting painfully across years with her two sisters. She remembered her faan's death and her Maester. She remembered being invited by Dorji Tashi to work in the palace as an assistant to Seldom Chime. Her eyes snapped open.

"I don't remember working for Seldom Chime. I remember being hired, but don't remember working there at all."

"How long?"

Penna swallowed. "Two years, give or take."

The words hung in the room for a moment.

Cadence sighed. "Wow. Well, that means that these vials probably include day to day memories and trigger memories."

"What are trigger memories?"

"They're the moments in our life that cut us the deepest emotionally or bring us the most joy. They have the power to change who we are as people. Trigger memories are kept here." He gently pushed back the hair from her right ear and tapped behind it, making her flinch. "If we put the memories there, you'll feel them more intensely than if we put them in the neck."

"Put it all in there. I want to feel all of it as much as I can."

Cadence bit his lip. "It might be too much all at once."

"Do it, Cadence."

He nodded a begrudging assent and uncoiled the tubing. He pulled an attachment and a needle from a drawer nearby and carefully assembled the hose, handing it to her.

"Hold this pointed up while I drop the vials in."

She watched her three memories be poured down the tube, Sai's first, then Tashi's, sending one last desperate wish that this worked; that this would make her feel how she imagined others felt. Whole was the only way she could describe it.

He turned to her and took the hose back, setting both of her arms face up in the blue gel. It was warm and thicker than she'd thought.

"This is going to hurt like hell, I imagine," he muttered.

With one last glance at her, he positioned himself behind her and inserted the needle, and flipped the latch on the machine.

She felt a wave of nausea, and the room around her faded.

Penna was in love. She couldn't help it. Head over heels, shooting for the stars, would take a dagger to the heart, in love. Was he her advisor's husband? Yes. But he'd never loved his wife. They'd been forced to marry by Seldom's faan. He was more a son to her than a husband. He told her that Seldom wouldn't even mind.

She was nineteen and had just landed an internship with Seldom Chime for work in the education system. She was playing shadow for a man named Aiditri. He hired and trained the Maesters for the Inner Ring children and had been one of the Maesters who recorded the original Sepa lessons on mathematics. Penna was passionate about both math and children. She knew her faan would have been so proud. He died in her last year of advanced mathematics.

Although Aiditri's job filled her with joy, her mind was drifting more and more often to the dark and brooding eyes of Sai San. He wasn't a smiling young man, but when he saw her, something changed in his face. He told her that something had changed in his heart.

Penna was in the Tropics Garden, one of their secret meeting places. They had been having an affair—she blushed at the thought of the word— for two months now. They never talked about the future. Both had thought about it, she was sure, but in the end had come up with nothing to say. They could never truly be together. Besides, their secret rendezvous dates were exciting. She wished she could tell Meera her secret, but Sai had made her promise to never tell anyone.

She sighed at the thought, clenching her palm to quell the urge to comm Meera. Then the crunching of sandals on pebbles met her ears, and she quickly fluffed her hair and struck a more appealing pose on the stone bench she occupied.

When he came around the corner into their little courtyard, his face did not light up at the sight of her. If anything, his eyes became even stormier. He came to her and fell on his knees in front of her, putting his head in her lap. She frowned, gently pulling her fingers through his silken black hair.

"Sai? What is it?"

He looked up at her, his eyes red rimmed with fatigue. "Tashi means to take you as his wife."

She sat back in shock, her eyes casting around the garden for something to say. "But... we only released his wife's stone last week."

He was nodding. "He had apparently decided on you as her replacement before her death."

She was shaking her head. "When?"

"He's planning to tell you tomorrow. He'll require you to run through a series of trainings and tests before he announces to the country."

"Tests?"

Sai scoffed. "He said that you are beautiful enough, but he needs to know that you are talented enough to serve him." His fists clenched around the folds of her dress.

"What does that mean?" she asked, aghast.

"I think everything. He wants to know how you will serve as a politician, as a cook, a masseuse, how well can you serve tea and dance for him... it's practically a geisha training," he muttered.

Her mind had caught on "politician." "But...what about my internship with Aiditri?"

He offered her a sad smile and cupped her cheek in a soft hand. "That is over, my love. Being Tashi's wife is a full-time position."

Her eyes filled with tears.

"And us?"

"This will be our last time together."

She jumped into his arms in a sob. She had just lost everything that made her happy. No more Sai... no more children... no more... and what now? Serving tea and dancing for Tashi? The thought made her sick and she pushed it away, clinging closer to the man before her. After her sobs had subsided, he started giving her soft kisses on the neck and running his hands all along her body. She realized that this would be their last time together, and neither of them would let it go to waste. This corner of the garden had seen them naked before. Sai had taken every mic out of the place to prepare for their first secret meeting. It was liberating to have no one listening; no constrictions.

As much as she wanted to enjoy his body, she couldn't shake her grief. She held tightly to him with quiet tears falling down her cheeks. When he was finished, he tucked his face in her neck, whispering feverishly.

"I love you, Penna San. More than the moon. You are the only one in the world who matters to me."

He pulled his face up to look at her. "I'm so sorry, my love, but you can't know about us anymore. It would be too much for you to keep this secret from Tashi." He kissed her fiercely. "Please," he whispered. "On some level, remember that I love you."

With those words, Penna felt a sharp stab into her side. She craned her neck in shock, immobilized by his body in hers, and could just see the leafy feather of a tranquilizer dart. Her eyes fell back to his in a last look of betrayal before rolling into the back of her head.

It seemed like moments later when her eyes drifted open. She could see a blurry outline of Sai, working at a machine with his back turned to her. She moved to reach out to him, only to realize that her arms were confined. She glanced down, the blurry edges of her reality sharpening. She found that her legs, arms, and head were all strapped down to a bed.

"Sai?" she croaked.

He whipped around. After a moment of staring at her, he rummaged in a case on the floor and came beside her. He kissed her forehead and stabbed her with a needle.

PENNA OPENED HER EYES. At some point in the process of receiving the first memory she had fallen to a sitting position on the gurney. She looked around her in horror. "This is where he took me," she said, and she choked on the words.

She had never felt so much love in her life as she had in that memory, but it hadn't been for Sai. She had truly loved her work. It had filled her with so much purpose. She could remember the joy of a child's eyes lighting up when they figured out a problem, and her own joy when discovering a new way to solve one. She had been a passionate person. Gone. He had taken it all from her. Did he know that he had taken it all from her? Not just him?

She turned and met Cadence's concerned face. Her eyes filled with tears. "I was—"

Her speech was interrupted by a second burst of liquid being pumped into her body.

Her eyes closed again.

PENNA HAD BEEN PRACTICING this dance five hours a day for the last week. She could do it in her sleep at this point. This was the final audition, as she called it, for being Tashi's wife, and it was also the most difficult for her. Dancing had never been anything she was remotely good at. Her sister Mishka had always taken the crowd's eyes off of her and Meera once the music started. That girl could mesmerize anyone with the gentle sway of her hips. If Mishka knew what she was up to, she would be very proud. Penna couldn't wait to tell her sisters of all the silly things she'd had to do to earn the engagement with the most powerful man in the world. Her cheeks flushed with pride. After two months of training, there was only this one last test. One more test, she kept thinking to herself, and you will rule the world. Then she would be free to talk to her sisters about whatever she wanted to.

Tashi had been close to her faan, Asaka, and had always been around during her childhood. He was like an uncle, in a way. Mishka had always thought he was funny, but Penna thought he was a little creepy. He was always watching her, just like he was now.

Dorji's eyes had heavy lids that almost drooped over his eyes completely, giving him an ever-intoxicated look. He had let his hair on the sides of his face grow wild while he tamed his beard in a braided tail. He stroked it now, watching her carefully.

"Stop," he said suddenly, stilling her mid-dance. Her arms were up with palms pointed out. She kept them there, frozen. What had she done?

"Come to me, girl."

She put her hands down and tried to walk as gracefully over to him as she could in the thick sandals. Because he was seated on a pile of pillows, his head was almost level with her stomach. He put his hands on her belly, pushing at it and looking at it from all sides.

Finally, he dropped his hands and cleared his throat. "What is this?"

Penna's hands covered her belly in embarrassment. "My apologies, Tashi San. I've been eating exactly what you asked me to, but my weight seems to rise. I... I thought I might see a healer about it."

Tashi rose to his feet. "You thought you might see a healer about it..." he parroted back. He was standing very close to her, huffing his breath in her face, his eyes glittering with malice. Suddenly Penna was truly frightened.

He grabbed the back of her robes and pulled her close with one hand. With the other, he lifted the front of her robes and shoved his hand up into her body. She gasped in shock and pain. She could feel him feeling around inside of her. He was nodding. "The healer has confirmed that you, little girl, have been very sick." He pulled his hand from her and released her back, only to bring a resounding backhanded slap across her face. She stumbled back.

"I—I don't understand, Tashi."

"You are meant to be mine alone. I wanted you to be brand new. But it seems you decided to play Rue around the palace." He grabbed her by the

collar of her robe and punched her in the face. The pain spiked around her head with bursts of light. She fell to the ground, gasping.

"I don't understand," she sobbed.

He lifted her roughly to her feet. "I don't understand" he huffed, "why, you thought you could make a fool of me."

She couldn't stop her sobbing, but he was suddenly calm. He traced a finger along her wet cheek. "We don't want anyone knowing about this, do we?"

She shook her head, without a clue to what he was referring to.

"I think you'll take to private quarters with an illness." He smiled cruelly. "And you, little girl, will get what you wanted." He squeezed her jaw painfully, "With this beautiful face, you'll be the most desired Rue we've ever had, pregnant or not."

Penna's eyes widened. "But, Tashi, I—I can't be pregnant. I've never even—"

28

———————

S EPORA

THEY'D BEEN FLYING in silence for a while, each deep in their own thoughts, when Ruby turned to her and patted her hand on the controls.

"Neither of us know if we'll see each other again, Sepora."

Sepora went to protest but Ruby put her hand up. "Just in case, I need to tell you something."

Sepora glanced at her. She'd never seen this look on her friend's face before. She was solemn as a starless night.

"You aren't the first girl I helped keep her own memories."

She glanced over at her again in surprise before reminding herself to keep her eyes on the horizon.

"Tashi and his men... sometimes they hide their pregnant lovers at the lake until the child can be born and smuggled into the SEPA Project."

Sepora's eyes flew to hers in surprise.

"No, you are not the only human to be smuggled into the project. Poor souls never know it."

Trying to grapple with this piece of information, Sepora turned back to the horizon.

"The women are obviously not used as Rues, and usually have no idea where they are. They stay on the top floor of Blossom House. I help them through their pregnancy and with delivering the babies."

Sepora was nodding with her jaw clenched.

"There was one girl, though. This girl, Tashi brought himself. He wanted her to be used as a Rue. He told me she was being punished. When he left, she cried to me that she didn't know how she could even be pregnant. She'd never been with a man. It was obvious to me that she'd been emptied before, and I told her as much. She was terrified, shaking like a leaf. She asked me, just like you did, to help her keep her memories this time. To not let her be trained. She pulled on my heartstrings. Enough that I made the biggest mistake of my life."

"What?"

"I helped her."

"That's what you should have done!"

"No." Ruby was shaking her head, her eyes filled with darkness. "It would have been a favor to her to make her a Rue. They used her nearly every night, and the girl never pretended to be trained. She fought every time. Some of the men complained to Tashi that her training was incomplete, and he came to see for himself. He didn't even ask me what had gone wrong. He liked it. He said it made for more of a challenge. After he found out, he started coming more often for her. She stopped fighting or crying. She stopped speaking to any of us. When she was here, she would just rub that growing belly of hers in silence."

"Dragons," Sepora breathed. She took a hand off the controls to squeeze Ruby's hand.

"When the time came for the baby to arrive, one of those idiot Rues ran off to tell the men. Both Dorji Tashi and Sai San were visiting at the time. The baby arrived and the girl held onto it like it was the very air she was breathing. I had never seen joy in her eyes before. She held that baby something fierce. Not twenty minutes later Tashi came and plucked it from her arms and handed it to Sai San. I'll never forget it.

"'Kill it,' he said. "The look on Sai San's face... He looked from Tashi to the girl twice, nodded, and disappeared into the forest." She nodded her head. "The scream that came out of her still haunts me."

Sepora and put a hand to her mouth in horror.

Ruby nodded. "Tashi whispered some dark words into her ears that she never told me and strode out. They left her there with me for a few more months, my guess is to let her body return to normal. She didn't say one word the entire time, but I stayed right there with her. I told her stories, braided her hair, held her at night when the night-mares came. I even bathed her when she'd come back from a night in Tashi's playhouse."

She took a deep breath and patted Sepora's leg. "Girlie, I'm not telling you this for nothing. Sai San, he would visit the lake a lot, too. He would come by Blossom House alone, usually late. Well past when the rest of the men had drunk themselves unconscious."

"Did he hurt her?" She whispered, hoping it wasn't true. She wanted her faan to be good, or at least, no more terrible than she already knew him to be.

"No. That was the interesting part. He didn't even speak to her. He would chat with me, but his eyes would constantly dart over to where she sat by the window. He would always be in a different degree of agitation. It was strange behavior, and it only lasted while the girl was here."

She sighed. "Sepora... when I was listening to him speak to you... I was thinking about that night the baby was born. The way he looked at Tashi when he was ordered to kill the infant. His face moved from devastation to fury so fast you would have to think you'd imagined it. I was so focused on the girl's pain, that I didn't think of it again. Sai all but told you that he's your faan today. What if that baby was his?"

Sepora swallowed hard. *What if that baby was his?*

"What if he never killed it, you mean?" she said tightly.

"He said that he'd tried to keep you safe by hiding you within the SEPA Project. He could have smuggled that baby to Meera San."

"He said that Tashi tried to kill me," she admitted quietly, keeping her eyes on the sky. She was thinking about her maan. How being pregnant with her had surely been the nightmare of her life.

"Sepora, don't look so down. This story has many silver linings."

She would have laughed if she hadn't felt so repulsed. "Really?" she asked skeptically.

"Yes," Ruby smiled softly. "First of all, we know who your maan is."

Sepora snapped her attention to Ruby's face.

"That girl's name was Penna San."

Sepora's eyes went wide with shock. "But that means..."

"Yes. That girl was also my daughter." Ruby's smile turned watery. "I missed so much of my baby's life, but I was there when she needed me the most, wasn't I? I was there when you were born."

29

C ADENCE

PENNA HAD STARTED TO CONVULSE. She'd been receiving the second memory for nearly twenty minutes. Her body was trembling and jolting with violent full body jerks every few minutes, and she was muttering and crying out. He guessed that this might be the one that took so much of her life away. How long would it take to remember?

His hand kept reaching out as if to calm her, but he always stopped short and snatched it back. Finally, he turned his back to her so he wouldn't have to watch. It was making his own body feel sick. Facing the wall, however, his thoughts were free to immediately question everything he had just done.

He had been trusted with secret information for less than a moon's turn and here he was, helping Penna get her memories back.

And yet, he reasoned, the Emptying of memories was meant to be possible for Sepas only, due to the extra memory pockets. These were simply to study transactions and movement in the Banjar. He was sure that the people of New Bhutan would be just as indignant and suspicious as he had been to learn that it could be done to anyone, and had been done to people they knew. Penna, for one. His bride to be, their new Heart.

Besides, you didn't tell her, he thought to himself. *She already knew. She had figured it out on her own,* so how could he be to blame?

You brought her here. You showed her where they might be.

Why had he done that?

When Penna awoke, what would she say to Dorji Tashi? What would Tashi say to him? He was imagining his title as Eye being stripped away and his faan saying he could never trust him to have a position of power. What would he do then? He didn't have the know-how to be a researcher in Luópán. He didn't have the patience to work in education or the interest in distribution. Would he take over an Inner Ring job as the gardener, enjoying his flowers as important people strolled by?

Cadence threw his head back to huff at the ceiling. He couldn't figure out why he had done something so stupid. Of course, he felt sorry for Penna. She didn't deserve to be tampered with. She was the daughter of Asaka the Just, not a Banjarian rebel. She deserved respect. Plus, if he was honest with himself, she was his only friend.

Penna let out a guttural cry from the gurney. She had long since fallen into a fetal position on the bed. Cadence whipped around to see her whole body jerking as if she was having a seizure. "Penna!" He ran to her side and lifted the upper half of her body into his arms.

It was at that moment that the door opened and his faan, the Dragon, the Heart of New Bhutan, strode into the room. He looked from Penna to Cadence twice, took a deep breath, and said quietly, "Set her down." He stepped quickly to the wall and flipped the latch to pause the transmission.

Cadence dropped her and stepped away, heart thudding wildly in his chest. She was still convulsing, her eyes rolled into her head.

"She's overloaded," his faan said. He touched his thumb to pinky and asked for Fai, Luópán's Emptier, to come to the Library Emptying station immediately. Then his heavy eyes landed on Cadence. "Penna was meant to be yours, you fool," he hissed. "I was giving her to you. Are you going to run to do her bidding every time she calls, or will you be the leader of this world?" He shook his head. "You disappoint me, Cadence."

He stepped away from the bed and watched her shake for a moment. "She's special. I know. I don't blame you for wanting to please her. Her and I, we have a special bond. But she needs a firm hand. She needs to be controlled or else she will control you. No son of mine will be controlled or manipulated. Is that understood?" He took the two steps it would take to stand directly in front of Cadence.

In almost a whisper, he added, "If she causes trouble like this again, I will have had enough of her. She will go away for good. Do you understand my words?"

Cadence swallowed, keeping his eyes averted from his faan's.

"Answer me, so help me."

"I do," Cadence pushed out. He was watching Penna, who had only now started to tremble lightly. He thought he saw her eyes fluttering open.

"Now get out," Tashi said. "We'll see you at the announcement."

Cadence inched backward, eyes on Penna. Fai nearly knocked him down in his hurry to enter the room.

He hadn't even realized his steps had taken him past the door until Tashi was shutting it in his face. He left him standing in the Library of Memories, dressed in his ridiculously elaborate robes. The man he had seen earlier busied himself at his desk, perhaps guiltily avoiding Cadence's gaze.

He stood frozen, thinking of Penna's eyes, and how they were probably opening.

30

———

SEPORA

SEPORA COULDN'T DISEMBARK in Tumail. She wanted to walk Ruby into the caves and make sure they welcomed her. She wanted to make sure she was safe. Ruby wouldn't let her cut the power. She reminded her of what she already knew: they were on borrowed time. They would be after her soon enough, and the sooner she left Tumail, the less likely they would know that she had been there at all.

She descended with a rocky landing, keeping the power on, and dove into Ruby's arms for a tight embrace. She was holding her grandmaan. She was someone's family, and they were hugging. She didn't want to let the moment go, trying to take in the smell of her hair and the feel of her arms.

"We'll see each other again," Ruby murmured into her hair. "You wait and see, girl. I'll bring my people and you bring yours." She pulled away and cupped Sepora's face, "And then we'll give them what they deserve."

Sepora had no idea how any type of vengeance could make up for what they had done to this woman. She nodded her head anyway, hoping that Ruby was right.

"Tell them that we're going to save Story, okay?" Guilt welled inside her. She wanted her to tell them that she had been made to do it. That she hadn't betrayed Story's trust, really.

But she had.

Finally, she said, "Tell them that the Sepas are not to be trusted... that New Bhutan is not to be trusted. And stay safe in there until I can come back for you," she added sternly. "Please."

"I trust in Tumail to keep me safe, girlie. You're the one I'm worried about. You'll come back?"

"Yes."

"And, Sepora?" She gently tucked a lock of hair behind Sepora's ear. "Will you tell Penna that I love her? That I'm still here?"

"If it takes my life," Sepora whispered.

Ruby cracked a small smile. "Now don't be so dramatic. I'll see you soon." She kissed her on the forehead and gingerly climbed down. After walking a few paces, she turned and gave a small wave. Sepora raised her palm to her, trying to memorize the lines of the woman's face and her long, thinning hair picked up with the wind. She took a deep breath and lifted the helio into the sky.

As she rose to fly away, she took in the view of Tumail. Her first home, in a sense. She knew the people there would welcome Ruby back with open arms. In Ruby's memories, everyone had loved her, just as much as they had loved Story. It was a hard life there, but the people were deeply kind to one another.

Looking over the landscape, her memories of Miracle came back to her full force. She remembered the first time he coughed that deep rattle of the Banjarguay. They'd had a proper Sepa Feast to celebrate Sepora's third arrival the night before, thinking that she had come to bring a large deposit of water. She had brought them water and other luxury items such as bananas, cold tea, buckwheat dumplings, aloo gobi, and several cases of their finest Bhutanese bread.

Story and Sepora were playing Fujii, a popular card game in

Tumail, and resting their full bellies when Miracle called for his maan. The cry sounded so unlike him that both women stood and came into the small bedroom they shared.

Miracle had pulled the small sheet over his body, even though the temperature outside had to be past a hundred and twenty. He let out that telltale rattling cough and told Story that he wasn't feeling well.

"Can you add to the mural tomorrow, Maan?" he said hazily. "I think I need to take a break."

Story sat down next to him, holding the back of her hand to his forehead. Sepora still remembered how in awe she was of her voice coming out so steady, knowing what she knew. "What would you like me to add, my love? I will add it."

Miracle had been painting a mural on the side of Tumail's common house over the last month. Each day, he would add a little drawing of something he loved in Tumail. The paint was made of vulture blood, sand, rock, and minerals from within the caves, so the colors were red, rusty orange, grey, and white. The drums were on it. The feasting table and dancer's fire. The little bugs that lived in the cave that the Tumailians ate were all featured (except for the purple ones, which he thought were disgusting).

He smiled his big cheeked smile, his forehead covered in sweat. "Can you draw you, Maan?"

Story's body jerked as though she'd been punched in the gut. "I can, my little Miracle." She tried to take a calming breath. "I can do that." She gently pushed the hair back from his head. "You go on, get some rest now. I'll head over to the market and bring you back a big glass a' cold water and some those juicy berries 288 brought us. Okay?"

He smiled up at her and coughed again. She sat bravely through the fit, kissed him on his forehead, and walked out of the room. She walked all the way outside before turning to Sepora, who had followed her. She looked at her in shock, mouth open.

"No one has caught it in months. No one has it, 288. He was fine, I —"

Suddenly the air began to ring with a solemn drum. It was the slow beat of the Banjarguay. Someone had reported an outbreak. Story fell to her knees in the sand, eyes staring blindly.

Sepora stood motionless, having no idea what to do or say or even how to feel. She was there to spy on Story, and possibly arrest her. Miracle had done nothing wrong in this world, though. He was just a little thing, painting and playing, showing kindness to everyone he met.

"Are you really going to market, Story?" she found herself asking. She knew that once it set in, the Banjarguay could take a life anywhere from a few weeks to a few hours.

Story jumped to her feet. "He needs some water. And he'll like the berries. I'll... I'll be right back. Maybe it will help." It was clear to Sepora that Story was panicking.

After taking a few steps away, she turned back, rushing to Sepora with a wildfire in her eyes. "Tell me now, 288, please, tell me Bhutan has the medicine for him."

Sepora stared at her helplessly. What could she say? She knew nothing about curing the Banjarguay. Seeing defeat, Story pressed her forehead to hers, taking a deep breath.

"Stay with him while I'm gone. I'll be right back."

And with that, she'd taken off at a run toward the common house.

Sepora remembered that it wasn't fifteen minutes later that Miracle's eyes and ears had started to bleed. His maan had returned and dropped the berries to the floor, rushing to his side as he drew his last breath.

Five people died that day, the most brutally fast acting strain of Banjarguay in Tumail's recent memory.

As Tumail twisted out of sight, Sepora found herself anxious to get back and see if Story had survived the escape from Qinghai Lake. She wanted to hear her friend's voice again. She realized suddenly that she was anxious to see Meera as well. It was in this moment of silence, flying high above the world, that Sepora let the reality sink in that she had a family. She wasn't just a number anymore, one of many silent Sepas. She was Sepora, and there were women she cared about. Children she cared about. *This is what keeping your memories does*, she thought. It was so much more painful to care than she would have imagined. She was consumed with it. And yet, she would rather die than give it up.

Suddenly, Ruby's theory about Penna San came back to her. Penna San, with her haughty stare. She remembered how her face had lost all color, her spirit all of its fight, halfway through the Sepa dinner in Potala. She looked like she'd seen a ghost. *Had she recognized me?* she wondered. Had she known somehow? With a jolt, she realized that Mecra must have known.

Meera! If Sepora was Penna's daughter, then... Meera San was her relative, too. This brought a balloon of joy to her chest that was just as quickly popped.

Meera knew. She knew this whole time that her niece was in the bunkers. She'd hidden her away and taught her to believe that she was subhuman. Should she be grateful? All she felt was anger.

Ruby didn't think that Meera was any friend to her either. Her criticism nagged at her. She wasn't Meera's slave. Meera was using what she could to seek justice. Wasn't she? She had asked Sepora to arrest Story and take her to the lake, but it had been her only option for finding out the truth. Finding the truth for everyone, right? Or was it just for the people of New Bhutan that Meera was concerned?

Honestly, how could she ever trust her?

Did Meera plan the dinner for Penna's benefit, knowing that she was reuniting maan and daughter?

And faan, she added as an afterthought. *I was sitting at a table with my family without even knowing it.*

As a Sepa.

As a slave.

Sepora was flooded with so many different ideas of who could or could not be trusted, but through it all, they had one common enemy. Dorji Tashi. Dorji Tashi had destroyed Penna and tried to kill her baby, had stolen Ruby from her own child and lover. He employed Meera to run the SEPA Project that enslaved so many. And it was Dorji Tashi who wouldn't let the Banjarians inside, safe from the Banjarguay.

Whatever she was going to do back in New Bhutan, it would include killing the Dragon.

The rolling dunes before her were playing with the setting sun. The waves of shadow and light pulled her attention, and she was suddenly reminded of a painting she'd seen in the bunkers as a younger Sepa. The red sun cast the exact same hues. It nagged at her mind, pulling at different memories.

She was moments away from connecting her thoughts when the lights in the helio shut off. She felt the tremble of power die beneath her feet and a sudden silence. For a terrifying moment, she was sitting in a box, high up in the sky. Then, in slow motion, the helio dipped and took a dive straight for the ground.

Too late, she thought, *They woke up.*

Just before the helio crashed into the earth, Sepora caught a glimpse of the cliffs outside the Sepa bunker winking at her from the horizon.

31

M EERA

Meera was exhausted. So tired, in fact, that she promptly fell asleep the minute the Rail embarked on its journey to the Sepa bunkers. She tried to keep her eyes open. She wanted to be there for Hui. She wanted to stay vigilant for Story. Her body, however, wanted a rest. Her mind must have disagreed, however, because the last few days came back to her in a distorted jumble of a nightmare, making her sleep far from restful.

In her sleep, she was in a dome similar to Luópán Hall. Celio was holding her hand, guiding her down through room after room in an endless swirl, each leading farther and farther downward. In one room, Mishka and Susu were kissing in a velvet purple chair. Their eyes had been sewn shut and blood was leaking out from between the stitches. She called after her sister, but the two ignored her. It was like a clear barrier had been placed between them and her cries just bounced back at her. Celio turned back to look at her frantically, urging her to keep moving. She found a room lined with three floor to ceiling metal cages, and in each was a different version of Penna. She was in an emerald green dress, a Sepa uniform, and naked. Each version was yelling at her, but she couldn't hear what they were saying. Celio left her side and rushed to the cages. She gripped the chains and shook them until it was Meera pulling at Celio, leading her away from the room.

They swirled downward, a claustrophobia gripping at her throat. They passed by what felt like hundreds of rooms. One with Tashi laughing, one with Faan and herself reading a story to baby Mishka, only to find that Mishka's bassinet held a chrysanthemum. One with a never ending hallway of glass boxes filled with Sepas.

Finally, Celio stopped short. They were at the very bottom of the dome, standing before a massive black door. Meera looked up and found that the dome had transformed. They were standing in the bottom of a very deep well, and water was dripping down the sides and puddling at her feet.

"We need to get through," she cried to Celio. Celio was quickly pulling at the belts and buckles that held the door. It swung open and Meera fell through it. It was pitch black in there, but she couldn't feel Celio next to her. She turned around to look back into the hall and found herself facing a glass wall. Beyond the glass wall was the well, now filled with water, and Celio's body was floating lifelessly in it. She put her hands on the glass, crying out in anguish. Celio's body drifted closer, and when her face was level with hers, the corpse's eyes snapped open and she let out a silent scream.

Meera's eyes opened. She blinked in the bright light of the Rail car and tried to stifle her gasping breath. As her eyes adjusted to the light and the Rail came into focus, she breathed a sigh of relief to see Hui curled up next to Story. The two of them were looking over his new encyclopedia.

"Its head is so hairy!" Hui was laughing.

"You only like these for the animals, true?" Story teased back.

Hui looked up smiling and noticed that Meera was awake. "Meera! Did you read about the buffalo?"

Meera yawned and rubbed her face with two open palms. "Hmmm. Not that I remember."

"It's the biggest animal I've ever seen!"

"New favorite?"

Hui scowled. "Never."

Meera smiled tiredly. This child was so resilient. He held his parents in his pockets and was still putting on a brave face, learning about new animals. Story had grown on her rather quickly as well. Right now, the young woman was turning the page in the book, pointing at different pictures and asking Hui to read what the captions said.

When she had first found her in the desert, she hadn't been sure if this was a risk she should take. Bringing an escaped rebel back into New Bhutan, Lhasa even, had seemed insane. She trusted Sepora's judgement. She was just as anxious as she was terrified to get back to the Sepa bunkers to hear Story's full report and begin planning a rescue for Sepora. Part of her wasn't ready to hear what kind of place she'd sent them to. She reminded herself that it had been the only option.

Besides, she thought stubbornly, the rebel *did* have to be contained. Story didn't feel like a dangerous rebel, though, ready to murder them all. Her eyes were wide with astonishment as Hui read to her about Bloody Mary.

"She burned her people?" Story asked in horror.

"Only the ones who followed a different religion," Hui said. "That's why we don't have religion anymore. It just caused fights."

Story nodded, her brow knit in concentration. After a moment, she said, "We still hurt people who are different, though."

She glanced at Meera.

Hui piped up, "Maester Fre called Banjarians barbarians, which is a word for people who don't follow the right way of living. But I told him that they never get a chance to live our way, so how can we call them that?"

"Wise words, Hui," Meera murmured. "What did Maester Fre say?"

Hui squinted, trying to remember. "I think he said I could be right, but that they're also dangerous to us." He looked up at Story. "You don't seem dangerous. You seem nice."

Story smiled, but it was Meera who spoke. "Who is 'us' and what is 'danger'? For that old Maester, danger could mean anything that threatens his role, and "us" could just mean him and those like him. Story was planning on attacking New Bhutan. That's why Sepora intercepted her." She looked at Story. "Who do *you* think you were a threat to?"

The words had come out more accusatory than she had thought they would. She was feeling defensive.

Story was nodding, staring at her without blinking. Her eyes glittered and Meera suddenly saw the power of a rebel in her. Then she broke contact and smiled down at Hui.

"I was no threat to you, little one," she said, ruffling his hair. "I don't think we were a threat to anyone. We just want to be safe and healthy. We want to be let in. Look out that window there." She pointed out at the rolling hills laid out between the Outer Ring's farms and the Sepa bunkers they were gliding through. "It looks like there might be space for a few more people to live in peace. That's all we want."

Hui looked at Meera. "Why can't they?"

Meera rested her fingertips on her mouth. It was so much more complicated than a simple question. A war started it. Then generations of fear built an *othering* that was at an almost species level. Resources. They needed every bit of what they made to survive. What if bringing in a new community of people disrupted the balance? There was the trading. The people of the Inner Ring had grown dependent on items from the Banjar, not necessarily for life but for quality of life, at least.

Meera was more sympathetic toward the Banjarian people than most. She saw them as humans in a tough situation, and she had always wanted to help. But she also didn't want a war, and saw rebels as just as much of a threat as anyone else. The SEPA Project was meant to help citizens of both worlds and keep rebels at bay. She had believed in her work without question.

Celio, on the other hand, had been full of questions. She was always encouraging Meera to see a little further, push a little deeper. She worked for the Family as well but would often question their actions in the dark of night, hiding from the Listeners under the covers.

Her dream came back to her then, full force. Celio's drowned corpse screaming at her. What did she want her to hear?

"Why, Meera?" Hui asked again. "Why can't they come in?"

Meera shook her head. "I don't know."

"Well, I think we should let them in," Hui said stubbornly.

Meera smiled tiredly. "You sound like your Aunt Celio."

The thought of Celio took Hui's mind in a completely different direction. "The paintings!" he cried. "Meera, will you still let me keep a painting? We left them all at your house." He turned to Story, suddenly solemn. "I'm going to live at the Sepa bunkers with you and be a Sepa operative."

Meera rolled her eyes. "Hui, I am positive that Penna and Cadence will want you in Potala Palace."

Hui ignored her, talking to Story. "Sepora said I would make a great operative."

"Well, she would know," Story smiled. "She saved me."

"And arrested you," Meera muttered.

"At your command," Story shot back.

Meera sighed. "We're all just doing what we're told, aren't we? Myself included."

Story leaned across the space between their seats and put a gentle hand on Meera's leg, startling her. She waited for Meera to meet her eye. "Maybe it's time we stopped."

They stared at one another for a moment before Meera gave a clipped nod.

There were only ten or so minutes left of the Railcar ride, and Hui spent it pestering Meera about which painting he could have and where he would hang it. She told him that she did, in fact, have a few at the Bunker that he could look at.

When they arrived, Meera coached Story on how to pretend to be a Sepa. She was dressed in the right robes and had to simply follow Meera with her head pointed toward the ground until they reached her room.

They delivered her to her bunker with her new name, Sepa 425. Meera instructed her to rest, get comfortable in the space, and she would collect her in an hour or so for a meal. They were all starving at this point, having last ate at Meera's in the hours just before sunrise.

She then led Hui to her own bunker. It was more spacious than the Sepa quarters. It had a small table and a sofa in addition to the bed. She told him to go ahead and unpack at her bed and she would take the sofa tonight. *If I sleep at all*, she thought to herself, thinking of her nightmare. She told him that she needed to check in at the Briefing Room and would collect them all for a meal as soon as possible. With that, she shut the door and took a deep breath.

When was the last time she had been alone? She walked down the sunset soaked hallway slowly, wanting to sit in the silence for a moment before chaos once again slipped over her life. It felt like she was close to solving everything that needed to be solved. Hui would soon be safe in Potala and Mishka and Susu had been properly put to rest. Story would be safe as a Sepa. No one would question the new recruit because they were seen as one; no one noticed them as individuals. Meera would have to keep an eye one her, of course, until they could send her home with a delivery gone wrong.

Penna was home, and by now would have her memories. Meera didn't know exactly what she would find, but she knew without a doubt that she would find something. Her sister had disappeared for over a year after moving into Potala. They had said she needed to be sequestered in a room high in the palace, the Plague Tower, they called it, as she had caught a deadly and extremely contagious virus. Viruses were taken very seriously in New Bhutan. The sick were kept well away from everyone else regularly. But she'd been gone over a year, and when she returned… well, she was different. She didn't care about anything she had before, including Meera. Her deep love for children and play was gone. Her excitement at solving problems was gone. Meera, once inseparable from her, was pushed away.

Sai's desperate call to hide the baby in the program had made her doubly suspicious, but Penna wasn't leaving her room for questions. She had thoroughly shunned and cut Meera out of her life. Whatever had happened, Penna didn't want Meera to know.

It was only in the last few years, as Sepora grew into a young woman, that Meera became positive of the truth. The girl was the spitting image of her maan, if anyone cared to really look at her.

That had made Sepora, the closest Meera had ever had to a child, into a vital tool. A tool who she'd been routinely sending off for slaughter. Sepora was well trained and determined, Meera reminded herself. She had the best shot of anyone in finding out the truth. And there was still hope.

Before Meera could swipe her palmpad at the Briefing Room door, it swung open and Kiro burst through, pulling Meera into an embrace that lifted her off her feet. After a tight squeeze, he let her go and took a step back, offering a formal bow.

"Glad to see you back, Sir," he barked.

Meera smiled. "Glad to be back. Let's go inside."

Once the door was closed, Meera jumped right in. "Any word from the desert?"

He shook his head regretfully. "Nothing yet."

"Any reports from Lhasa on our movements?"

"No one heard your morning journey to your retired honeycomb, but there were reports of your visit to Susu's. Cadence San had asked for Penna's palmpad to be tracked down and found it as it was leaving Susu's. Everyone knows by now of the loss." He lifted his hand as if to squeeze her shoulder but dropped it. "I'm sorry for it, Meera. To lose a sister…"

He had enough experience with that, she thought, Celio's face drifting across her mind. "Yes, well," Meera responded. "At least they didn't spot Penna any earlier. We were lucky."

"I transferred the recordings in your Rail to the empty one behind it, as you instructed, so you weren't recorded coming here. Did you bring the Banjarian back?"

"I did. That's why I am here, really. I need you to stay here in the common room tonight and coach her. I want her to ease into the training sessions tomorrow as if she's always been here. She'll need an introduction to all the lessons you will be doing tomorrow."

"She would need to go to Loupan for Sepa pockets."

Meera scoffed. "We are not really going to make her a Sepa!"

"Will you send her back to the Banjar as a trader without them?" he asked, incredulous.

Meera nodded. "I plan on returning her to Tumail. We can add her number to the list of Sepas who died on duty and leave her there. She'll be happy to be home free, I'm sure."

"But we know she was organizing against the Family."

Meera cocked a brow at him. "And what, exactly, are we doing?"

Kiro kicked his head back in surprise. After a moment, he smiled and said "Research."

Meera shook her head. "It's all muddled now, isn't it? The good guys and the bad guys. I need to know what they're doing at that base. I feel like the answers must be there."

Kiro smiled softly. "Thank you for doing this. It's all Celio wanted."

They had mourned Celio's death together, before Kiro had told her about Celio's suspicions about Tashi. She'd never told Meera, maybe afraid that Meera was too close to the Family to keep it a secret.

"Did the Banjarian tell you anything about the base?"

"Not yet. We haven't had much of a chance with everything that's happened with Mishka. And Penna," she added to herself.

"What happened to Penna San?"

"She..." Kiro didn't know about Penna's origins. She had kept that a secret from everyone, including her own wife. "She had a breakdown after finding Mishka's body."

He nodded solemnly.

"I want to bring Story in now, but I don't think we should talk in front of Hui. The poor child will have too many secrets to carry back to the palace with him as it is. But my first priority right now is to feed us."

He smiled. "Let me take care of it. I'll send a meal to Hui's bunk and three here. I'll pick the Banjarian up on my way back."

She sighed. "Perfect. Thank you, Kiro."

"At your service, Meera San." With that, he hurried through the door. Just before it closed behind him, Meera shot to her feet.

'Kiro! Why don't you take care of the food and I'll pick up Story. I think she'll feel more comfortable to walk with someone she knows."

With a quizzical look on his face and a slow nod of assent, he left, walking a few feet ahead of her until he switched directions. She hurried on toward Story's bunk, bewildered at her own feelings. Kiro was one of her very best friends, one of her only confidants. And yet. And yet she didn't trust him to be alone with Story. How could anyone trust a Bhutanese to be kind to a Banjarian rebel?

When she came to Story's bunk, she found her sitting straight up on her cot, staring at the wall across from her. Meera was again struck by how small these bunks were, no larger than her broom closet in the Su Song Dome. Story turned to give her a stony glare.

"I see you now," her gravelly voice spat, "You going to lock me up in this."

"I'm not locking you—"

"That door locked 'til you come through."

Meera looked back at the door, "Well, that's just an automatic lock for the safety of the Sepas."

"If it's for them, why isn't the lock on their side?" She stood up and there wasn't room for a step between them. "Take me back to Tumail," she said quietly, her voice rippling with a threat.

"Story, it's safe here. I—"

"I am not your slave, Bhutan." She grabbed Meera's chin tightly. "And I will not be kept in this box."

Meera was frightened but felt a thick wave of shame flow over her. This was a box. She'd been keeping women in these boxes for years.

"Story, I—I came so we can talk about the base and Sepora. Will you agree to do that if I take you to Tumail afterward?"

Story eyed her suspiciously. "Where's the boy?" she asked finally. "Is he boxed up in one'these as well?"

"No! He's... well, he's eating in my room."

Story nodded slowly, taking this in and deciding if it was true.

"Alright then. Let's talk." She released her chin and took a small step back to give Meera room to turn around.

With a shaky breath, Meera left the bunk and led the way to the Briefing Room.

Kiro was already back, setting up the listening equipment on the center table. When they came in, he looked up and smiled. "Dinner is on the way, Meera San." He looked at Story, his voice losing all of its warmth. "Have a seat."

"Who you now?" Story demanded.

Meera stepped in, guiding her to the table by the elbow. "This is my dearest friend and assistant, Kiro. This is the person who kept my honeycomb and the Rail we took silenced."

Story squinted at him and gave a decisive nod of approval, sitting down.

"What are you doing with all that?" Meera asked Kiro, taking a seat next to Story.

"Setting up to record the conversation."

"Don't you think we should keep this as undocumented as possible?" They were trying to silence all of their conversations, but he was gearing up to record the most sensitive one of all.

"Meera San," he said gently, 'to silence this moment would be to protect us if this doesn't go well. But to record it could aid in protecting everyone else." He tilted his head at her. "We will need proof of what he's doing if you truly want to stop him."

"Stop who?" Story demanded.

"Dorji Tashi," both said at the same time.

"The Dragon?" Story asked in disbelief. "You two are plotting to take down the Dragon?"

Meera was rubbing her jaw, still tender from Story's grip. "Not necessarily," she said finally. "We're really just after the truth."

Story frowned at her in confusion and Meera realized she owed Story an explanation. "In the last few years, we've noticed things shifting. People in both Rings are disappearing from their homes. Systems are breaking down and no one is fixing them. Several families in the last month never received their supply delivery. And the Sepas," she glanced at Kiro. "The Sepas are disappearing right and left."

To her surprise, Story barked a laugh. "No food? People disappearing? Sounds like you're getting a taste of the Banjar."

Meera blushed crimson but powered on. "Well, we hope that the marriage between Cadence and Penna could turn the tide for an alliance between New Bhutan and the Banjar. There's a rumor that Tashi is going to hand over the Heart to Penna."

Story's eyes widened. "Penna? That Tumailian is about to be the Dragon?"

The words came out in slow motion for Meera as she realized that no one had told the Banjarian they had been forced along for the ride to keep Penna's origins a secret.

Kiro was looking at her, brows raised in surprise.

Meera kept her eyes on her hands as she cut them through the air, detailing her plan and ignoring Kiro's look. "Penna is the key. We have to convince her to allow the Banjarians within the barrier. "

She gave Story a meaningful glare before continuing. "I lied and *told* her that she was born a Banjarian. I thought it could do something to start a shift. I thought if she saw herself in them she would have some empathy." She threw a pointed glance at Kiro and added, "I know she seems like a monster, but she used to be good. She could be good. My faan, Asaka the Just, believed in her and so do I. I just thought that—"

"Your faan was Asaka the Just?" Story interjected, sounding astonished.

Meera coughed, nodding and hoping that Story wouldn't reveal anything else.

Kiro sounded equally taken aback when he asked, "You convinced Penna she was born Banjarian?"

"I think so."

Kiro, nor anyone else, need know Penna's secret. It was her secret to share.

She shot Story another meaningful glance, hoping she would pick up on the game she was playing. She didn't.

"But when Penna saw the vul—"

"I know we have a lot to process," Meera interrupted, "but my first priority right now is getting Sepora off that base. Can you tell me what you saw?"

Story bit her lip and nodded.

"I saw... a lake." Story closed her eyes and leaned her head back. "A shimmerin', blue and green water that went longer than you could see. Men were swimming in it. And there were trees. There were green trees all around it, like the Earth come to life; like in a legend. The colors... I've never seen anything, or even dreamed anything, so beautiful."

Meera frowned. That couldn't be right.

She exchanged a dubious look with Kiro. A lake? That was impossible.

"We landed and 288 was taken one way; I was taken another." Story continued, oblivious to Meera's reaction. "The man threw me over his shoulder. I was... my wrists and my legs were bound. My mouth, too. I could only see the ground. It was made of stone, with bits of brown and green falling from the treetops. We came to a small building and he took me down; down some steps into a cool, damp place. He told me they would be back for training in an hour. Before that happened, though, 288 was thrown in as well, looking beat up around the face."

Trees, now? First a lake and now trees. She was starting to think this might have been a waste of time. None of it made any sense. She'd had suspicions that it was a prison. It would explain why people were going missing. But this...

"Story..." she began, "I need you to give us the facts. The truth."

Story cocked a brow at her. "If you're not going to believe what I say, then why you asking?"

"But...a lake? The earth outside New Bhutan is dry. That's why we bring you water."

Story huffed and then laughed. "It would be hard to believe if I hadn't seen it with my own eyes."

She met Kiro's gaze again, this time with a touch of hope. A lake. Water, in the Banjar.

If it was true, then everything—everything—had changed. The world had changed.

And Tashi had kept it a secret.

Her rage at Tashi and joy in this news of Earth coiled together to constrict her heart until she felt like she couldn't breathe.

Story put a hand on her chest, concern knitting her brow. "You okay?"

Meera took a shaky breath.

"Were there other captives there?" Kiro asked.

Story shook her head, keeping an eye on Meera but taking her hand back. "Just me and 288 until the man came to train us. 288 broke his face open, though, and told me to run. She said take the lake all the way to the Eastern corner and to head for Tumail. To call your name once I had it in my sights. I made it to the edge of the trees with no incident... She was screaming her head off to distract them. Then... I was standing in a line of trees out of sight from the houses, far away from anything or anyone but the water and the trees."

Still trying to regulate her breathing, she looked up to meet Story's gaze.

"It was like nothing you could imagine. In one direction, it was just trees and water for as far as you could see. I thought Miracle might walk out of the water any minute, that place was so much like a dream. It was so hard to turn away and run the other way, straight into the desert, but I did. I ran straight toward my death."

"Straight into the desert?" Meera repeated.

Story nodded.

Meera's head fell into her hands as she tried to sort it out. "There wasn't a gate or door to exit the barrier?"

Story shook her head. "There was no barrier, Meera. It was just a few rows of trees and then some dry grasses, and then desert. I looked back a few times just to make sure it had been real, and there it was."

Kiro sat down next to her. "And there were Banjarians *swimming* in the water?"

Story shrugged. "Hard to say where they were from. 288 and I saw them as we landed in the helio. So. That's all I know."

"What did you mean by "train" you?"

"I never had the chance to find out."

Meera glanced at Kiro. "Labor?"

He shrugged. "It's possible…"

"But with that timeline, I would have picked you up the same day you were taken. What are you leaving out?" Meera challenged. "It was nearly two weeks before you called my name."

Story took a deep breath and leaned back, eyeing Meera steadily.

"She asked you a question," Kiro barked.

Meera lifted a hand to stay his interruption and waited.

"This whole story could be a fabrication, Meera. You can't trust a thing she says."

"She's not lying," Meera mused, keeping her eyes on Story, "but she is leaving something out."

Story was a force to be reckoned with, and their silent staring match lasted longer than she'd expected it to.

Finally, Story caved. With a quiet venom in her voice, she asked "Do you know who you are to me, Meera San?"

"Do tell."

"The enemy."

Meera snort-laughed. "The enemy? You are aware that I run the Project that brings you food and water? That I am the one keeping the barrier open for trade with your people?"

"At what price?"

"Excuse me?"

"I've never seen you delivering food or water."

"It's not that simple—"

"It is. You've decided the path you take is noble, even as you step over the bodies of these Sepas to walk it. Even as you charge the Banjarians prices they must risk their lives to pay. Did you know that in Tumail, we lose people just as often to the mines as we do to starvation? More than we do to the Banjarguay? Our bravest and strongest are lost on quests to find trinkets for your Family. So don't say you are bringing us food and water as if you're a damn messiah back from The Old World."

Kiro went to respond and Meera again held up her hand in protest.

"Okay," she said quietly. "So I work within the system I was given and do the best I can. It isn't perfect. That's why I am here. Now stop deflecting. Where were you those two weeks?"

"My point is, I don't trust you. You believe doing good can come at the cost of other people's lives. Makes me question your values. Where I was will not help or hurt your plans to save her, so that story's stayin' with me." She fixed them with a glare. "Now, what will you do to help Sepora?"

Meera gritting her teeth in frustration. Didn't this fool know that every detail mattered? Her words had stung enough, however, for her to let it go for now. "Well," she said tightly, "it's certainly not much to go on. Could you tell at all what they were doing besides swimming?"

"No. We saw a lot of buildings 'round the lake, though, so they're doing something."

Meera looked at Kiro. "If there's no barrier, then the idea of a second dome is out."

Kiro nodded.

"And if Dorji didn't build a second dome, then it must be a prison. Why would prisoners be kept at a real *lake*? A natural water source... it could change everything. Are you sure it was a real lake?" she asked Story skeptically.

"You could always go see for yourself," she replied dryly.

Meera rubbed her face with both palms. "You're right." She turned to Kiro and said again, "She's right. If there's no barrier to get through, we would just need to go the same way Story left and ease our way in. Besides…I need to see this for myself."

"And what if you're caught and brought back to Potala to face Tashi's judgement?"

"I'm practically his daughter. What would he do?"

"He'd throw you right where he threw us," Story said flatly.

A Sepa came to the door with their food then, a steaming platter of red rice and mashed eggplant for them to share.

Meera almost melted in relief. "I'm starving."

Story raised a brow at her and again Meera felt the heat rise to her face. The embarrassment didn't stop her from diving into the food. Story, on the other hand, merely picked at it.

"Not to your taste?" Kiro asked mockingly.

"We only eat one meal in Tumail. I won't be hungry until morning."

Kiro dropped his eyes awkwardly.

At least I'm not the only one acting a fool, Meera thought wryly.

There was a sudden pounding on the door. Meera stood, casting an uneasy glance at them. Kiro reached his hand out to Story, beckoning her away. She followed him and let him tuck her into a large cabinet built into the wall. Nodding her approval, Meera opened the door with her heart pounding.

Her body sagged with relief as Hui darted around her and ran to the table, holding a cup of fried okra in one hand and his new encyclopedia in the other.

"Kiro!" he cried in excitement, "You will never guess what I found!" Each word was punctuated by his efforts to put the book on the table, open it, and find the page.

Story unfolded herself out of the cabinet and came to sit at the table with Hui.

Hui found the page he was looking for and smacked the book triumphantly, looking at Kiro. When he only stared at the picture drawn inside, he frowned.

"Don't you remember? It's the thing from the trading log! You told me you didn't know what it was. It's here! In the encyclopedia."

Meera was watching Kiro carefully. His face had gone pale and she could see his jaw working with tension. She glanced down at the book.

"What is it, Hui?"

He cleared his throat dramatically. "It's called a respirator mask but it's in the biological warfare section because that seems like the best picture they could get. Biological warfare is invisible, that's why." His eyes widened dramatically at the word "invisible."

"You've seen this?" she asked Kiro.

"It came in as a trade from the Dredgers a few years before you started. The palace was anxious to pick it up. They asked that the trade remain off file." He looked ashamed of himself, but Meera understood why he would have kept it from her. She would have kept it from him, too. "I drew it in the book anyway, for my own record, but didn't add who took it."

"What is biological warfare?" Story asked, looking at the picture with distaste.

Hui read the description aloud. "Biological warfare is the use of airborne chemicals or disease to kill an enemy in war."

"That's how the super powers killed each other in the Great War," Meera murmured. She looked at Story. "They wanted to kill the people but keep the land, so any sort of traditional weapons were off the table. Unfortunately for them, the illness spread out of control and ended up infecting almost everyone."

"And," Kiro added, "it still does. Those diseases still infect the earth and reach out to infect the people."

Story's face went pale. "The Banjarguay."

Meera nodded solemnly.

"The respirator mask provides clean air from a tank on your back so you can survive around the disease," Hui explained.

Meera frowned at Kiro. "So why was the palace anxious to have it?"

Kiro shrugged. "I don't know."

32

———

S EPORA

SOMEONE WAS SCREAMING. Sepora tried to open her eyes, but she found them to be too heavy. She reached out in the dark, trying to find the source of the sound, but could only feel unfamiliar objects. She strained to open her eyes with all her might, and they fluttered for a moment before falling closed again. In that moment of sight, it was only a bright red world. Taking a calming breath, her body and mind started to come to, and she realized with a gasp that she was in excruciating pain.

Her eyes inched open as she tried to sit up, but the slight movement caused a wave of agony to ride up her leg and left side. The blurred objects around her began to spin. She turned her head to the side and retched. Panting, she tried opening her eyes again, careful to keep her body still.

The objects around her were not only distorted from her blurred vision. What were once knobs and dials were now a mashed pile of metal. She was still in the helio, but it had been crushed around her. A large pillow of sorts had inflated in front of the dash, protecting her from the impact and shattered glass on the other side. It was covered in splats of blood and vomit and emanated a deep orange glow. Gingerly, she looked down at the rest of her body.

Kinsu's robes were soaked red and a massive shard of glass was protruding from it along her side. Sepora thought dully that it would have been nice to have pillows along the side doors as well as the front. Her leg was twisted half around, caught under the warped metal of the chair.

She took a shuddering breath and thought for a minute, giving herself the steps to get out of this, no matter how painful it might be. Almost methodically, she began.

The first step was to take off the top of her robes so she could use the sleeves to staunch the blood at her side.

Gritting her teeth, she tried to pull the sleeves down behind her without sitting up. The pain made reality ink away for a moment and she had to pause. *You can't go to sleep, 288*, she thought. After a few more deep breaths, she tried again, this time managing to quickly pull off one side with a scream of pain.

Breathe.

She pulled the fabric under her waist and tossed the ends up over her stomach. The whole ordeal took several tries, black webs inching across her vision with every movement. She was thinking about Penna for some reason. Poor Penna, always forgetting.

Wake up, 288.

Sepora let out a few frustrated sobs. She didn't think she could do it, but knew she had to. Holding the fabric in one hand and gripping the glass shard in another, she wrenched the glass from her body.

Tie it.

She obeyed, knotting a tight cinch around her waist before passing out completely.

Sepora dreamed she was sitting on the couch in Blossom House with Penna San. Penna was staring unseeing out onto the lake, with dark bags under her eyes and bruises along her arms. Sepora was braiding her hair. They were quiet, the only sound the soft lapping of the water against the shore. Sepora felt at peace. Without warning, Penna's hand snapped up and grabbed her wrist, stopping her movement. She turned and looked her in the eye, her expression terrified. Urgently, Penna cried "Wake up!"

Sepora's eyes snapped open to find that she was gasping sobs. Settling her breathing, she tried to look at her leg without moving her head. She had been flung out of her own chair and was half in Ruby's, half on what was once the dash. Her left leg was free to move around, but her right foot and calf had been smashed as the seat was crushed. She would have to pull the seat up if she were to move at all.

The wound on her side made it nearly impossible to bend forward and pull the metal with her arms, but her left leg had some potential. She craned her leg so that her foot could inch between the chair and her other leg. Gritting her teeth, she strained her foot forward. The metal didn't budge. Her foot wasn't strong enough. Cursing, she tried inching her body into a fetal position, trying to get closer to the chair with her hands. Her fingertips grazed the lip of the chair.

You can do this, 288. One last push.

With a guttural scream, she bent into a full crouch, grabbed the chair with both palms, and pulled with all her might. The feel of the metal moving was so slight, she wasn't sure if it had even happened. She brought her body back to where it had been, panting.

After a few minutes of getting her breathing under control, she tried to wiggle her trapped leg. Shuddering with the pain, she pulled on her thigh.

With another yelp, she watched her mangled leg come free of the chair. Nausea overtook her and she vomited again, this time unable to turn her head.

She thought about how grateful she was that Ruby wasn't here with her. Ruby was safe in Tumail. Sai San would be coming for her, though. He must have deactivated his palmpad from a distance, shutting the clearance for use of the helio off. She wondered if the palmpad could be tracked at this distance. Reaching into her pocket, she felt for the thin stick. To her satisfaction, she found that it was smashed into little shards. He probably could guess where she was headed, but at least he didn't know for sure.

Either way, she needed to get out of sight fast. He would be coming for her.

The helio was on its side; the door facing the ground was crushed and had left a hole for her to ease out through, but moving feet first was not an option. She tilted her head back and looked at the other door. This one was tilted toward the sky and had received little damage. She would just need to open it and pull herself out.

She reached her arms up and pushed on the door with a grunt. It inched open and then fell back again. A frustrated sob slipped from her lips.

You giving up now, 288? I thought you were a real Sepa, not a Bhutanese baby.

It was Kiro's drill sergeant's voice in her mind, yelling at her to stop being so weak.

She pushed again, this time adding some leverage by pushing with her right leg. The door flung open and stayed there. Sepora resisted the urge to bring her arms down to rest and instead gripped the open rim along the door.

The pain of the next few moments was so severe that Sepora must have blacked out, because when she next opened her eyes, she was splayed out on the baking sand near the crashed helio and both her side and leg were screaming in pain.

She opened her eyes and tried to take in where she was. Outside the bubble of the crashed helio, she found that the sun was nearly gone. Its fiery red burned low in the sky, causing the desert's dunes to be striped with red, orange, and lines of dark shadow. On her right, the wall of the barrier began and arched steeply into the sky. She was only a few hundred yards away. About a mile past the dome, she could see the cliffs that marked the beginning of New Bhutan and the small line of buildings that was her home, the Sepa Bunkers.

She rolled onto her belly and pulled her arms up, fists before her face and elbows akimbo. Inch by inch, she began to drag herself toward the dome. With the friction of the ground, her cinch soon loosened and then fell off altogether. She could feel the blood draining from her body with every minute, but she kept pulling. She just had to make it to the dome.

When they had approved the SEPA Project and opened the barrier, they didn't want to take any chances of Banjarians breaking in. Every door was a hundred feet in the sky, accessible only by helio. At ground level, however, there was a strip of tech for identifying a clearance to enter. This was made for Sepas or Bhutanese who may have been trapped outside the barrier somehow and need to get back. It would alert the Briefing Room that someone was at the gate.

With a few feet to go, Sepora started to lose consciousness. Half of her mind was in the desert, while the other was in her mind's eye, watching Penna in the Blossom House.

She was rubbing her pregnant belly absently. Sai San was sitting just behind her, blood pouring from his palms. He rubbed her arms lovingly, as if he couldn't tell that he was smearing blood over those bruises. He kissed her neck, but she ignored him, still looking like her mind was a million miles away. Sai reached around and grabbed her face, pulling it to face him. "I named you," he whispered fervently. "I named you. You're all that matters to me."

"I named you," Sepora whispered to herself. She was stretched out along the cool texture of the dome, bathed in the last rays of sunset. Her eyes fluttered open and she thought about how beautiful the Banjar truly was. Red and gold and black, the ground rippling across the Earth forever. She remembered the painting, set in this exact spot, where the skeletal remains dined on Bhutan bread. Death's feast.

She imagined her body added to the painting, a small skeleton lying before the table.

It felt like where she belonged, like she had never intended on heading anywhere else.

She looked to her left and was surprised to see Penna sitting next to her in the Banjar, looking at her with a soft smile playing on her lips. Her bruises were gone.

"Just raise your arm high, Sepora. It should reach the strip."

"I can't," she whispered.

"You can. We are all counting on you."

Sepora's eyes filled with tears. Penna was right. Ruby needed her to get her memories back to her. The Rue's needed to be liberated.

She had made a vow to Miracle that she would discover the truth about the Family. She would find out if they had lied about having a cure for the Banjarguay, and if they had, she would bring that cure to the Banjar. And now, Sepora needed to ask Meera if the pieces she was fitting together in her brain were true.

She needed to live.

Blinking away her tears, she found that Penna wasn't there after all. The sun fell below the horizon and suddenly the Banjar was dipped in darkness.

With one last cry, she lifted her arm into the air.

PART V

THE FEAST

33

M EERA

She was thinking of when a lover's hand is less than an inch away and you feel that distance so fiercely it's as if you're already touching anyway. That's what it felt like tonight with Celio. She felt so close to her. So close that if she just turned her head fast enough, she would see her sitting there beside her. She could feel that excited energy she would get, urging her to keep pushing.

She leaned back in her chair, dropping the study of her notes in frustration. The plan to have everyone get some rest in a bunker hadn't worked out. Story had flat out refused to sleep in the locked Sepa bunker, so Meera had offered her the sofa in the Briefing Room. Hui wanted to wait for her to go back to her rooms but had fallen asleep before she and Kiro were finished. Unfortunately for all of them, she still didn't have the finish line in her sights.

She and Kiro were sitting at the briefing table, drawing and writing on the board behind it. So far, they had made a map of the lake base as far as they could see it from Story's retelling. Seeing it drawn out, she had been able to give them a few more details on shape and size. They had created a list of strange happenings that could mean something along the left:

Prisoners are to be "trained" by a young man. No prisoners in sight

A real, swimmable lake exists

There is (presumably) no barrier over the lake base

Sepora said to mind the trees. Possible danger?

Susu and Mishka perform gishiki shinju, leaving a suicide note with the maxim on it. Possibly blaming Tashi?

She had added the last one after Hui fell asleep.

"It's not much to go on, is it?" Kiro asked.

"No. It isn't. But at least we have a map. I think I'll take a helio when the moon's almost gone. Anyone at the lake will likely be asleep. I... I can probably find that room Story and her were locked in. Maybe they took her back there."

Kiro tapped his charcoal on the table. "Meera..."

"Yes?"

"I just wonder." He rocked back in his chair a bit. "I've known you for a long time. I know you are a passionate person, but... Sepas go missing all the time. They are meant to be disposable. They're built to do the job until they die, and honestly, 288 lasted longer than most."

She winced at that thought. She had sent all of those children out there. She had been appointed to take over the SEPA Project after years of dedicated work and training. Everyone had been so proud of Meera. Even Celio. She would be the protector of New Bhutan. And according to Celio, the protector of the Banjarians as well. *But what about*, she thought now, *the Sepas? Who was protecting them?*

She swallowed. "What's your point, Kiro?" she asked, already knowing.

He shrugged and raised his brows. "Why her? Why would you risk your life to go save this Sepa?"

"This Sepa was sent to retrieve sensitive information by me. I sent her in there," she could barely say the words, seeing how horrible it was for the first time. With a sick churn in her gut, she admitted that her fear for Sepora had been half manifested by her guilt. "I sent her in there," she started again, "so I could find out what Tashi was up to. I wanted to protect the Bhutanese from whatever he was doing."

"And it didn't work, Meera, so let's make a new plan. One that doesn't include risking your life." He tried to tuck a strand of hair away from her eyes, but she brushed him away, jumping to her feet.

"And why is risking my life so terrible when we care nothing about hers?"

Kiro raised his hands helplessly. "Because," he said, "that's their way. That's where she belongs. They all go one way or another out there, Meera." He was looking at her like he had never seen her before; speaking to her as if she were a confused child.

At her angry silence, he continued. "Meera, they are serving New Bhutan and the Banjar. Without their help, the Banjarians would have died a long time ago. We are doing what we are able to do for their wellbeing."

"Did you know the doors to their bunkers lock them in?"

"Of course. I run the bunkers."

"Well what if they need to use the latrine, Kiro? Or see the moon in the middle of the night?"

"They swipe their ID chip and request to." He let out a sharp laugh and threw his hands up. "They're happy here, Meera. It's better than what happens to the other extra children in New Bhutan."

Meera stopped and peered at him. "What do you mean, other children?"

She watched him realize he'd said too much. "The Quántóu," he said quietly, knowing there was no way to lie to her.

"Quántóu? How could a Quántóu's fate be worse than a Sepa's?"

Kiro was nodding slowly as if he was talking himself into something. Finally, he looked at her and shrugged. "All I know is they disappear right and left, too."

Meera stared at him for a moment before turning abruptly and adding that fact to their list.

Quántóu disappear from New Bhutan.

She stared at it, thinking again that if she just turned around fast enough, she was sure she'd find Celio right behind her, looking at it too. Instead of turning, she found herself writing.

Celio dies.

She felt Kiro's body stiffen beside her. He still didn't talk about his sister.

"Why is that on the list?" he asked thickly.

She turned to him. "There are different ways that people disappear. My sister disappeared from our lives last night, and we don't know why. Celio disappeared from our lives. We don't know why."

"I don't thin—"

His voice was cut off by a sharp whirring sound at the Listener board. A small beeping began under the whirring, and both got progressively louder. Kiro looked at her, eyes wide in astonishment.

"Someone's at the gate."

Meera ran to the Listening board with Kiro close behind her. The scanner read the identification chip.

"It's her!" she cried, barely believing it to be true. "It says 288 on the identification tag." She turned to him with tears in her eyes. She blinked them away, trying to think.

"We can't know what to expect," she said. "Get Story into the Blue Room and take Hui to bed in my bunker. I'll be back." She turned to leave but he grabbed her arm.

"Be careful."

She nodded and rushed out.

The Family kept four of the seven helios in the world. Yutan kept two for delivering produce, and the Sepa Bunkers had one. It was parked in the fields on the opposite side of the gardens, so Meera had a distance to cross. She crossed it at a flat out run.

Although her breathing was ragged and her heart racing, her hands were sure and steady as they lifted the helio into the air and flew straight for the barrier. Kiro had accepted the request back at the

Listener's wall, raising the gate in the dome. Small blue lights erupted around the edges of the gate, creating a guide for the helio.

"I'm coming, Sepora," she whispered.

Meera had never been outside the barrier after dark.

Maybe she had been scared to be at the mercy of the universe without a dome over her head; to have nothing between herself and space. She realized this when the helio exited, gasping aloud at the difference. The dome was meant to be barely discernible, but it was still there. In New Bhutan, there were two lights that lit up the night. The moon and one star.

The clarity of this night's sky exploding across the desert was the most beautiful thing she had ever seen. The endless void before her seemed to be swallowing the world. She forgot for a moment her urgent purpose. Her helio hung in the air, stilled, as she took in the layers of stars and the barely discernible dance of black, blue, and purple that made up this marvel before her.

She had been lied to. She pulled her gaze from the stars and looked down and out at the rolling hills of the desert; this stunning expanse of earth. She felt as though she'd been wearing a blindfold all her life, and only in this moment ripped it away.

She swung her helio around slowly, letting her light reveal the dips and turns of the sand. It was in that turn that she was snapped to her senses by the sight of a helio smashed to bits in a dune. Her heart jumped into her throat and she swept the desert, looking for any sign of Sepora outside the wreckage. She was just thinking she should lower the helio near the crash and look for a body when she saw her against the barrier, crumpled on the ground. A wide circle of dark sand bled out around her.

Her stomach dropped. She rushed to land next to her, grabbing the first aid kit from behind her seat.

Jumping from the helio into the night, she rushed to Sepora's side, careful not to look up for fear she would fall into the sky.

The girl was unconscious but still alive. She was breathing shallowly. After saying her name once, Meera thought better of trying to wake her up and just set to work.

The wound in Sepora's side was small in diameter but obviously deep. Meera opened the first aid kit she'd brought along and found a bottle of water and a bottle of antiseptic. She cleaned the sand from the hole as best she could, poured on the antiseptic, and opened her stitch kit. Taking a moment to quell the shaking in her hands, she began to sew up Sepora's flesh. It might have made her queasy if it had not been Sepora's life at stake. The stitches were poorly done but training only went so far without any hands-on practice.

She used bandage tape to wrap around her waist and keep the stitches tight. To her relief, she didn't see any red blots leaking through.

She scanned the rest of her body for wounds. She had a few cuts on her head, a gash in her palm, and her leg was twisted around the wrong way. Meera used scissors to cut away the robes she was wearing, realizing that they were men's robes.

She glanced back at her face curiously, as if she would explain. The leg needed equipment she didn't have in her first aid kit. She tried wrapping it, but it didn't do much. She glanced back at the helio, realizing she was going to have to carry Sepora and lift her in. If she could just get her to the bunker, she would be fine. Sepora's face was pale and Meera tried to forget how much blood was on the ground. She would be fine.

Meera picked her up like a groom carrying his bride and placed her as gingerly as she could in the second seat. Rushing to the other side, she jumped in and set them into flight. It was then that Sepora's eyes fluttered.

"Meera."

Meera's eyes filled with tears of relief. "I'm here, my girl."

"Penna." Sepora's eyes were closed, her head lolled to one side.

"Penna is okay, too," Meera said, having no idea why Sepora would be saying her sister's name.

"Meera?"

"I'm right here. Rest now. We'll talk soon."

Sepora's chest heaved with dry sobs. "I know. I will."

Meera glanced over and realized that Sepora wasn't talking to her.

She pressed her thumb to pinky. "Kiro."

"Boss."

"Bring a gurney out to the landing pad. I got her, but she's in bad shape."

She quit the comm and glanced at Sepora again. Her eyes were open now but stared out into the night unseeing. "Sepora?" she cried, terrified that the girl was dead.

Her eyes closed, causing a single tear to run down her cheek.

"Meera... take these memories. Every one." She panted at the effort, eyes still closed. "Take them before I'm gone... and... they're gone."

"You're not going anywhere, Sepora."

Meera was landing the helio on the cliffside and Kiro was already running toward them with the gurney. He picked her up with ease and strapped her safely in, heading back to the briefing room. "Did she say anything?" he asked as they ran.

"Not really. She crashed a helio out in the desert."

Kiro whistled. "A fighter."

Meera just nodded, hoping that fighting spirit wasn't going to give up yet.

"I think we should take her to the Blue Room with Story," she said suddenly.

"There's a hospital ward here with—"

"She stole a helio. How did she do that?"

Kiro looked at her. "She used someone else's palmpad."

Meera nodded. "They're probably on their way to find her and bring her back."

"Blue Room," he agreed.

In the Great War, the bunkers had been equipped with hidden shelters underground. They were meant to protect soldiers if there was a bomb dropped. In the Last War, the war along their border as the barrier was being finished, a general had made the bomb shelter into a secret hideaway by creating hidden doors under the floorboards and covering up the original doors.

He had known that anyone who'd had any access to a bomb was

now dead. The people at their door were beggars at this point, fighting for their lives. He'd had a great sympathy for them and used the Blue Room as a place to smuggle them in during the fight. During the Last War, Banjarians were living right underneath New Bhutan's briefing room. Of course, that was before they were considered Banjarians. Then, they were just people.

Meera and Kiro knew about this because one of their prized relics was the man's journal. It was Celio who had found the journal long before they had met. She had done a dramatic reading of it for them, bringing everyone to tears.

As the years passed, Celio had become more radical. She would be working, but always picking up tidbits of information about the Banjar and Tashi. She would come home and pour it out into her paintings or, if she hadn't been inspired, would read the encyclopedias and the Trading Logs, looking for something to be suspicious of.

The Blue Room was a secret among the three of them. It had been long forgotten by the palace and was the perfect place to hide two refugees. The trapdoor was under the heavy table in the center of the room. Kiro had already pushed the table aside and brought Story down, so the hole was open for them to carry the gurney down. The Blue Room earned its name from the lights set into the brick circling the perimeter of the room at ankle and waist height. The "room" was in fact a maze of rooms, common and private spaces, kitchens, and even a toilet system like they had used in the Old World (disabled, of course). Now, all waste was recycled on site.

As they lumbered awkwardly down the steps, Story rushed to their side. "Is she alright?"

"No," Kiro barked. "Can you get water for her? There's a supply in the ice box."

"Where's the ice—"

"Go!"

Story nodded, glancing at Sepora's inert form before running up the steps.

"Where are we taking her?" Meera asked, leading the gurney.

"Let's keep her on the gurney. We don't want to move her around much. By the lights along the wall. I want to check her wound."

"Meera?" Sepora breathed, eyes closed.

Meera's eyes filled with tears of relief. "I'm here."

"Empty me."

"You're safe now."

"Empty me."

"Sepora. You don't know what you're saying."

Sepora's eyes opened and her palm stretched out toward her.

Meera took her hand and crouched down next to her.

"I'm their daughter," she said thickly. "You're my family, Meera. And Hui." Tears rolled down her cheeks. She took a rattling breath, eyes closed.

Meera's eyes went wide with shock. After years of wondering *what if*. What if? She felt at once validated and sick.

Sepora took a moment to catch her breath before opening her eyes to glare into Meera's. Her face twisted into the ghost of a smile. "Now you need to take it. Take it all."

Meera tried to speak, but Sepora stopped her.

"You need to know. You need to see." Her eyes were closed again. "The painting... the painting. We break bread."

Story came running down the stairs with Hui in tow.

"We have water!" Hui shouted, running to Sepora's side. At seeing her, concern immediately bled across his face.

Sepora opened her eyes and smiled faintly. "There you are," she said to him.

"Why is he here?" Kiro demanded angrily.

Story put her hands up helplessly. "I didn't know where the water would be."

Kiro grabbed the water from Hui, cursing under his breath, and asked Sepora to tip her face and drink. The effort made her slip back into unconsciousness.

Kiro began to unwrap her side tape, casting a glance at Meera. "Go upstairs to the Emptying Room and bring down the equipment. Story can help you carry the board."

Meera's eyes widened. "I'm not going to empty her! You know that memories don't come back the same. They're jumbled and pieces are missing. And we need to know what she knows now, from her. We can't just store that information in a vial."

Story stepped between them. "288 knows what she's giving up. If she thinks it's worth it, it is."

Meera cast one more pained glance at Sepora and nodded, running up the steps. Sepora was not going to die.

She's not going to die, she repeated to herself. *I just got her back.*

The Listener's board burst into life as she was rushing past, making her cry out in surprise. It lit up and there was a crackle of sound. A broadcaster's voice was welcoming them to a required message.

The mic switched to a booming amplification of Cadence's voice.

"There has never been a woman more qualified to be my bride. I am thrilled beyond bounds to welcome New Bhutan in joining us tonight, as we celebrate our love and our engagement."

Cadence's voice was traded out for Dori Tashi's boisterous laugh, making Meera's skin crawl. "New Bhutan! What a pleasure it is to celebrate with you tonight. This is a special evening for me. My son is engaged to a beautiful woman. And, if you must know, I have decided to give that beautiful woman a very special wedding gift. My own heart!" He was slurring his words and laughed at his own joke. "Oh no, don't worry, I won't be stealing her away. I mean that as of tonight, I will be retiring as your Heart."

There was a moment when the stunned silence seemed to crackle through the system. It was as if all of New Bhutan had held their breath.

"My reign has been long and peaceful," he continued. "The people of New Bhutan have served me well, as I hope I have served them. It is time for this Heart to slow its beat. Tonight is not just about an engagement, but about a change in rule, a brighter future. I am passing my Heart to the great Penna San, as soon as these two are wed! To Penna San! Long may she beat!" he cried.

A chorus of "long may she beat" swelled through the speaker along with the roar of applause.

Meera nearly fainted in relief. *He's handing Penna the Heart.* It was all she had hoped for. With Penna as ruler, they could change everything.

Penna's voice, however, sliced Meera's hope like a dagger across the throat. It was flat and cold.

"I will serve you well, New Bhutan. I will work alongside your Eye, my beloved husband, to protect you from the Banjar more than ever before. New Bhutan is in grave condition." She paused for a moment to let her words sink in. "We've seen attacks. We've seen infiltration. The opening of our barrier has let in the monsters." The crowd fell dead silent, hanging on her every word. "You've seen the people disappearing from their beds. We see it, too. Your great Dragon has trusted me with the task of stopping them. It is with a hopeful Heart that I promise you great change in the future. Under my leadership, we will no longer rely on the Banjar for help. We will close down the SEPA Project, and we will close the barrier. That is my promise to you in my reign. Never will we need fear the Banjar again."

The crowd went wild with cheers, making a stingingly sharp screech erupt from the speakers.

Meera stood in shock, her head spinning. *How could she?*

Cadence took the mic back, his voice and nervous laugh revealing his own shock. "That is my passionate bride for you, Bhutan! She won't let you down. Now, enjoy the music, the dragon dancers, and of course, the spirits. Let's dance to greet the sun!"

34

———

C ADENCE

CADENCE WAS HAVING what might be his first panic attack. The laughing crowd swayed before his eyes, the lantern lights stabbed sharply at his vision, and his breathing was coming in tight gasps. His faan was clapping a man on the back next to him and his bride-to-be was standing still as a stone, staring out at the crowd with a small smile stamped on her face. Seldom Chime sat near Penna, watching her with a concerned frown.

He lifted a hand in a casual salute and turned away, breaking into a jog once he'd left the stage on Bankhar St. He ran to the left of the palace, seeking isolation near the deserted fire dragon fountain. He fell to his knees, body bent over the marble pool, and splashed water on his face.

After a few minutes, his breathing caught up with him. The water stilled and he could see his face reflected in the moonlit pool. The face of a failure. Cadence the Weak.

Dorji Tashi had told him to leave the Emptying Room. They would see him at the celebration. He had shut the door between them just as Penna was regaining consciousness. What could Cadence have done? He could have kicked the door open and told his faan that he wasn't leaving Penna's side. But he hadn't. He could have asked his faan what he intended to do with his bride, but he hadn't. Instead, he returned to Potala and was swept up into the approving and disapproving of different details for the party. Should the lanterns glow purple or red? Should the musicians play directly before the speech or after? Should there be a song playing during the speech? How much water should they offer, or should they keep it at spirits? Will they be available for interviews?

He had replied no to that last, having no idea if Penna would be feeling better. He told himself that Tashi was making sure she was safe and that her pain had stopped. He had known, though, with Kinsu in tow and the firm closing of that door, that Tashi might steal what she had just gotten back.

What he hadn't imagined was the truth. The Penna that greeted him on the stage was not Penna at all. His feisty friend had strong armor, but after so much time together, he could see right through it to the person underneath. This person had none of that. Her eyes were like stones, only lighting up at the thought of closing the barrier; igniting only in hatred for the Banjarians. Tashi had promised him that he would never fill anyone but a Rue. Why had he been stupid enough to believe him?

The moment of Tashi bursting into the Emptying Room played in his mind over and over.

"This is where he took me," she had said. Had she meant Tashi? How terrible it must have been to wake up to him there and Cadence gone. What a hero he had turned out to be.

She had spoken after her first memory had gone through. Then the second memory had made her start to convulse. Either it was too much in one sitting or truly horrific. There was no way for him to know for sure. The third memory... Cadence sat up straight, meeting eyes with the water dragon above him. The third memory never took.

What if it was still in the machine now? He glanced back toward Bankhar Street, still glowing with light and laughter. He looked the opposite way, where Luópán Hall rose into the night like a mountain, dark but for the reflected light of the party bouncing off glass. If he could find the third memory, at least Penna would have some of herself back.

Determined, he stood and started to make his way to Luópán's doors. Halfway down the path, his palmpad lit up. Fearing it was his faan looking for him, he made a plan to say he was on the other side of Bankhar Street, dancing, and he would catch up with him later. Instead, however, Sai's name lit up his palm. He pressed thumb to pinky.

"Cadence! Thank Dragons." Sai San's voice was desperate and rushed. "I've been trying to contact Tashi for over an hour, but he ignores his pad."

"Sai San, you're not at the party?" Cadence tried to make his tone casual.

"No. I'm in Qinghai."

His mouth twisted. He'd thought as much.

"Cadence, I need to speak to Dorji. Is he near?"

"He is not, and probably wouldn't be much help if he was. He's enjoying the spirits of the night."

Sai was silent for a moment, obviously weighing his options. "Cadence, fly a helio out here and pick me up."

"Sai, I'm at my own engagement party."

"Yes, I'm aware, but we have a security breach on our hands. It's... it's your Rue, in fact. Ocean."

Cadence's heart skipped a beat. "What about her?"

"She's gone awry. She poisoned us with extract from the sleeping darts, cut my identification chip out of my hand, and stole our only helio."

A broad smile broke across his face. She must have got her own personality back, he thought. That will teach them.

"Oh my," was all he could manage with a straight tone.

"She's probably headed back to the Sepa bunker. Sepas always run home to Meera. I need to get there and intercept her. Bring her back here."

The smile fell off Cadence's face. "I thought you had taken her back to the bunkers yesterday. Why does she need to be at the lake?"

"The girl's a criminal, Cadence! She attacked and nearly killed Kinsu and myself. Even without that attack, she's obviously learned too much about us. To let her go back, we would need to perform a complete Emptying. We would have to take out everything to make sure that we didn't miss anything classified. If Meera got her back as a shell, she would have questions. We just have to keep her here, Cadence. That's it. So get your ass out here before it's too late."

"I'll be right there," he said hollowly, and closed the connection.

Then it was just the gurgling of the dragon, the faint music of the party drifting over the grounds, and the winking panels of Luópán Hall.

He could still try to get Penna's third memory while he had a chance. Or he could do as he was told and grab a helio to pick up Sai San, hoping that 288 had already gotten away. Or he could turn around and walk back to the party, forget about the lake and the memories and dance with his people.

Who are you going to be? that voice inside asked him again. Cadence the Brave? Cadence the Loyal? Cadence the Coward? He was remembering Seldom's advice in the gardens. A meaningful life is simply caring about something and working toward achieving it. He squeezed his eyes shut for a moment, and opened them, giving a decisive nod to the water dragon. He turned and broke into a run, heading for the helio pads.

35

———

M EERA

The Emptying Room was next door to the Briefing Room, with a door on the inside that connected the two. Kiro was the trade coordinator, but he was also one of the few trained Emptiers and had the equipment for an emergency.

Story swore as they entered the room. "What is this?" she asked in wonder.

Meera sighed. "It's an Emptying Room." At Story's frown, she added "In the case of an attack on a Sepa like this one, or an illness, we can do an emptying here. Usually, a Sepa is only Emptied annually at Luópán Hall and the memories go straight to their Librarians for analysis."

Meera thought she was being kind by explaining, but Story was glowering at her. "They're your spies? They listen to everything we say and then bring it back for you?"

"And our traders," she replied stubbornly, trying to brush off the sting of her work being painted so ominously. She motioned Story to the back wall. "This is the board. We need this, the hoses, vials, and those needles."

Story crossed her arms, looking at the equipment with disdain. "How do you see the memories that are taken?"

"You inject them into your own mind," she muttered, hoping she wouldn't ask if she'd ever done it. Story would just judge her for never having the procedure done herself.

Instead, Story just nodded grimly and said, "I'll take the board if you can get the rest." As they were hauling it out of the room, she added. "I can't believe you Bhutanese. You send people to bring us life, paint them as our heroes, and all the while they're there to monitor us. Are you taught to be that sick, or are you born with it?"

Meera gritted her teeth and ignored her. In silence, they managed to bring down the station and set it up behind Sepora's cot. Kiro was restitching the wound in her side and Hui was standing bedside, watching the process in horror.

Meera set to work inserting the needles into Sepora and hooking the vials to the other side of the board.

"Can you put the memories in one of us once they're out?" Story asked.

"No. Not unless they emptied us first. After age ten, a person's body becomes a tangled web, with childhood memories crossing with adolescent and adult memories. We add extra memory pockets when Sepas are children so we can work with those spots. With an unaltered adult, you would have to erase their memories without any real certainty that you're getting the ones you want."

Hui's brow furrowed with sympathy for the Sepa children. He would be ten soon. "Does adding the memory receptors hurt them?"

Meera gave him a pained expression. "Yes," she admitted quietly. "But they don't remember it after their first assignment."

Story was shaking her head.

"But what about Aunt Penna?"

Meera's jaw clenched. "It's not that it *can't* be done. It just can't be done well or safely. Whatever they are adding or taking away from my sister is less controlled."

Hui was trying to take that in when the whirring and beeping of the alarm sounded.

Meera gasped.

Story whispered, "They're at the gate?"

But Kiro was frowning. "That's not the front gate alarm. That's the landing pad." He looked to Meera. "They're already inside the barrier."

"Who is?" Hui was looking from person to person with a terrified expression.

Meera felt panic claw up her throat. At a run, they could be here in under a minute, "Story, hide in one of the rooms in the back."

For once, she immediately obeyed.

"Hui." At this, she bent down next to him. "I need you to pretend you don't know anything about Sepora or Story or the Blue Room, okay?"

He nodded, eyes wide. "Mission accepted," he breathed.

"Kiro, stay here and finish the Emptying. I'll try to get them out of here."

"What are you going to say? There's a crashed helio out front!"

Meera looked at him for a moment. "I don't know."

She turned to run up the steps, guiding Hui by the hand, and instead ran straight into a panting Cadence San, dressed in thick and plush purple robes trailing several feet behind him.

She stepped back, staring at him in shock as he took in the scene. As his eyes found the Emptying board, he strode over and pushed Kiro aside, flipping the latch of the machine off. He cupped Sepora's face for a moment before turning to Meera.

"What are you doing?" he demanded, looking around. "What is this place?"

Meera put up her hands in surrender. "Cadence San, there is so much you don't know," she said gently. "This girl will disappear if you take her to Sai San. She's not just a Sepa."

Hui jumped between them. "Cadence San! Sepora is really hurt. She might die!"

Cadence whipped around and inspected her again, taking note of the stitches across her side.

Kiro said quietly, "Meera did her best, but she's lost too much blood."

"Is Sai with you?" Meera asked.

Cadence turned. "I'm not here to take 288 to Sai."

Meera took another step back in confusion. "Then why... why are you here?"

He took a deep breath, as if trying to decide what to say. "Sai San told me what she did. I was told to pick him up and bring him here."

Meera tensed and Hui spread his arms across the length of the bed protectively.

"But I'm not," Cadence added, looking back at Hui. "I... I want to help her. Can they hear us in here?" he added, looking around the room.

"No. What do you plan on doing, then?"

"First of all, I'm not going to let you empty her again."

Meera took a steadying breath and said "Sepora asked us to take her memories, Cadence. She doesn't want them to die with her."

Cadence took the few steps to close the gap between them.

"You don't know what it does to them," he said fiercely. "You don't know." His eyes were full of pain. He turned back to look at Sepora. "We...we have a hospital wing at Luópán Hall. They have blood for transfusions. I'll take her—"

"No!" Meera and Hui both shouted at the same time.

Meera put a hand up to silence Hui. "We are not giving her to the palace, Cadence. They won't ever let her go."

"She's going to die if we leave her here, yes?" Cadence asked with gritted teeth. He raked a hand through his hair. "Tashi and Penna are still at the party, along with everyone else in Potala. Sai San is trapped at—he's unable to come after her. No one will even know I was here."

"Would you even know how to help her when you go there?" Meera demanded.

"I..." Cadence was looking around as if the answer would be on the walls. "Yes! I have a friend—the florist—who works in the hospital wing. I'm certain he will help us."

She could tell he was convincing himself as much as them.

Everyone turned to look at her. Meera bit her lip. She knew it was up to her to make a decision. She knew her answer but didn't want to admit it. In the end, she had to do whatever it took to keep her alive, even if it meant giving her up.

She nodded her head. "You can take her, but only if we empty the memories first."

Cadence's face twisted in pain. "You don't know what you're saying."

"I know I can't trust you to keep her safe if your faan comes asking for her. She wanted us to have them and I won't deny her that."

She'd hit a nerve. His face paled as if she'd punched him in the gut.

"Turn on the machine," he said quietly, still staring at Meera.

Kiro flipped the latch.

"You better have a plan to get these back to her," Cadence said quietly.

Meera lifted her chin bravely. "Get her back to me safely, and I'll have her memories."

He turned back to the gurney, lifting Sepora's hand into his.

Story emerged from a back room. "How do we know he's not going to take her and send a bunch of Family Members to take us and the memories to the lake?"

Meera swore. "Hiding," she muttered. "A concept we need to review."

"Who are you?" Cadence asked, looking her up and down.

"I'm her friend."

"And my friend," Hui piped in. He smiled at Story, adding, "He's not going to take her back there. Can't you tell?" At this, he smiled at Cadence. "He likes her."

Everyone looked at Cadence in surprise, Meera in particular.

How could he? When could he...?

He offered Hui a pained smile and turned back to Kiro. "How much longer? We need to get her in the air now."

"She's almost finished." He pointed to the edge of the board. Cadence looked around the rim and saw four vials nearly filled. He nodded and turned to Meera.

"Sai San told me she stole his helio and his ID chip right out of his hand. Where are they?"

"The helio's just outside the barrier. I'm assuming the chip is out there, too."

"You need to get rid of it. Burn it. Bury it. I don't care. They can't know she came this way. I'm going to send a helio to pick him up as soon as 288 is safely hidden. That will give us a head start but not make him suspicious of me. I'm supposed to be finding him a ride right now."

"How much time will we have?"

"An hour at most."

"She's finished," Kiro interrupted. "Get her out of here."

They unhooked her and Meera helped Cadence lead the gurney up the stairs.

As they left Story, Hui, and Kiro in the Blue Room, balancing the gurney between the two of them, Meera was barking orders at Kiro for getting rid of the helio. They jogged across the grounds as fast as they could without jostling the gurney. Cadence lifted her into his helio and gingerly strapped her in. Once Cadence had boarded, Meera paused him with a hand on his knee. "Protect her with your life," she said.

In the dark of night, Cadence frowned at her. "Everyone called her Sepora in there."

Meera sighed. "Because that is her name. You will hold that secret as close as you hold her."

"Penna said she knows her," he pressed. "Do you know anything about that?"

Meera stepped back. So Penna had known.

"Did she find her memories in Luópán?" she asked, wondering what secrets about her sister would have been hidden there.

Cadence paled. "She did." He looked at her square in the face, shame darkening his eyes. "But Tashi took them away again."

Meera's jaw tightened with anger, but before she could speak, Cadence interrupted. "I'm not going to let him hurt either of them ever again," he said. "I'm going to get both of them back."

She threw a pained glance at Sepora. "You better."

"Get rid of the helio. He'll be on his way soon." With that, he was in the air.

36

————

H UI

Kiro had flown the eight Sepas currently in the bunkers out past the barrier using multiple trips with their helio. They were at work in the dark of night, breaking down and burying the helio one chunk at a time. Hui had wanted to join them, but Meera had said it was too dangerous for him to be out beyond the barrier.

Story said he was sulking, but he maintained that drawing soothed him. He had set up near the window that overlooked the cliffs, drawing the lines of rock he could see from Kiro's floodlights. Story was resting on the sofa, and Meera was sitting at the briefing table, back in its place over the trapdoor, staring at the line of vials.

"You know, I don't think staring at them is going to work," Story said from the couch.

"Very amusing," Meera replied dully.

Story stood up and came to sit opposite Meera, her expression softening.

"She's going to be alright. She survived the lake and a helio crash. She can take whatever happens in a palace."

Meera was still looking at the vials. "She wanted me to know what was in here. She said my sister's name and... and she knew about Penna and Sai. The last thing she said to me was 'we break bread.'" At that she looked up at Story, a pained expression twisting her face. "It keeps coming up. Susu said it, and now Sepora? I keep feeling like I'm right on the edge, you know? Celio's telling me to keep pushing, to open my eyes, but no matter how hard I try, I just... I can't see."

Hui had stopped drawing and turned his chair, watching his aunt. He'd never heard her sound so hopeless. It reminded him uncomfortably of his faan.

She startled him by decisively slapping her palm on the table. "What if we comm Kiro and ask him to send up one Sepa. We give all of Sepora's memories to her and interrogate her. Then we can take them out again." She looked at Story for approval, but Story was leaning back in her chair, eyeing her.

"Every time I think I like you, you go and say something like that."

"What?"

"You just tinker with people's minds like they're yours."

"I would use mine in a heartbeat if I could!" Meera spit back. "My body isn't modified to accept memories properly. Sepas are made to retrieve and give them."

"No," Story shook her head. "They are made to live, just like us, but you changed them."

Meera leaned her head back in frustration. "What can I do, then? What if I use their memory receptors this one time? We're in a bit of a dire situation, if you haven't noticed." She straightened, her hands palm up as if begging for scraps. "What if I promise to never take another memory again?"

Story laughed. "Woman, look at yourself. You're a Family official begging a Banjarian rebel who just escaped prison for her approval. You know you don't need it. So who are you really asking?"

Meera's palm went to her face and she rubbed her mouth as if to keep in a cry. Story reached over and took the hand down, tucking it in her own.

"You might not see what's in those vials, honey, but your eyes are wide open to what you've been doing. You can't just turn a blind eye now."

Meera gave a tight nod, staring at Story's hand folded over her own.

Hui looked away and back at his sketchbook. He skimmed through, finding the drawing from Sepora tucked inside. He rubbed his thumb along the bottom, smudging the secret number. His first moment of espionage. It felt like so long ago. Before his aans had died. Before Aunt Penna turned out to be Banjarian or he met Story and realized rebels could be nice, too. Before he knew that Sepora might lose her life. There was so much more to their lives than he had imagined.

He closed the book decisively and stood up, crossing over to the table in three strides.

"It's going to be me," he said calmly, his voice sounding stronger than it ever had.

Both women turned to him with very different expressions. Story was smiling like a proud maan, but Meera looked completely taken aback.

"What?" she asked.

"'I'm the right age to add the extra receptors, so I'm the only one here who could take the memories in without losing anything when they take them out. The only one who can willingly, at least," he added, nodding to Story.

"Hui," Meera said, "We have no idea what these memories could contain. You could see things that... that you aren't ready to see."

"I'm ready."

"And the pain... the surgery is..."

"If they can do it, so can I, Meera." He skipped over his usual "auntie" to prove that he was old enough.

Story was smiling broadly. "I knew you would do it, little one." She turned to Meera, "He can take it."

"You're just a child," Meera protested.

"How old are Sepas when you send them to the Banjar?" he countered.

Meera's eyes fell to her lap. "As young as eight."

Hui put a hand on her arm. "I can do this. We need to do this."

Meera closed her eyes. "If we could just ask a Sepa…"

"Story's right, Aunt Meera. The Sepas never have a choice. But I do."

Meera opened her eyes and took in his determined face.

"Well, I don't know if it is even my choice to make." She took Hui's hands in her own. "If you at any point decide to change your mind, there is no shame in it."

She lifted her palm to call Kiro back. With one last glance at Hui, she added "You have no idea how much this will hurt."

Hui's jaw clenched. He wasn't just scared. He was terrified. "I can handle it," is all he said. He glanced at Story for support, and her warm smile strengthened his resolve.

They hadn't moved the Emptying station, so the three of them heaved the table back over and opened the door. The musty cold reached out and clawed at Hui. When he had first descended into the room he had felt a sense of excitement and urgency to see Sepora. Now, it was with slow, determined steps that he returned, feeling like he was walking into his grave.

He let out an audible exhale. *Stop being so dramatic*, he thought. *You'll be like a Sepa after this; a real spy fit with the equipment to keep memories. And you'll know what happened to Sepora. We can help her once we know, and we can start a new life.*

He sat on the bloody cot, thinking about what that new life might entail. Maybe he would make such a good Sepa that he and Sepora would become partners. Maybe Story would stay as a Sepa, too.

Kiro's feet came pounding down the stairs. He looked at Meera like she was insane. "This is really your plan? With a Family boy? We have eight perfectly capable Sepas out there digging right now."

Meera hopped off the gurney where she had been sitting next to

Hui. "I'm finished playing with people's minds, Kiro," she said quietly.

Kiro rounded on Story, pointing an angry finger. "I know this was you," he accused.

He looked at Hui, "This is too dangerous. The surgery could kill you. It could damage your memories. And the ones you get... if you get the wrong memories all at once and you could lose your mind. I did a complete Emptying. I took everything Sepora had from when she turned ten on. What's left will be jumbled because of how many times she's been emptied. Are you sure you're ready to take that all in?"

Hui resisted the urge to bite his lip. "I am."

"This is insane," he breathed, appealing to Meera again. "The boy doesn't know what he's saying. He's just lost his aans. Of course he feels reckless."

"It's not recklessness," Hui said quietly, realizing his own truth as it came out of his mouth, "it's purpose. I want to do something for us. For her."

Kiro shrugged helplessly. "Fine. We can't do the surgery here. Come up to the Emptying Room where it's sterile." He turned to Story. "Stay down here, and if you can, clean up the cot. Meera, bring Sepora's vials down here and ready the machine. If Cadence San is right, we have less than thirty minutes before Sai San arrives."

Hui gave one last look at Story and Meera, letting his terror peek through his eyes for only a moment, then turned to follow Kiro back upstairs.

Kiro stopped by the large table and pulled open a drawer, bringing out a small bottle, then led him to the Emptying Room. "Get on the cot," he ordered.

Hui obeyed.

Kiro started to belt down his ankles and wrists. "You can't move during this, so I have to strap you down. You might think you can hold still, but once I start, you'll be fighting for your life." He held the bottle to Hui's lips. "Drink."

He obeyed, then coughed at the sharp burn in his throat. "It's awful. What is it?"

"Spirit Tea. Now bite on this and keep it there." He set a flat paddle of wood between Hui's teeth and gently pushed him to a resting position, strapping in his head.

"Scared yet?" he challenged grimly.

Hui nodded yes.

"Want to stop all this?"

Hui shook his head no.

Kiro sighed and tightened the strap.

"Good luck, kid," he said. Then he pulled a jar of blue liquid from a cabinet and extracted a long, thin blade.

Hui squeezed his eyes shut and waited. A moment later, the paddle dropped from his mouth and he began to scream. His screams sounded far away, as if he were listening to them from the opposite side of the tunnel leading into the bunkers. Eventually, it was so quiet that they stopped altogether, and he was floating in a dark silence.

After what felt like years, or maybe seconds, the darkness was punctured by Penna San's snarl across a dinner table. He could see her from his point of view as well as from another's, and felt both annoyance and fear spike inside him. She faded and he saw himself, a feeling of love and a heavy sadness blooming in his chest. He watched his own face begin to shift, and it was a different boy, much younger. The child reached out and put two pudgy hands on his cheeks, pushing the skin around and twisting his own face to match. He burst into a fit of giggles, making Hui's heart soar. The boy turned away and was suddenly standing at a large wall, drawing crude pictures with the dust of stones. Hui stepped closer to inspect the art but a storm cloud covered the sun and the child looked up in fear.

"The Banjarguay," a woman behind him said. He whipped around and saw Story standing there, holding the child's limp body in her arms. She was walking away, up a narrow cliffside, blood dripping from his face to create a trail behind her.

There was a cackling laugh behind him and he whipped around again, finding an old woman sitting at a window looking out on a huge body of water. "Look around you, sweetie," she said, "the air is fine." The woman's smile faded and she pointed behind her. "They'll be here any minute." A bell had appeared and she reached up and pulled it. The sound sent terror shooting up Hui's back and he turned again, only to find that he was in a red hallway, hands bound behind him. He felt a firm grip on his wrists and looked up to see Dorji Tashi leading him along. He leaned down, his hot breath smelling of onion and gravy, and whispered in his ear.

"You will make a fine gift, won't you?" He grunted in agreement with his own statement. "And then I'll have you, too. Would you like that?"

Hui felt like he might retch, but he said, "More than you could imagine."

The man laughed and shoved him through a door.

On the other side, he saw Cadence, sleeping. He came to his side and sat down. Cadence opened his eyes and cupped Hui's face. "I'm going to get you out of here, okay? We're going to get you back. Not one of them is going to touch you, I promise."

Hui wanted to tell him so much then, but he couldn't say a word. He fought to open his mouth but felt like there were stitches across his lips.

Suddenly he realized that Meera was stitching his mouth. "You have a name, you know," she said tenderly, as she laced the thread through his bottom lip. "It's Sepora."

"I named you!" a man behind her bellowed. He stepped closer and came into focus. His palms were bleeding. It was Sai San. "She's everything to me," he whispered fervently.

Hui was scared, but then a gentle voice whispered in his ear.

"You don't have to go back, you know." It was Ruby, inviting him to come live in Tumail. "Tell Penna I love her? At least I was there for that."

"If it takes my life."

But it wasn't his voice. It was Sepora's.

And then Penna was there, younger. She was screaming for a

baby that was being taken away from her. Hui held her back, trying to hush her.

Sepora! You need to wake up now.

He turned to find a desert evening stretched out before him, and in the rolls of sand stood a dining table heaped with...

Hui's eyes snapped open.

He was in the Blue Room. He could tell immediately because of the damp air. The blue lights along the perimeter cast a thin glow, but the trap door was shut. He was hyperventilating, his chest punching the air. He realized that a hand was clamped tightly over his mouth, and he looked over in terror. To his relief, it was Story. She had one hand over her own mouth and was nodding.

We need to be quiet, she was saying.

He remembered making the exact same motion to her after they saw the lake for the first time. But he wasn't him, then. He was Sepora.

He nodded that he understood, feeling sick with deja vu. He laid his head back and closed his eyes, trying to piece together the swarm of memories crowding his brain. Through the cloud, he began to hear muffled voices from the floor above. His eyes opened again and he shot a glance at Story, brows raised in question.

She nodded and looked toward the ceiling.

Hui strained his ears to hear what they were saying, but he could only make out their tones. Had they hid the helio in time?

After half an hour or so, two male voices disappeared. They heard what sounded like Kiro and Meera speaking for a while. Another twenty minutes and they heard the table being pushed to the side.

Meera came down first, rushing to his bedside.

"You're awake! How do you feel?"

Hui squinted in the sudden light, not sure how he felt. "Heavy," he said finally. "Was that Sai San?"

Meera grimaced. "Yes, with his henchman. They didn't believe us, I don't think, but what can they do? They searched every bunk. I believe they're headed to their second guess, Tumail."

Hui shot into a sitting position. "Ruby!"

Meera stepped back, bewildered. "Ruby?"

"I left her there," he said frantically. "I told her they would go there," Hui fumed.

Kiro had come down the stairs and put a hand on his arm. "Hui. It's very important that you keep Sepora's memories and your own separate. You need to remind yourself which ones are truly yours and which are not. Okay?"

Hui nodded, his terror gone as fast as it had come, leaving in its place a skull splitting headache. "Can I come upstairs?" he asked weakly.

"Yes, I believe we're safe for now," Meera said, concern knitting her brow. "But you shouldn't walk yet."

Story picked Hui up in one swoop, holding him to her like a toddler. They made their way upstairs and Kiro and Meera put the door and table back. Late afternoon light was streaming through the window.

"How long was I asleep?" he asked, still squinting.

"A day." Kiro answered. "Cadence must have held Sai San off somehow."

Story set Hui in a chair and they all sat around him, staring expectedly. Meera picked up her graphite pencil, ready to add to the list.

Hui was taking deep breaths, trying to organize his thoughts into a coherent story, but he couldn't. He was a little hungry, and a little nauseous. He glanced at the list Meera had already made, his heart constricting when he saw that she had added his aans' gishiki shinjū.

PRISONERS ARE TO BE "TRAINED" by a young man. No prisoners in sight

A real, swimmable lake exists.

There is (presumably) no barrier over the lake base.

Sepora said to mind the trees. Possible danger?

Susu and Mishka perform gishiki shinju, leaving a note with the maxim on it. Possibly blaming Tashi?

Quántóu disappear

Celio dies

HE CLOSED HIS EYES.

"They're slaves," he said. "All of them. The Banjarians, the Sepas, even traitors from New Bhutan. I...I don't know about the Quántóu. The men and older women...they work in the buildings on the opposite shore. The women... they're a different kind of slave. They're called Rues." He opened his eyes, swallowing.

Everyone was staring at him intently.

"It means flesh. They... they have to be naked with them."

Meera brought a hand to her mouth.

"But...they like it, kind of. Palace, or Ruby, she taught me—her—how to pretend. They didn't train me."

"What?" Story asked.

Hui rubbed his face with both palms in frustration. "They train them with a Filling procedure. By giving them new memories. The memories give them a love, a kind of obsessive love, really, for the men. They would do anything for them. And they give them memories of what they can do with them, so they know."

"Dragons," Meera breathed, horrified.

Hui had clenched his eyes closed again, trying to sort it all out. "Penna was there, too. She was pregnant. Ruby helped her." Hui's eyes flashed open as panic again overtook him.

"Meera, we have to help Ruby! Sai San will kill her."

Story was looking back and forth between them.

Meera had gone pale. "Sepora wants us to understand the memories first," Meera said slowly. "Let's get through this and then—"

"Hui," Story interrupted. "You don't mean Ruby the Warrior, do you?"

"Story," Meera groaned. "I'm sorry, but we need to get through the entire account before we start branching off topic to Banjarians you may have known. I know it's difficult, but we need to stay focused."

"Maybe this *is* what Sepora wanted us to know," Story countered. "She wanted us to know that Ruby needs our help. You don't know who Ruby the Warrior is, do you?" Story was looking at her with surprise and a hint of pity.

Hui had put his head back down on the table. The mention of Ruby had brought his mind swirling deeper into confusion. He was holding a baby girl protectively to her chest as the man he loved asked to take her away. He could feel a pressure building up behind his brow. This wasn't Sepora. This was someone else. He tried to fill in the blank for himself. My name is...My name is Ruby the Warrior. Yes, I'm going to tear down the barrier. I'm going to... Hui shook his head. There was so much swirling just beyond reach.

"Yes." Hui said, his eyes closed. "I am Ruby the Warrior," he whispered.

Story's hand was on his shoulder, and he opened his eyes to see hers wide with excitement.

"Meera San!" She jumped from her seat, whooping with joy. "Ruby the Warrior!" She nodded happily at Hui. "No need to fear for her if she's in Tumail. They'll hide her well."

Meera sighed. "Well, now that we've established that. Hui, please, Sepora said something about a painting. Do you remember a painting?"

Story sat down, her voice distinctly calmer. "Maybe it was Miracle's painting. That's in Tumail."

"Was it?"

It took a moment for Hui to realize that Meera was asking him. He lifted his head and squinted, trying to peel back the layers of memory.

In his mind, Hui could see the little boy working on the mural. His heart swelled with love.

"I... I see three paintings," he said finally. "The mural is there. Sepora wishes she could paint because she wants to add to it. She," he looked at Story, "she wants to paint you."

Story swallowed. "Yes. That was Miracle's last wish before the Banjarguay took him."

Hui could see her holding Miracle as he died. They were in a small shack full of sand and the smell of blood. The boy's eyes had begun to bleed.

He reached his hand across the table and squeezed hers for a moment, really looking into her eyes for the first time. "I'm so sorry, Story."

Her lips twisted for a moment, but she just nodded.

Pulling back, he glanced at Meera. "There's another mural. This one is at the lake. It's of..." Hui blushed. "Naked women. Dorji Tashi was there, and... I'm scared here."

"*Tashi* was there?" Kiro asked, incredulous.

Hui watched Meera's jaw clench. Sepora knew to watch for that tic to judge her emotions, and so now did he. She was furious.

"And the other?" she said tightly.

"The other is a Celio painting, but I can't tell if it's my memory or hers." He squinted again, a sharp ringing in his ear. "I remember just seeing it yesterday and being scared of it... but I also remember hating it... there's a lot of emotion around it that I don't think is mine."

"Which is it?"

"It's in the desert. There's a table in the center with five people sitting at it. They have dress robes on and the table is full to the brim with food, but... but the people are skeletons."

"The Last Meal," Meera breathed. She shot out of her seat. "It's in my bunker!" she cried over her shoulder and ran out.

Hui looked up and saw that Meera had been writing down everything he had said in shorthand on the wall. He didn't like seeing these experiences boiled down into phrases. He put his head down and let his mind sink into the memories.

"Who knows about the lake, Hui? Can you tell?" It was Kiro.

Hui kept his head down. "Dorji Tashi and Sai San were there. Cadence was there, but he wanted to help her."

"*Did* he help her?" Story asked.

"Not really," Hui said grimly, looking up and meeting her eye. "She thought he would, but he never came back."

"Do you think he'll protect her this time?"

Hui gave a small shrug. "She still trusts him."

"Is there a barrier over the lake?" Kiro asked, causing Story to roll her eyes.

"No," Hui said, frowning with concentration. "She asked Ruby about it and she laughed at her."

Meera came back into the room, lugging a large painting along with her.

Hui closed his eyes again. "Auntie Meera. Before the crash, Ruby told her about Penna. She knows that Penna is her maan... and," he felt a flare of excitement in his chest that was all his own. "And she's my cousin!" At Meera's pained expression, his excitement dwindled. Sepora's suspicions weighed on him. "Did you know, Meera? Did you know she was your niece?"

Meera paused, resting the painting against her legs. "Yes," she said heavily. "Penna disappeared for so long. The night Sai brought the baby to me, I knew it must be his. He kept whispering the name Sepora, near hysterics. When Penna finally returned and she was so different, I suspected. But I was hurt that she never told me; wouldn't even look at me. We went our separate ways, but I created 288's Sepa identity and kept Sai's chosen name close to my heart. It wasn't until she was older that I became almost certain. They have that same fierce expression."

"How could you let her go to the Banjar, though? To be a Sepa?" Sepora's deepest emotions were coming to the surface, and his childish innocence brought it pouring out. He knew she wouldn't approve of him asking so bluntly, but he had to know.

Meera didn't say anything for a moment, her eyes flickering between Story and Kiro, who were both staring in stunned silence.

"Sai told me that Tashi wanted the baby dead and begged me to hide it. I was doing all I could to protect her."

"Why didn't you tell Penna, though? She's your sister." He pressed, knowing he was pushing her limits.

"Penna was gone," she said sadly. "Just like she is now. She came back and didn't want to see me. She quit her studies and went straight to work as an apprentice for Tashi. I didn't know who Penna was anymore. Sai had told me to hide 288 completely, for her safety, so I did."

Hui, hearing Ruby's story in his mind, knew this was far from the truth.

"It was only years later that I began to suspect that maybe Penna didn't remember. The more I worked with Sepas, the more suspicious I became. I tried to ask Seldom about the Emptying. If it could be done on naturally born people. Her denial was brisk, quite the opposite of her normal affect. She was lying.

"I tried to talk to Penna about it without revealing I had Sepora. I asked her what had made her decide to work for Tashi. I asked her where she had been. She became frustrated and angry, and it ended with her having her Quántóu throw me out of the palace. We...we didn't talk for several years."

She glanced at Kiro. "It was only after I became the Sepa Coordinator, just before Celio passed, that I was invited back by Tashi. He wanted constant updates."

"Did Sai San ever ask about the baby?" Hui asked. Had Sepora's faan wondered how she was faring, at least?

Meera looked at him, "No," she said simply. "Although we would meet a meaningful eye now and then. Especially when I brought her to the Sepa dinner."

"Why in New Bhutan would you take that risk?" Kiro asked.

"Once she was older, I started seeing the resemblance. I've seen Sepas be triggered to remember things that should have been emptied. I believe that with the right stimulus, some shred of every memory remains to be revived. I wanted her to see Sepora. I thought it might shake her awake."

"It did," Hui said. "I remember her staring at me—at Sepora, I mean. She'd gone pale. She looked sick."

"Yes, it drove her to start looking. But it was all a waste. They were broadcasting the speech to announce the engagement tonight and I heard Penna speak. She said horrible things. She said that she would close the SEPA Project and the barrier to keep the Banjarians out."

Story's face paled. "That would be the end of Tumail."

"You think they altered her again?" Kiro asked.

"Of course they did," Meera said. "That's why Dorji Tashi's handing the Heart over to her. She'll do whatever he wants her to do."

The sentence reverberated in Hui's mind painfully. She'll do whatever he wants her to do. "Aunt Meera," he said, his eyes squeezed shut. "You can't leave Penna alone with Tashi. No matter how much she tries to shut you out."

"Hui, she's the Heart. I can't—"

"Meera!" he interrupted harshly, Sepora's thoughts seeming to burst from him, "You don't know what he did to her. You don't know why Penna became who she did; why you lost your sister." He took a deep breath and opened his eyes to meet his aunt's. "Tashi has been altering her memories more than you think. She's been through so much. She was... she was a Rue for Tashi for over a year." His eyes were full of pain. "But it was different. She... she didn't have the training." He was Ruby now, holding Penna through a nightmare. His eyes filled with tears. "They ripped her apart."

Meera's hold of the painting slipped and it crashed around her, the glass that had been protecting it shattering. "What do you mean?" she asked tightly.

"You know what he means, Meera," Kiro said tightly, "don't make the boy say it." Hui glanced at Kiro gratefully. Every muscle in the man's body looked flexed with anger.

Meera was surrounded by shards of glass, shaking visibly. "I will kill him myself," she said fiercely.

Everyone sat silent for a moment, each enveloped in their own dark thoughts. Hui was thinking about what a person could do with the power to alter a mind. Not delete it but change it. It was the stuff of nightmares. He knew Sepora thought so, too. He started to swirl into confusion over what he felt and knew verses Sepora until he felt dizzy. He put his head down. There was something else. It was the crash. Sepora looked out over the desert and thought of the painting. She knew it was important but couldn't quite figure out why.

"I need to see the painting," he said, keeping his head down.

Meera looked down as if she'd almost forgotten about it. She picked it up and lugged it to the wall they were creating the list on, propping it up for everyone to see.

"Celio painted that here," Meera explained, her voice hollow, "in the last days before she died. That's why I keep it here, hanging in my room. At first it hung in here, but Kiro doesn't like it. She'd been in one of her moods all week. She'd locked herself in our private quarters. I had to sleep on that sofa," she gestured across the room. "It's a reminder of what the Banjarians have to live through. She was so consumed with Banjarian rights near the end."

Hui lifted his head to find Story was staring at it, deep in thought. He looked at it, too. It was the one Sepora had thought of right before and after the crash. Why, though?

"Looks like a welcome feast to me," Story offered.

"A Sepa welcome?" Kiro asked.

Story nodded. "Every time a Sepa comes, they bring a big feast of food to smooth the deal over. Everyone loves them for it, welcoming their arrival like a gift from the Gods. They fight to gain favor with the Sepas so they can have a spot at the table, not realizing that they could be getting that food all the time if we stood up to New Bhutan. Idiots," she scoffed.

Meera frowned at the picture. "It could be any dinner, though. No one is wearing a Sepa robe."

"It's in the desert," Story countered, "and the Banjar never has that much food without a Sepa's welcome feast."

Kiro chimed in, "The robes suggest wealth. Maybe it's meant to be the Family, feasting when New Bhutan has died around them, and we all live in the Banjar."

Hui studied the painting and found he could hear Sepora's voice in his head, thinking.

We break bread, Ruby had sang to Sepora.

"The bread," Asaka had whispered. Asaka... Ruby's memories were deep, brief snatches in a swirl of others. Sepora hadn't seen all of them yet. She didn't know...

"The bread," he said suddenly. "Look at the table."

The food on the table was a feast of fruit and grains, but a pile of bread loaves was front and center, with the lighting making it look almost as if it were glowing.

"The bread is always the main course," Story explained. "We have nothing like it and it fills us up so fast."

"We break bread,' Meera murmured, meeting eyes with Kiro. "Not bones, to thrive."

Kiro's expression darkened. "New Bhutan will stay alive," he finished.

"When was that maxim created?" Meera asked no one in particular.

Glad to be of use with his own knowledge, Hui piped in. "Maester Fre said the Resting Dragon, Raju, wrote it."

"The same man who created the SEPA Project," Meera said softly.

She closed her eyes and grasped the nearest chair as if she might faint.

"Meera, what is it?" Kiro asked.

Meera was nodding her head. She picked up the graphite and went to the board, writing alongside her old list with body turned so they could see it.

A lake discovered.

Not looking at them, she said thickly "It means the Earth is healing itself. It means the Banjar is livable." She cast a pained glance back at Story before turning back and continuing to write.

A bio war mask brought to Luópán Hall.

She turned and looked at Hui. "It means the old Dragon's men could have been learning about biological warfare. Learning from the men before the divide." She turned back, reading her words aloud as she wrote them.

"The SEPA Project approved and the maxim created by the same man."

She turned and stared at Kiro.

"What if they created the SEPA Project for something else? What if it wasn't about trade at all, but control? If they knew the Banjar could become another livable land... without the help of New Bhutan..."

Avoiding Story's eye, she turned and wrote again.

Banjar sees population losses to the worst bout of Banjarguay in history just after the SEPA Project sends out its first traders.

She read it aloud and Story immediately responded, her voice full of all the fear Meera was feeling.

"That run took out half Tumail."

"And what if," Meera added quietly, pressing her forehead to the wall, "What if no one left alive could remember if there had always been the Banjarguay or not?"

Yes, yes, Hui thought. *Asaka said...*

She was letting her words sink in for a moment before continuing. The room was dead silent.

Hui knew she was right. He watched her work it out in silence.

She circled 'Susu leaves a note with the maxim on it.'

"We break bread," she whispered, "not bones to thrive, New Bhutan will stay alive.'" She gave a sharp, hysterical laugh. "He put it in his damned maxim."

Taking a deep breath, she turned back and wrote her last clue.

Sepas bring feasts of Bhutanese bread to celebrate a good trade.

She sucked her lips into her mouth and dropped the chalk to the table, her eyes filling with tears and immediately spilling over.

Hui felt Sepora's pain hiccup in his chest as he watched his aunt cry.

"The Banjarguay is... in the bread?" Kiro asked.

Story stood up behind her. "You're killing us," she whispered.

Meera didn't turn around, but stood aside so everyone could take it in.

"That can't be right," Kiro said, but his voice teetered with uncertainty. "We've never been involved in sending out trades. We don't decide what goes out or how much." He looked at the others.

"But Celio did," Meera said softly. "She worked in the distribution department in Yutan."

She picked up her chalk and slowly circled the words 'Celio dies.'

Their eyes all rose to the painting she had left behind. In the silence, Story's voice whipped the air.

"*You* killed him?" she asked, her throat choked with grief and betrayal.

"Seven years of sending Sepas out with deliveries," Meera said hollowly. "How many died when her message was right here, warning me?"

"I would kill you right now," Story said fiercely. "Both of you, with no hesitation."

Hui felt panic rise up in him. "They didn't know, Story."

"I won't," she finished, glancing at Hui. "I know I need your help to stop this."

No one spoke for a long time. Meera was staring unseeingly at the painting. Kiro was staring at Meera. Story had pressed her knuckles into her mouth, as if afraid her hands would attack Meera on their own.

Finally, feeling Sepora's grief heavy inside of him, Hui broke the silence.

"If the Sepas deliver the Banjarguay," he hesitated, watching his hands on the table. "Then Sepora brought it to Miracle, didn't she?"

37

M EERA

Meera could almost hear the sound of Penna's cold voice announcing the closure of the SEPA Project echoing off the cliffside. That voice was not to be taken lightly. After she'd finally put the pieces together, finally seeing what Celio had wanted her to see, Meera had run from the Briefing Room. She'd run right back to the helio field that looked out into the Banjar. She hugged herself as that voice reverberated in her mind.

Standing alone on the edge of the world, Meera knew two things. She couldn't give up the Sepas to the Family now. They were loyal to her and could be used as a meager army if it came to that. She winced as she thought of Story's reaction to her thoughts. They could be used; these creatures they had created. Still, she knew, they would be better off with her than in Tashi's grasp.

She also knew that her only path from here would have to be to find out the truth about the Banjarguay and do all in her power to stop it. So many had died at her hand already. How many Sepas? How many Banjarians? She had no way of knowing, but she could feel their hearts, beating alongside hers; a thousand hearts pounding against her chest until it felt her body might tear in two.

She would be running south. With the Sepas at her back, they could make their way on foot. Yutan, pressed against the Broken Oceans, was the source of all of their water. Although the ocean was deadly after extended exposure, Yutan had the only equipment in the world that could pump, funnel, purify, and distribute usable water. The Yutan workers ran the funneling of ocean water from below the barrier. They cleaned it and delivered it to the farms of Midland, Lhasa, and the bunkers to be delivered to the Banjar. They prepped and packed all trades with the Banjarians, using their helio to bring deliveries.

They also, of course, baked and packed the bread. The grains were grown in Midland, and the harvest was delivered to Yutan. Celio had always spoken fondly of her time there, saying it was a place full of laughter, not like stuffy Lhasa.

Meera had no idea how she would discover the truth, but she had a burning need to find someone responsible. Someone else to blame.

She cast one glance along the barrier, out over the cliffs into the void of the Banjar. She'd been thinking about Penna and Sepora for so long. Her main objective had been to bring them together and help Penna see the truth. They had come so close. And now? She was powerless to save either of them. It was all up to Cadence now. Besides, the manufacturing of the Banjarguay changed everything.

She said a silent goodbye to Sepora; a wish that she be safe from harm, before turning and jogging into Kiro's control room. Everyone seemed to be sitting just where she'd left them, just as in shock as she was.

Everyone but Hui looked up as she entered, who was staring inward.

"Penna is coming to close the Bunkers," she said matter of factly, sounding much stronger than she felt. "If I'm correct about Tashi's intentions, her drive to close us down is simply so Tashi can gain control of our Sepas. She will be coming to take them from us. We need to bring the Sepas in and brief them for a new mission. You can tell them the details while Hui and I gather all the food and supplies we will need—"

"Meera." Kiro interrupted. "What is the new mission?"

She stopped to stare at him, incredulous. "What else? Do you know how much blood is on our hands, Kiro?"

He leaned back on his heels. "Ah. We are going to Yutan."

Nodding curtly, she moved toward the door. "On foot."

"On foot?" he called after her, causing her to pause again at the door.

"The Rail system will record our passage and the bunker helios have trackers. You can bet my sister is coming after us. The last thing we want is her coming to Yutan." She turned to Hui, gently putting a hand on his shoulder. "It's time to go."

He stood slowly, the weight of multiple lives on his shoulders. Story stood to follow but Kiro stopped her. "Shouldn't she stay with the Sepas?"

The question caught her off guard. That had been the plan, but somehow she didn't think it was right to hide Story away with strangers. Not now. She squared her shoulders. "The SEPA Project is dead. Story belongs with this rebellion, whatever risk that might be to us."

"But, Meera—"

"It's the least I could do for her," she snapped, a slight note of hysteria creeping into her voice. She swallowed it down. This was no time to break.

She turned and led Hui and Story back to her bunker, ignoring Story's heavy stare. She rummaged through a closet and tossed them three traveling packs. "I need you both to pack what resources you can into these. We'll need water and dried foods. I'm sorry, Hui, but everything else will have to be left behind." She squeezed his shoulder. "Including the encyclopedia."

"But, Meera—"

Meera's palm glowed and she hastily tapped thumb to pinky.

Kiro's urgent voice came through her palm. "They're here."

She thought they had a day, at least, to get a head start on their journey. Time to disappear.

She slammed her palm shut. "The Blue Room! Go! Bring the packs!"

She pushed them out and the three of them ran at full speed down the steel walkways and back into the Briefing Room.

Kiro had already crammed the eight Sepas on base inside, still filthy from burying Sai San's helio.

The trio stopped short as all of their faces turned as one toward them, so eerily the same. She let her eyes rove over their faces... taking in their unique features, trying to see them as individuals. She pledged in her mind that she would get to know every one of them on their journey if they got the chance.

They didn't.

Kiro had already pushed the table over and thrown open the door to the Blue Room. He grabbed her arm and started to pull her down.

"The Sepas first!" she ordered.

Tightening his grip on her arm, he forced her down the steps, ushering Hui and Story after her. "If Penna believes you're using the SEPA Project to kidnap her people, you will be arrested on site!"

Meera was protesting about the Sepas, but Kiro was shutting the door and scraping the table back over. Once the hatch closed, she fell silent immediately. Fear for those left above tied her tongue.

Moments after the table shifted, Penna's voice licked through the air. She must have been pleased to find them all congregated in the same place. "Kiro," she spat, "and Meera's monsters."

She paused, possibly looking for her, before adding "I need to speak to Meera at once."

"She left last night, My Heart." Kiro spoke with an impossibly calm authority. "Right before your announcement to close the Project. She was taking Hui back to the palace, as promised. Do you remember?"

There was a pause, where Meera held her breath. Would she remember? Did she even know that their sister had died?

"Hui?" Penna's voice quavered with a sliver of uncertainty.

"After the ceremony for Mishka, Meera brought Hui here. But she knew that you would welcome him to live in Potala." She could hear the careful pace in his words. *Remember*, it urged.

Silence stretched while Penna struggled with how to respond. Meera knew then that she did not remember the last two days. It filled her with so much rage she wanted to burst out of the Blue Room and hold her sister tight.

When Penna finally spoke, her voice was cold and strong. She chose not to respond to Kiro's news. "Meera is charged with treason against the Family, as are you."

She'd directed her next words to the Quántóu she must have brought along with her. "Collect them all."

Hui was clutching at Meera's legs as chaos broke out above them. Feet pounded the floor and an occasional thump of something larger, a body, slammed onto the ground. There were no cries or screams. Neither Sepa nor Quántóu would show any weakness. It was just noise until she heard her sister's voice again. "Find Kiro and Meera."

So Kiro had escaped.

Her Sepas had not been so lucky.

Silence descended on the Blue Room as Penna's party departed. Hui had sunk to the ground at her feet and was in his own web of thoughts. Story was standing just below the trap door, ready to fight if it opened.

Meera was already in battle, fighting a rising black wave of hysteria.

She'd lost her Sepas to whatever Tashi had in mind for them. She'd lost her wife after Celio found Tashi's secret. She'd lost her baby sister to death and Penna to something arguably worse.

These facts, her brain could handle; a checklist of every face she'd never see again—a series of images in her brain that she could catalogue: *This is the mistake you made to lose this person. This is how you were too blind or too stubborn.*

This, she could quietly hate herself for.

But these facts were merely making up that tumultuous ocean; the rolling and pounding waves creating the storm that set the stage for what was coming—that mammoth black tidal wave inking out the sky.

The bread.

It wasn't one face, or two. It was hundreds. She'd been killing people for years, blind enough to believe that the use of Sepas was for the greater good.

Her body began to tremble. If she could have asked Story to steady her, she might have succumbed to tears and let the pain out. From a distance, she could feel her chest pumping for air. The trembling had grown to a violent shudder. In a blurry haze, she recognized that Story was with her now, saying something. It made it worse. The concern on her face, on the face of a woman whose child she, Meera San, had murdered. One face in hundreds.

She let out a strangled cry, like something dying and clutching onto their last moments of life.

Hui had come to stand with Story, and they looked at her with concern but said nothing. Meera knew that they felt her anguish was well deserved. More than well deserved. She'd killed Story's son. She had mangled the mind of Hui and he could see firsthand every evil she had done to Sepora. Her sister had been tortured by the man she affectionately called Uncle, and she'd never done anything to find out what had happened. She had killed people. Enslaved people. Working with Tashi all the while. She wanted to crawl out of her body and run away from everything she'd done.

She lifted shaking palms out before her, certain that they would be covered in blood.

All she could see was the faint outline of tech, the best technology the Family had to offer for Meera San, a Family Official.

The wave crashed.

Hatred inking out her thoughts, she lurched across the room to the medical supplies they'd used on Sepora. Sepora, her resolute, resilient niece, who she had raised as her own as best she could, only to send her to her death. She opened the kit and pulled out a scalpel.

Dorji Tashi had used her and her sister equally, even if he'd used different techniques.

She would never be his tool again.

With a guttural scream, she stabbed the blade into her palm repeatedly, desperate to remove any connection to the Family from her body. Dimly, she heard Story holding back a protesting Hui from stopping her.

She didn't feel the pain, even when she could see that the hand was nothing but a pile of blood and mangled flesh. She wished she did. Suddenly Kiro was back and holding her arms down, slipping a needle into her neck, and she was gone.

A few hours later, she opened bleary eyes to find a bandaged stump where her hand had been. She looked at it gratefully and fell back into a dreamless sleep.

Meera slept until late morning, a mere four hours since Penna's departure, before awakening with a start. Her groggy mind was slammed with urgency. She was alone in the Blue Room, the hatch to the upstairs open. Ignoring the searing pain in what had been her hand, she rushed up the stairs. Story and Hui were both asleep on the sofa. Kiro was tying up the last of her four large packs set out on the table.

He stopped when he saw her, and they stared at each other in silence.

"I'm so sorry, sir,' he said heavily. "I hoped the Sepas would defeat her. I used them to fight back instead of hiding them, as you commanded."

She held his gaze with an unforgivingly blank expression.

"I disobeyed orders, Meera," he continued, weakened.

"And now, the Sepas are gone," she said flatly.

He flinched at her accusatory tone.

"The eight that were here, yes," he said, "but most were on assignment. There are forty-seven out in the Banjar. We may be able to do a round of pickups before—"

"Penna will have used our helio to fly them all back." she said coldly. "So unless you plan on picking them up on foot, I suggest we forget about them for now."

Story had woken up. "Forget about them?" she asked, incredulous.

Meera glanced back at the sofa. "For now," she said tiredly. "I am sure that they are already being rounded up by palace Quántóu, just as they were here. We will have to find a way to help them later." She tried to soften her face to reassure her, but only managed to soften her tone when she added, "All of them." Reluctantly, she turned back to Kiro. "How did you get away?"

Kiro explained that the Quántóu had come prepared with sleeping darts, a weapon the bunkers had never been allotted. He ordered the Sepas to fight and, much to his relief, they followed his orders against Penna. But the darts were too much and too fast. At least one Quántóu was knocked unconscious before the other two managed to shoot every Sepa down. Amidst the chaos, Kiro had slipped out a door on the backside of the control room.

Penna left with every Sepa they had, and Kiro had turned tail and hid. She was nodding her head with what she hoped was blatant disapproval, trying to ignore the dizzying pain in her arm.

"What will we do now, sir?" Kiro asked.

Meera gingerly lifted her bandaged arm up, studying it as she thought. "I'm going to Yutan. They can't trace me anymore and no one there will recognize me. I'm not changing course."

"I'm coming with you," Story said firmly.

Meera nodded her assent, locking eyes with the girl. She'd only agreed so easily because she knew Story wouldn't be denied. And... and because of Miracle. Meera had killed Story's child. The woman was a walking reminder of her crimes. As much as she hated to admit it, she might need that reminder.

"And me, Meera? Will I come with you?"

Meera turned an icy glare on Kiro. "No. You will hide out with Hui until Cadence sends you word on Sepora. I will make sure Cadence knows what to do when she wakes if you can keep Hui safe until then." She looked grimly at Hui's sleeping form. "As much as I would have preferred not to bring him into this, he is our most precious asset right now." She turned to Kiro. "Once she's ready," Meera gave a silent wish that that day would come, "you will bring Hui to Potala and transfer Sepora's memories back."

Kiro blanched. "But, sir, how—"

"We will have to trust that Cadence will find a way. Sepora needs her memories. We will smuggle her into the Banjar and she will find the remaining Sepas if there are any to find. She will rescue them with the help of the Banjarians. Once she tells them of the palace's hand in the Banjarguay, they will stand with her."

"If they don't kill her for bringing it to them for so many years," Kiro said, exasperated.

"They won't." Story offered. "They know who the real enemy is. We've held enough Sepas as they died to know that they are just as much a victim to New Bhutan as we are."

Meera winced, grateful for the pulsing pain in her arm. She turned a hard glare at Kiro.

"Figure it out, Kiro. And don't disappoint me again."

She turned away from him, happy to lay blame at someone else's feet; to be angry instead of heartbroken. She kneeled next to Story and Hui, gently pushing her nephew's hair back.

He opened bleary eyes, and for a moment, it was clear that he didn't remember where he was. It was hard to watch the dawning in his eyes.

"Hu? May I have a word with you? Can we take a quick walk?"

He scrambled to his feet and Meera felt another swell of guilt. There were circles under his eyes, darker than any ten-year-old should have to bear.

She caught Story looking warily from Meera's arm to Hui and realized with a jolt that she didn't trust Meera with him. Hui followed Story's gaze.

"Are you feeling better, Auntie?"

Her lip trembled but she coughed away the emotion. "Yes." She tousled his hair. "I'm so sorry you had to see that, Hu."

He wrapped his hand around her remaining one and gave her a tired smile. "I've seen worse."

That did not have the soothing effect he'd imagined. With a grim nod at Story, she led them both back to her private bunkers.

Not more than an hour later, the party split up. Kiro and Hui would follow the mountain ridges East toward Paro, where the ancient Bhutan cliffside homes would provide refuge. The women would head South, straight through Midland to Yutan.

With a tearful goodbye to Hui and a hesitant embrace from Kiro, Meera walked away from them for what she hoped was not the last time.

Story walked silently beside her for the first few hours as they hiked up the dry mountains that separated Lhasa from Midland. Meera was too consumed with her own thoughts to notice.

She was thinking about what she'd said to Hui.

There hadn't been much time for second guessing. It was this moment or never that she made her move.

In her private bunk, she used her personal Listening equipment to craft a message to Cadence that Hui was charged to deliver. She made him swear to keep the message private from everyone, including Kiro. This would have to be Cadence's choice, and his alone.

Now, she doubted her decisions. She was delirious, panicked, depressed, and manic all at once. Was that the best time to be making world altering decisions?

But what could she do?

The bread is the Banjarguay.

The Banjar is healing.

What other conclusion could she have come to?

After a few more hours of hiking in silence, Meera had to shield herself from a sudden blinding sun. They had crested a peak and could see out into Midland. She cast a sidelong glance at Story, trying to judge if she might need a break, but the woman was standing tall with a broad smile on her face.

"In good spirits?" Meera asked incredulously.

"Yes," Story murmured, closing her eyes.

Meera looked around. Beyond the hills lay an endless land of green. The world's last forests and miles of farmlands drawing patterns of color stretched on the path before them.

"We're going to give this to the Banjarians," Story said, gesturing out at the view before them.

Meera felt her stomach drop.

Are we?

Are we going to shake the very world?

There was no turning back now.

She wondered if Story understood her enough to have guessed what she had sent to Cadence, or if she was simply daydreaming.

The words on the tape swirled in her brain over and over.

Whatever it takes, Cadence, destroy the barrier. Destroy the barrier.

With one tape, she may have risked the life of every person living in New Bhutan.

But then Story opened her eyes and smiled at her, the late morning light igniting her eyes, and Meera felt herself offering a weak smile back.

"Whatever it takes."

PART VI

DRAGON'S FIRE

1

EPILOGUE

D ORJI TASHI

DORJI TASHI WAS DRUNK. He relished the freedom spirit tea brought him. He could laugh at his own jokes without second guessing if anyone else thought it was amusing. After a few cups, he could feel that ever present tension in his shoulders melt away, the hard edges of the world soften. He'd spent the majority of his life watching with held breath, always waiting for the moment when someone would realize that he didn't have what it took to run Lhasa. And then everything would be taken from him. He couldn't bear the thought. It kept him on constant edge.

It was his faan and uncle first; always watching his every move with a slight edge of disappointment. Then his wife, Kiba Chime, with her soft suggestions. As if her tone could mask her meaning. You don't know what you're doing, Tashi. Let me handle it, Tashi.

Tonight, watching Penna make the speech he'd influenced her to make, he knew that he would never have to worry again. Finally, he was in complete control. With all three branches under his thumb, he could finally breathe easy. He had consumed more spirit tea than ever, toasting every strange face that swam into his view. To Penna and Cadence, long may they reign! To Sai, my most faithful advisor!

At this thought he paused his steps, causing the two Quántóu holding him up to almost trip. "Well, he never questions me," he slurred to Zeesha, the girl on his right. "I have my doubts about him, but he never questions me!"

"Why would he?" the other girl murmured. He lifted his head to look at her, throwing what he hoped was a flirtatiously cocked brow.

Zeesha tightened her grip on him, propelling him up the sloping incline.

"Cadence, though..." he continued, glancing back at her. "Betrayal at its finest!"

Dorji could recognize weakness. He saw it in his son from the beginning. The way he'd mourned his maan; nearly a year of sniveling and crying out in the night. The way he'd clung to Seldom like he was a baby, not a seven-year-old. Choosing song as his craft, just like his maan. The child had no determination. No grit. He was a dreamer. Dorji wasn't surprised in the least when he betrayed his own faan for Penna. He had been surprised to find out how.

What had Penna discovered that led to her search? *Well, there was no asking her now*, Tashi thought ruefully. Cadence would need to be questioned. He would need to be reminded of his role.

Tashi let out a loud sigh of satisfaction. If controlling Cadence was the only barrier to achieving his goals, he had nothing to worry about.

"Let's get you inside, Tashi San," Zeesha said calmly. "We're almost there."

They were leading him to his private chambers. It was on nights such as this that he would have preferred that the Dragon be housed at the bottom, rather than the very top of the palace. This thought made him pause as well, earning him an exasperated sigh from both of his Quántóu. This may be his last night in the Dragon rooms. *For now*, he thought with a grin. They were the best, and Tashi wanted only the best.

Of course, there might be a long period before he returned, but that time would be spent in the altogether superior luxury of Qinghai Lake. This made him fall into a fit of laughter. He made to swat the girl to his left on the bottom but missed, making him laugh even harder.

Soon, they were passing the two Quántóu standing guard at his doors and making their way through the common spaces, all well-lit for his return. He had red silk sheets on his bed, and suddenly he could feel himself being wrapped in them, their cool touch a soft kiss on his body. They had, apparently, removed his robes as they put him in bed. He thought that they must have been hurt that he hadn't even noticed as they did it; that he may not be interested in inviting them to stay. He called out for them to come back and sit with him, half his mouth pressed against the bed, but they did not respond. Suddenly the room was plunged into darkness, with only his heavy breathing for company.

It was only in these moments, after his Quántóu turned down the lanterns and left him in the dark, that Dorji would remember how much he didn't like being drunk. And he certainly didn't like being alone. In the dark, the world began to rocket around his head. With a grunt, he untangled himself from the sheets and stumbled to the ground. He crawled to the washroom and threw up in the water basin. Even in his stupor, he refused to put his head near the squat toilet. Although the drop was an impressive sixty feet before waste hit the insects that would work to recycle it, he could still smell it.

After throwing up several times, Dorji pulled himself to his feet and poured some water from the freshly filled pitcher onto his face, leaving it to drip down his mustache and across his chest. Feeling slightly more alert, his thoughts returned to Penna.

As they always did.

Before Asaka was gone, he would bring his three daughters to the palace to play in the gardens while the two men talked. He would struggle to focus on the Eye's words as the girl with fire eyes would flash glances his way. It was clear to him that the girl was just as curious about him as he was about her. She haunted his dreams, distracted his plans. When he shared his wife's bed, she would transform into the girl before his eyes.

Once Asaka was out of the way, he convinced Seldom to take the girl on as an apprentice. There, he could always watch her. Penna; his only weakness.

Like all great men, he would pass what he treasured onto his son. It was true that she had been soiled; had not been fit to be his bride. But, still, she belonged to him. First body, now mind.

He splashed more water on his face before easing himself out of the washroom, carefully gripping the doorframe.

Penna would be his again, once he'd taken back the palace. It was years from now, he was sure, but Tashi was patient. Especially when the waiting would be spent with Banjarian women, who somehow never failed to remind him of her.

He inched his way along the wall to the far side of the room and eased his wrist along the trick panel. It opened to reveal his private Listening board. Even in the dark, he knew which switch would turn on the sound of Penna's Apprentice quarters. He flipped it on every night he was in Potala. The mics were nestled in her headboard, close enough that he could hear her gentle breathing as she slept. Sometimes, she would breathe hard in a dream, making his own pulse quicken. Sometimes, she would cry out his name, fear choking the words. The sound sent shudders of pleasure up his spine.

She did not dream this time. Her even breathing was a testament to the quality of her recent Emptying. No memories plagued her subconscious.

Not to worry, he consoled himself. In time, he wouldn't need to rely on her dreams to remind her of him.

With this thought, he fell into daydreaming about his plans coming to fruition. He slipped into a drunken sleep before he got past the part when his new Sepa army would bring thousands of Banjarians to Qinghai. One face after another, eager to help him, eager to love him, believing in him without any shadow of a doubt.

It was only a few hours later that the steady pulse of a comm in his wrist pulled him from sleep.

Eyes still closed, he tapped pinky to thumb.

"Tashi San!"

It was Sai, his voice harsh with disapproval.

"Eh?" he grunted, eyes still closed.

"Are you on your way to the lake?"

"I'm in bed, you fool. It's not yet light out."

"Didn't Cadence tell you I was in need of an emergency helio? That a Sepa has gone rogue?"

Tashi opened one eye. The image of Cadence swam before his mind. "He might have said something, yes…"

He heard Sai's exasperated sigh. "Tashi, I need you to wash your face, take a shot of coffee, and get in a helio as soon as possible."

Tashi yawned. "Someone's feeling rather powerful this morning…"

"I don't mean to be insubordinate, Tashi San, but if we don't act quickly, the secret of the lake is out."

This brought Tashi to a sitting position. "What's that?"

"Palace and 288 escaped, sir."

"Palace?" he asked, disbelief erasing all sleep from his mind. He was already up, pulling on robes. He yelled for a Quántóu to bring him a coffee before hastily turning off the Listening equipment and closing the cabinet, silencing Penna's gentle breath.

"288?"

"Yes, sir," he replied in a tight voice. "They must be silenced… I recommend immediate execution."

"Execution? Dragons, Sai. When have we ever done that? A full Emptying will suffice. I had a thought to keep that Sepa at the lake anyway. Where are they now?"

Sai was silent for a moment.

"Sai? Where are they now?"

A Quántóu was handing him a strong cup of black coffee while another wrapped him in fresh robes.

"We believe they are headed to Meera, sir, at the bunkers."

Tashi cursed. "I'll send a helio out for you and it will take you to the bunkers. We'll need a way to discredit Meera, in case she already knows. I wondered if Meera had an idea. When Penna returned from Mishka's ceremony and went straight for her memories... I had a feeling."

"Penna did what?" Sai asked stiffly.

"Penna found her memories. We were alerted by a staff member and took them back. But Meera... Meera might know. How did they escape?"

"They poisoned Kinsu and I and stole our ID chips."

Tashi paused, suspicion tickling his senses. "I see."

"They used the ID chips to steal a helio."

"My, my." Tashi batted the Quántóu away and out of his rooms.

"Okay. Sai, I need you to find them and bring them back to the lake. Tranquilize them. I don't want any mistakes. Get the rogue and leave Meera to me."

"What will you do, Sir?"

"Visit my sweet Penna. The helio will be there within the hour. Be ready."

He tapped forefinger to palm and laid back on the bed, head swimming.

After a moment, he started laughing. Palace! That sneaky old wench. Never would he have thought that she would betray him. Serves him right for being soft, for believing for a moment that loyalty would come from years of service. That love could exist without force.

He ordered his new Quántóu to take the family helio to Sai San. The coordinates were pre-programmed in. He had a moment of regret sending her to the lake so soon. Once a Quántóu took the journey, they could not return. That one had shown promise, too.

Groaning, he started on his way down to Penna's quarters. His steps were slow and careful as he tried not to agitate his pounding headache. Nodding to Penna's Quántóu posted at the door, he found that he still thrilled at entering her rooms. She was still sleeping, nestled into a tight ball beneath perfectly smoothed teal silks. Her private quarters had a balcony, and the early morning sun illumi-nated her face in a warm glow. He eased himself onto his knees next to the bed and leaned his face within inches of hers, feeling the tickle of her breath.

"Penna San," he whispered.

Her eyes opened, and for a delicious moment, those gloriously green eyes were filled with a dark horror at meeting his own. Then, just as quickly as it had appeared, the look was gone, replaced by pure adoration.

"Tashi," she said warmly, "This is a surprise."

He sucked in a shuddering breath, trying to control himself. "It's your sister," he said roughly. "Meera has betrayed us all. We need our new Heart to act immediately."

She sat up, keeping her silks tight around her body. "What happened?"

Tashi knew what would make her the angriest. He loathed it, but he knew that hating something doesn't make it any less true.

"She ordered her Sepas to attack Sai San. They are in open rebel-lion against the Family."

Penna's hand went to her mouth in horror. "Is he safe?"

He burned to say no. The traitor was dead. *It's me. It's me for you now, and you will love me and only me.*

But he had to wait.

Tashi could be patient.

As long as what he wanted was on the other side.

ACKNOWLEDGMENTS

Special thanks to my team of friends and family who helped bounce ideas for this story around for the last two years! To my first readers and endlessly supportive parents, Debee and Mark; this book would not be here today without you bugging me for the next chapter! To my second round of readers, Julie and Josh, thank you for helping me work out missing pieces in scenes, characters, and world building. This story would not be the same without you. And thank you to my dear friend, Melissa, and my amazing editor, Marni MacRae, for making sure my grammar was looking acceptable! Thank you to my son, Poe, and my partner, John, for listening to me rant for months as I verbally processed the story and the characters. Big thanks to PoeX Designs, Ray Sunshine, and Kat Murphy for all of the amazing Sepa art that brought my vision to a new format.

And lastly, thank you to everyone who stands with the people who are othered, who fight against injustice in all its ugly forms, and who break all the Sepa rules; the ones who wonder, speak out, and stand up. Thank you.

ABOUT THE AUTHOR

Jillian Moody grew up acting out imaginary stories; pirates on the river, fairies in the woods, and ghosts in the bathroom. She loves to write fiction that questions society's norms around gender, sexuality, and equality. The Sepa Series explores social norms, xenophobia, and women's rights, all topics that tug at her mind daily.

Jillian spends her time teaching, writing, dancing like nobody's watching, and creating art. She lives with her family in Milwaukie, Oregon.

Previously, Jillian won the Best Horror Short Fiction Award for her story "To Be a Woman" through *Ooligan Press*. Her short horror and dystopian stories are featured in the anthology *Once Upon Another Time: Fresh Tales from the Far Side of Fantasy and When All That's Left are Stories; Diaries of the Dystopia. The SEPA Project* is the first in her trilogy, The Sepa Series.

Connect with the Author

www.jmoody.art
INSTAGRAM: @freedomreadersmoody
TIKTOK: @ms.moodywrites

The wash house of Potala Palace was packed with the sweat and chatter of aging Quántóu. They would spend their final years there, scrubbing shade curtains and the underthings of palace residents on washboards. The place was too thick with steam to see across the pool. Moist heat soaked them through within minutes, so most didn't bother to wear much clothing. Their undyed robes were discarded along the floor, only their heads wrapped up to hide that they'd taken down their Quántóu braids. Get to be their age, they'd complain, and the braids felt more and more troublesome. Zeesha was sure it was only that *they* had lost their discipline.

She couldn't really blame them, though. Active Quántóu slept in rooms below the wash house, but they never lingered on their way through. It was worse when she was already gasping and sweating from an intense training session. Zeesha's rank as the Heart's personal Quántóu gave her some privileges, one being to choose her time of day with the personal trainer. She chose just before sunrise so she could be at Tashi's side before he woke. It was merely a bonus that exerting herself in the relatively cool air, the sky still a dark greenish purple, left the morning's energy running through her veins. Her body rippled with strength. She wanted to climb those jagged mountains in the distance, but instead, as always, she'd returned to the sticky heat of the wash house to pick up Pa.

The heat wasn't the only reason she lingered in the archway. She hated seeing the once respected Quántóu, her childhood heroes, reduced to wash maids. And yet, that was the way.

If you were lucky.

Quántóu had a reputation for simply disappearing.

She glanced irritably at the empty arches that led from the wash house down to the bunk rooms. She hoped to find Pa standing there, only just emerging from her sleeping shift. That girl was always late. She yawned, causing a few nearby elders to smile at her.

"Morning," she said, tipping her head.

"Zeesha," one said, smiling a toothless grin, "Come sit, love."

Wiping the moisture from her brow, she reluctantly obeyed.

"How is it in the palace this week?" the woman asked. "We heard Penna San's Quántóu arrested several Sepas! Our Pa was included in the action!"

She grimaced, grabbing a straying lock of the woman's hair and braiding it absently. "Yes, Olka, I heard that too. It is not our business to know, however, so we should keep what we hear to ourselves."

"Hmm-hmm. I hear the Dragon has left again, too."

"Strange times," her friend murmured.

"Very strange!"

"Penna San or Tashi?" Zeesha asked, despite herself.

"Oh my," Olka laughed. "I'll have to get used to a new Heart. I meant Tashi San, of course."

"What will we call him now?" the other woman asked.

"I say we keep calling him the Dragon. Everyone knows Penna San is the Snake!"

"Olka," Zeesha interrupted. "Did you hear where Tashi San went?"

She sniffed. "We really should keep what we hear to ourselves. Wouldn't you agree, Sia?"

"Agreed," her friend murmured, a glint of amusement in her eye.

Zeesha smiled, rolling her eyes. "Okay, fine. Have you seen Pa?"

"Pa is here," a sleepy voice came from across the pool.

Zeesha turned to see her, a wisp of a girl with a perfectly round face, stretching her arms high.

She scowled, mopping the steam from her brow. "Let's go."

"Important palace business to get to," Olka said to Sia.

"Very important."

They both snickered.

Zeesha grabbed a towel that was hung to dry and tossed it into the soapy pool. "Missed a spot on that one, Olka."

She could hear them laughing as she led Pa out.

"Those two are no help whatsoever."

"They make you smile," Pa teased.

"Hm."

As they crossed the long bridge on their way to the palace's main building, the women switched their conversation to Chimeegüi, the Quántóu sign language. The wash house was just as loaded with gossiping Quántóu as it was with Listening equipment, and past the bridge, a Family member might catch them using nonverbal communication. That made the long bridge that connected the wash house to Potala their special space. This daily walk was the only time they felt truly alone.

Using her hands to speak, Zeesha wasted no time.

"What happened out there?"

Her friend's sweet face had bloomed purple and yellow from temple to chin. Bruises were quite common among Quántóu, but Pa was the exception. Penna San was not a violent keeper.

Pa sighed. "It wasn't pretty. Nyra is in Luópán's hospital, she was beaten so badly."

"*Hospitalized?*"

She nodded. "The others are in similar shape to me. We had sleeping darts, but they were so fast. So fast and so strong."

Zeesha frowned. "Tashi was sure we would be stronger."

Pa tilted her head in thought. "Stronger, maybe, but not as... methodical."

Zeesha took that in. "The Memory leaves little room for strategy," she conceded before putting a reassuring hand on Pa's shoulder. Still, her jaw twitched with jealousy. She spent most of her days waiting outside Xīn Dome for a man she knew might not appear for days. If he did appear, she would instantly wish to be back to standing guard. Pa was allowed to sit in her keeper's private rooms and had been on an adventure outside the palace; had actually *fought* the Sepas. She'd been able to *use* the Memory.

"Penna must have been proud of you." She knew that Pa and Penna San had a bond most Quántóu didn't understand, Zeesha included.

A happy blush did not brighten her friend's bruised cheeks, however. "She could not be happy with anyone right now, I don't think," she signed sadly. "She is not herself."

"How so? Is she ill?"

"Maybe."

"I'm sure it's difficult business to take over the Heart's role. And having to arrest her own *sister*. How terrible."

She couldn't help imagining Pa and her thrust onto different sides of a battle. Would she be able to arrest her if Pa betrayed the Family? She wasn't sure.

"She did not succeed in arresting Meera San, thank dragons," Pa continued.

"Thank dragons?" Zeesha repeated, her steps halting. "Why would you want her to fail?"

Pa paused and glanced around with uncertainty. "I... can you keep something between us?"

Zeesha frowned. "Of course."

"Penna San was missing before the announcement. For *two days*."

Zeesha's brows shot up.

"She ordered us to stay in her rooms until her return, but never came back. When she did arrive, it was no more than an hour before her announcement speech. And..." Pa looked over the shallow moat for a moment, her hands pausing their words to wring one another nervously. "And Tashi himself carried her in. She was unconscious."

"What?" Zeesha exclaimed aloud. She clapped a hand over her mouth.

Where had she and Tashi been just before the announcement? She thought back. Tashi was being fitted for a new robe for the event when he'd received an urgent comm from the Memory Library. He'd rushed away and asked that she make sure the garment be finished.

"He ordered us to wait outside the door," Pa continued. "Usually, Penna San will at least nod hello to us, but when she left her room an hour later, it was like we didn't exist. She's been like that ever since. When she does ask for something, she snaps or screams. She's been crying a lot, too. I can never tell minute to minute what she will be like. Did *you* see her with Tashi at all?"

It was clear that Pa had been dying to ask her about this. Zeesha wished she had more to offer. "I remember him leaving abruptly that night. He must have gone to find her. I can say for certain that her disappearance had nothing to do with him. He was surprised by the comm."

Pa raised a brow at her and Zeesha flushed with embarrassment. Pa had lectured her for years on her constant defense of Dorji Tashi. No matter how deeply he tormented her, she would always provide excuses for him. He'd been stressed. She'd been careless. Pa had exchanged her long lectures for small shakes of the head and brow raises, and Zeesha wasn't sure if that meant she finally understood or she'd just given up.

They were nearing the end of the bridge. "Pa," she began, trying to change the subject, "has Penna San said anything about Tashi's plans moving forward?"

Pa smiled apologetically. "I know you're anxious to know where you will go now that Penna is Heart, but she hasn't said anything. I promise to tell you right away if she does."

Zeesha nodded. "Of course."

They walked a few more paces before Pa stopped short, signing with excitement. "Nyra will be out of service for a while. And even when she returns, Penna may not want her. She *failed* in our mission! Her trial scores were obviously misleading. If the Dragon isn't in need of you anymore, maybe Penna will take you on! We could work together!"

A little spark of hope flared in Zeesha's heart, but it was quickly extinguished. "We don't know that the Dragon will be wanting to let me go."

Pa tweaked her nose before signing. "Have hope." With that and a big smile, she turned to leave, heading up the path toward the palace. Zeesha turned right, toward Xīn Dome.

Could she be reassigned to a different Family member? The thought hadn't even occurred to her. When Tashi announced his retirement, Zeesha's first thought was that he would be in the palace more, lounging around in his private rooms and demanding company. The thought made her stomach clench painfully. That worry hadn't gone away this morning, but she'd been slightly comforted when the first thing he did was leave.

She couldn't believe he could *walk* after consuming so much spirit tea the night before. He was up well before sunrise, demanding that her latest partner, Neta, ready the helio and that she, Zeesha, bring him coffee. Neta was new and disgustingly eager to make a good impression. It was working, because once again, Tashi had chosen the new Quántóu to fly over her. She'd received top marks in flying and had always been seen as his primary Quántóu, and yet he never, not once, had chosen her to be his pilot.

The pathways of Potala had become all too familiar to her and she was convinced she would live every day of her life here, never flying beyond those mountains or even visiting the Rings. The claustrophobia of that thought was slightly alleviated by the knowledge that every other Quántóu of Tashi's had come and gone, and she was still here. Their promotion could have led to something so wonderful it was beyond her imagination. She could be the pity of them all, standing outside Xīn Dome until she retired to be a wash maid.

But at least the people who cared for her knew where she was.

No one had a clue where the advancing Quántóu disappeared to, and they never came back.

Standing outside Xīn Dome may not be as exciting as traveling alongside Tashi, but odds were they safer.

Curling around the last palace tower, the dome loomed into view, glittering black in the early morning light. She sighed, sneaking in one more yawn before taking her place near the entrance.

It wasn't that standing guard outside Xīn Dome was so bad in itself. It was knowing that the only thing she was guarding was Tashi's deception. He liked everyone to think he was in there, working away at top secret projects for days at a time, but his Quántóu knew the truth. He had left Lhasa.

Xīn Dome contained the entrance to an ancient tunnel that led into the mountains. The dome had been built over it to allow for the Dragon to make a speedy escape if a rebellion reached the palace gates. No rebellion had occurred, but it didn't stop Tashi from frequently escaping. No one knew where he went. The helio rides ended at a rail station just north of Lhasa every time. Sometimes another helio would be there. Other times Tashi was dropped off alone in what appeared to be the middle of nowhere. She was not supposed to know this, but the Quántóu had gained their share of secrets over the years. How could they not?

Along with nearly everyone else, graduated Quántóu were not allowed inside Xīn Dome without Tashi as escort. It was only for the Heart, his closest advisors, and the young Quántóu in training. Quite the waste of space if you asked her. So the Dragon's Quántóu must stand in the heat, day in and day out, waiting for someone who was unlikely to come out any time soon.

If she was Penna's Quántóu, she might be pouring her a fresh glass of orange juice and sitting on a shaded balcony. She shifted her weight to the other foot, already uncomfortable. Her favorite daydream to slip into during these shifts was one where Tashi rewarded her for her loyal service with a pair of shoes. He would be in one of his jovial moods, when his smile was celebratory and he wanted her company just for conversation. In the fantasy, he would reward Zeesha with shoes for being the best Quántóu in New Bhutan. Pa thought it was a depressingly small fantasy, but Zeesha had learned a long time ago that dreaming about the impossible was the best way to torment yourself. At least this was possible, if still extremely unlikely. She watched the Luópán Hall workers pass in beautifully crafted sandals and shifted her weight from one foot to the other. During the training years, they made sure to harden a Quántóu's feet so they wouldn't feel the heat as much, but imagining the support on her knees was enough to make her legs shake. She was just settling into the fantasy, Tashi coming toward her with a package wrapped in red cloth, when Cadence's honeyed voice made the image fade.

She always heard him coming before she saw him. That gentle tone, wishing everyone who passed a happy morning. From his direction, she knew he was heading back from the gardens. It was the place he haunted when he was troubled, searching for answers in rose buds and the soft hum of bees.

She frowned. It was much too early for him to be there. He was known to sleep several hours past now. The sun had barely risen and the only people around were Palace Quántóu, cleaning and pruning the paths to perfection for the arrival of the Luópán Hall employees.

What plagued him so much that he couldn't sleep? What had he thought of Penna's move to arrest the Sepas? She knew how worried he'd been that Penna would undermine him at the Sepa dinner, and she'd gone so much further, arresting them without his consent on her first day as Heart. She wondered how Cadence was feeling about the marriage alliance now.

Jealousy for Pa whipped through her again. When Penna married, Pa would be spending most of her days with Cadence.

But maybe... if Tashi gave her away, maybe Cadence would finally accept a new Quántóu. He'd been dragging his feet on it for months. Would he remember their time together as children and ask Zeesha to take the honor? Her mind immediately jumped to lounging in the gardens by his side, chatting about the day. Unlike every other Family member, Cadence spoke to Quántóu as he would to anyone else.

But no, Zeesha was sure he was still mourning the loss of Teka.

She liked to think that he wouldn't accept a replacement until he'd uncovered the truth of where his Quántóu had disappeared to.

Teka, Pa, and Zeesha had shared a bunk during their training years and roomed together ever since. They were family. Zeesha was Kiba Chime's Quántóu in the beginning, replacing one who had recently disappeared. Kiba was distraught and refused a new servant. Instead, she selected a young Quántóu so Cadence could have a playmate. They'd been just about the same age, Zeesha being a couple years older. Most of Zeesha's time was reserved for training in Xīn, but when she was with Kiba, the Brain would bring Cadence and her to the gardens. At the time, the children assumed Kiba loved it there. It wasn't until later that she realized Kiba was probably keeping them there to be discreet. It wasn't normal, or acceptable, for a Family child and a Quántóu to be friends.

They played together until Kiba's early death, when Zeesha was seven, at which point the Dragon reassigned her to himself. Teka was assigned to Cadence when he turned ten. From then on, Cadence and Zeesha had resorted to sneaking around, then the occasional comment in passing until eventually, their friendship was forced to fade. It was only through Teka's gossip that she learned about Cadence's life.

Then, a few months ago, Teka had joined the masses of missing Quántóu.

Quántóu disappearing was nothing new, but when it happened to someone you were close to... well, suddenly it felt very personal.

Cadence rounded the corner, his eyes blinking in the sudden sunlight. He shielded his face as he passed, nodding her way. "Morning, Zeesha!"

She nodded curtly. "Morning, Sir San."

He was carrying a freshly soiled pot fit to bursting with three or four different plants, each topped with brightly colored blossoms.

He slowed as he passed. "No word from Tashi yet?"

"No, Sir San."

He paused his steps, shifting the pot to one arm. "And yet, you are still here, waiting patiently." He gave her that lopsided, apologetic grin that she *knew* he knew the power of. She bit the inside of her cheek to keep from smiling back.

He squinted in thought for a moment before setting the pot on the ground and carefully picking a flower from it, a perfectly pink azalea. "Now," he said as he worked, "I don't usually condone cutting a flower from its root. Why limit the life of something so precious?" He stood, holding the flower. "However, *occasionally*, its beauty is magnified by the right setting, and must make the sacrifice. A shorter life, lived beautifully, is better than a long and dull one, wouldn't you say?" He moved toward her. If it had been anyone else, she would have moved to break his neck. In the case of Cadence, she held her breath.

He met her eyes and smiled, waiting to see if she would object, before tucking the flower behind her ear, careful to tuck her braids back as well.

"There," he said, stepping back to analyze his work. "Now you have two jobs. Waiting for Tashi and brightening Potala's day with your beauty." He winked at her, picked up his flowers, and walked away.

Her hand found the flower as she watched him go, petting the petals that were soft as silk. A flower, so precious, would live a shorter life if plucked from where it'd been planted, but at least it would see the world outside its garden. She was thinking about flying again, up and over the bridges, and out of Potala Palace. Being promoted to pilot might be dangerous, it might even shorten her life, but at least she would have lived.